Scarlet Cloak

Jean Plaidy, one of the pre-eminent authors of historical fiction for most of the twentieth century, is the pen name of the prolific English author Eleanor Hibbert, also known as Victoria Holt. Jean Plaidy's novels had sold more than 14 million copies worldwide by the time of her death in 1993.

For further information about our Jean Plaidy reissues
and mailing list, please visit
www.randomhouse.co.uk/minisites/jeanplaidy

Praise for Jean Plaidy

'Plaidy excels at blending history with romance and drama'
New York Times

'Outstanding'
Vanity Fair

'Full-bodied, dramatic, exciting'
Observer

The Scarlet Cloak

JEAN PLAIDY

arrow books

Published by Arrow Books 2009

4 6 8 10 9 7 5 3

Copyright © Jean Plaidy, 1957, 1969 and 1985

Initial lettering copyright © Stephen Raw, 2008

The Estate of Eleanor Hibbert has asserted its right under the Copyright, Designs and
Patents Act, 1988 to have Jean Plaidy identified as the author of this work.

First published in Great Britain in 1957 by Hodder and Stoughton Ltd, under the pseudonym
of Ellalice Tate

The Random House Group Limited
20 Vauxhall Bridge Road, London, SW1V 2SA

www.rbooks.co.uk

Addresses for companies within The Random House Group Limited can be found at:
www.randomhouse.co.uk/offices.htm

The Random House Group Limited Reg. No. 954009

A CIP catalogue record for this book
is available from the British Library

ISBN 9780099533030

The Random House Group Limited supports The Forest Stewardship
Council (FSC), the leading international forest certification organisation. All our
titles that are printed on Greenpeace approved FSC certified paper carry the FSC logo. Our
paper procurement policy can be found at www.rbooks.co.uk/environment

Mixed Sources
Product group from well-managed
forests and other controlled sources
www.fsc.org Cert no. TT-COC-2139
© 1996 Forest Stewardship Council
FSC

Typeset by SX Composing DTP, Rayleigh, Essex
Printed and bound in Great Britain by
CPI Cox & Wyman, Reading, RG1 8EX

❧ Contents ❧

Fanatic fools, that in those twilight times,
With wild religion cloaked the worth of crimes!

John Langhorne, 1735–1779

We have just enough religion to make us hate, but not enough to make us love one another.

Jonathan Swift, 1667–1745

They that approve a private opinion, call it opinion; but they that mislike it, heresy: and yet heresy signifies no more than private opinion.

Thomas Jobbes, 1588–1679

PART ONE

ANDALUSIA
Spring, 1572

❧ Chapter I ❧

ANDALUSIA – SPRING, 1572

At the window Señorita Isabella de Ariz sat fanning herself. Beside her were her two women, Juana and Maria. They were clearly anxious; it was rarely that their young lady was allowed so much freedom.

'Sit well back,' commanded Juana.

'It would be unwise for these gipsies to see you clearly,' declared Maria. 'Who knows what evil thoughts might enter their heads!'

In the *patio* a fountain played; the scent of the flowers was exquisite and the sun shone hotly on the white flagstones.

Juana continued to grumble to Maria. 'Who allowed these gipsies to invade the *patio*? Who, I say? Was it that lazy Tomás? He should not think this will be allowed. There will be some questions asked when Don Alonso returns home.'

'Have done, Maria,' said Isabella. 'They wish to show us their dances, and why should they not?'

'They wish to lure the gold out of our pockets. What else besides, I wonder!'

'They must live,' said Isabella.

Juana shook her head at Maria. Their young lady was

3

growing wayward. Perhaps it was as well that soon she would have a husband to command her.

She was often restive during the long days spent behind the *persianas*; she no longer took any great pleasure in her needlework; even the most beautiful altar cloth with the blue and gold embroidery of the saints no longer delighted her. 'I am tired . . . tired of sitting here . . . day after day, and nothing happening,' she said.

'And what should happen to the daughter of a great nobleman, Doña Isabella?' she was asked.

'Nothing, I suppose,' she had answered. 'Nothing at all. She rises early and says her prayers; she hears Mass – oh, not in the church, oh no! She must not be allowed to do that; that would be too adventurous! She hears it in the private chapel which is only a flight of steps and a passage away from this room; and then she does her lessons and a little embroidery. What else is there for her to do?'

'Would you have her roam the countryside like a peasant or a gipsy?'

'Sometimes I envy the peasants and gipsies – those girls with their bare dancing feet.'

Such words were shocking and the women would exchange glances and shake their heads. It was indeed time their Isabella was married. She was sixteen – so old enough – and clearly fretting to exchange the life of a carefully nurtured young lady for that of a wife and mother.

She was no longer content to sit at her window and look out on the *patio* or gardens which were shielded from that burning sky by the leaves of the palm trees; she was no longer content to enjoy from the window all that colour and beauty which came from the pimienta and orange trees, to delight in the air

4

which was perfumed with the delicate scent of orange blossom, to look beyond at the vineyards and watch the grapes ripening in that white soil which by the breeze was blown on to the grapes and made the wine in the country surrounding Jerez the best in the world. She wanted to be out of the house, mingling with the people who passed along the road; she delighted to watch the pedlars and the gipsies on their journeys from Seville and Cordoba, from Malaga, Granada and Cadiz.

And now here were gipsies dancing in the *patio*. And, in the absence of the master and mistress of the house, it had been Doña Isabella who had said that they might amuse her with their dancing.

'And who knows that they are not robbers?' murmured Juana. 'Do you see the knives in their belts?'

'They all carry knives,' said Isabella. 'I have watched them on the road. Each man has his *faja*. It is necessary. What if he should be called upon to defend himself on his lonely journeys?'

Juana and Maria shivered expressively and raised their eyes to the ceiling.

But now Isabella was leaning forward a little, for she had seen the young gipsy girl, who was demanding attention by that abandonment which was outstanding even among gipsy dancers. Her skirt was red and tattered, her brown feet were long and narrow; she carried herself with dignity for all that her blouse was torn and a brown shoulder gaped through the tear. Her hair was black as only a gipsy's hair could be; her eyes enormous, sparkling, flashing with curiosity; the large rings swinging in her ears brushed her shoulders.

She was endeavouring to call attention to herself. Isabella knew that those flashing dark eyes had seen her at the window and, as their glances met, Isabella was aware of an appeal in that of the gipsy girl. It was not only the *pesetas* which would be flung to them, for which she was asking, it was for something more.

A man had caught the girl by the arm, and she was whirled backwards to take her place among the dancers in the *fandango*. But she was reluctant, and as she was drawn back she had turned her head and was still seeking to hold Isabella's attention.

Neither Juana nor Maria had noticed the young dancer, and Isabella was glad of that. In that whirling crowd she sought for the girl; but she was small and it was not easy to pick her out. Isabella sat intent, watching the sensuous movements of the dancers. She saw the gipsy girls with cast-down eyes, feigning indifference, pursued by the men; she saw the dark eyes gleaming; the sudden flash of teeth as a gipsy girl gave up the pretence and threw herself wholeheartedly into the game, which was pursuit, capture, surrender.

The music had reached a crescendo and the lutes of the two musicians were suddenly silent. The dancers stood where they were, as though some god had turned them into stone at the very climax of capture and surrender. For a few seconds there was complete silence in the *patio*. Isabella's heart began to beat fast; she felt a strange sense of significance in the hot sun, the scent of flowers, those figures as though cut out of stone struck lifeless there.

Then suddenly there was movement from below. The gipsy girl, whom Isabella had noticed, sprang forward; she looked up at the window at which Isabella was sitting and she began to dance. This was the *farraca*, slow, stately. She was imitating the gestures and postures of the matador. Sinuously her young body swayed from side to side; the figures about her seemed still to be cut out of stone, so motionless they were. By her movements and that strange power of hers the gipsy brought into the *patio* the torrid excitement of the *corrida*. Watching, Isabella was completely fascinated. Now the girl was in danger; now she had narrowly escaped death; now she was triumphant; it was as though she stood before them waving the scarlet *muleta*, accepting the acknowledgement of the crowds.

Isabella had leaned forward. 'Bravo! Bravo!' she cried.

But Juana and Maria were laying restraining hands on her, and a man had stepped forward to join the girl. This was the *flamenco* – the quick dance which was so called because it had reminded people of the manners of the soldiers returned from the Flanders wars. Noisy, impromptu, it portrayed the arrogant temper of ravaging soldiers bent on pillage. The man was angry with the gipsy girl; that was clear to Isabella. So much was conveyed in their dancing; it was their very means of expression. Roughly he caught her as they danced; angrily she drew herself away. The musicians had begun to play more wildly and the people were clapping their hands. The gipsy had taken her ebony castanets from the pocket of her skirt. Angrily they clashed, keeping in time with the musicians.

There was no surrender this time; the girl kept her anger; she tore herself free of the man; it was as though they were driving themselves to a frenzy. Then suddenly a man from the crowd, a dark-haired gipsy, in whose belt was a bigger knife than those carried by the others, came forward and joined the dancers; he danced, lightly flicking his fingers before the younger man's eyes; then in a second the whole band of gipsies was dancing and the young girl was lost among their swaying bodies.

7

Juana had come to the window now. She threw down money.

'Go now,' she said. 'In the kitchens you will be given food. It is enough. The lady is tired.'

The dancers stopped abruptly; there was a scramble for the money; in a very short time the *patio* was empty and there was nothing left of that strange scene but the sunshine and the scent of the flowers.

❧ ❧ ❧

They called blessings on the house as they departed, and Isabella looked in vain for the gipsy girl whose dancing had so impressed her.

She turned from the window.

On the return of her parents Juana and Maria would feel it their duty to tell them what she had done. She would be scolded.

She shrugged her shoulders. It was done; and she believed that not much longer would this house be her home. She would live on an estate some few miles south of the town of Seville, between that town and Jerez de la Frontera; and as a married woman she would be able to visit her parents often. She would have more freedom when she married Blasco – or Domingo. Which would it be? Domingo was the elder, but they must know that it was Blasco who had been her friend in the days when they had been children and played together. Often she had spoken to her parents of Blasco. They knew her feelings, and they loved her dearly; their ardent wish would be to see her happy.

It was some years since she had seen either Blasco or Domingo, for, as there was to be a match between Isabella and one of them, their parents had thought they should not spend their childhood together. Five years ago she had ceased to visit the Carramadino estate and, although Señor Gregorio and Señora Theresa Carramadino came to the house to visit her family, they came alone; and when her parents went to the estate near Seville — as they had this day — they did not take their daughter.

Did they — Domingo and Blasco — often think of her, as she did of them? Did they remember the games they had played when they were very young? Blasco had been bold even then, more like a man than his brother, although he was the younger. Domingo was two years older than Blasco, and Blasco two years Isabella's senior. It had been Blasco's custom to kiss her hand when they met, and he would lift his head slowly, his black eyes giving her looks which seemed to add years to them both and to exclude Domingo from their presence. Domingo was gentle, he talked of being a priest, for he had not thought then of marriage as Blasco had. Blasco talked of adventures, of Cortes and Peru and the wonderful discoveries of new lands he would make for the glory of Spain, and the treasure he would bring back to share with King Philip. Often she had wondered what would have happened if she and Blasco had been allowed to continue meeting.

Had she thought too much of those boys? There had been little else to think of.

What a contrast between the freedom of that gipsy girl and the sheltered life of the noble lady! Faint rebellion was stirring in her. It was due to the gipsies. Juana and Maria were right; she should never have watched their dancing. It was more than dancing; it was an expression of their way of life.

Sitting working at the altar cloth she had felt contented with her life. She had known that she would be married soon; she had not thought then how Blasco had excited her and how she had enjoyed most those occasions when he and she had escaped, from the solemn Domingo. She was wondering now whether the young gipsy girl would be forced to marry where her parents wished. No! She could laugh at the idea. That girl would never be forced to do anything she did not wish. She remembered how her teeth had flashed when the young man had stepped forward to dance with her.

She wondered then what life would be like for herself in the Carramadino home. Gradually she would take the reins from the hands of Doña Theresa; she would be the lady of the house. If she were forced to marry Domingo, Blasco would still be there.

The door was flung open suddenly and Maria hurried in.

'Here is trouble!' she cried. 'Tomás went to the cellar to bring up wine, and look what he has found there! Juana, bring her in. Bring her in, I say, and let Doña Isabella see what can happen when we bring gipsies into the house.'

Isabella had risen; the altar cloth had fallen to her feet. Juana had come in; she was dragging the gipsy girl with her.

Isabella caught her breath and stepped forward. She was standing on the altar cloth but she was unaware of this; she was unaware of everything except the brown-skinned girl who, seeing her, wrenched herself free of Juana's grip and threw herself at Isabella's feet.

'What does this mean?' demanded Isabella.

'She had come back to rob the place,' said Juana.

The gipsy turned a venomous look on Juana. 'You lie!' she spat out.

'If you did not come back to rob, for what reason did you come back?' asked Isabella.

'I did not come back. I did not go.'

'So you hid yourself in the cellar when the others left?'

The girl smiled, flashing those white and perfect teeth.

'It was easy. They cared for nothing but the food and drink.' A disgusted smile curved her lips which gave place to amusement as she thought of how she had fooled them. 'Dogs!' she cried, snapping her fingers. 'They are dogs.'

'They are . . . your people,' said Isabella. 'They will come back to look for you.'

'You can pay them money for me. That will satisfy them.'

'The girl should not be in Doña Isabella's presence,' said Maria. 'Take her away, Juana. Take her away.'

The dark eyes were turned angrily on Maria. 'I will talk to the lady,' said the girl.

'Are you in trouble?' asked Isabella.

The gipsy nodded.

'Leave us alone,' said Isabella to her two women.

'Doña Isabella, are you mad? The girl might murder you.'

The girl lifted her skirts and took out a knife which she wore in a belt beneath them. Juana and Maria recoiled. But the girl held the knife out to them. 'Now you see . . . I could not harm the lady.'

Maria took the knife hesitatingly. It was a *faja* such as those worn by most men in their belts.

'It is to protect myself,' said the girl, her eyes downcast. 'It is for that I carry the knife. Lady, let me speak to you alone.'

'That you shall certainly not do,' said Juana.

But Isabella commanded: 'Yes, I would speak with this girl. She has something to tell me, I know. She was trying to tell me when she danced in the *patio*.'

The gipsy smiled; the two women looked at one another.

'I order you to wait outside the door,' said Isabella. 'If I need you I shall call.'

They hesitated but, seeing their young mistress's determination and realising that she was no longer a child, and that with the master and mistress away from the house she was assuming a new authority, they retired.

Isabella turned to the girl.

'What is your name?' she asked.

'Bianca, lady.'

'Bianca, why did you do this?'

'I want to live in a house like a lady. I no longer wish to be a gipsy girl. I wish to sleep with a roof over my head and wash at the pump; I shall be clean and wear fine clothes and serve you all the days of my life. I saw you at the window and I wished to be of your household, so I danced to tell you so . . . and to tell you that I have left the gipsies.'

'You would never stay in a house. Gipsies never do. They want to be free. Bianca, you must follow them as fast as you can. You must go before it is too late to catch up with them.'

Bianca planted her bare brown feet firmly on the floor and shook her head. 'I will be your servant.'

'I have servants.'

Again there came that flashing smile. 'But never such a servant as Bianca will be.'

'Why do you want to live within four walls and sleep under a roof?'

'Because I am afraid of Pero.'

'The man with whom you danced?'

Bianca nodded and her eyes narrowed. 'I hate Pero. I will not take Pero, and if I go back to my people I shall be forced to. He is always there . . . watching . . . trying to catch me alone.

My lady does not understand. But he will catch me one day . . .
one night . . . and he would do that to me which would make us
married. And then he would beat me as he does the dogs; he
would kick me out of his way. And when he wants love he
would say "Come hither", and when he had finished I would
be as a dog again. No, I *will* not have Pero!'

'He will come here to look for you.'

'Not here. He would not believe I would stay in a house.'

'Bianca, I am not the mistress of the house.'

'Not?' Bianca's dark eyes were very wide. Fear crept into
them. 'It is not one of those two . . . those black crows, eh?'

'You mean Doña Maria and Doña Juana,' said Isabella
severely. 'No, it is not one of those. It is my parents who are
away from the house until tomorrow.'

'They will not come back till tomorrow? Then I will stay
the night with you, and I will show you what a good servant I
shall be, and then when they come back you will implore them
that I may stay.'

'Matters are not arranged thus in a house like this, Bianca.'

'But we will arrange them!' The girl had thrown herself at
Isabella's feet, had taken her hand and was covering it with
kisses. 'Lady, lady, let me stay. If you do not I shall starve . . .
or Pero will find me. Should I be Pero's dog?'

How expressive was that small oval face, the eyes so big, so
pleading, so full of woe at one moment, so full of hope in the next!

Isabella thought of the brutal gipsy boy; and she longed to
keep the girl with her, the girl who knew more of life than she
had ever learned, the wandering gipsy who longed to sleep
under a roof for a night.

She did what she would not have dared do yesterday. 'You
may stay for tonight,' she said.

Isabella lay in her bed and watched the stars through the window. She could not sleep that night. Bianca was in the room adjoining hers. Maria had insisted on locking the door. Maria had said: 'We are left in charge of you. What your father and mother will say when they return, I dare not think. A gipsy in the house! A stranger! How do we know what evil plots she carries in her head?'

How did she know? Isabella asked herself. She knew that she wanted Bianca to stay with her; she knew that when the door had been flung open and the gipsy had been brought to her she had felt a lifting of her spirits.

Now she thought of the previous evening when Bianca had gone to the pump and washed herself, shrieking with sudden laughter as the water tickled her. Her hair was free from lice. She was proud of her hair; she had combed and cared for it, had picked a flower from the *patio* to set in it, and she looked lovely in spite of her rags.

'Bianca,' Isabella said to her, 'you must have clothes. You cannot stay in the house dressed like a gipsy.'

Isabella had thought: I will make her look like a servant, and then it will seem to my father and mother that she *is* just another servant. If I am to marry I shall need to escape from nurses and duennas and have a maid. Why should it not be Bianca?

She wanted Bianca with her. She wanted to learn something of all that emotion which Bianca had displayed in her dancing. She could teach Bianca how to behave in a nobleman's house, but Bianca could teach far more than she learned.

So she dressed Bianca in the dark clothes of a servant. How

odd she looked in the sombre black gown with the earrings dangling from her ears, for she refused to part with them; and she would not put shoes on her long bare feet. She kept the castanets in the pocket of her black dress, but Maria would not return her knife to her.

She tossed her head and laughed at that. 'I should not be needing it here in a great house,' she said. 'It is not in great houses that people carry knives. That is for the gipsy encampment.'

They talked a little that evening, but that was not always easy, for Isabella spoke the Castilian language and Bianca the gipsy patois. Yet they understood each other.

Bianca said: 'As soon as I entered the *patio* and saw my lady at her window, I knew I had come home. A gipsy knows such things. This is my home and you are my mistress, and I who was free will be free no longer, for no one is free when they love. And I shall love my lady and protect her with my heart and soul, with my whole body.'

'You speak with great extravagance,' Isabella told her.

'No, no. It was a call for help I saw in your eyes. You, lady, need Bianca, and because of Pero Bianca needs you. That is how love starts. It is a need.'

'When my parents return . . .'

'They will say, "Here is the very good servant of our lady daughter."'

She will soon be gone, thought Isabella, for my parents will never let her stay.

So she tossed and turned on her bed and continued to think of Bianca.

15

The next day Señor Alonso and Señora Marina de Ariz returned to their home. Isabella stood in the hall beside one of the pillars, on which were carved inscriptions in Arabic, and received her parents with the ceremony due to such an occasion.

Her father kissed her solemnly and her mother embraced her with the utmost tenderness. On either side of Isabella stood Juana and Maria.

'Ah, my daughter,' said Don Alonso, 'your mother and I are happy to be with you once more.' He laid his hand on her shoulder. 'Come with us and we will all drink a glass of wine together, for your mother and I are in need of some refreshment.' He turned to the duennas and said: 'We would be alone with our daughter.'

He led the way into the small room – intimate and hung with silken cloth woven to represent the triumphs of the great Emperor Charles, father of King Philip. Although it was morning and the heat of the day was some hours off, the *persianas* shut out most of the daylight.

Isabella knew what they would say to her, but now that she was in the presence of her parents she seemed once more the timid girl she had been before the coming of Bianca.

'We have been in long consultation with our great friends Señor and Señora Carramadino,' began her father. 'We have news for you, daughter; and we trust that it will bring as much pleasure to you as it does to us. The Carramadino estate is a good one,' went on her father. 'I have never seen such olives, such grapes as grow in their vineyards. They are both rich and noble; and, my daughter, there is no family in the whole of Andalusia which could offer more to a young lady.'

Her mother was watching her eagerly. Isabella said softly: 'No, Father.'

'You are a good girl,' went on Don Alonso; 'and rarely have you given your mother and me cause for anxiety. As you know, it has been a great sorrow to us that we have had no sons. All our hopes have been in you, daughter. And now that you are a young woman, it is time that you married; and into what better house could you marry than the noble one of Carramadino?'

'You are not surprised, Isabella?' said Doña Marina. 'You guessed the purpose of our visit?'

'Yes, Mother, I guessed it.'

'Ah, that is why we see you looking so serene,' said her father. 'My child, Señor and Señora Carramadino are as eager for the match as we are. Domingo has asked your hand in marriage.'

'Domingo!' The name escaped her lips, although she had done her best to suppress it. 'Domingo, Father?'

'The elder son of a noble house. He will share his father's estate with his brother one day, but the larger share will go to the elder. All the vast estates will be Domingo's, and it will please us greatly to see you, daughter, the mistress of such fine lands.'

They were waiting for her expressions of joy; they were waiting for gratitude. But she was unnerved. Domingo! Solemn Domingo from whom she and Blasco had run away to hide. It was Blasco whom she had loved as a boy.

'Well, Isabella?' said her mother.

'It is your wish,' said Isabella slowly. 'This is what you have arranged for me.'

There was fatality in her words; there was despair in her eyes.

Her father turned from her. If she were going to protest he

had no wish to hear those protests. He could not impair his dignity by explaining to his daughter; that was a task for women. Let her mother explain, plead, force, if necessary. That was her affair.

He went out and left his wife alone with their daughter.

'My dear child,' said Doña Marina, 'it would seem that you do not realise the extent of your good fortune.'

'It is great good fortune to mate with the Carramadinos, I know, Madre. But when the boys came here, and I went there, it was Blasco who became my friend.'

'Blasco! He is the younger son, my child. Your father would not allow you – his heiress – to marry with a younger son. Why, it is long since you saw either Domingo or Blasco. Because you took a fancy to Blasco when he was a boy, that does not mean that you would do so now.'

'Has he changed then . . . so much?'

Doña Marina shook her head impatiently. 'I cannot believe this is my daughter speaking. Your father was hurt by your lack of response, your lack of gratitude for all that he has done for you.'

'I am not ungrateful. I know he has my good at heart. I know that he feels it will be best for me to marry Domingo because he is the elder.'

'Well then, be happy, child. Enjoy your good fortune. Oh, what an estate! And what a beautiful spot in which to live! Moreover you will be near us, dearest. I could not bear that you should go far from us. I have always wanted to keep you safe with us . . . close to us. It is because you are an only child.'

'Madre, when will the wedding be?'

Doña Marina smiled. 'So you want a wedding, eh? I will tell you we shall have a wedding such as has never before been seen in these parts. There will be a *fiesta* for the whole neighbourhood.'

'Madre, what said Domingo?'

'Domingo! He is beside himself with delight. He remembers you well, as you remember him. He says he has never ceased to think of you since those early days; he has been longing for this time when we should consider you of an age to marry.'

'And Blasco?'

'Blasco is delighted in his brother's good fortune. He also rejoices.'

Isabella felt the tears touch her cheek. Her mother was looking at her in dismay. Then suddenly Isabella threw herself into her mother's arms and lay sobbing there.

'There, there, my *niña*, my *hija*. Madre is here. Madre will let nothing harm you. You must not fret, my darling, my little *favorita*. There are happy times ahead. You will marry, but not be too far from your home. That is what makes your father and me so happy.'

'Madre . . . Madre . . . I *am* afraid. Domingo . . . he is so solemn. He never laughed with us.'

'It is good for a man to be serious, my child. That means he will make a good husband. If a man is ready enough to laugh with one woman he will soon be off, laughing with others. You have seen these brothers, and Blasco charmed you with his laughter. Believe me, my dearest child, it is not only because Domingo is the elder son and heir to his father's estates that we find such pleasure in this match.'

'But, Madre, there are some we feel drawn to, even though they lack the virtues of others; there are some we love for themselves.'

'And you were ready to love Blasco, eh? You knew that one

day there would be a match between our family and that of the Carramadinos, and you said to yourself: "That is good. I will love Blasco." '

Isabella was silent; she knew that she must marry Domingo. What was there for a girl to do but obey those in authority over her? She knew that her childhood had been a happy one, that she had enjoyed great love and consideration from her parents; as an only child perhaps she had been over-indulged, but there was one law which was unalterable in the house of her father, as throughout all the noble houses of Spain: the strict obedience of daughters to their parents.

She remembered Bianca, and for some reason the memory of the gipsy lightened her spirits. She thought: When I go to my new home, she will be with me. It is from her that I shall learn what I must expect of my marriage.

She turned to her mother then, and Doña Marina was pleased to see that she seemed calmer.

'Madre, yesterday gipsies came to the house to show us their dances; and when they left, one of them – a poor little girl, a little younger than myself – hid herself in the house and asked that she might become a maid to me.'

'My child!'

'Madre, please do this for me. She pleaded so sadly. She was so unhappy with the gipsies. There was a man who was threatening her. She begged me to take her in – and last night she slept in the house.'

'But a gipsy! She will be no good in the house, my daughter.'

'Then if she is not I will rid myself of her; but until she has proved herself to be useless . . . may I keep her with me?'

'This is a strange request. I will ask your father, but I am sure he will not agree to keeping a gipsy in the house. The other servants would not like it; and what were Juana and Maria doing to allow you to see the gipsies dance?'

'You must not blame them. The fault was mine. I insisted. I commanded. I wish to help this girl. Oh, Madre, how I wish it! If she were unhappy, I feel I should be unhappy. I should remember all my life that I had failed to help her when she was in need.'

'She has told you her tales, I see. Gipsies are notorious liars.'

'Madre, I do not think she lies. If she were with me, she could help me prepare for my wedding. I could take her with me as my maid . . . my personal maid. I would train her. And she is of my age, so that I should feel less lonely . . .'

Isabella's lips trembled and her eyes were filling with tears.

Doña Marina said quickly: 'I see that you have set your heart on helping this girl. I will speak to your father. It is a great concession you ask, but he has always been indulgent towards you. It is always first with your good and then with your wishes that he concerns himself.' She shook her head. 'But I cannot say what he will think of having a gipsy in the house; yet perhaps if I tell him that you wish for an extra servant, a maid who will help you with your wedding plans . . . perhaps then, at such a time, he will be ready to grant this strange request.'

Isabella embraced her mother once more, and she thought: To them I am a child still. They ask me to make no difficulties in bringing about this marriage with Domingo; and in exchange for my passive obedience I am to keep Bianca.

🌹 🌹 🌹

Bianca was riding towards Seville with Juan, one of the grooms. They were taking a message from Señor Alonso de

Ariz to Señor Gregorio Carramadino, and it concerned the wedding which was now definitely to take place. Bianca rode pillion, and as they went she sang a wild gipsy song which set Juan's senses tingling, as it was meant to do. Bianca was pleased with her new life. It was pleasant to be maid to a great lady, and to such a lady as Isabella – that was indeed bliss. There was only one thing which Bianca feared, and that was that when she ventured from the house she would meet gipsies who would know her and tell Pero or his friends and relations what had become of her.

She snapped her fingers when she thought of Pero. 'Dolt, and dolt again!' she would murmur. 'He thought to conquer me with his great powerful hands. His hands are those of an ape, and his mind that of a sloth or a worm that burrows blindly in the ground. And because he has such strength he would think to crush me . . . me . . . Bianca!'

Bianca was not to be crushed. She was to be cherished, as the confidante of the lady Isabella. She would live in a house, wear fine clothes and set a light glowing in the eyes of all men who beheld her. Mingling with the gipsy fire and passion in her nature was a gipsy pride; and with it grew dignity.

Not for her the wandering life, not for her begging by day, the camp-fire by night; never would Bianca submit to one such as Pero just because, in his brute strength, he had caught her unaware and given her his child.

No! Bianca would be free – no less free of gipsy laws than of the laws of Spain. She would be slave to no man. When she worked it would be for love. For love was free, to be given at will, to be withdrawn at will; and only thus could one as proud as Bianca serve another.

When she had first seen the gracious house, with its walls

golden in the sunshine, she had loved it. How delightful the scent of flowers in the *patio*! How enchanting to stand in the hot sunshine and let the water from the fountain trickle over her fingers, and to wonder what went on behind the *persianas* which shut out the brilliant sun and the hot light of day. And then at the shaded window the blinds had been lifted and, sitting back in the shadow, was the lady – soft-eyed and beautiful, her dark hair gleaming beneath her mantilla, and her hands dazzlingly white, it seemed to the brown-skinned gipsy, against the black silk of her gown. Pero would be far away by now. He would never find her. And each day she grew closer to her young lady, each day had something new to teach; and now, when Isabella married, she would go with her to her new home; she would live with her on the great estate of Carramadino, whither she was riding now with Juan.

Foolish Juan, he too had his dreams. They amused Bianca. Did he think then that they would bring him satisfaction? Well, there was no harm in his dreaming. He was no Pero to be feared.

They followed the gleaming river – the lovely Guadalquivir – and Juan pointed out the ships to her. He was proud of them, as every Spaniard was, because it was these very ships which were bringing conquest to Spain. It was only ignorant gipsies who knew nothing of these things. Bianca was a gipsy most eager to learn.

So, as she rode behind Juan, she listened to his talk of the Spanish galleons which sailed the world and brought back treasure and were bringing new empires under the dominion of great King Philip. Had she never seen the processions which passed through the streets of great towns to honour the returning adventurers? No, never! Then she must. One day he, Juan, would take her into Granada or Seville or perhaps Cordoba, and she would see among the glories of Spain, all the slaves who had been brought home from those far-off territories. She would see great things.

'I see, Juan, that you are ready to be very good to a poor gipsy.'

'Oh, Bianca, indeed I am. There is nothing I would not do for a poor gipsy girl like you.'

'Please to remember I am no longer a poor gipsy girl. I am Doña Isabella's personal maid, and that is something to be, my poor Juan. It is a far better thing to be than a poor groom; to comb the hair of a lady is a nobler task than to groom a horse.'

'You are right, Bianca,' said Juan humbly.

'Then please to remember it.'

And she despised him, as she despised all humility; she dismissed him from her thoughts and continued to dream.

In this house, to which she would come for the first time, she would eventually live. It was beautiful, she had heard; it was a house which had once been a palace of Moorish kings, and when the last of the Moors had been driven from Granada and King Boabdil had been sent in exile to Africa, the Carramadinos had taken possession of their palace and the fertile vineyards which surrounded it; and thus they became one of the richest families in Andalusia. It was for this reason that the Doña Isabella's father was so eager for her to marry into that family and that the old Moorish palace should be her home.

They were approaching the estates and she could see the acres of vineyards stretching out before her. The river was shimmering in the heat although the long hot summer had not yet fully begun.

Now she could see the palace, and she caught her breath at its beauty. It looked golden in the sunshine, like a Moorish temple set among the vineyards. She was filled with longing to be there. She had a mission to perform; it was for this reason that she was here. She was going to see Domingo, and she was going to tell Isabella exactly what he was like.

In the bag which was strapped to her back was an embroidered kerchief – a present from Isabella to Doña Theresa. It was not to carry a present that she, Bianca, had come; it was to spy for her mistress. She was no humble carrier of kerchiefs. No! She was on a mission of diplomacy.

Now they had reached the gates of the palace and it towered above them, dominating the landscape.

Two grooms appeared and came towards them. They exchanged greetings with Juan and smiled warmly at Bianca, who allowed herself to be helped to dismount. They jostled with each other for the privilege, and that was how it should be.

She gave them a warm glance of appreciation and said: 'Take me to Señora Theresa Carramadino if you please.'

They knew whence she came. They were ready to do homage to the maid of Doña Isabella who would one day be their mistress. Their eyes gleamed, for they would be ready to welcome Bianca to their house even if she were not maid to their prospective mistress. Juan had presents and messages for the master of the house, but it was to Bianca that they gave their attention.

So Bianca was taken into the hall which was like the hall of that house which she now regarded as her home, but grander. It was cool in the hall, and the marble columns, like Arab poles, which supported the roof, were more elaborately carved than those of her mistress's house. There were servants to conduct her to the presence of Doña Theresa and to look askance at the big brass rings which hung from her ears. What manner of maid was she, they were asking themselves; she had the brown skin and bluish black hair of the gipsy; she had the graceful gait of one, and her feet were bare. Strange servants were employed in the house of the lady who was to become their new mistress.

They were conscious of Bianca's beauty, and that in her which was different from themselves, and Bianca was pleased that this should be so.

Doña Theresa was not pleased. She had heard of the girl, for Isabella's mother had told her of the incident; Isabella was kind-hearted; the gipsy's sad story had appealed to her; and because Isabella was eager to train the girl as her maid, she had been allowed to do so. Doña Theresa had made up her mind as soon as she set eyes on Bianca that she would not long stay in her house. Such a girl would cause great trouble. She would never behave with the decorum expected of a servant; there was arrogance in the tilt of her head; moreover, those sinuous gestures, which might be inbred and therefore impossible to eradicate, would be a cause of perpetual disturbance among the menservants.

So Doña Theresa's reception of Isabella's maid was cool indeed.

She accepted the kerchief; Bianca was asked to wait while she wrote a note of thanks.

Bianca spent the time of waiting looking about the room. There were real carpets on the floor, and the hangings were more elaborate than she had ever seen before. There were wonderful pictures worked on them – pictures of great Ferdinand and Isabella in splendid robes, their feet resting on the heads of conquered Moors. It was very splendid, but Bianca was already disliking the proud woman whose feelings towards her she very quickly interpreted. There would be an enemy in the house.

'Take this and give it to Doña Isabella,' she was told. The white hand, on which jewels gleamed, placed the note on a small table; it was as though the woman feared that it might come in contact with Bianca's brown one. 'Before you leave, you may join the servants. They will give you refreshments.'

But was she going to the servants' quarters to drink wine and eat servants' fare – the black pudding which these people ate with such an appetite, or a dish of *olla podrida*? Was she to sit beside one of the grooms or the housemen, and to see the looks she had seen in the eyes of Juan and those who had brought her to the presence of the odious Doña Theresa? Was she to allow them to put their thighs close to hers as if by accident, to let their hands linger on her person? Indeed she was not. She had her mission to perform; it was not as though she had ridden hither merely to deliver a kerchief.

So she hurried from the room and crossed the great hall, dodging from pillar to pillar, using each as a temporary shield. She was going to see if she could catch that glimpse of Don Domingo and carry back with her such glowing accounts of him that Doña Isabella would cease to be afraid.

Clearly she could not stay in the house where a servant might come upon her at any moment, so she slipped out and, keeping close to the house, made her way stealthily round it.

She went through *patios*, under archways, keeping in the shade of the awnings, and came to a delightful garden in which orange trees and palm trees grew; she had passed the servants' quarters; she knew this because she had heard their voices; they

27

were laughing, and she thought she heard Juan with them; she could smell the onions in the *olla podrida* and was glad she was not with them. She passed through a *patio*, swiftly and silently, and now she had come to another wing of the house. There was quietness here and she realised that that part of the building before which she was standing was not of the same age as the rest of the palace; it was not built in the Moorish fashion, and she saw that it was a chapel. Cautiously she approached and climbing to a ledge was able to look through the long narrow glassless slit, and she saw that within was indeed a chapel. There was the altar; there was the confessional: and there was the great carved figure of the Virgin in her robes of blue. And as she looked she saw that someone was kneeling in prayer before the altar, and that it was a young man.

She was aware at once that her quest was ended, for Isabella had made her her confidante and had talked of the boys, Domingo and Blasco; Bianca was certain therefore that this young man was one of the sons of the house; his garments proclaimed him to be so; and she knew that he could not be Blasco, so must be Domingo.

He was dark-haired and his head was bent so that she could not see him clearly. He remained motionless; he was evidently deep in prayer.

She was alert watching him; she would wait here until he moved; she must see him clearly, for she would have to tell Isabella so many things about him.

Now he had risen and she saw him clearly. He was of medium height, his face pale and stern; he was very serious and looked as though he was still in communion with the saints. His lips were moving as though he was still praying.

He is too serious; he will be a stern husband, thought

Bianca. But I will tell her that he is handsome, for he is in some measure. And I will tell her that, as he goes to pray when no one watches, he must indeed be a good man.

He was coming out now; Bianca pressed herself against the wall; she was fortunately hidden from sight by the stone ledge, but if he should turn to the right he would surely see her.

She began to frame excuses. She would tell him that she had lost her way, that as a gipsy she had not dared enter the chapel but had wanted to see what it was like inside. She would tell him that she was Isabella's maid and that her mistress was very fond of her. Then he, wishing to please Isabella, would surely not be stern with her.

But there was no need to think of further excuses, for he had turned to the left. She stayed where she was, listening to his retreating footsteps.

Then suddenly, as she was about to leap to the ground, she heard a rustle from behind an old pepper tree, and a young man appeared. She was so startled that she slipped. He had leaped forward and caught her as she plunged down.

She was looking up into a pair of black flashing eyes and a mouth that was full yet mocking and, she decided, cruel.

'Well,' said the man, 'you are caught, my beauty. What are you doing – trespassing, eh?'

'I am not trespassing. I have every right to be here.' He held her at arm's length but his grip was firm. 'Ah . . . gipsy!'

'Please take your hands from me.'

'Not until I hear who you are and what you are doing here.'

'I ask the same of you.'

'Then you are impertinent as well as a gipsy. Do you know what I shall do with you? I shall take you to the whipping post. It is a way we have here with trespassers.'

Now she knew. She recognised him. She felt the blood rush to her face. He had noticed the change in her; he was watching her with some amusement. 'Blasco!' she said.

'Señor Blasco Carramadino, to impudent gipsies,' he said.

'So you are Blasco. Then he, the other one, *was* Domingo.'

'I shall need an explanation,' he said, 'before I release you.'

'You are tearing my gown.'

'Gown! 'Tis a grand name for it.' He picked up her skirt with one hand, holding her firmly with the other.

She kicked.

'Gipsies carry knives, and the girls hide them under their skirts. I must make sure you do not stick a knife in my back when I release you.'

'I have no knife.'

He held her against the wall and laughed at her.

'I shall have to search you to discover whether you speak the truth.'

She kicked him again, but he caught her foot and she fell to the ground.

She was on her feet immediately. 'Please to know that I am the personal maid of Señorita Isabella de Ariz.'

'That interests me,' he said, 'while it does not excuse you for trespassing in our private chapel grounds.'

'It was not so. I . . . I lost my way.'

'And you climb a wall to look through a window to find it! Come, you had better tell me why you were looking through that window.'

'I shall not.'

'Well,' he said, 'you are Doña Isabella's maid; you rode over with a message doubtless; and because you have the nose' – he flicked it lightly with his forefinger – 'for prying into what does not concern you, you climb walls and look where you should not. But it is a charming nose, so I will forgive you this time because . . . well, because you have wicked eyes and cruel feet, and I verily believe that you would kill me if you could because I have made you my prisoner.'

'Let me go, and you shall not die.'

That made him laugh; he threw back his head when he laughed, and thus she found her opportunity. She wrenched herself free and ran.

But he was after her, and although she was fleet so was he. She heard his low laughter close behind her.

She was running blindly; she did not know which way she had gone, when she had turned away from the house. She had reached a garden; she skirted it, deftly leaping over a statue; but as she did so she caught her foot in the intricate carving and went headlong into some pomegranate bushes.

She was caught.

'What a devil!' he said. 'What a spitfire you are, my little *gitana*!' He had thrown himself down beside her and put his arms about her. He kissed her suddenly, full on the mouth. She would have struck out but she was pinioned. 'That is for a clean gipsy; the first I ever saw. Why,' he went on, 'if you took those baubles out of your ears and covered up this brown skin of yours you might be mistaken for a lady . . . that's if you did not kick so.'

She was not easily afraid of men, and this was not the first time she had been so pursued; but she was afraid of some feeling he inspired within her. She felt that this was not the first time they had met; she had come to know him through Isabella's talk of him.

She said slyly and with mock humility: 'So you, a great gentleman, would chase a poor serving-girl?'

'There are some things,' he answered, 'that all men pursue.'

'You mean . . .?'

'You ask unnecessary questions,' he answered. 'You know.'

She smiled at him in a sultry way; she saw his eyes gleaming; he was off his guard. Suddenly she leaped up; she was lithe and she had a good start of him. She ran as though a lion pursued her and she was in fear of her life.

She saw the house, the chapel; this was the way she had come.

There were the servants' quarters. She quickly found a door and dashed inside.

She saw them all sitting at the long table.

Juan cried: 'It is Bianca! We wondered where you were, Bianca.'

❧ ❧ ❧

Bianca was quiet during the journey back.

As soon as they arrived she was summoned to Isabella's apartment.

'You saw him?' asked Isabella.

'Yes, I saw him. He is handsome and he is good. I saw him praying in the chapel. I crept away from the others and I climbed a wall. Through the window I saw him. He did not know I watched. But I saw him clearly, and I know that he is a good man.'

Isabella was silent; she continued to work on the altar cloth which she hoped to finish before her marriage.

After a while, she said: 'And, Bianca, did you see anyone else?'

'Yes,' said Bianca. 'I saw the other.'

'Blasco?'

'Yes it was Blasco.' Bianca rose and threw herself at Isabella's feet; she took her mistress's hands and kissed them. 'He is not good. He is ugly. Oh, you are indeed fortunate that it should be Domingo.'

'Ugly? Blasco? It could not have been Blasco.'

'But it was. I . . . I was told. Someone told me. He is very, very ugly . . . and he is not good. I know because I was told.'

'It is not true,' said Isabella, 'certainly not true that he is ugly. I am sure of that. As a boy he was taller than Domingo, and he seemed older and more handsome. Everyone said that he would be a fine man.'

'He is bad,' said Bianca. 'I know he is bad.'

She took the cards from the pocket of her skirt.

'I will read the cards,' she said. 'I will see if they will tell me what I already know. Ah! Here he is. The dark man. He is evil. But he will not harm you because he cannot come near you. And here is your good angel – that is the good Domingo. He is dark too.'

'Then if they are both dark, how do you know which is which?' demanded Isabella.

'I know. I do know,' said Bianca fiercely.

Bianca continued to think of him; and that night she dreamed that he had caught her among the pomegranate bushes, and when he kissed her she did not run away.

❧ ❧ ❧

Domingo was completely unaware that he was being watched. Kneeling before the altar he was praying for courage that he might not fail in that way of life which he believed it to be his duty to follow. There were so many times when he had felt that the priesthood was the only life for him; and yet he knew that, were he to follow that calling, he would never escape from that desire to be in this house again, master of the vineyards, a husband and father.

There were times when he stood in this chapel and sang praises to God and the saints, when he was exalted and felt that he would ask nothing more than a life of service to the Church. Then he would remember childhood days – wine harvest and the merriment of the villagers at such times; he would think of the gardens which he often tended himself, the roses which bloomed all the year round; and he knew he would never be happy away from the Carramadino country. He wished to be a priest who was also a man; a man who was also a priest.

He had always believed that one day he would marry Isabella. That had given her some special charm in his eyes from the very first days when he had seen her – a baby in her cradle.

So if he became a priest, if he entered a monastery, he would not only be haunted by his longing for his home, but there would be an even greater hunger, that for Isabella.

He had discussed his feelings with his father. It was for this reason that as yet no definite arrangements had been made for the marriage. His father and his mother had joined together in persuading him where his duty lay. They had but two sons; they hoped they would have many grandsons; but they were a family not noted for fertility. There was Blasco; but he was a younger son; and they wished the elder to make himself master of their house and lands; they wished him to marry into the noble house of de Ariz. The marriage had been discussed when the little Isabella was in her cradle, and Don Alonso would not be eager to give his daughter to a younger son.

So not unwillingly he had let himself be persuaded. But

there were doubts. There were days when he thought longingly of the quiet of monastery walls, of a life which was ordered by the ringing of bells, of solitude, of dedication to prayer. But never far from such thoughts would be the dream of the gracious life lived in this old house; he could picture Isabella beside him, beautiful Isabella who, from the days when it had been hinted that one day she would be his wife, had seemed to him especially vulnerable, frail, in need of his care.

There were days when the sun shone warmly and the grapes were ripening, or he heard the song of the harvesters, and he knew that in the vineyards, when the rejoicings were at their height and the darkness came, the workers – men and women – would be lying together out there in the cool of the evening, making love in that abandoned way which followed the ceremony of rejoicing; and then he would wish to be as they were, and he would know that in some measure he was. At such times he put on the hair-shirt beneath his doublet, and he would wear it all through the heat of the next day. But although such measures gave him temporary satisfaction he continued to be pulled either way.

How strange was the quietness of the chapel! Yet as he prayed there he had a feeling that he was watched. It could not be. None came to the chapel at this hour. Perhaps he was being watched by his own uneasy conscience.

Was he in his heart rejoicing because for filial reasons he must choose the secular life? Did he wish to be a priest because he knew he lacked the brash courage of such as his brother Blasco? Was he as sensual as any of the grooms who were on the alert for a willing serving-girl? He was tortured by self-doubts.

Again he was conscious of those watching eyes. Prayer –

concentrated prayer – was impossible. He murmured: 'Oh Holy Mother, intercede for me. Help me to know myself. Help me to live this life I have chosen with the same devotion to duty as I should have followed in a monastic cell.'

He rose and looked about the chapel. Foolish thought! There was no one there.

He had learned something this morning. He had wished for the recluse's life because he feared he lacked the courage to live any other as he longed to live it.

He was afraid of the future. He had discovered his fear; that was why he fancied he was overlooked and mocked.

❦ ❦ ❦

Blasco, picking himself up from the pomegranate bushes, was cursing the gipsy. Now, why did she run away at such a moment? What were gipsies for but to enjoy such fun as they might have had together? What a gipsy this one was! He remembered a gipsy he had known when he was a young boy of barely fourteen – tall, buxom, with similar flashing eyes and blue-black hair. What initiation there had been then into pleasures such as now had become commonplace with him, but none the less desirable and necessary for all that! This girl had reminded him. Not that they were alike; they were gipsies, that was all; and there the resemblance ended. There was something about this girl which he believed was going to prove unforgettable.

He laughed aloud.

She would be in the house when Domingo married, for she was Isabella's maid. He would have his opportunities with the girl, and something told him that he would not go unrewarded.

It was because he knew they must meet again that he

allowed her to escape him, and slowly picked himself up from the pomegranate bushes.

He continued to think of the gipsy. He thought also of Isabella. It was many years since they had met. He had been away at the university in Salamanca, and there he had indulged in amorous adventures with students of similar tastes. He had roamed the streets late at night in the fashion set by Don Carlos, the heir to the throne, though, unlike the adventures of the Prince, those of Blasco invariably ended in the seduction of a not unwilling victim. Don Carlos had been a monster; Blasco was one of the most charming young men in the university town and there had always been many to show tenderness towards Blasco.

He had not thought about Isabella until he had come home and heard all this talk of marriage. Then, it was true, he had felt faintly piqued; he remembered the rather shy dark-haired girl who was to be his sister-in-law and whom he himself had loved when they were children.

Had he been told by his parents that he was to marry Isabella de Ariz he would have been delighted, and very willing to ride over to her home and play the lover.

But no – it was to his elder brother that the heiress must fall.

Poor Isabella! Domingo was half in love with the saints, and it would always be so.

And what was Isabella like these days? Was it true that she had grown into the beautiful young lady his parents praised, or was that merely the talk of parents anxious to inflame the desire to marry in a son who was toying with becoming a priest? Were his parents crying their wares as the *turron* sellers did in the market? 'So sweet! So well flavoured! There is not better *turron* in Alicante or Tarragona!' Was that how it was?

How amusing to ride over to the de Ariz house and discover!

Oh, but that might be a breach of good manners. Should the prospective brother-in-law call at the house of his brother's bride before her bridegroom?

He laughed to himself. Was the real reason for his desire to visit Isabella that he might see the gipsy again?

He walked slowly through the gardens.

He was thinking of them both – Isabella and the gipsy, the one with faint regret, the other with growing desire.

🌹 🌹 🌹

In the great reception room the pillars were decorated with festoons of flowers; there were roses freshly gathered that morning; the room was filled with the scent of them.

Isabella stood with her parents to receive the visitors. Señor and Señora Carramadino embraced her warmly. And behind them stood the two young men. Isabella recognised the taller, whose eyes flashed with a merry humour, as Blasco. Domingo lacked that air of enjoying life and the suggestion which went with it that everyone who was with him must share that enjoyment. Domingo seemed stern and forbidding.

'My son Domingo will have much to say to you, Isabella,' said Señora Carramadino.

Isabella lifted her eyes to that pale face. Domingo took her hand and kissed it. 'Yes,' he said, 'there is much we have to speak of, Isabella. And here is my brother waiting to greet you.'

Blasco took her hand now; his pressure was warm; his smile brought back memories.

'Why, Isabella,' he said, 'you have not changed at all.'

'Nor you, Blasco.'

So affectionate was his expression that she could almost believe that he was the one who was to be her husband. How differently she would have felt if that had been so! Apprehensive she might have been, but joyously so; not fearful as she now was.

There were other guests, for this was the formal betrothal. Neighbours had come from miles around to witness it; and there were gentlemen even from the Court of Madrid staying as guests of her parents and the Carramadinos.

There was to be a banquet in the great hall; and after that there would be dancing; the dances would be stately, far different from those Isabella had seen the gipsies perform.

Domingo stood beside her while with her mother she received their guests.

How gracefully she bowed to them! How charming she looked! It was small wonder that the eyes of Señor and Señora Carramadino sparkled with gratification when they surveyed their prospective daughter-in-law in her rich home.

It was Domingo who took her hand and led her into the banqueting hall; and they sat together on the right hand of Señor Carramadino. Blasco was on the other side of the table and Isabella was aware how often his eyes rested upon her. Over his goblet again and again their eyes would meet, and his seemed to convey a message to her, a message of regret and longing. It was as though he said: 'Do you remember, Isabella, how when we were young we said we would marry? Ah, if only I had been my father's elder son!'

Domingo whispered to her: 'Isabella, you are not unhappy? You are not afraid?'

'No, Domingo.'

'You do not shrink from me? I am not distasteful to you?'

'But no, Domingo.'

'You should not be afraid. There is nothing to fear. We will be good to each other, Isabella.'

'Yes, Domingo.'

She did not know what she ate. She stared with unseeing eyes at the *cochinillo* and the other roast dishes. She knew that the cooks had been busy for two days preparing the feast; she knew that they were sweating with anxiety lest all should not be done to perfection. Yet she was unappreciative of their efforts. The fish and the meat, the savoury dishes, all were wasted on her; she stared at the grapes and melons, the peaches and green figs, but she did not see them; she could see nothing but Blasco – Blasco and Domingo.

When the meal was over they went to the great hall to dance. The musicians had already settled themselves on the dais; her father led out Doña Theresa, and Señor Carramadino led out her mother; and Domingo took her hand. They danced the stately measures and again she remembered the wild abandonment of the gipsy dancing, and she wondered: Why did Bianca lie to me?

It was later when she danced with Blasco. She knew that her hand trembled as he took it; and he was aware of this.

'Isabella,' he said, 'how lovely you are! I had forgotten how lovely.'

'I am glad that you find me so,' she answered.

'I never forgot you,' he told her. 'Ah, Isabella, what customs there are in this land of ours – what solemn senseless customs! Your family is destined to be linked with mine and, because of that, three little playfellows must cease to meet. I wonder why they prevented our meeting. How much easier it might have been if we had known each other all through the years between, eh? Then you might have married a man whom you knew as well as you know the members of your own family, one whom you had come to love. Ah, but I think mayhap our parents had wisdom. For they knew that had I known you, and had Domingo known you, then should we both have fallen deep in love with you. You could not marry us both, Isabella.'

She was startled. She did not know that this was the way young men in Salamanca talked, that there was little behind the earnestly spoken words but a desire to natter and make pleasant conversation. She was thinking as she danced: It should have been Blasco. I knew it should have been Blasco. He was the one I loved when I was a child; he is the one I could love, now that I am a woman.

Doña Theresa was watching her younger son. She knew him well; he must not be allowed to see too much of Isabella. She would speak to Gregorio. They must remember that their very attractive son was by nature a philanderer.

Blasco's attention had wandered slightly; he had caught a glimpse of a face at a window. His heart leaped with sudden expectation. She had a passion for looking through windows. Somewhere out in the warm, scented garden the gipsy was lurking.

Desire swept over him. He thought of the upward flash of her eyes, of the darting bare foot which he had caught in his hand when she would have kicked him; he thought of the feel of her body as briefly they were together among the pomegranate bushes; and while he continued to talk to Isabella, his thoughts were with the gipsy.

Now the music had stopped, and he conducted Isabella back to her parents. 'I see that Domingo is longing to lead Isabella in a *corranto*,' said Doña Theresa.

Domingo somewhat unhappily took Isabella's hand.

The music began and they went out into the centre of the hall while others fell in behind them.

Blasco slipped behind one of the pillars and stood in the shadows away from the light of the torches which lined the wall.

Domingo was saying: 'I am but a poor dancer compared with my brother, I fear.'

'Oh, but you dance very well,' said Isabella perfunctorily.

'He learned such graces at Salamanca. My father said he had greater aptitude for such studies than for those concerned with books. But, says my father, he has learned that which will stand him in good stead at Court.'

'He is going to Court?'

'My father thinks a place may be found for him there. My father has already spoken to Ruy Gomez da Silva and, as you know, there are many who say that Ruy Gomez is the chief adviser of the King, for Philip is a strange man. There are some who say he is happier at prayer in El Escorial than with his councils of state. Isabella, do you believe that possible?'

'I have heard it said that it is so.'

'Mayhap he often wishes that he had been born the son of a simple man, that he might have become a priest,' went on Domingo. 'It is a problem which may have presented itself to others – not only to the King.'

'Mayhap,' agreed Isabella.

'But he has faced it courageously, has he not? Often he must long for the quiet of El Escorial; yet it is said that never has he been known to neglect his duty. Duty must come before desire, must it not, Isabella? And when a man has decided where his duties lie, mayhap he can build a very pleasant life for himself.'

'Oh yes, Domingo,' said Isabella. 'I am sure you are right.' She was looking about her, looking for Blasco, but he was no-where to be seen.

※　※　※

She must have been waiting for him but she had not seen him leave. Blasco knew just where to find her. She would have climbed on to the ledge; she would need to in order to look through the window. He would steal up behind her and pull her down.

It was as he had thought; he could see her bare feet against the stone of the wall. Silently he came, and she did not hear him because the strains of the music filled the *patio*.

He caught her and she gave a little scream but none heard that either, for he had pulled her down and was holding her against him, his hand over her mouth.

'There is no longer need to look,' he said. 'He for whom you search is here beside you.'

She dug her teeth into his hand and he snatched it quickly from her mouth. She wriggled, but he held her firmly against the wall.

'Devil!' he said. 'Gipsy devil! You must be taught not to bite your betters.'

'I bite when I wish, and I have no betters.'

He caught her chin in his hand and held her face so that she could not move. 'You have to be taught many things, my little *gitana*.'

'Let me go, or I'll scream and all shall know you are here with me.'

'Scream then! Scream! I'll tell them I have caught a beggar who had climbed the wall to steal the ladies' jewels.'

'You would not dare.'

'I dare a great deal. How your heart beats!' He thrust his hand into her bodice, and she kicked. But she was excited and had no real will to escape him.

'Let me go,' she said; but he was full of knowledge, and he was quick to sense her slackening resistance. He thought: It will be sooner than I expected. Tonight. Why not?

Then he bent his head and kissed her mouth.

'What do you want?' she cried, breaking free. 'Why are you not in there dancing with the ladies?'

'It is a waste of time to ask questions when you know the answer. I am here because I like better to kiss willing little gipsy girls than to dance with ladies.'

'Willing! Willing! You said willing?'

'Aye, most willing!' he said; and he lifted her in his arms.

'Where are you taking me?'

'To find a pomegranate bush.'

'What if those people knew of this?'

'What if they knew? The gentlemen would lift their shoulders a little and the ladies would smile behind their fans. They would say, "But, of course, he is so fond of pretty girls even if they be gipsies . . . and since the gipsies are so willing, nay, so eager . . ."'

'You lie.'

'Do I? Do you intend to fight very fiercely then?'

'I am not afraid of you.'

'Certainly you are not. You are willing and eager.'

'I shall tell my lady how you have treated me.'

'It will make amusing telling, I doubt not.'

He held her firmly in his arms and was walking determinedly away from the house.

'I tell you I shall call for help. Do you want to have us caught like this?'

'No. Nor do you. That is why you will not call for help.'

'If I called they would not believe me. They would believe what you said about my trying to steal the jewels. There are many in that house who would be ready to believe the worst of a poor gipsy girl.'

'You are wise as well as beautiful.'

'Do not think to win me with soft words.'

'You love soft words, as you are ready to love me. Pray be still. Direct me to a place where we can enjoy our solitude. It is years since I was at this place, and there are doubtless changes.'

'Here. Put me down here.'

'Then you will lead me to the spot?'

She nodded, and he set her on her feet. She ran then, but he had held tightly to her skirt. There was the sound of tearing material, but he still held her. He lifted her with one arm and carried her across the *patio*; he went through a gate and into the gardens. 'You see,' he said, 'you are not to be trusted.'

He paused by the acacia bushes which grew near the wall of the garden, and he put her down by them and threw himself beside her, holding her there. She could smell the sweet smells of the flowers and the earth, and she felt dizzy with excitement. He had aroused in her a desire to match his own. She was wise enough in these matters to know that it was useless to hide it. He kissed her again. He whispered: 'You did not tell me your name, little gipsy.'

'Bianca,' she said.

'Bianca,' he repeated. 'We must meet often, Bianca. I have never ceased to think of you since we last met. All during our journey here I thought: I shall see my little gipsy. And that is why I wished to come.'

'It could not be true,' she said.

'And after the marriage you will be at my father's house. Bianca . . . Bianca . . . that pleases me.'

She did not hear what he said; there was a singing in her ears. For this she had fought Pero; for this she had left her own people; for this she had given up the freedom of the wandering life.

In the distance she could hear the music; above her she could see the stars.

Bianca cared for nothing now – not for what had happened in the past, nor for what would happen in the future. She felt that her whole life had been leading to this moment.

He was saying her name softly. 'Bianca . . . Bianca . . .' And she put her arms about his neck; she heard him laugh in the darkness – a laugh of tenderness and triumph, and she was glad.

🌹 🌹 🌹

Bianca was helping Isabella to her bed. The mantilla lay on the stool and Bianca was unclasping the necklace of rubies from her mistress's throat. Isabella said little.

She is sad, thought Bianca; she is sad because it is Domingo who is to marry her, and she hoped that it would be his brother.

Bianca felt dazed; she forgot that she was in her mistress's room; she imagined that she was out there in the dark scented night. Over his head she had seen the stars and never before realised that there was beauty in the heavens; she felt that she was reborn; that all her senses had been awakened with the birth of one.

'It was a wonderful banquet,' she said softly, for Isabella must know nothing of the adventure she had shared with Blasco this night; and often Isabella had laughed at her because she talked so much. 'And you were happy to have the good Don Domingo at your side?'

'He is a good man, I am sure, Bianca.'

'A very good man,' said Bianca firmly.

'Though quiet, and he looks a little stern, but I do not think he will be.'

'No, he will be good and kind – never stern,' said Bianca. And she was thinking: He said: 'Do you sleep with the servants?' And she had answered: 'No. They would not wish to sleep with a gipsy.' That had made him laugh. 'No? I'll warrant there are many among them who would give ten years of their lives to do so.' And she had told him: 'The servants sleep all in the great room below the hall. The women on their pallets, one side; the men on the other. For myself I sleep in a small room which leads from that of Doña Isabella.' He said then: 'Tonight when the house is quiet you shall come to my room, and we will lie together there until the dawn.' 'I dare not.' 'You would dare anything.' 'And if it were discovered?' 'Never think of discovery until it is a fact. Take your pleasures, and count the cost when you are asked to pay for them.' 'That is what you do?' 'That is what I always do.' 'I could not do it.' 'Then would you force me to come to you?' 'You would not.' 'Would I not? You will see. 'Twould be better if you came to me than I to you.' 'I could not,' she said. But she would.

Isabella was looking at her. 'What is the matter with you, Bianca?'

'The matter? Nothing is the matter.'

'You were just standing there staring at me.'

'Oh . . . It is because you are to be a bride and so happy. Don Domingo will be the best husband in the world. It is in the cards.'

'Oh, those cards! I believe you make them say what you wish them to.'

'You love him – Don Domingo?'

'Does love come so quickly?'

Bianca was silent. Something came – some wild impelling passion; but perhaps that came to people such as herself and Blasco – not to such as Isabella.

Again Isabella was watching her, wondering at her thoughtfulness. 'Love can come quickly,' said Bianca; 'but the love that comes more slowly is often that which lasts longest.'

Isabella was in her bed, looking up at Bianca who stood beside it.

'When I marry, Bianca,' she said, 'you shall be with me. I shall need you because in some ways you are very wise.'

'Shall I douse the candles?' asked Bianca.

'Yes, please.'

'Then I will go to bed. I am very tired tonight.'

'Good night, Bianca. Sleep well.'

'Sleep well, Doña Isabella.'

Bianca went into the small antechamber which led from Isabella's room. She sat for some time looking at her guttering candle. Then she undressed and put on a robe which belonged to Isabella; it was of ivory-coloured velvet and, with her black hair falling about her shoulders, she knew she looked very beautiful.

She was glad that there was a door in this small room of hers which opened into the corridor, for it would not have been easy to have escaped through Isabella's room. And what if

Isabella came to look for her in the night? What had he said: 'Take your pleasure, and consider paying when payment is demanded.' She smiled, for she knew that nothing would have kept her from him that night.

She opened the door and looked out. All was quiet; she went stealthily along the corridor, mounted the staircase, and within a few minutes had opened his door.

He was waiting for her; he caught her in his arms and kissed her with passion; then, first admiring her in Isabella's ivory velvet robe, and then without it, he said: 'You were long in coming. I was just on my way down to you.'

And from that moment she did not care if she were discovered. She was ready to take his doctrines for her own, to follow him in all things.

She would take her pleasure. She was powerless to do otherwise, for when she was with him her world was composed of his pleasure and hers — and she would not think of consequences. Payment would be made if payment should be demanded. There could be no thought of anything at this time but the transcendent joy of being together.

❧   ❧   ❧

In four weeks' time the wedding was to take place, but there was anxiety in the Carramadino palace.

Don Gregorio had had many secret talks with Doña Theresa, and they concerned the wedding and their son Blasco.

'He rides towards Jerez often,' Theresa told her husband. 'I have had him followed. He has been away from home for several nights. I know him well, and I know that his head is full of plans.'

49

'You cannot think that he has some notion that he can snatch his brother's bride!'

'Blasco is capable of any folly. Do I not know how it always was when he was a boy? Blasco must have excitement. He must always be the centre of plots and intrigues. You have educated your son as a courtier, Gregorio, and a courtier he has become. Had he been destined for Isabella she would not have seemed so desirable to him as she now does. It is to see her that he so often leaves home.'

'And Domingo?'

'And Domingo – there is another. Domingo is half priest. If we do not take care he will be wholly so, and there will be no marriage for that reason. Why, were he to realise the extent of Blasco's schemes, we should have him standing aside for his brother's sake. No! It will not do. Domingo shall marry Isabella, and Blasco must be given another occupation.'

'Do you not think that, as Domingo seems set on being a priest and Blasco on marrying Isabella, it might not be better to let them have their way?'

'Nay, Domingo is meant to be the lord of the estate. Once he is married, this desire for priesthood will leave him. When his first child is born he will give himself up to the delights of being a father. He will serve the estate better than his brother could. Remember your great-grandfather!'

Don Gregorio remembered. There were many children in the neighbourhood who carried Carramadino blood, and that was due to Gregorio's great-grandfather – another such as Blasco. For the peace of a village, such a man as Domingo were better its lord.

'Then,' said Don Gregorio, 'arrangements must be made. Ruy de Gomez is sending one of his men to see me this week.

He will have a proposition to make. There is to be a place for Blasco in Madrid. It might be well that he should take it before the wedding.'

'It might indeed.'

'Then it shall be arranged.'

So it was that, when a few days later Señor Diego de Cos arrived at Carramadino, he had a long and secret talk with Don Gregorio and as a result Blasco was summoned to his father's presence and told that Señor de Cos had come to take him back with him to Madrid.

Blasco, who but a short time before would have welcomed the idea of travelling to Madrid, was now reluctant to leave his home.

Bianca was unique, he told himself; he had thought to indulge in a passing love affair, yet he was finding it impossible to keep away from her. Often he called at the house some miles south of Jerez; he sought every pretext for doing so; he knew that his actions were giving rise to comment, but he could not help it; he had to see Bianca. There were many passionate meetings between them. Sometimes he stayed at an inn not far from the house – in the disguise of a merchant – and he paid that innkeeper much money to admit to him a certain lady who came in a long, concealing cloak. The innkeeper was prepared to do a great deal for money and, as Blasco had threatened to slit his nose and cut out his tongue if any learned of his visits to the inn, there was less danger in this enterprise than there might have been, though it was necessary for Bianca to leave the house late at night and return to it in the early morning. It was fortunate that she was as resourceful as she was. She was the perfect mistress and he felt he could have been content with her all his life. So when there came the summons to Madrid it was most unwelcome. He toyed with the idea of taking her with him and was wondering how this could be accomplished. He had visions of arriving at the Court with a gipsy mistress. The King was solemn and a great respecter of convention. It seemed that a difficult task lay ahead of him.

'You must be prepared to leave within a few days,' said his father.

'I could not be ready so soon,' said Blasco. 'I must have more time. Let it be after the wedding.'

'These are the King's orders,' said de Cos.

Later, when they walked in the gardens away from prying eyes, de Cos said: 'The King has many enemies; they threaten his great empire. But the greatest enemy in the eyes of the King is the Heretic.'

''Tis so,' said Blasco.

'There is one country which gives him great concern, and it is that which is ruled by a red-headed bastard.'

'I know of whom you speak,' said Blasco.

'The King has plans . . . many plans. He may wish that you go abroad to work for his cause.'

'That is what I would wish with all my heart,' said Blasco.

He was thinking that it would be easier to have Bianca with him if he were not attached to the solemn Court of Madrid.

'These English,' said de Cos, 'would challenge our power on the seas! There is this man Hawkins. What is he doing now? Taking men from the west of Africa, shipping them to the West Indies, and selling them to our settlers there. And at what a profit! This might be called legitimate business, but the fellow's a pirate. He sails the seas with his cut-throats, looking for our vessels returning home with treasure for Spain; he intercepts them and diverts them . . . to his red-headed bastard of a mistress. And what does she do? Folds her hands and says it is none of her business – that is what she tells our ambassador. But she makes little secret of the fact that she honours her pirates and is happy to take the greater part of their plunder.'

'Is it to England that His Majesty would send me?'

'I know not. He hates them. By all the saints, one day we shall grind them beneath our heels, we shall break the bodies of these heretics until they cry for mercy and beg to be allowed to accept the comfort of the true Faith.'

'Amen,' said Blasco. 'But could I not stay here a little? It is not every day that a brother marries, you know.'

'The King will brook no delay. Do you know the latest exploit of these robbers? This Hawkins and his young nephew, Drake, are not our only enemies, you must know. The whole country mocks us. Now the bastard has confiscated money which the Genoese bankers were sending Alba to pay our troops in Flanders. I tell you, the King grows restive. He is going to put an end to these irritations. He is going to show these people what is meant by the might of Spain. So be ready to leave, my friend; and do not delay. Delay in the King's service is dangerous.'

So Blasco knew that he must go.

🌿 🌿 🌿

In the tiny inn bedroom, in which he found it difficult to stand upright, he told Bianca.

'Do not think that we shall not meet again. I have but to go to Madrid; then I shall send for you, and you will come to me. I think we shall go over the seas . . . mayhap to England.'

'You will send for me? You swear it?'

'I shall send for you, and you must come to me.'

'I will leave all to do that.'

'It will not be long; I swear it. How could I live without you!'

'It must not be long, for how could I live without you!'

'Bianca, I swear there never was one like you.'

'But there have been so many!'

'It is because there have been so many that I am sure.'

'You have but to send for me,' she told him, 'and wherever I may be, I will come.'

❧ ❧ ❧

Blasco did not leave Seville until three days before the wedding.

He had delayed as long as he could but now he had spent his last night with his gipsy mistress, and he rode out in the morning, before the sun was hot, on the journey north to Madrid.

In the capital he was received with respect and, before he had been in the city twenty-four hours, he was commanded to ride out to El Escorial where the King himself would see him.

This was beyond Blasco's imagining. He had been ambitious for a place at Court, but since he had met Bianca he had been careless of such honour; yet this summons from the King drove from his mind even his longing for Bianca, and he was filled with unaccustomed nervousness at the thought of what it might mean.

He lost no time in riding out to the great palace-monastery, that austere structure which stood bleak and forbidding against the granite of the Sierra de Guadarrama. He was apprehensive as he passed through the gates and into the formidably imposing building in which King Philip spent the greater part of his life. Why has this mysterious man, aloof, and relentless, this fanatic in religion, the devotee of duty, sent for *me*, wondered Blasco. And he began to search his memory for some misdemeanour which in the mind of an ascetic man might seem a major offence. He learned later that many experienced such feelings when they were to enter the presence of Philip of Spain, whether it was in one of his palaces at Madrid, Valladolid or in El Escorial itself.

He was led through white corridors which aroused in him a claustrophobia more because of his own state of mind than because of the low vaulted ceilings, past guards who stood so still they might have been stone figures, past mute pages who looked as though they felt it would be a sin to smile or speak in such a place. Through great chambers they went, whose floors were paved with white and black marble, past Saragossa bronzes and on to the library in which, seated at a table, was the King himself.

He was a small man with pale blue eyes and hair so fair that Blasco was not sure whether it was white or not. Blasco went forward and knelt. He was bidden to rise in a voice devoid of emotion, and Philip with a wave of his hand indicated to all those who were in the room that he wished to be alone with the newcomer. Blasco stood up and at attention.

The King stared at the papers before him, and they were alone for several seconds before he spoke. Then said the King, still keeping his eyes fixed on a paper before him: 'You are Blasco Carramadino of Seville?'

'Yes, Your Majesty.'

'You are eager for a place at Court?'

'Sire, I am eager to serve Your Majesty.'

The cold blue eyes studied him briefly.

'You will leave Spain within the next few days for Paris.'

Blasco bowed.

'Your going will be quiet. I have chosen you for this task because you are not known here. You are an obscure young man. In Paris you will be a Spanish nobleman of no great importance. It should not be known that you come direct from me.'

'It shall not be known, Sire.'

'I wish you to take a message to a person there of very high rank, but this message is one which you will deliver by word of mouth. It is of too important a nature to be committed to paper or to be passed through any channels through which it might be expected to come.'

'I am honoured, Your Majesty, to be chosen for the task.'

'It is by no means a hazardous one, and you will be but one source through which the message will reach the Queen Mother of France. It is of the utmost importance that you do not speak of this to another person. It is secrecy I ask of you, Señor Carramadino, not great cunning or even bravery.'

'Sire, I will serve you and Spain with all the wits at my disposal.'

'Then listen carefully to me. You will make your way by degrees to Paris, and when there you will seek some means of speaking to the Queen Mother of France. It must not, of course, be at an audience which she might grant you and at which there would doubtless be others present, either visible or not visible. It must be at some moment when you may whisper to the Queen, perhaps in a dance, perhaps on passing near her. You must seek the moment; but this you must do on your own account, for were I to ask my ambassador in Paris to give you certain privileges you would immediately be a marked man. It is for you to use your cunning, and I have heard that you have a native wit. At the Court of France you will be a Spanish nobleman of excellent family, and as such you should, if your behaviour is correct, be received at Court.'

'I foresee little difficulty in achieving that which Your Majesty desires of me.'

'Let us hope that your belief in your own powers will be warranted,' said Philip dryly. 'The message is not a long one. It is this: "Continue with the arrangements for the wedding and, when you have them all about you, the moment for you to prove your friendship will be at hand."'

'That is all, Your Majesty?'

'That is all. Memorise it. Repeat it just as I have said it to you. Every word is of importance.' Blasco repeated the King's words.

Philip nodded. 'Go back to Madrid,' he said. 'Present yourself at the Palace. You will be taken to one of my ministers. You will repeat the message to him. If you do so to his satisfaction he will tell you to leave for Paris the next day.'

Blasco bowed low.

But the King had already turned to his papers.

🌿 🌿 🌿

It was but two days before that fixed for her wedding and Isabella awoke with foreboding. Seated on the floor, waiting for her to awake, was Bianca. Bianca had her cards spread out before her and she was frowning over them.

What was she seeing in the cards? Isabella wondered. Bianca often saw what she wished to see, but why should she be frowning today? And why had she seemed so remote, so sad all during the previous days? Where was her vitality, that quick and sparkling joy of living which was so essentially Bianca?

Isabella said: 'What do you read in the cards, Bianca?'

Bianca shook her head; there were tears on her cheeks.

'Bianca, you are worried about the wedding. It is so near and yet . . . and yet I cannot believe that I shall marry Domingo.'

'Why should you not?' asked Bianca. 'Everything is in readiness. What could happen in two days to stop your marriage?'

Isabella smiled secretively. Some time within the next two days Blasco would arrive. He would tell her that he could keep silent no longer. He would tell her that since his parents and her parents would never consent to their marriage they must ride away together. She saw herself riding pillion, riding far away . . . perhaps to Madrid, yes surely to Madrid for Blasco had been commanded to go there and he dared not disobey a summons from Court. They would be married in Madrid and Blasco would do so well that King Philip himself would congratulate him. Then her parents and his parents would be so pleased that they would welcome them home. Domingo would be happy; he had always wished to be a priest rather than a husband. They would all be happy for ever more.

Bianca was picking up her cards and dropping them into her pocket. She knew the way Isabella's thoughts were running and she felt very tender towards her.

Isabella said, seeking to speak lightly: 'They tell me that Don Blasco will not be at my wedding.'

'It is so,' said Bianca. 'They say he has left for the Court.'

'I cannot believe that he will not dance at my wedding,' said Isabella.

'Yet I heard from Tom as that he has already left his father's house.'

'Perhaps it is not true,' said Isabella.

🌿 🌿 🌿

The house was quiet. It was the time of the siesta.

That morning Señor and Señora de Ariz had left for Carramadino. There were certain settlements to be made. The wedding would take place in two days' time. In the kitchens the cooks were busy; there was much running to and fro, and fragrant odours drifted into the *patio*. The pillars in the great hall were being decorated with leaves and flowers; the great table in the banqueting hall was being prepared for the hundreds of guests who would attend the wedding.

Isabella had not yet risen from the siesta. She had not slept; she had lain behind her sun-blinds; and all the time she was alert for the sound of horses' hoofs, for she still believed that he would come. He was so daring. Had he not always been so, even as a child? It was not possible that he could be less so now.

And his eyes had told her so clearly what his lips dared not. He had remembered their childhood.

He must come soon, she told herself. There is a little time yet. He has not yet gone to Madrid. He will come for me and we will travel there together.

🌿 🌿 🌿

Bianca stood at the door shading her eyes.

It was foolish to look for him. He was miles away. Perhaps

he had already forgotten. He would find many to charm him in the great cities.

The sun was dazzling but the heat of the day had passed; and as Bianca stood there she thought she heard in the far distance the sound of horses' hoofs.

She pictured him, riding through the gates, calling her name as she had heard him call it so many times – softly and urgently.

It sounded as though there were many horses.

Perhaps the first guests were close to the house.

Bianca turned and went inside. It was time that Isabella was awakened from her siesta.

She entered Isabella's chamber. Isabella was lying on her bed, her eyes open.

'It grows late,' said Bianca. 'The Señor and Señora will be home quite soon. Indeed, I think I heard them coming.'

'They could not be here so soon. They would not have ridden so far in the heat of the day. They will be another two hours yet. Bianca, is it not strange how the time seems to go so slowly! It would seem as though I were eager for my marriage – so leaden are the hours.'

'It is a strange time for a young lady. It is a new life waiting for you, and that is why you have these fancies. Life at Carramadino will be much as life is here, only there you will have a husband. That is the only difference.'

'Perhaps that is so. Listen! What is that?'

'It sounds like riders at the gate.'

'It may be that some of the guests have arrived early. I must go down to greet them. Bianca, help me make myself ready to receive them. I will wear my velvet gown, I think.'

As Bianca took the gown and was helping Isabella into it,

there was a shout from below followed by the sound of strange voices. Someone screamed. That was one of the servants.

'Something is amiss down there,' said Isabella; she had begun to tremble. 'I must go down at once.'

Bianca thrust her mistress's fan into her hands from force of habit, and they turned to the door; but even as they did so they stopped and stood quite still for they heard heavy footsteps on the stairs.

The house was full of noise now. Pandemonium had broken out in a sudden burst. Above this were the recognisable voices of the serving men and women – the cries of the men and the screams of the women.

'We are set upon by robbers,' said Isabella, and she put her arm about Bianca as the door was flung open, and the tallest man either of them had ever seen stood surveying them. His hair was blond and his eyes as blue as the sea that washed about Cadiz; his skin was weather-beaten, and his mouth shrewd, cruel and sensual. He looked what he was – a man who had faced death so many times that he had ceased to be in awe of it.

He said something in a tongue which neither of them understood, and it was Isabella who was the first to realise who the man might be. She had heard of these men – these pirates from a barbarous island to which their noble land had once been allied through the marriage of their King and its Queen. It was an island which many felt belonged by right to Spain; but it was ruled over now by the King's sister-in-law, a red-headed woman, a heretic and an enemy to Spain.

This woman's subjects, aided by her, were becoming the greatest menace on the seas, and on occasions on land. There had been incidents not only in Spanish possessions but in Spain itself. These raids were carried out with speed and precision; but surely they had never taken place so far inland as this.

The man laughed suddenly. He said: 'By God, two women, eh! And charming, both of them. But they must wait.'

Isabella, who had not understood a word said: 'Who are you? How dare you come into my room . . . ?'

He laughed; she saw then that the sword he held in his hand was stained with blood, and she could not take her fascinated eyes from it.

'Don't be afraid,' he said. 'We don't put women to the sword.'

Then he strode over to them and took Isabella by the arm. Bianca tried to force herself between them. He laughed and with a quick gesture thrust her aside. She slid along the floor, and for a few seconds she lay still watching him.

He had put his hand to Isabella's neck almost caressingly. Isabella stood perfectly still; her horror was such as to strike her helpless. Then his hand snapped the gold chain on which hung a diamond, and he put the chain and the diamond into his pocket. He touched her then, felt her body as though he were searching for more jewels; then he laughed afresh and took her chin in his hands.

Bianca could bear no more. She flew at him; she began fighting with hands and feet and teeth. If she had only kept her knife, if she had not allowed those fools to take it from her, she would have plunged it into his heart, and that would have been an end to the foreign pirate.

But he had picked her up with one hand as though she were a stray dog. He held her so that her face was on a level with his and looked at her with approval. Then with one hand he felt the rings in her ears and laughed again. 'Worthless!' he said.

'Brass rings. The maid, eh? You shall both come along with me, though I did say I'd take only one, for, by God, it's hard to say which I'd have, till I've proved you both.'

Now he pushed them both aside and went to the door. He roared an order, and two men came running. One was small and dark and there was the look of a Spaniard about him. The other was tall — though not so tall as the first man.

He shouted orders and the small dark man said in Spanish with a foreign accent: 'Stay where you are and do what you're told. You'll not be hurt if you do. Show us your valuables. Where do you keep your jewels, eh? You must be quick, for the Captain is in a hurry.'

Bianca cried: 'Tell him I'll kill him. Tell him I'll kill him.'

Two men appeared at the door. They carried rope. The Captain signed to them, and one seized Bianca, the other Isabella.

Isabella cried: 'What are you doing? Who are you? How dare you?'

The man who spoke in Spanish said: 'You should submit to the Captain's orders, lady. He might kill you if you do not. He is an English pirate and he is in a great hurry, for he has ridden too many miles from his ship. He comes here for food and wine and all the treasure he can find. He will not kill you because you are young and handsome, but if you try to make trouble he might change his mind.'

Bianca cried: 'And who are you who are helping him in this? What do you think your punishment will be? You shall be hanged from a tree for your work in this.'

'Lady, I could do no other.'

The Captain roared again and it was clear that he was telling them to be quiet.

But Bianca would not allow herself to be tied up. She bit and fought; she tried to reach Isabella, but a gag was thrust into her mouth and she was soon trussed and flung aside with Isabella lying beside her, while the men stripped the apartment of all valuables, stuffing their pockets and bags which others brought into the room.

Captain Ennis March watched them. He was in acute danger and he knew it. He was too far from his ship for comfort. He and his men had ridden ten miles through the heat rather than go back empty-handed; and they would ride ten miles more before the adventure was done with. He thanked God the ride back would be in cooler conditions. It would need to be, for they must go much more slowly; they had some jewels, some gold plate, some food and wine and about half a dozen women.

It was not much, but there was some honour in having raided the land of Spain itself. When he got back with his booty – and women to prove what he had done – he would perhaps find many who would be ready to back him on a bigger enterprise. He dreamed of Mexico and Peru.

But he was not there yet. He was a gentleman of fortune and he did not flinch at great odds, but he had much on his mind at this moment. He had longed to raid Cadiz itself – that port into which sailed the ships from Spain's great Empire – but the place was too well protected for him to hope to make a successful raid. Had he been wise in landing a few boats at a quiet spot and riding inland, looking for a big house like this one? That remained to be seen.

The treasure was not what it might have been if they had had better means of getting it back to the ship, but the men had grown restive after several months at sea and determined to have some of the spoils which were enriching Spain.

He had warned them that the raid must be a quick one. There would be no dallying ashore with the women, and any man who touched a drop of drink would be killed by the Captain's own hand or, worse still, left behind for the Dons to deal with. They should have their wine and they should have their women, but not till they were all safe aboard.

Now he yelled to his men: 'Faster, you sluggards. Do you want Don Philip's armies to find you here? On with your work and we'll be sailing by nightfall.'

🌹 🌹 🌹

Isabella believed that the horror of what followed would never leave her as long as she lived.

She and Bianca were taken down to the waiting horses and were tied on to one of these. Isabella saw that four of the serving-maids were with them – the youngest and the most comely. She also saw other things – the bodies of one of the grooms and one of the housemen lying on the marble *patio*, and she knew that the stains on their clothes were blood.

She saw Juana weeping on the stairs and being roughly thrust aside by one of the men. She saw Maria run forward as she, Isabella, appeared, and try to drag her from the men. Maria received a blow which sent her reeling to the floor.

The horses were laden with silk and velvet hangings which had been roughly torn from the walls of the house; there were mules, each carrying saddle-bags, which already having been loaded were being sent on in advance.

And at last she and Bianca, together strapped on a horse, were led away with the others.

Isabella had fainted; but Bianca looked round and saw the flames of the burning house as they rode away.

They were in a rough cabin on board a ship.

The ropes which had cut them had been removed, for there was no possible fear of their escaping now.

With them were the four maids who had been brought to the ship with them.

They were all frightened, and it was to Bianca that they looked for comfort, for Bianca was less afraid than the others although she more readily guessed what their fate would be. Bianca's anger and hatred were so fierce that they swamped her fear.

If I but had my knife! she thought. And she remembered foolish Juana weeping on the stairs, and Maria who had made her feeble effort to protect her mistress and had been knocked into unconsciousness for her pains.

I would have had my knife in his back, thought Bianca. One of them at least would have fallen to my knife. But it was taken from me. Fools! Fools!

Isabella said: 'What will become of us? Bianca, what will become of us?'

No one answered. Not even Bianca.

She knew that soon the men would come. They were eating now, eating the fine foods which had been cooked for the wedding, drinking the wines with which the bride should have been toasted. And when they had had their fill of those dainties they would wish to enjoy others.

Even now there were stumbling footsteps outside the cabin door.

The door was wrenched open and Captain Ennis March stood there surveying them all with malicious amusement.

But his eyes were on Isabella. Isabella had been the lady of the house, and he was the captain of the ship.

Bianca knew that he marked Isabella for his own. He would have seized her, but Bianca had sprung forward, her eyes flashing rage, and she had placed herself before Isabella. The Captain's eyes kindled. He looked from Bianca to Isabella and then back to Bianca as though he could not make up his mind. He laughed suddenly.

Then Bianca knew that he had decided.

II

Domingo was praying before the *prie-dieu* in his bedchamber, which was more like the cell of a monk than the bedchamber of a Spanish nobleman, heir to a vast estate.

The walls were bare of ornament; there was nothing but the cross on which was a carved figure of a tortured Christ. He had been in prayer ever since the departure of Isabella's parents. Two days from now, he had thought, and I shall be Isabella's husband; then there will be no turning back. It is my duty.

Father Sanchez, the priest resident in the Carramadino household, knocked gently at his door. Domingo rose from his knees and bade the priest enter.

Father Sanchez was sad; he was the only member of the household who regretted Domingo's choice, for he saw in Domingo a sad loss to Holy Church.

'So, my son,' he said, and his voice was reproachful, 'the final settlements are signed, and you are determined.'

'Father, I am unsure. I know not which way to turn, but I remember that it is a son's duty to obey the wishes of his father.'

'My son, you have two fathers – one on Earth and one in Heaven.'

'I could not believe it was God's will that I should leave this world, Father. If I could have had some sign, none would have more readily rejoiced.'

'The call of the flesh had you in thrall, my son. Your bride is fair; your estates are fertile. Ah, it was a hard choice for a man to make. But is it not said in Holy Scripture that it is easier for a camel to go through the eye of the needle than for a rich man to enter the Kingdom of Heaven?'

Domingo covered his face with his hands. 'If there had been a sign . . . a sign . . .'

'Ah!' said the priest with an ironical laugh. 'How easy it would be for us if we were *led* along the righteous path! Then we might live our lives with the utmost sloth, for what need would there be for us to find the way and overcome the obstacles which are there to test us?'

'It is too late now. This marriage must go on. Only a miracle could prevent it.'

'Or your own will, my son.'

'At this late hour?'

'Many halt at the very gates of perdition.'

'You would call this perdition – this desire to please my father and to live the life of a normal man?'

'In one whom God has chosen to serve Him, I would, my son. The hand of God has touched you and the voice of God has said: "Follow me." And you have turned your eyes away from God to the rich vineyards of your father and the beauty of a woman.'

'That is not so, Father. There are times when I long for a life of seclusion, when I yearn to give myself entirely to the service of God.'

'It is not too late. There has as yet been no ceremony.'

'It is too late, Father. I have sworn to make this marriage. There is a command which says, "Honour thy father and thy mother." '

'There is another which says that God is a jealous God.'

'Father, pray with me.'

They knelt together and there was silence in the room.

❧ ❧ ❧

A rider was in the courtyard. His horse was flecked with foam and distressed from the long ride. The rider leaped from his horse, flung the reins to an open-mouthed groom and cried: 'Take me to the Señor at once . . . at once, I say!'

Señor Carramadino and his wife came hurrying through the great hall.

The rider did not pause to give them the ceremonial greetings. He cried: 'Terrible news! The house of Señor de Ariz has been sacked and burned. I have ridden with all speed to tell you . . . to ask your help. It was a band of English pirates . . . and they have taken the lady Isabella . . .'

Gregorio cried out in anger: 'So it has come to this! The rogues have dared even do this.' Then he said: 'And Señor and Señora de Ariz?'

'They are distraught, Señor. The Señora runs through what is left of the house, calling for the lady Isabella. The Señor bade me come to you and beg you for help. He knows, from one of the men who was wounded and able to tell him, that it was English pirates who came just as the siesta was ending.'

Señor Carramadino clapped his hands, and a servant came hurrying to his side.

He said: 'Tell the grooms . . . without delay . . . to saddle all the horses.' Then he shouted: 'Men . . . Men . . . come hither! There is work today. We are riding south this instant. We go to the aid of our friends.'

Señora Carramadino who had stood pale-faced beside her husband said: 'I will tell Domingo. He will wish to ride at the head of you all.'

She walked straight into her son's room. Domingo and the priest, who were on their knees, rose as she entered. They were astounded, for they rarely saw the calm Doña Theresa disturbed; now her lips were twitching and she was so pale that she looked as though she were about to faint.

'Domingo,' she cried, 'a terrible thing has happened. Prepare to ride to the house of the de Ariz at once. English pirates have attacked the place in the absence of Señor and Señora de Ariz. They have robbed the house and set it on fire. Domingo . . . they have taken Isabella.'

Domingo had begun to tremble. The thought of violence had always horrified him.

'Quick, my son! There is little time to lose. You might catch the pirates yet. You must ride with all speed to the house of our beloved friends. They will be waiting for you.'

Domingo nodded. He said: 'I will go at once, Mother.'

For a brief second he met the eyes of Father Sanchez, and he read in the priest's eyes the thoughts which were in the priest's mind.

Nothing but a miracle could save us. This is the miracle. The ways of God are truly marvellous and mysterious. He has chosen you, Domingo Carramadino, to give your life in His service.

With his father, Domingo rode at the head of the group of horsemen headed south towards Jerez.

Don Gregorio's face was white with fury.

'By all the saints,' he cried, 'are we, none of us, to sleep soundly in our beds? Are we, none of us, to leave our homes and families for a few hours without fearing these English pirates? I trust that ere long we shall teach them a lesson they will not readily forget.'

Domingo said: 'They have raided the coast before.'

'The coast! Yes. Our fortified towns. Yes. That is different. But to creep so far inland as this . . . it is unprecedented. How did they get the horses? What devilish bravado! By all the saints, if we had but caught them. And we shall . . . we shall . . .'

'They will have had many hours' start of us, Father.'

'They do not know the country. It is said that they are unaccustomed to the heat. Who knows, we may yet get them. We *must* get them. What of . . . the women?'

Domingo shuddered. His mind was often his enemy; it tortured him with pictures he would rather not see; it conjured up possible events which made him sweat with fear.

I hate violence! he told himself. That is it; I cannot bear violence. The sight of blood sickens me. Oh, for the peace of a monastic cell!

Now that seemed bliss, the end of all desire; cool stone walls, the comfort of the cross, tho hours of meditation, the bells calling him to complines, melodious voices which echoed in the chapel in such a way as to suggest that the atmosphere was holy and that there was truly life in the carved images of Christ and his saints.

If he had chosen wisely, he would not have been here now;

he would not be in a position where he might be called upon to face an English pirate.

He pictured the man as he rode along. He would be vulgar – as the English were – quick with the sword, fearless as pirates must be, careless of pain and suffering inflicted on himself or others. How could he, Domingo, a gentle person with the soul of a priest, enter into combat with such a man!

He had shut his eyes. Instinctively he was calling on the saints – the saints who seemed more real to him than the people with whom he came into contact in his daily life. He shuddered with horror as he realised the content of his prayer. 'Holy Mother, let me not meet the pirates . . .'

What was the meaning behind his words? Let them escape. Let Isabella and the women they have taken suffer at their hands . . . anything, but let me not be called upon to face the pirates.

If he were wholly priest he would be a happier man. It was because he was partly priest and partly man that he suffered so. Even as he prayed, the man in him was calling the priest 'coward'.

You hate violence. Why? Because you fear pain. You are afraid of the English pirate; he represents Life, and you are afraid of life. Life is often cruel, often violent, and you, knowing yourself inadequate, are afraid to face it. The walls of the monastery cell are comforting because they are a shield against life; you love those walls because, not only are they a comfort, they are a disguise. You may soothe your conscience with piety; it is a beautiful cloak with which to conceal your ugly fear.

He tried not to think of Isabella, and what might be happening to her now.

'Father,' he said, 'we shall never overtake these pirates.'

'We shall. We must. Were our people sleeping, that they could let them ride so far inland? Who gave them the horses in the first place? There could not have been so many of them. Surely some of those who saw them on the road would have given the alarm.'

'These pirates are desperate men, Father. It may be that they inspired such fear into those who saw them . . .'

'Are Spaniards cowards then, my son?'

Domingo felt the blood rush into his face. He said: 'There are cowards in every land, Father.'

'Then, by the saints, I'd let such men suffer that revenge which I have planned for pirates. Any man who played the coward at such a time should be hurled from the rock of Toledo.'

They rode in silence until they saw before them the town of Jerez de la Frontera lying between the ranges of hills; about them stretched the ochre-red earth in which the olives flourished. It reminded Domingo of blood; and the white soil of the vineyards made him think of Isabella deflowered.

As they rode through the town Señor Carramadino called to the people to follow him, that pirates had raided the house of his friend, and all Spaniards should rise in arms against the English dogs.

'*Si Señor! Si Señor!*' cried a woman running beside his horse. 'Our men have already gone. A messenger came from Señor de Ariz. They have already gone in pursuit of the dogs, and to bring the lady back to her father.'

'That is well,' cried Gregorio; and a grim smile curved his mouth. 'Come, Domingo, a few more miles and we shall be at the house.'

They could smell the charred wood as they approached.

Soon the air was polluted with smoke from the still smouldering building.

Gregorio dug his spurs into his horse and they galloped the last few miles.

Among the debris in the courtyard they leaped from their tired horses and Gregorio shouted: 'Is anyone there? We are the Carramadinos, come to help you.'

Doña Marina came running to them. Both Domingo and his father were shocked at her appearance and scarcely recognised her; she seemed to have put on ten years in the last hours. She threw herself into the arms of Gregorio, forgetting the etiquette of a lifetime in this tragic moment.

'My dear, dear Marina . . .' said Gregorio. 'My dear friend!' At first Marina could only shake her head. She had not wept before, but the sight of Gregorio and Domingo set the tears flowing.

'It . . . is more than I can bear,' she sobbed.

'And Alonso?'

'He lost no time. He has gone to the coast. He has taken with him as many men as were left. Others from Jerez have since ridden by. The whole countryside has been roused.'

'And we too will go, Marina. We'll not rest until we have brought Isabella back to you.'

'I dare not think . . . I cannot . . .'

'Nay. We'll bring her back. We'll cut the heart out of the English pirate when we have despatched him . . . oh, and it will be a slow despatch. And you, Marina . . . what can you do here? My poor friend, what is left to you?'

She said: 'We have no home, Gregorio . . . but if our daughter were restored to us that would seem of small account.'

Gregorio called one of his men to his side. He said: 'You

will remain behind. Take Señora de Ariz back to Carramadino with as many of the women and wounded who are able to ride with you. They can do no good here.'

He turned to Marina: 'Theresa is waiting to receive you, my dearest friend. She will look after you. Now we need fresh horses. Are there any men about? We will see what fresh mounts can be found, and then we go with all speed to the coast. I would not miss the end of that English dog for all the wine of Jerez.'

Marina raised her eyes to Domingo's face, and the grief he saw there made him flinch.

'Domingo,' she said. 'I am glad you are here, Domingo. You will bring her back to us. You . . . you, Domingo.'

He bowed his head: 'I will do it, Señora, I *will* do it.' And he felt brave suddenly; for a brief moment he longed to meet the English marauder face to face. But almost immediately he mocked himself. You would fail if you met him. He is an adventurer; he would run you through and toss your body aside before you could as much as draw your sword.

Then came the comfort, the beautiful balm.

'I could bring Isabella back,' he told himself, 'only if it should be God's will.'

So they reached the coast, and Domingo knew that he would not have to put his courage to the test. They found the distracted Don Alonso – like his wife prematurely aged.

He wept when he saw them, and when Gregorio told him that Theresa would now be looking after Marina he could only say: 'My daughter . . . my little Isabella . . . what has become of her?'

The people of the small village not far from the coast where the pirates had landed told them of what had happened.

It was in the morning – an hour before noon – when disruption broke upon the little village which was suddenly full of strangers, big men, with ruddy skins and crude voices, brutal men who had respect for neither God nor man. They had entered the little church and stolen the more valuable of the ornaments there; they had defiled the altar, for they were savages who did not seem to know they stood on holy ground. Then they had terrorised the village; they had stolen horses and asked questions as to the direction of the nearest great house; they had left a few men there to search for valuables, and ridden away. The villagers had not wanted to tell – but it was not easy to keep silent while a sword tickled the throat – and they had told of the coming wedding and directed the pirates to the house of Señor de Ariz. It had been unavoidable, for these were cruel and desperate men indeed.

Some of them had seen the return of the men; many had seen the ship sail away.

'So it is too late,' said Domingo. 'They have taken Isabella.'

Alonso covered his face with his hands.

'I shall never see my daughter again,' he said, blankly.

Gregorio, who was by nature a man quick to anger, cried: 'We shall not allow these dogs to do this to us. We will avenge this raid. We will do to them what they have done to us. We will bring Isabella back . . .'

Alonso shook his head, but Gregorio had turned to Domingo. 'You forget, Alonso,' he said. 'Domingo was to be her husband. Do you think he will allow this to happen . . . do you think he will lose Isabella like this?'

Domingo had begun to tremble.

'Ah, my son,' said Gregorio. 'I know your feelings. You tremble with rage. You long to take ship at once. You long to raid those barbaric islands and bring home your bride. Have no fear, my son, this shall be done. This shall be done.'

Did his father mean this? Or was he talking for the comfort of Don Alonso? How could he go to England and bring Isabella back? How could he begin to look for Isabella?

But he said: 'Father, I will go. I must bring Isabella back.' And the man within him, who would not be blind to the truth, said: With what vehemence you speak, my cowardly Domingo! Is it because you are aware of the impossibility of this task?

♘ ♘ ♘

Gregorio insisted that Alonso should stay a night in the inn which was close to the water-front. Alonso had been all for making straight for Cadiz.

'Can I rest, thinking of Isabella in the hands of that . . . that . . . ?'

'My dear friend, Isabella *is* in his hands. The need is now for well-considered rather than hasty action. Come, drink this wine. Would to God I had a potion with me that would make you sleep. But rest, my friend. Try to accept what cannot be helped, and let us do all in our power to think of a way to bring your daughter back to us.'

'I would go to England. I would appeal to the Queen.'

'The Queen! The woman who now holds money from our Genoese bankers! She would do nothing for you. She applauds these pirates of hers. Moreover, she does not feel friendly towards us Spaniards. No, that is not the way.'

Alonso thumped his fist on the table. 'I cannot rest here. I must go in search of my daughter.'

'Listen, it may be that some know who this pirate is. Tomorrow we will go to Cadiz and we will discover, if it be possible to discover. Then, if you go to England, you will at least know the name of the man for whom you are searching.'

Alonso was quiet then.

'It may be,' went on Gregorio, 'that some of those people who were unfortunate enough to see the man may have heard his name mentioned. If this were so we should have something to work on. But you are exhausted. And we cannot ride into Cadiz this day. We will be up tomorrow early. Meanwhile we will question the villagers further. For the love of the saints, Alonso, let us be calm.'

'Very well, we will question these people,' said Alonso. 'We will discover all that we can, and tomorrow we will ride into Cadiz. I cannot stay here while my daughter is in the hands of those men. I must do something. I shall sail to England tomorrow. I must. I cannot stay idle, thinking of my daughter in their hands.'

'You are too late, Alonso, to prevent their treating her . . . as a slave.'

The veins stood out on Alonso's temples. He clenched his fists and said: 'No matter what has happened, I must bring my daughter home. Domingo, you will come with me. You . . . who love Isabella, and whose wife she was to be . . . you will come with me.'

Domingo faltered; then he said: 'Yes, Don Alonso, I will come.'

❧ ❧ ❧

The night was still; the stars seemed to hang low in the dark sky; they were brilliant tonight; on the horizon the red planet shone.

Domingo walked along by the shore and looked out to sea. Not so many hours ago the English ship lay out there. Not so long before that Isabella had been taken aboard. Now there was no sign of the ship. Whither had she gone?

He threw himself down on the scented earth and listened to the gentle ripple of the water below him.

Tomorrow he would sail out of Cadiz harbour. He pictured what would happen. He would ride into the town with his father and Don Alonso, and the tale would be told of the abduction of Isabella. Men and women would gather about them; they would condole and their eyes would flash and they would cry: 'Death to the English dogs!'

Then they would say: 'It is small wonder that you who are her father and you who were to have been her husband cannot rest until you have brought her back.'

The villagers whom they had questioned were certain that they had heard the name of the pirate-in-chief. It was Captain Mash, or something like that. He had been addressed thus on several occasions.

There would be no difficulty in finding a ship to carry them to England and they would sail across seas infested with pirates; there would be horror and bloodshed. They would go to that land of barbarians – they who could not even speak the language. Alonso's grief had robbed him of his common sense. How could he go to an alien land and demand his daughter?

'Holy Mother,' prayed Domingo, 'I asked for a miracle. Is this the miracle? Is this the answer? But if I am to sail from Spain on this hopeless quest I shall sail to almost certain death, for what account could I give of myself if I met these robbers?'

He roused himself and listened for he could hear footsteps coming his way.

A voice said: 'Don Domingo?' He felt relief sweep over him, for the voice was that of Father Sanchez.

'I am here, Father,' he called.

He saw the plump figure of the priest in his dark *soutane* coming towards him.

'Father! So it *is* you.'

'Indeed yes, my son. After you left,' said Father Sanchez, 'I fell on my knees and thanked Saint Peter for the miracle.'

'But for Isabella to suffer so! Is that one of God's miracles?'

'The saints suffered for the love of God. Mayhap one day when she realises that she has been the instrument of God, she will rejoice in all that she has suffered. God has marked you for His service.'

'I have promised to sail away from Spain with Don Alonso tomorrow.'

'What good can he do by sailing away from Spain?'

'He will look for Isabella, and I shall go with him.'

'Look for Isabella! In a ship sailing the seas!'

'He thinks they may have taken her to England.'

'And how could you find her there? Your duty has been clearly shown to you.'

'My father would think my duty lay in another direction.'

'Your father is a worldly man. But God has marked you for His service.'

'How can I refuse to accompany Don Alonso? He would call me a coward.'

' "Blessed are ye when men shall revile you . . . for My sake!" Let us leave this place at once.'

'And return to Carramadino?'

'Nay. Let us ride to Valladolid, to the Seminary there. It is what in your heart you wish for. God has removed the woman from your path. God has shown you the way.'

'My family have sustained a terrible tragedy through their friends' disastrous loss; could I add to their troubles?'

'Could you spurn the Lord Jesus? Come, ride with me now. There will be a great welcome for you in the Seminary.'

'I feel that it is wrong for me to leave in secret. I crave for the life of the priest. I know that I long for it as I never did for anything else in my life. But to go now . . . when this has happened!'

'This is the time. God has clearly shown you it is to be so.'

'My father would call me a coward. He would think I am afraid to meet the English pirate.'

'Shut out these worldly matters, my son. Your pride is great. Subdue it. It matters not what others say of you. God has chosen you for His servant. To ignore His command could lead to eternal damnation.'

'Oh Father, I am a weak man, I fear. I long to ride with you to Valladolid, yet if I did I should be tortured day and night, for I should know that I was a coward and that I was afraid to leave Cadiz tomorrow.'

The priest was silent for a few moments, then he said: 'I see a way in which you could accomplish both your desires and vanquish fear. It may be that God, in His great wisdom and knowing you as you cannot know yourself, has set you this task to perform. "Go to Valladolid now," God commands you. "Give your life to My service." The King has great interest in the Seminary. As you know, the King is a deeply religious man who has dedicated himself more wholeheartedly to the service of the Catholic Faith than to his own crown. There are many priests who leave Spain for England. They arrive by boat at some secluded spot where friends are waiting to help them. They travel the countryside, staying in the houses of friends who wish to celebrate the Mass or to have their friends and family converted to the true Faith. There is great work in England that priests may do for the love of Holy Church. It may be that this is God's will; He will purge you of your fear; He will give you an opportunity of overcoming that fear, and it may be that in His great plan He wishes you to be the one to bring Isabella to her parents. It may be that when you are a priest, when you have learned to speak the English tongue, you will be sent to England and, going from house to house, you will be the one to find Isabella.'

Domingo's eyes were brilliant.

He said: 'It is the will of God. I see it now. To leave Cadiz tomorrow would be madness. But to go from house to house – a priest, speaking English – that would be a different matter. How long would it be before I should be ready to go?'

'A man does not become a priest in a year, my son. Great tasks are not accomplished so easily.'

'It is true,' said Domingo. His spirits were lifted. He was seeing the way before him, and he could walk it without shame.

It would be a long time before he could leave for England. By then he would have learned to conquer fear.

He said: 'I will write to my father. I will explain what I plan to do. I will tell him that I shall learn to be a priest, and that when I have become one I shall have means of finding Isabella. I shall tell him that it is folly to seek to find her as her father wishes to do. Don Alonso is crazy with his grief and he does not think clearly. I will tell him that, and when I have written my letter I shall meet you, Father. Where shall that be?'

'In the lane, half a mile from the inn. I shall have horses ready. We will make our way north to Valladolid.'

❧ ❧ ❧

They had passed through Salamanca with its pale yellow buildings which had been baked a golden brown by the heat of the sun, and headed north to Valladolid. The journey was long, for they must rest during the afternoons; but under the influence of Father Sanchez, Domingo felt more at peace than he had for a long time. He had even shut his mind to the fate of Isabella. She was suffering as the saints suffered, and had not all the saints rejoiced in those pains which made them holy? Father Sanchez's doctrines were comforting; thus would it be through the long months ahead while he learned how to become a priest, and if his conscience worried him, if that voice within him raised itself to tell him that he was a coward, he would answer that all his study was to enable him to be a priest, a priest who would undertake the most dangerous of tasks – that of going into a heretic country and ministering to those Catholics already there, and endeavouring to turn others to the true Faith.

And so to Valladolid, past the Plaza Mayor, past the house in which, more than sixty years before, Christopher Columbus had died in great poverty – on to the Seminary.

❧ ❧ ❧

In the small and comfortable room which was occupied by Father de Cartagena, the Superior of the Seminary, Father Sanchez sat drinking from a goblet of wine. This was comfort indeed, and Father Sanchez liked comfort. This was different from taking gulps of wine and water from the *porron* which was made of skin and was the only way of carrying liquid refreshment on a journey. Father Sanchez could smack his lips with pleasure, for he was pleased with himself. He had done what he had set out to do and, although at times he had felt he was far from achieving his goal, he had brought Domingo de Ariz into the Seminary to begin training as a priest.

'Well done! Well done!' Father de Cartagena was saying.

'Ah! There were times when I thought my task was to end in failure.'

'But you ever had a persuasive tongue, Father Sanchez.'

'It was the employment of my tongue in prayer which served me better than any persuasive words I spoke. I prayed for the miracle, and the miracle occurred. But for the raid by the English pirates, Domingo de Ariz would be a husband now and lost to priesthood for ever.'

'God is good,' said Father de Cartagena. 'Nothing could have been more opportune. The fact that He sent the English pirate is a sign of His will. His Majesty is eager that more priests should be trained for service in England. A man who has suffered at the hands of the English will be excellent material.'

'He is a fearful young man, Father. He is afraid of shadows. He is not entirely sure of his vocation. He has confessed to me that he is a coward, and he fears that his desire to lead the life of a priest may be due to a fear of the world.'

'We need courageous men for service in England.'

'But it will be many years before he is qualified for such service. That is as well. He is a young man who could not be content if he thought he had turned his back on the battles he should fight.'

'He will have many opportunities of proving his courage when the time comes. Come, let me fill your goblet. These priests whom His Majesty wishes to send to England are often more than priests.'

'Spies for Spain?'

'Spies indeed; and more than that. They are Spanish agents who work not only for the Faith but for the glory of Spain. It is becoming more clear to us all that under His most virtuous and Catholic Majesty these two are one.'

'So while our young Domingo would train as a priest he would also train as a Spanish agent?'

'My friend, as a priest he will be received into the houses of Catholic noblemen. There he will have daily contact with the great families of England. These families will protect him, and, while he makes good Catholics of them, he will show them how much more advantageous it would be to live under a Catholic sovereign than a heretic, herself a bastard.'

'These arc deep matters, Father de Cartagena. They would seem matters of state rather than of Holy Church.'

'They are one, for the King has one great desire, as you well know. It is to see the Catholic Faith triumphant throughout the world. This woman – and that it should be a woman is past all understanding – is the greatest of our enemies. It is one of our King's dearest wishes to see a Catholic England. Do not forget that there is a Catholic Queen in England now; she is the prisoner of the Bastard. Many would wish to see her on the throne; many would give their blood to bring this about. We are not without friends. But we work with caution and in secret. At this moment Mary the Queen of Scots is at the mercy of Elizabeth. It would be the simplest of matters for the Queen of England to cut off the head of her Scottish cousin. But she will do no such thing. She is no gentle woman . . . far from it. She is a fiery, ruthless woman who would stop at nothing to rid herself of her greatest enemy. But she will not act against the Queen of Scots because to do so would be to act against Royalty itself, and she fears to create such a precedent. So she keeps the Queen of Scots as her prisoner. But we are watching and waiting, and with God's help the great desire of our King and all true Catholics shall become a reality. You see, we need such as Domingo Carramadino – not only to go from us to preach the Truth, but to help set in motion great political schemes.'

'It would be well not to speak to him of these matters at present. Let him settle into his new life. Let it gradually dawn upon him.'

'You are right, of course. Nor should we in any circumstances talk to him of these secret matters. He has many years of arduous training ahead of him before he is fitted to go forth and offer solace to Catholics in a heretic land. Send for him now. It would be well for me to have a word with him.'

❧ ❧ ❧

Father de Cartagena embraced Domingo; then he gripped his shoulders and held him at arm's length, looking with affection into his face.

'My son, it gives me great pleasure to welcome you here among us. There is no greater pleasure to be found than in the service of God.'

'I know it, Father.'

'My son, you are come among us, and for a long time you will live within these walls. You will learn the abnegation of self; you will learn to sacrifice all worldly desires to the service of God. It is a hard life. A life of prayer and meditation. You have considered well what lies before you?'

'I have, Father; and I know it is the life for me.'

'That is well. While you are with us you will converse with an English student. He will be your almost constant companion, that you may make yourself fully conversant with his tongue. Why, in five years' time you will speak English as an Englishman speaks it. I know your history. You were to have been married, but God chose you for the Church and He gave a sign which has clearly indicated that He commands you to follow Him.'

'That is so, Father.'

'But you are uncertain of your vocation. You are a priest who doubts himself. You are not as strong as some men are. You shudder and turn from violence. Fear is something which those in the service of God must learn to overcome.'

'I know it, Father.'

'So, my son, God has worked a double miracle. He has smitten the house into which you would marry, and has shown you clearly that marriage is not for you. At the same time He has brought about a need for priests to do His work in a barbarous country. There are several here who are training as you are training. When the time is ripe and when you are mature, you will go to England.'

'When would that be, Father?'

'Not for many years. Priests are not made in a day, my son. Much learning, much meditation is needed before they are accepted into God's service. They live for months within the quiet walls such as these. They spend many hours, weeks, years, in meditation and prayer. And then – and only then if they are judged worthy to go into the world – do they go. During your stay with us, you will mature. You will learn to know yourself. When the time comes for you to go to England you will be a different man from that one who now stands before me. I see you rich in knowledge of God's wonderful works, I see you strong, all fear cast off.'

Domingo was overcome with emotion; he knelt and kissed the hand of Father de Cartagena.

'Father,' he murmured. 'Father, forgive my emotion. I feel that I have come home, and that I am at peace.'

❧ ❧ ❧

The days passed. The months passed. They were days of great peace. Each morning he rose with the dawn. Long hours were spent in prayer and meditation. There within the Seminary in that city of Old Castile with its many memories of the past embodied in its beautiful buildings, he had come to contentment.

He was at peace with himself, for he had stilled his conscience. He had postponed that which he feared until he would have the strength to meet it. One day he would go to England, and there he would face danger, but that was some years ahead of him and a man could change in that time.

When he rose in the mornings to the sound of bells he would feel a great gladness settle upon him. He believed in God's miracle; he had ceased to suffer because Isabella might be suffering. As he wore his hairshirt, Isabella must wear her torment. She must come to contentment in suffering as he must for the glory of God.

There were rumours in the Seminary. Events were moving fast. Priests visited them from time to time – fully-fledged priests who were strong enough to leave the nest and try their wings in dangerous places. There were intrigues afoot, and there was a certain confidence throughout the Seminary that before long a successful rising in England would turn the Tudor woman from the throne and set the Stuart there in her place.

Then would Domingo go to an England which was Catholic and a friend of Spain. Then would he go, not in secrecy, not hiding in the houses of Catholic noblemen in fear of his life, but to be received as an honoured guest.

There came letters from his family. His parents were hurt that he should have run away at such a time. His father had written to him at the Seminary begging him to give up his idea of becoming a priest and come home to do his duty on the estate. Domingo had tried to explain. He had written: 'Blasco will manage the estates. He is more suited to that work than I am. Let him cease to be a courtier and return home to Carramadino.'

And now they were reconciled. He had chosen, and it might be, thought Domingo, that God had shown them that they had been unwise to try to turn him from his desires.

This letter had news for him.

❧ ❧ ❧

'My son,' his father had written, 'I trust this finds you well and as devoted to the life you have chosen as you could wish to be. I have no need to say again that, should you wish to return home, we shall welcome you most warmly. I have sad news. Señor Alonso de Ariz met his death a short while ago. As you know, he has been sailing the seas since his great tragedy searching for his daughter. The ship on which he travelled met an English ship. She was boarded and, as she carried no treasure, the English would have let her go; but Alonso, poor, tragic man, insisted on drawing his sword. He was instantly slain.

'Doña Marina has been with us since the tragedy. But now that her husband is dead she seems to have roused herself. She seems to have come to the conclusion that Isabella will never be returned to her and that she must reshape her life. Therefore she has stirred herself and is making rapid plans for rebuilding the house. She talks of bringing Don Alonso's brother's young child, a boy, to live with her that she may bring him up as her heir — for he has little to hope for from his own parents, being the youngest son of a large family. This is good for her. It seems to have given her a new reason for living.

'And so life goes on, my son.

'We have no news of Blasco. But we understand that he is on a mission for the King in a foreign land and that we must rejoice that our son can thus serve his country. We shall rejoice still more when he returns to us. Then we hope he will soon marry and fill this house with children. In new lives we can forget the past; and that is what we, no less than Doña Marina, must do.

'The past is done with. The future lies before us.

'Adieu, my dear son. Your mother and I will never cease to love you.

'Your father, Gregorio Carramadino.'

Domingo pictured life in his old home.

It would be as though there had never been a young girl named Isabella.

PART TWO

PARIS
Summer, 1572

♣ Chapter II ♣

PARIS – SUMMER, 1572

Blasco was riding north; with him was a gentleman of the Court, Gabriel de Ayala, who would accompany him to the French and Spanish border; each had a manservant with him.

De Ayala was a sober middle-aged man, interesting up to a point because of the adventurous life he had led, but of such solemn demeanour that Blasco felt it very necessary to curb the freedom with which he was apt to express himself.

The memory of his visit to El Escorial stayed with him. He had returned to the Palace of Madrid where he had been received by one of the King's ministers; he had repeated the exact words of the message he was to convey by word of mouth to the Queen Mother of France, and the minister had impressed upon him the seriousness of his mission.

'You are a young man to whom a certain levity is second nature,' he was told. 'It may be that His Majesty has chosen you for this mission for that reason. You have not the looks of a young man who would be chosen for a serious mission. Keep up that impression, but remember this: it is dangerous not to obey to the letter the commands of His Most Catholic Majesty.'

Those words stayed with Blasco; they sobered him. He had dreamed once or twice that he was walking the cold low-vaulted corridors and that he was approaching some terrible doom which he had earned because he had failed to carry out the wishes of the King. He had awakened sweating from the dream. It had its roots in his brief experience in the granite building which was more like a monastery than a palace; it had its roots in the mute statue-like figures of the guards and pages, in the cold appraising gaze of the King. Philip of Spain was a King whom none of his subjects would dare disobey.

As they rode along he begged de Ayala to tell him of Paris – that was a safe subject. It was right and fitting that a young man bent on a mission to Paris should wish to know something of the city to which he was going.

'You will find the French very different from us Spaniards,' said de Ayala. 'They are a vociferous people. They cannot say *one* word if half a dozen will do; they like noise and excitement. They are extravagant in the extreme, extravagant in all things, in their garments, in their food, in their speech and manners. They would kiss your hand while they were planning how best to destroy you. You will have to keep your eyes open, Señor; you will have to have every sense alert. And on no account trust a French man . . . or woman. You may find some hostility. There are always those who prove hostile to strangers. But you are well provided with money. Take care that you are not robbed. If you keep your head you should do well in Paris. But, above all, beware of women.'

'And the *Court* of France? Is it as our Court in Madrid?'

'It is not! Never were two Courts more unlike. His Most Catholic Majesty sets the example of dignity and decorum. There is no such example in France. The French are immoral, and, it would seem, feel little shame in immorality. The King is young and his mother is the most important person at the Court. But you will see these things for yourself, though it will not be for you, a foreigner, to judge or blame – nor even to express an opinion. You will find that there are many enemies of our country in France. Some of these you will clearly see; they are the Huguenots, and at their head is the Admiral Gaspard de Coligny and Jeanne, the Queen of Navarre. But these you will know as our enemies. They are the heretics and therefore easily recognisable. But you may well find that those, who by nature of their religion should be our friends, may also be our enemies. The Queen Mother is a strange woman. Our King is unsure of her. But you have your orders.'

'Yes, I have my orders,' said Blasco. 'What of the town itself?'

'A town of winding streets set on the banks of the river Seine, a cluster of buildings, some of great antiquity, a town of churches and taverns, of great prisons such as the Bastille and the Conciergerie. But you will do well to keep clear of those. It is a town of restaurants and pastry cooks, for I tell you the French are mightily fond of their food. It is a town of shops where gowns and jewels and all manner of garments may be bought. For, more than any nation, the French love to adorn themselves. There are beautiful churches too – Sainte Chapelle and Notre Dame; and almost every French nobleman has his *hôtel* in Paris. The noblemen and women are extravagant in the extreme; the poor are wretchedly poor. Contrast! Contrast! There is always contrast. The French will laugh one moment, weep the next, they will love you and hate you, all within an hour. That is France. I have seen such brawls in taverns as I never saw elsewhere. There was one I remember . . . It was a place called L'Ananas . . . I saw a man run through with a knife. Whether he expired or not I do not know. His body was taken away. I never heard the outcome.'

'Such things have been known to happen in our Spanish inns.'

'Ah! I see I cannot explain this difference to you. It is something you must discover for yourself.'

The journey was a slow one. They passed through Zaragoza, pausing at an inn in the Plaza to eat roast sucking-pig and drink *manzanilla*, and to fill their *porrons* with the wine. On the balconies women sat in the shade, fanning themselves and driving off the flies. A pretty young girl served them and was clearly taken with Blasco. Strangely enough he had no fancy for her. His thoughts were all for Bianca. Matias, whom he had brought with him as his servant – a young man of not more than seventeen years with an eager innocence which had appealed to Blasco – watched the girl with admiration.

Blasco was amused. Matias seemed younger than his years. He had told Blasco that he came from a village not far from Toledo, and that it was only two days before Blasco had engaged him to act as his servant that he had arrived in Madrid to seek his fortune.

De Ayala dozed over his wine, and Blasco called Matias to him.

He said: 'A pretty girl, eh? The one who waited on us.'

'*Si Señor*,' said young Matias, smiling his shy and eager smile.

'She waits outside in the *patio*. She knows there is nothing more she can bring us. Why do you not go and talk to her, Matias? Would you not wish to do that?'

'But *si Señor*.'

Matias bowed and went off. A few minutes later Blasco heard him in conversation with the girl.

He went to the room which the innkeeper had put at the disposal of the nobleman from Madrid, and he lay there on a couch, gazing at the blind which could not completely shut out the fierce rays of the sun. If he had had Bianca with him he could have been perfectly content. Ah, if he could exchange the pompous de Ayala for her, what bliss that would be! But she should soon be with him. He had been making his plans as they journeyed north. As soon as de Ayala had left him he would despatch Matias south with orders to bring Bianca to him in Paris. L'Ananas. He had found out the name of that tavern, and there Matias should bring Bianca. If only he might have sent Matias on his way south immediately, how glad he would have been!

Yet he dared not send Matias back now. He was afraid of what this solemn man might say and do if he told him that he wished to have his mistress with him in Paris. Who knew what tales he would carry back to Madrid? There might even be some plan to prevent Bianca's coming to him.

He longed for her; no other could satisfy him. This girl at the inn was a case in point. At any other time he would have passed a very pleasant hour with her, and would doubtless have seduced her before he passed on. Now – and on account of Bianca – she had no charm for him. So she was left to poor innocent Matias.

He slept lightly and a few hours later he rose and went downstairs. He was amused to see that Matias was sitting in the shade with the girl.

De Ayala was ready to continue their journey, so they left immediately.

'And how fared you with the lady?' asked Blasco lightly, as Matias strapped the *porrons* to his saddle.

'Ah *Señor*, she is very beautiful, and I told her so.'

'Words!' said Blasco. 'Words! They are all very well, my poor Matias; but it is the deeds which bring pleasure. But do not look so sad. Who knows, perhaps you will one day ride this way and pause at the inn in the Plaza of Zaragoza. Mayhap then there will be more time, eh, Matias?'

Matias smiled his innocent smile. '*Si Señor*,' he said.

%% %% %%

At the frontier, as had been arranged, de Ayala and his man took their leave, and turned back towards Madrid.

As soon as they were out of sight, Blasco pulled up his horse and said: 'Matias, I have an errand for you to perform. It is of the utmost importance, and you must set out on it without delay. You must ride back the way we have come with all speed. But do not go into Madrid. Do not go into any town where you might be recognised, and you must on no account meet with Señor de Ayala and his Pablo.'

'What does the Señor wish of me?'

'I wish you to ride south of Madrid until you come to the town of Seville. When you reach Seville you will be near your destination. I wish you to ask then for the house of Señor Carramadino. It is some four miles south of Seville. When you have reached the house you will look for a certain woman there. You cannot mistake her – she is a gipsy, although she is dressed as a servant. She wears great rings in her ears. You must not let anyone but this woman know from whom you come. To her you will say: "I come to take you to my master, Blasco. We must leave with all speed." I tell you this, Matias, it is to my home you will go, and the woman is the maid of my brother's newly married wife. I shall give you money – a great deal of money. Guard it well and do not linger in lonely roads, or if you should stop at an inn let any know how much you carry. You will need it all. When you reach my home, find the woman quickly and bring her to me. You will have to find your way with her to this spot and then travel northwards to Paris. She will help you find the way, for she is quick and clever. When you reach Paris you will bring her – her name is Bianca; Bianca, the gipsy, remember that! – to a tavern to which anyone will direct you. It is called L'Ananas. Matias, I rely on you. Do this and you shall be my servant all the days of my life, and yours. You will find that I am a good master ever ready to reward those who serve me well.'

'*Si Señor*.'

'Now repeat to me what you have to do and then . . . off you go. The sooner you return to me, the greater will be your reward.'

'*Si Señor*.' Matias repeated the name of the gipsy, the name of the house where he would find her. 'Bianca . . .' he repeated. 'Bianca . . . the gipsy. And L'Ananas.' Yes, he would remember that. His one wish was to serve the Señor with all his heart.

❧ ❧ ❧

Matias was happy. He was in the service of a great lord who had promised that he should serve him for the rest of their lives. They had laughed at Matias in his village when he had said he would go to Madrid and make his fortune. They would not laugh so much now, for he, Matias, was to all intents and purposes a rich man. He carried more money concealed about his person than any man in the village had ever seen in the whole of his life. His village was south of Madrid. Perhaps he could pass through it. It was not far out of his way, and he

99

would stay just long enough to show them the money; for unless they saw it they would never believe him.

But before he reached Madrid he came to the town of Zaragoza, and he thought then of the pretty daughter of the innkeeper who had seemed to like him so much; so, instead of skirting the town, he decided to pass through it, for after all a man must rest during the hot hours of the day, and his horse must be watered and fed.

He came to the Plaza. It looked exactly as it had a few days before, when he had been here with his master and that nobleman and his servant from Madrid. The flies were as fiercely insistent; the women still sat on their balconies fanning themselves. And how their eyes lit up at the sight of a handsome young boy!

Matias was beginning to realise that the world outside his village was very appreciative of him. There were two qualities he possessed which the world greatly admired: youth and good looks; and now that he also carried a great deal of money on his person, and was on an important mission for his master, he felt grand indeed.

He went to the inn. He sat under the shade of the awning and called for wine. She brought it to him and she lingered.

'It is the señor who was here with us but a few days ago!'

'It is so. And you remembered?'

'Ah, Señor, we do not see so many like you that we should forget.'

He said: 'Would it be possible for you to sit down here and drink with me?'

'My father permits it for important customers, Señor.' How happy he was, sitting there in the shade with the innkeeper's pretty daughter opposite him.

She said: 'You are riding on, Señor, or shall you stay awhile?'

To stay awhile! That was inviting. It was not possible to get very far with such an acquaintance in a few short hours. But of course he must not linger. His instructions were to ride to the house of the Carramadino with all speed. But there was no need to tell her that. She no longer saw him as the servant of a nobleman; she was looking at him as though she believed him to be a nobleman himself.

'It is as yet undecided,' he said.

That seemed to please her. She was clearly suggesting that she would be delighted if he stayed.

He asked her name. It was Blanca. That excited him. Blanca! Bianca! That seemed to him significant, but perhaps that was because he was already under the spell of *manzanilla* and the eyes of the pretty Blanca.

He paid for his wine, and he could not resist flourishing his purse before her eyes. How they widened! Now she believed him to be a gentleman of some fortune.

She laughed at him slyly. 'So it was a pretence, Señor, that you were the servant of that other?'

He did not deny it. With a knowing smile he ordered more *manzanilla*.

She told him that her father had special apartments to be set aside for noblemen who wished to pass the hours of the siesta under his roof. They were splendid apartments, but not beyond the purse of one such as himself. Should she lead him to them?

Why not? He had money to pay for such service, and none would expect a man to ride on during the heat of the day; he would rest, and that would make him very fresh for the journey ahead of him. He would soon make up for any time that he had lost.

So she led him to the room in which was a couch; it was the very room where, not so long before, his master had spent the hours of the siesta while he had sat under the awning looking fondly at the pretty Blanca, never dreaming that soon he would return to her father's inn in the guise of a lord.

'Here is the room, Señor.'

She stood before him smiling, and he took her suddenly into his arms and kissed her.

⅋ ⅋ ⅋

Blasco continued his journey through France, through towns and villages, past vineyards which were not unlike those of his own land. But here there was a softness about the countryside which the Spanish landscape lacked; the temperatures here were not so extreme, the people were more pleasure-loving. There was one thing he had discovered about France in which it differed largely from his own country; that was the divided opinion on religious matters.

He kept silent unless he was with Catholics, for he was quick to sense the tension which existed throughout this country; it was almost as though there was a civil war in progress, a secret war which would suddenly cease to be secret.

There were certain towns which seemed to be entirely Huguenot. He saw churches from which many of the statues had been torn down, and in such towns people looked at him suspiciously.

'A Spaniard. Recently come from Spain!' They would avert their eyes; it was clear that to such people the Kingdom beyond the border was their most bitter enemy.

He had heard that a group of Huguenots, going to worship in their simple way, had been set upon by the Catholics and the death of many had been the result. And as he travelled further north he became increasingly aware of these differences.

One evening he came into a small town not far from Orléans and looked about for an inn at which he might spend the night. He noticed that there was great activity in this town, which was unusual for such a small place, and when he called at the inn he was told that there was no room for him.

He was astonished, but the innkeeper quickly explained: 'Monsieur, our little town is full. It is unfortunate that you should have chosen just this day to ask me for a room. It is due to the fact that Her Majesty the Queen of Navarre rides to Paris, and all those in her retinue must be found accommodation for the night.'

'So the Queen is here now?'

'Yes, Monsieur . . . on her way to Paris.'

Blasco was thoughtful. He was wondering whether he might join the Queen's retinue, and so be directed to Paris and at the same time perhaps ingratiate himself with some powerful person in that retinue who could help him achieve his mission.

He dismounted and asked the innkeeper to see that his horse was watered and fed.

'With pleasure, Monsieur,' said the innkeeper. 'If you are determined to stay the night here it may be that, if you do not mind spending it in a small room in a cottage, you could find that.'

'I should be thankful for any room, however small and humble,' said Blasco.

'Then walk on a hundred paces, and you will come to the cottage of Madame Ferronier. Tell her you come from me. It may be that she can offer you shelter for the night.'

'I am grateful,' said Blasco. 'Take care of my horse. You will be well paid, my friend. I shall go at once to the house of Madame Ferronier.'

'And, Monsieur, if you would care to return to my inn I can promise you good meat and wine.'

'I shall do that.'

As he came towards the cottage he saw a young man approaching, and it soon became clear that both had the same object in view. The young man was a year or so younger than Blasco; he was soberly dressed and looked as though he had ridden far.

His expression was pleasant, and he greeted Blasco with a friendly smile.

'It would seem,' he said in French which Blasco recognised as similar to that which he had heard in the South of France, 'that you and I are bent on the same mission.'

'A room at the cottage of Madame Ferronier?'

'Yes. That is what I seek.'

'And I.'

Blasco laughed. 'Is it the only available room in this place?' he went on.

'It would seem so.'

'Then one of us will be unlucky.'

'You are not French, Monsieur?'

'No, I come from Spain.'

The faintest shadow crossed the boy's face, but his smile remained sweet. 'You are on your way to Paris?'

'How did you guess?'

'Everyone is on his way to Paris.'

Madame Ferronier had come to the door; she was a small, squat woman with suspicious eyes. Yes, she said, she had a room. It was small and there was a pallet in it. She would wish to be paid in advance, and as there were two of them to share it she would want a little more than if there had been only one.

They looked at each other and smiled. Then the French boy said: 'Shall we look at it?'

Blasco nodded, and Madame Ferronier led them into the dark cottage. There was one room above and one below. They climbed the narrow spiral staircase which led straight into the room. There was no door and one tiny window. On the floor was a pallet and the place was none too clean.

'You must have it, Monsieur,' said the French boy, 'because you are a guest in our country.'

'Certainly not,' said Blasco. 'You take it. I could go on or sleep under a hedge. It would not be the first time I have done that.'

'The woman thinks we might share. Monsieur, if you will take the pallet, I shall be very comfortable on the floor.'

And so it was arranged.

Blasco went back to the inn and ate a good meal of meat washed down with burgundy, and afterwards he made his way back to the cottage of Madame Ferronier. The young man was already there. He had spread out his cloak on the floor, and as Blasco entered he declared that it would by no means be the most uncomfortable night he had ever passed.

'We should know each other's names,' said Blasco. He told his.

'I am Pierre Lerand of Béarn.'

'And you are travelling with the Queen's suite to Paris?'

'That is so. My father is with us, and my young sister Julie. It is our first visit to Paris. Julie is very excited. She is young – so young. And you, Monsieur? You also have business in Paris?'

'Business? I fear not. I am an idler. My father has estates in Spain and he wishes me to see the world a little before I settle down. So, I ride to Paris, for we have heard that to know the world a man must first know Paris.'

'The capital of France is a worldly city, so I have heard.'

'That seems to give you some anxiety.'

'My sister is very young. It might be that it would have been wiser to have left her in Béarn.'

'It is not always easy for a foreigner to find his way. Do you think I might join your party . . . become a humble follower of your Queen and so ride with you all into Paris?'

'But you are a Spanish gentleman and, I doubt not, a Catholic.'

'Does that mean that I should not be welcome?'

Pierre Lerand showed his distress. 'The Queen of Navarre is one of the leaders of the Huguenot party.'

'And you?'

'I . . . I am a Huguenot.'

'But you do not hate Catholics?'

The boy's brow was wrinkled suddenly. 'I would prefer not to hate anyone.'

'Then you might forget that we are not of the same faith, eh? Could we not both forget it?'

'We could try, Monsieur.' The boy hesitated. 'But if you would ride with us . . .'

'Oh, I shall not attract attention to myself. I shall not indulge in swordplay with those whose faith is not mine. I have loved a great many people in my life and hated some, but I have never yet considered the religion of those whom I loved or loathed.'

'You come from Spain, Monsieur, and there are many

Catholics there. In France at this time there are a great many Huguenots. It has been the cause of much strife throughout the land.'

'I have seen it even in the short time I have been in France.' Blasco shrugged his shoulders. 'I pray you, let us forget it. Let us prove that Catholic and Huguenot can share a room in amity.'

'Yes,' said the boy, 'let us do that.'

Blasco removed his sword and laid it on the floor. He loosened his doublet and took off his boots. He decided to undress no further.

Pierre took off his boots and jacket and knelt to say his prayers. Blasco watched him in the light of the candle with which Madame Ferronier had provided them; he thought how young he looked, how earnest.

When Pierre had finished his prayers he rose.

'Shall I blow out the candle?' he said.

Blasco nodded.

There was faint moonlight in the room, and they were silent for a while. Then Pierre said: 'If you are what you say, a young man travelling for his education, I do not think our Queen will refuse to allow you to accompany us. She might appoint someone – very likely myself – to make you see the error of your ways.'

'I can see that we should pass the time between here and Paris in the most pleasant discourse.'

'She is a tragic Queen, and much unhappiness has come to her. She is a widow now. She dearly loved her husband although he was cruel to her. He was weak, and she is strong; he all but handed her over to her enemies. There was at one time a plot to capture her and take her to Spain. There she might have been burnt at the stake as a heretic. That plan was foiled.'

'I am glad of it,' said Blasco.

'It makes us a little suspicious of Spaniards.'

'It must do so.'

'So you must forgive me if I have seemed to be over-cautious.'

'You have every right to be so; but you have been nothing to me but gracious and courtly.'

'All Her Majesty's hopes now rest in her son, young Henri, but he is wild and I fear may cause his mother much anxiety. Already he has had many mistresses. It is a source of great anxiety to the Queen. None will be more eager than she for the marriage.'

'The marriage?'

'Between her son and the Princess Marguerite of France. It is for this reason that we are journeying to Paris now. There are settlements to be arranged.'

Blasco had begun to feel excited.

He said: 'So the King of Navarre is to marry the Princess of France.'

'It is a match which has long been talked of between them. But my Queen does not trust the Queen Mother. She would not allow Henri to leave Béarn. He did not mind. He was deep in a love affair with the daughter of a humble citizen. He cares not where he picks his mistresses. But the Queen commanded him to stay. She fears that if the Queen Mother were to have him in the Louvre she would make him her captive. They say that all who come near the Queen Mother fear her, that she is a strange and silent woman, and that none has ever really known what goes on in the mind of Catherine de' Medici.'

'So it is to sign the wedding contracts that your Queen now makes her way to Paris,' mused Blasco.

'Yes. But I tire you with my talk. Good night, my friend. Sleep well.'

'Good night, my friend,' said Blasco.

He lay on his pallet and for a long time did not sleep.

He was excited because of this talk of the wedding; it made sense of the message he was to deliver. This was the wedding to which King Philip had referred.

At last he slept and, when he did, he dreamed that he was standing in that great chamber in El Escorial and that he knelt before the King; he was commanded to look about him, and when he did so was no longer in the monastic palace of his sovereign; he was in the village near the church and people in sober habits were streaming out of it. Among them was Pierre Lerand with the sweet and innocent smile on his face, and as he, Blasco, watched, Philip was beside him, thrusting a sword into his hand, commanding him to run it through the boy's body in the name of the Catholic Faith.

He awoke sweating. He sat up on his pallet. In the moonlight he saw the boy sleeping on the floor; he lay on his back and he was smiling peacefully.

The next morning both Blasco and Pierre were startled out of their sleep by the sound of knocking from below on the floor of their room. It was clear that they had slept late, for the room was full of light.

'One waits for you here below,' called Madame Ferronier.

'I did not mean to sleep so long,' said Pierre, rising hastily.

'Did you sleep well?'

'I woke now and then.'

Blasco laughed. 'Ah, you were uneasy. It is not everyone

who would have shared a room with a foreigner and he a Spaniard. Who waits for you below?'

'It may be someone from our party, urging me to make haste.'

'I propose to go to the inn, collect my horse, wash myself if maybe and eat. What say you? Will you come with me, and be my guest?'

'There is nothing I should like better . . . if there is time; but first I must see who is waiting for me and what news is brought.'

They put on their doublets and their swords and went carefully down the narrow staircase.

Standing in the room below was a young girl of about fourteen. She was tall and slender, and her straight fair hair fell about her shoulders. Blasco knew at once that this was the sister of whom Pierre had spoken; she had the same youthful and innocent look as her brother.

'Pierre . . .' she began. Then she stopped, seeing the stranger.

'Monsieur Carramadino and I shared a room,' Pierre explained. 'There was only one room, and two of us needing it . . . so it was inevitable.'

'Monsieur Carramadino?' said the girl slowly.

'At your service, Mademoiselle,' said Blasco.

'You are not French?' said the girl.

'I come from Spain.'

She recoiled slightly.

'I am sorry my country does not find favour with you,' said Blasco with that charm which came to him as naturally as breathing. 'But that I myself should not, makes me desolate.'

'Julie!' said her brother in dismay.

Julie said: 'It is no use saying I am pleased to see him if I am not. He is a Spaniard and the Spaniards are no friends to us.'

'Julie is fierce in her opinions, as you see, Monsieur,' said Pierre. 'Please forgive her.'

'There is no need to apologise for me, Pierre,' said Julie sharply. 'If it were necessary I should be capable of doing it myself.' She turned to Blasco. 'Monsieur, we do not like the Spaniards in Béarn. We forget not their plots against our Queen.'

Blasco bowed. 'I greatly regret these plots, Mademoiselle, even though I am completely ignorant of them.'

'You speak like a child, Julie,' said her brother. 'Are *we* to blame for all the actions of the men and women of Béarn?'

'The Béarnais have never behaved as the Spaniards do!' said the girl.

'She is so young,' said Pierre, apologetically.

Julie looked impatiently at her brother and Blasco said quickly: 'It is a great pleasure to meet someone of such fixed opinions. I find those who share mine intolerably dull. Mademoiselle Julie, you and I will have some interesting talks together, I doubt not. I am accompanying you to Paris.'

Her eyes softened a little. She looked, Blasco thought, like a young martyr. She was easy to read, and it was clear to him that she was wondering whether she might snatch his soul from perdition during the ride to Paris.

'You have the Queen's permission to ride with us?' she asked.

'Not yet. I am about to go to an inn where my horse has spent the night. Will you and your brother accompany me? I doubt not that the landlord will have a good meal waiting for me. I told him last night that I should need one.'

The girl's eyes sparkled, for after all she was little more than a child. 'Mayhap it would be churlish to refuse,' she said.

And as they left the Ferronier cottage and walked towards the inn, Blasco was conscious of her eyes constantly upon him. He knew from her zealous glances that she had marked him for conversion.

❧ ❧ ❧

During the journey to Paris Blasco, for the first time since he had met her, ceased to think constantly of Bianca. This girl amused him – not as Bianca had, of course; she did not arouse desire in him; she was too young; she was merely an innocent child assuming the airs of an adult. Her quaint accent was enchanting while her forthright manner appealed strongly to him.

Over their meal at the inn he had decided to employ a little cunning. He knew how the minds of the zealously religious worked; he had had the experience of contact with his brother Domingo. He therefore intimated that although he was a Catholic and a Spaniard he was very interested in the Reformed Religion. He even allowed it to be assumed that it was for this reason that he had come to France.

Now he knew there would be no difficulty. The girl and her brother would arrange that he should ride with them and, as their father was in close attendance on the Queen, before the company left to undertake the last part of their journey to Paris he had been received by the Queen herself and told that he might accompany them.

It was good fun to ride beside the young Julie and answer her questions, to listen to her stern preaching which came so oddly from such young lips. He thought how fine and fair her skin was, and how she would be enchanting in a year or so, prim little firebrand that she was. He was grateful to her; he allowed her to preach to her heart's content, for when he was with her he forgot in some measure his yearning for Bianca.

And so they came to Paris.

As he rode among the followers of the Queen of Navarre through the gates of the city, Blasco was conscious of an interest and excitement which no other city had ever aroused in him. They crossed the bridge and came to the Île de la Cité; they crossed the Quai des Fleurs and he saw the Gothic towers of Sainte Chapelle and Notre Dame; he saw the tall, slender houses with their grey roofs, and near the Cathedral a huddle of narrow streets with the contents of evil-smelling gutters running down the cobbled paths; he saw small wooden hovels which seemed on the point of collapse, their overhanging eaves shutting out the light and air.

The air seemed filled with the smell of food; and standing at the doors of their shops to watch the procession pass were the *restaurateurs* and *pâtissiers* surrounded by lively groups of customers. There were beggars squatting by the river, their hands outstretched, their wailing voices rising and falling; groups of people stood about, some silent, some chatting in their voluble way.

All watched the woman who rode with her young daughter at the head of the procession, and there was tension everywhere because the Huguenot Queen of Navarre was riding into Catholic Paris.

The procession was making its way to the Louvre and Blasco had decided that here in Paris it would be against the interests of his master for him to be accepted as one of the party. From now on he must walk with the utmost care.

None must guess that he came on a mission for the King of Spain. He must quietly insinuate himself into Court circles; and to arrive as a member of the Queen's retinue he, a Spaniard, would attract immediate notice.

He had told Julie and Pierre that he intended to slip away, as soon as they arrived in Paris, and find a lodging for himself.

As the procession moved forward he turned into a thoroughfare on his right, and rode away so unostentatiously that his going was unnoticed except by his two young friends.

He had made his plans. He had long decided that he would find a lodging not far from that tavern to which he had ordered Matias to bring Bianca. There he would have the tavern under constant surveillance, and immediately Bianca arrived in Paris they would be together.

He was directed to L'Ananas. It was a tavern at which he could not stay the night; for he saw that the people who were drinking there were not those with whom a young nobleman, hoping to be received at Court, could associate.

But at the corner of the street was an inn of a better type and he rode into the courtyard, where he was received with pleasure by a garrulous host who assured him that he was indeed far-sighted to have found a lodging in good time. 'For, Monsieur, now that we have distinguished visitors in Paris, depend upon it, in a few hours' time there will not be a room to be had for love or money throughout the city.'

Blasco chose a room which gave him a good view of L'Ananas; it was small and low and he had to stoop to enter it; but he said it would serve his purpose well, and he paid the innkeeper in advance a much larger amount than the man was accustomed to receive.

'I am expecting to be joined by a lady,' said Blasco. 'It may be some weeks before she arrives.'

The innkeeper's lively eyes were warmly sympathetic. 'Then,' went on Blasco, 'I shall need a larger room . . .'

'Monsieur shall have the best in the house.' The innkeeper rubbed his hands together, and it seemed as though the thought of the lady's coming pleased him more than the money Blasco had paid in advance. 'And is Monsieur sure that this room satisfies him? I have a larger and a better . . .'

'This suits me well,' said Blasco. 'I like the view. And could I eat now?'

'Monsieur shall eat a meal such as he has rarely enjoyed in his life. It is his first visit to Paris?'

'It is,' said Blasco.

'Then it shall be our pleasure and our honour to show Monsieur how we Parisians eat.'

'What of the inn across the road there? L'Ananas, is it?'

'Ah yes, Monsieur.' The innkeeper shook his head. 'It has not a very good reputation. There are brawls most nights at that tavern. It is these . . . er . . . Monsieur is from Spain? They say that the Spaniards are good Catholics almost to a man.'

'I am a Spaniard and a Catholic.'

'Then Monsieur will understand. There is constant trouble in Paris. A man says a word which another overhears. He insults the Faith, and then . . . swords are drawn. It is what happens frequently at such places as L'Ananas. Ah, Monsieur, it is a time of anxiety for us innkeepers. Trouble blows up and a man's place is wrecked, and he powerless to prevent it. But with the coming of the Queen of Navarre there is a new hope throughout the City.'

'Paris is eager for the proposed marriage of the Princess and the King of Navarre?'

'Monsieur is puzzled. Should good Catholics, you say, be pleased to see their Princess married to a heretic? Monsieur, there are some of us humble folk who long for peace.' The innkeeper looked furtively over his shoulder. 'And we believe, Monsieur – those of us who are good Catholics – that our Princess will turn the King of Navarre from his religion to hers.' He lifted his shoulders. 'But a marriage between Catholic and Huguenot should bring peace. Peace . . . Peace . . . It means much to us poor working folk, Monsieur.'

'I understand that. Let us hope that the marriage will take place.'

Again the innkeeper lifted his shoulders. 'Who can say? There have been such plans made since there were Princes and Princesses for whom to make them. The Princess Marguerite – our Margot, as we call her, Monsieur – she is a merry one. And not a little in love with young Henri de Guise. Ah, to see those two riding together – which I have seen often in these streets – that is a sight to please the eyes. Monsieur de Guise is the handsomest man in France, so think we people of Paris, and our Margot thinks so too. There are these rumours. They are lovers, those two. They are married in all but name. You would not doubt it to see them together. They are young, so much in love – it is difficult to restrain themselves. There are rumours that the Queen Mother – that Italian woman whom all good Parisians hate with all their hearts, Monsieur – has caught them together in the early morning after their night of love and beaten poor Margot black and blue because of it.' The man laughed. 'Ah, but they are young and beautiful and in love. And is not Monsieur de Guise a good Catholic? And is he not more beloved in Paris than any man in France? But I doubt not it will be a good thing if this marriage takes place, for the welding together of Catholic and Huguenot is what our poor country needs to put an end to much bloody strife . . . I talk too much. But Paris is content, Monsieur, that the Queen of Navarre comes hither to discuss her son's wedding to our Princess.'

Blasco followed the innkeeper down to the parlour where a savoury pie, among other good things, was put before him, and there was burgundy to drink with it. The food and wine had a different flavour from that to which he was accustomed, but he had to admit that the French could be justly proud of their food and drink.

Having taken the edge off his appetite he began to think again of the reason for his being in Paris and of the strange message that he had to deliver to the Queen Mother. The marriage to which King Philip had referred was clearly that of Princess Margot and Henri of Navarre; but why should Catholic Philip – fanatical to a degree – wish to see such a marriage? Why should he wish to honour the King of the little province of Navarre by marriage with the Princess of France, when that King was – if he were anything like his mother – fiercely Huguenot?

It was incomprehensible, and he felt that that which he did not understand was full of sinister implication. He was sobered by the thought that he had a part – even though it might be a small one – in a plot which he could not understand.

After his meal he sauntered out into the town. He wandered aimlessly along the south bank with its convents and colleges; he climbed the hill of St Geneviève.

During his stroll it seemed to him that there were many

prisons in that city. He passed the old building of the Conciergerie with its towers and courtyards; he saw the Great and Little Chatelet built at the end of the bridge which connected one bank of the city with the other; and in the Rue Saint-Germain l'Auxerrois he came upon yet another – Fort l'Evêque; and at last the Bastille itself.

He stood looking at the grey stone fortress with its eight pointed towers, and saw the cannons which projected from the ramparts; he gazed for a while at the dry moat which surrounded the prison, and the two drawbridges which connected it with the Rue St Antoine. Then he shivered and turning made his way towards his lodging, but before going to his room he went into L'Ananas.

There were all types of people in the tavern. Some were clearly men and women who might have been of the Court; there were also liveried servants, pages and soldiers playing dice.

Blasco called for wine and listened to the people about him. They were talking of the visit of the Queen of Navarre and what it would mean to France if the marriage took place.

This night, thought Blasco, all Paris must be talking about the coming wedding.

※ ※ ※

The next morning Blasco presented himself at the Palace of the Louvre and asked two pages, who were playing dice on the steps, to take a message from him to Monsieur Lerand. Very leisurely one of the pages rose and intimated that it was beneath his dignity to go on such an errand unless he were well paid for it.

Blasco suppressed a desire to knock the boy down, and gave

him money instead. Blasco was learning a great deal since he had been on the King's business. He was assuming a more cautious personality and only now did he realise how often in the past he had acted on impulse.

The boy disappeared and after a long time returned to say that Monsieur Lerand was not at Court but that for a consideration the other gentleman – indicating the page who was sprawling on the steps – might discover where he was lodged, since he was a follower in the suite of the Queen of Navarre.

Controlling further irritation with what he congratulated himself was marvellous restraint, Blasco paid over more money and eventually learned that the Lerand family were lodged in the Rue Béthisy.

He made his way thither immediately, and there was received by Julie. She seemed younger than he had been imagining her, as she stood before him, directing her stern gaze upon him.

'Have you been to Mass this morning?' she demanded.

He said that he had.

She recoiled from him, and then, as though determined to hide her natural repulsion for one of his faith, she said earnestly: 'I hope you will soon come to the truth, Monsieur Carramadino.'

'I believe you are wondering whether you will be the one to lead me.'

Her face turned slightly pink. 'If God has chosen me for that task I should be honoured.'

'Shall I precede Him by choosing you myself? Would that help?'

'You blaspheme,' she said.

'What a prim little girl you are! Do you never laugh?'

'We are not put on this earth to laugh, Monsieur.'

'Are you sure of that?'

'Absolutely sure, Monsieur.'

'When we are very young it is easy to be sure. As we grow older we are filled with doubts.'

'That is because you have not seen the truth.'

'Whose truth?'

'What do you mean? How could there be more than one truth?'

Pierre came into the room. He was delighted to see Blasco, and greeted him warmly.

'Your sister has already begun to save my soul,' said Blasco. 'I confess I did not expect such an early attack.'

'You must forgive her. She is over-zealous.'

'And you are not then, Pierre?' demanded his sister.

'Julie, I remember that Monsieur Carramadino is our guest. I offer him refreshment.'

'You are generous indeed,' said Blasco lightly. 'One offers me salvation, the other refreshment. At the moment I am sure Mademoiselle Julie will forgive me if I content myself with refreshment.'

'Julie, will you please have wine brought for Monsieur Carramadino?'

'You will not let him talk to you of idolatry, Pierre?' asked the girl anxiously.

'Julie, you must trust me. It was scarcely fitting for you to receive a gentleman alone, you know.'

She flushed again. 'I . . . I did not think of him as a gentleman, I fear.'

'Only as one of those wicked idolators,' said Blasco, with a smile. 'There is a difference, I suppose.'

Julie went out, and Pierre smiled warmly. 'You must forgive my sister. She is very young and has seen so little of the world. In Béarn we live simply. We have our house which is close to the Queen's Palace, and life is lived very differently from the way it is in large cities. We are of the Court yet we live like farmers; and the young people are brought up in the simplest fashion.'

'You have no need to apologise for your sister. I find her enchanting. I am deeply honoured that she should be so concerned for my soul.'

A servant brought wine and they talked of Paris; and later the two young men went out to walk through the City.

Pierre said: 'I have news for you. The Queen of Navarre gives you permission to join her suite at the Louvre this evening, where the Queen Mother is giving a ball in her honour.'

Blasco expressed his grateful thanks.

He thought: I am progressing well. Who knows, tonight I may see the Queen Mother and have a chance of executing my duty.

When he had delivered the message, when his mission was performed, he would feel free again, free to be himself. And when Bianca came to Paris – ah, then he would be perfectly content, for he would be able to assure himself that, whatever the meaning of King Philip's message, and whatever part he had played in matters of state, he had merely done his duty as a subject of his King.

❧ ❧ ❧

Never had Blasco witnessed such brilliance; never had he seen so many beautiful women so brilliantly attired. He was astonished at the colour of their dresses – scarlet and blue, silver and gold – and these dresses were low-cut and tightly swathed about the bodies of those who wore them in a manner which was completely strange to him. The jewels were dazzling. He had heard of the lavish extravagance at the French Court but he had not believed it could be so great as this.

The *sal de bal* was lined with flambeaux; and it seemed to Blasco that the men were as brilliantly clad as the women, and some were perfumed and painted, he could swear.

He realised that in his sombre garments he was conspicuous as a Spaniard, for in his dark doublet he was differently attired even from the Huguenot guests in their simple garments.

He would never have an opportunity of whispering those words to the Queen Mother, dressed as he was.

He was in the company of the Lerands who, like himself, were astonished at what they saw.

There had been a banquet to which he had not been invited, and now the guests were all assembled in the *sal de bal* where the dancing was taking place.

The dancing of these people fitted their clothes; it was extravagant, stately, yet entirely seductive.

Julie was standing beside him, her eyes wide, her mouth a shocked circle.

'Are they not beautiful, these ladies?' he whispered.

'They would not be in God's eyes,' she answered.

'Then I am fortunate to have the eyes of a man, for I find great pleasure in contemplating them.'

'Pleasure . . . Pleasure! You think of nothing but pleasure.'

'Of what should I think?'

'Of God, and His works.'

'But would that not be pleasurable contemplation? Did not God create everything?'

She turned away angrily, and he laid his hand on her arm. He felt her recoil, and he was immediately conscious of the desire to make her love him.

He thought: How Bianca would like to be here tonight! And she would dance as none of these fine ladies could dance; and she would put them all in the shade with her beauty.

Pierre was whispering to him. 'There is the Queen Mother herself.'

Eagerly Blasco looked; he saw a middle-aged woman, with a pale, flat face, a woman who looked as if she were over-fond of the delights of the table; she was dressed in black and made no attempt to vie with the beautiful ladies about her, wherein, thought Blasco, she showed her wisdom.

He could not take his eyes from her face; its thick white skin, its expressionless eyes, that faint smile about the lips, all repelled him. He thought of the stories he had heard of those beautiful women who now surrounded her, and who were known as her *Escadron Volant*, and whom she commanded, it was said, to use their beauty in order to lure men's secrets from them.

Beside her was the Queen of Navarre – herself not a beauty, and sombrely clad after the Huguenot fashion; but what a different face that was, and how one realised, seeing the two women side by side, that the Queen of Navarre, for all her hard looks, was a good woman, while from the other emanated something which was essentially evil.

Now another woman caught his eye and he could not turn his gaze from her. She was clad in scarlet velvet with her black hair flowing about her shoulders. No other woman present wore her hair in that fashion, and this in itself set her apart. The red velvet was cut lower than was evidently the custom, and the sparkling black eyes of the woman were defiant and mischievous.

'The Princess Margot is determined to show her disapproval of the match,' said a voice close to Blasco.

'Poor Margot!' replied his companion. 'To think she must take the oaf from Béarn! They say his manners are those of a peasant, and if we may judge by those of his subjects who are here tonight I'd say they were right. All know she longs for de Guise, who has been her lover since they were children.'

Blasco watched the hot blood flame into Julie's cheeks; she had turned and was about to speak, but Blasco grasped her arm so tightly that she winced, and before she had recovered, the man who had spoken had moved away.

'Haw dare you!' demanded Julie.

'To prevent your making trouble for yourself and your friends.'

'Did you hear him call our King an oaf?'

'You are too serious.'

'That is what I would expect one as frivolous as yourself to think.'

'Here frivolity is the order of the day. When you are in Paris you should behave as a Parisian.'

'Never!' she cried.

'Why not? They are an attractive people.'

'In the eyes of such as you, I daresay.'

'Look at the beautiful Princess. Is she not a delight to the eye?'

'She is brazen. She is a wanton. That is clear. I do not wish to look at such as she is.'

'You stand alone, Mademoiselle. Almost every eye in the room is turned upon her.'

'Then pray turn yours.'

'I! I thought you wanted to save me from too much pleasure. But look! A dance is to begin. Ah, this is the *branle des lavandières* of which I have heard. The dancers clap their hands to represent the washerwomen on the banks of the Seine. Come, Mademoiselle, dance with me.'

'Dance! We do not dance. To dance is sinful.'

'How you love sin, you puritans!'

'Love sin!'

'You are so preoccupied with it, and it is a fact that people concern themselves most with what they love best.'

'You seem to mock me.'

'Then I must not, for that will give you pleasure. You enjoy being mocked. It makes you feel blessed and virtuous. But pleasure is bad for you. I must remember that.'

'Monsieur Carramadino, I think it would be well if you did not call on my family any more.'

'What! Will you let my soul suffer in torment and do nothing to save it?'

'I fear you are beyond redemption.'

'All the more credit to you if you snatch me from perdition, you know.'

She turned away from him, saying: 'I am going to ask Pierre or my father to take me to our lodging.'

'The sight of so much pleasure is too much to be endured?' A sudden impulse came to him. He placed a hand on her shoulder and went on seriously: 'Mademoiselle, tomorrow I will call at your lodging. Do you think that you and Pierre would talk to me . . . seriously?'

'You mean that you wish to learn more about our religion?'
He nodded.

Her face softened suddenly. She said: 'You will be welcome, Monsieur.'

He looked from her to the dancers. He thought: What am I doing? Can I never be in the presence of a girl without wishing to seduce her? Something was urging him to this.

It was the dancers in the sinuous, sensuous movements, the clap-clap of their hands in the *branle des lavandières*; it was the beautiful young Princess, defiant and angry, passionately unhappy because she was to be forced into a marriage with the King of Navarre when she was in love with another man; it was the sense of evil which emanated from Queen Catherine de' Medici. And was it also the tension he felt about him? Or was that just something which did not exist beyond his own mind? He alone knew of the message he must deliver from his King to the flat-faced Queen Mother of France, and he knew this proposed marriage was no ordinary marriage, that there was an underlying significance of which his King and Catherine de' Medici were aware. Perhaps he merely needed that diversion which Bianca alone could give him?

He felt a need to escape. And at the moment the pursuit of this innocent and prim little Huguenot seemed the only avenue open to him.

🌹 🌹 🌹

A week had passed since his arrival in Paris.

There was still no sign of Bianca and Matias. Often he would sit at his window looking out on L'Ananas with longing eyes. He had come to believe that as soon as Bianca arrived in Paris all his restlessness would disappear. He had presented himself each day at the house in the Rue Béthisy. It was pleasant to sit beside the youthful Julie and listen to her reading to him, to watch her eyes widen as she talked to him of the doctrines of her religion.

She soothed his desire for Bianca, and she thought she was saving his soul. She angered him while she attracted him. He despised her primness while it appealed to him. Often when she would be talking of the Scriptures he would be thinking of her, her piety forgotten – Julie in love. She would be fierce in her emotions, he believed. All that fire which she squandered on religion would be diverted. Could it be? That was the question that concerned him.

But when he left the Rue Béthisy he would still be thinking of Bianca, and he would look in at L'Ananas and ask if any visitors from Spain had called that day.

He was walking past the shops on the quay opposite the Louvre when he saw a woman approaching him; she was plump and dressed in black, and she wore a shawl over her head as the working-class women wore when they went out to do their marketing.

But there was something about this woman which attracted his attention. Her face was almost hidden by the shawl and as she passed him she stared ahead; but there was in that face that which was unmistakable: the white skin, the dark eyes, the flatness of the features and the faint smile which betrayed nothing as it played about the mouth.

'By all the saints!' swore Blasco under his breath. 'That was the Queen Mother.'

He halted and looked after her; she was going slowly on. Now he was certain. He had studied her well on those occasions when he had seen her, and had been baffled as to how he could possibly approach her and, without seeming to, give her the message from his King.

What was she doing, walking the streets of Paris like a woman on her way to the market?

What did it matter? Here was an opportunity such as he would never have again. He could walk a few paces with a woman in the street and none notice, and walking thus he could discharge that duty to perform which he had come to France.

Hastily he looked round and saw that she was turning, in her ponderous way, into one of the shops.

He walked swiftly to the shop, but paused on the threshold. If she had decided to venture out incognito she would not thank him for recognising her; moreover, how could he tell her what he had to say before shopkeepers?

He decided then that he would wait for the Queen Mother to emerge and then walk up to her and give her the message from his King. When he was close to her he would be sure who she was; but he was certain now that he had made no mistake.

He took up his stand close to the shop. The minutes passed slowly: fifteen minutes, twenty passed.

An old woman wearing a shawl similar to that worn by Catherine de' Medici passed by. She was coming from the market and, as she passed near Biasco, she dropped a package, and when he stooped and picked it up for her, she thanked him and blessed his handsome face.

He asked her what was sold in the shop, saying it was strange that there was no sign to indicate. She looked and grimaced.

'It is René, the Italian, who lives there. He is *parfumeur* and glove-maker to the Queen Mother and there are some who say he makes more than gloves and perfumes for his mistress!'

'What sort of things?'

'Monsieur, how should I know? I am not of the Court. Strange things have happened at the Court since we have had Italians in this land. It is nothing new, I tell you. There is not a soul in Paris who does not ask how it was she became the Queen of France. King Henri, her husband, was not King François' eldest son, you know. But then that eldest son died when he drank a draught from the cup brought him by his Italian cupbearer . . . and then the Italian woman became the Queen.'

'You are bold, Madame,' said Biasco, 'to say such things.'

The woman spat over her shoulder. 'All Paris says them. When she appears in the streets, there is silence or insults. Paris has never loved Italians, and the Italian woman is worse than any.'

'I am a stranger. I know little of these things.'

She laughed and passed on.

He continued to watch the shop. Now it occurred to him that she travelled abroad thus because she feared the insults of the people. Was it true that they greeted her with a hostile silence when she went into the streets? If that were so it was not so very strange that, when she wished to visit her *parfumeur* or glove-maker, she should do so as a woman of the people.

His heart leaped, for she had left the shop and had started to walk in the direction of the Palace of the Louvre.

He was after her; he walked past her, and turning sharply came face to face with her. He was so near and his turn was so sudden that he had taken her by surprise. Now he had no doubt whatever that he stood before the Queen Mother of France.

He said quickly: 'I understand Your Majesty's desire to remain unrecognised. I chose this opportunity because it seemed heaven-sent. I come from Madrid on the instructions of King Philip, and I have a message which is to be delivered to you when none can overhear; therefore I trust Your Majesty will pardon my accosting you thus.'

He saw the smile on her flat face. It conveyed nothing; it might have been interest, pleasure, contempt – he could not be sure.

She said: 'Pray walk beside me until you have delivered your message.'

He did so, and when he had spoken, she said: 'Thank you. I understand. You may tell your master that I commend you for your astute delivery of his message. Leave me now – nay, no ceremony, please. Good day to you.'

She went slowly on.

Biasco hung back; he touched his forehead. He was sweating.

❧ ❧ ❧

A few days later, when the innkeeper brought bread and wine to Blasco's room, he was filled with excitement. He was trembling as he set them on the table.

'Why, Monsieur . . . such news! The Queen of Navarre is dying.'

'This cannot be so. She was well yesterday.'

'But she is dying. There are crowds outside the Hotel de Condé where she is staying. They are all Huguenots, they say. They are crowding into the apartments there. It seems we have a goodly number of Huguenots here in Paris.'

'What ails her?'

'Ah, Monsieur, that is the point. What ails her? None

knows. She has signed the marriage settlement. Everything is clear now for the marriage to go ahead. Last night, I hear, she fell into a fever, and now she has lost the use of her limbs. The Huguenots are in an ugly mood.'

'They suspect . . .'

The innkeeper nodded. 'They always suspect at such times, Monsieur. And since we have had Italians in France . . .' He lifted his shoulders as though there was no need to say more. But he could not resist saying more. 'There are some who are saying that she was well until she put on a pair of perfumed gloves – a gift of Queen Catherine.'

'Gloves!'

'Indeed yes, gloves. A beautiful pair of gloves fashioned by René, the Queen Mother's glove-maker, who has his shop on the quay.'

Blasco did not speak. He felt impotent and angry. He was a puppet; he performed certain actions; he did so because he was commanded, and he had no notion what part he played in a major tragedy.

'If the Queen dies there may be trouble,' said the innkeeper. 'I shall barricade the lower parts of the inn at once. A man has to look after himself.'

Blasco stared at the innkeeper. He did not see him; instead he saw the woman emerging from the shop of the Italian glove-maker. Then the innkeeper said something which sent all thoughts of gloves and the two queens from his mind. 'There was a message this morning from L'Ananas, Monsieur. It was for you. It is a Spanish gentleman, who speaks no French . . . very difficult to understand. The good God knows how this message would have come to you but for the fact that I had made it my business to tell them at L'Ananas to expect it.'

But Blasco was not listening. He had made for the door and was running down the spiral staircase and across the road to L'Ananas.

❧ ❧ ❧

Matias faced him, and Matias was mournful.

'And Bianca?' were Blasco's first words.

'Señor, I could not bring her. She was not there to bring. She had run away.'

'Matias, what are you saying? She was gone! But where? Where? Did you not discover?'

'None knew, Señor. I questioned the servants, but not the lady of the house. That was your command. I asked, what of Bianca, Bianca the gipsy, who had come with her mistress to the house when she married. And I was told – not by one but by many – Bianca had gone away. None knew whither.'

Blasco turned away. He could not bear to look at Matias. All those days and nights when he had sat at his window watching the tavern for the return of Matias, all that longing for Bianca . . . to end in this! It was unbearable.

'Señor . . .' began Matias tremulously. 'Señor, I did what was asked.'

But Blasco had turned and hurried back to the inn on the corner of the street. There he shut himself into his room and would see no one.

❧ ❧ ❧

Matias followed uncertainly.

When he reached the inn he sat in the courtyard, wretchedly waiting.

The innkeeper came out to speak to him, but Matias had no

French and the innkeeper had no Spanish, so they could only shake their heads at each other.

Matias gratefully accepted refreshment. He had wept often during the journey from Zaragoza to Paris. He despised himself, but if he had been made a fool of once he would not be again.

Blanca had been charming and costly. He had stayed with her a week, and it had been enchanting – until the money that should have taken him to Seville and back was spent and Blanca's demands on his purse became more extravagant. But, Matias told himself, I am a wise man, so I knew when I must leave Blanca and make my way to my master in Paris. So many of the fools from my village would have spent all before they had the wisdom to think of the future. Then they would have found themselves without the means of reaching their master.

Of course he could have said he had been robbed on the way. But how much more plausible was the story of the gipsy girl's leaving her mistress's house. Gipsy girls never stayed in houses. So it was probably true that she had run away. He was wise, this Matias. He knew this without going to Seville to make the discovery. So there was nothing wrong in dallying with Bianca at Zaragoza if, out of his wisdom, he could bring the same news to his master after living the life of a nobleman in Zaragoza, instead of riding many hot miles to Seville.

There were times when Matias could believe he had actually ridden to Seville, that he had discovered for his master that the gipsy had really run away.

So now he sat in the courtyard of the inn, eating his pie and drinking his wine, and coming to the conclusion that he was, after all, a very fine fellow.

He snapped his fingers. Gipsies! Innkeepers' daughters!

What if one of these disappointed? The world was full of others!

Paris was sweltering under the hot August sun. In the streets knots of people congregated; they grumbled, they clenched their fists. The theme of all conversations was either the death of the Queen of Navarre or the wedding plans which were still going forward.

Even Catholics declared that here was another murder to lay at the door of Catherine de' Medici. The old familiar pattern, they said. 'My dear sister of Navarre, here is a gift from me – a pair of beautiful perfumed gloves made by my own Italian glove-maker.' And so the poor lady puts them on. She is not destined to wear them for long. No sooner do the deadly things touch her skin than she is doomed to die. It is not the first time poison has been conveyed through gloves. Nor will it be the last while we have Italians among us.

Such were the murmurings at street corners, and even the young King – the poor little madman who was writhing, it was said, in his mother's strong hands – seemed for once to turn against the woman whom he feared, and ordered an exhumation of the body of the Queen of Navarre.

'An abscess on the lungs,' was the verdict.

'Abscess on the lungs!' cried the people of Paris. 'Ah, these physicians are careful men. They do not wish the *morceau italianiẓé* to be slipped into their wine, you know. This is an evil thing. Paris is Catholic, but Paris deplores this murder. The Queen of Navarre was a heretic, a Huguenot, but she was a good woman – as far as her religion would let her be – and she came here in good faith. We like not these Italian ways.'

But the Queen Mother did not seem to care. She smiled when she heard the reports, so Blasco heard; and her invitations to the son of the Queen of Navarre to come to Paris and marry her daughter were warm indeed.

Had Blasco not spent long hours in mourning for Bianca he would have been deeply conscious of the general unrest. He felt listless. Each day he visited his friends in the Rue Béthisy and, feigning to condole, he listened but half-heartedly to their mourning for Jeanne of Navarre and their accusations against the Queen Mother.

Julie was passionate in her denunciations.

'The Queen Mother destroyed Queen Jeanne because she feared her,' she cried. 'She wishes to make our King Henri a Catholic, and she knew she could never do so while his mother lived. Ah, Monsieur Carramadino, I wronged you. You are sad, even as we are. Ere long you will be one of us.'

And she would sit beside him and point with her finger at the words which were written in the books she wanted him to read.

He would study her young smooth face and try with all his might to banish thoughts of Bianca.

🌫 🌫 🌫

It was a hot August night. Blasco was restless. He had visited the house in the Rue Béthisy that afternoon and he had listened to the loud lamentations of his friends. They could talk of nothing but the accident to their leader, the Admiral Gaspard de Coligny, whose house was only a short distance from their own in the Rue Béthisy. The Admiral had been walking home from a council meeting which the young King had attended and, as he was passing through the narrow street which adjoined the Rue Béthisy, shots had been fired at him from the window of one of the houses. The first shot had whizzed past him to become embedded in a wall, but there had quickly followed another which had shot off one of his fingers before grazing his arm and coming to rest in his shoulder. Almost unconscious, the Admiral had been carried into his home, and it had been feared he would not survive for he was an old man.

Now in the Rue Béthisy angry Huguenots gathered about the Admiral's house waiting for news of their leader. The King had sent his own physician; the King loved the Admiral for, in spite of Charles's madness, he recognised the virtue and strength of the great Huguenot leader who was admitted throughout the country – even by those who did not share his views – to be one of the most noble figures of the age.

All that day the Lerands had talked continually of the virtues of the Admiral, of the terrible loss to their cause if he should die; they asked what was the meaning of these outrages. Jeanne of Navarre called to Paris only to meet her death; the Admiral called to Paris to be shot at; and it was only by the flimsiest chance that the bullet lodged in his shoulder instead of his heart. What next?

Blasco was weary of the continual preoccupation with these matters. Why could they not live in peace with one another? In his own country there was the Holy Inquisition; its *alguazils* came by night to take their victims, but there was not all this noisy and continual wrangling about religious differences.

He longed for Bianca. No one else could replace her. He was no longer interested in the fierce little puritan with the smooth skin. She seemed childish; she seemed dull, simply because she was not Bianca.

He came through the inn and went up to his room. There were several people in the inn; they looked at him furtively as he passed through. He did not see them; as he mounted the stairs to his room he was thinking of Bianca's secret meetings with him at the inn not far from Jerez.

He had decided that tomorrow he would leave Paris – tomorrow or the next day. Why should he delay? His work was done. He could present himself at the Palace of Madrid and tell that high official, by whom he had been instructed before he had left his country's capital, of how he had delivered the King's message to the Queen Mother of France. There was no point in staying now. But when he reached his home, would he be any happier? Every time he passed the chapel he would think of her. Where was she now? Had she gone back to her own people? Was she lying under the bushes with another lover now? In Spain he could search for her. And in Spain there were many gipsies. Were they so different from Bianca?

Yes, tomorrow he would leave.

The wedding had taken place a few days ago. He had been among the crowds and had seen the flamboyantly lovely Princess Margot married to the man from Béarn. An ill-matched couple, he had thought them. She, Parisian to her finger-tips; he somewhat coarse, seeming to be a peasant for all his royal blood, full of vitality, his eyes lazy yet humorous, his mouth shrewd yet sensuous; scorning the elegance of the Parisians, he wore his hair *en brosse* in the rough Béarnais way. Blasco had seen the marriage on the threshold of the great cathedral of Notre Dame, for it must needs be performed outside the church since Henri of Navarre was a Huguenot and therefore could not be married in a Catholic cathedral.

The tension of the atmosphere had penetrated his longing for Bianca as he had stood there close to the western door of Notre Dame. These people were expectant; waiting for trouble?

He had the feeling that at this moment they were placated by the ceremonies such as this one, which they loved, and that because of this they were ready to mingle, Catholic with Huguenot.

Blasco shrugged with impatience.

Had they not lives of their own to lead? Must they concern themselves with the bold-eyed girl whose glances kept straying to the tall and handsome Duke of Guise while she knelt beside her husband? She was enjoying herself, he believed; she enjoyed the sympathy of the crowd. If he could believe all he heard of this young woman who was now La Reine Margot he was sure she would not hesitate to be unfaithful to lover or husband.

But he was leaving tomorrow. In time his adventures here in Paris would be nothing but a memory, significant only because it was in this city that he became aware that he had lost Bianca.

The innkeeper was knocking at his door.

'Come in,' he called.

The man came. His lips were twitching with excitement. He held one hand behind his black.

'Monsieur,' he said. 'I must talk with you.'

'Say on.'

'You have been with me for some time, and I have an affection for you. That is why I come to you thus. Monsieur, you must understand that Paris is a dangerous city.'

'Ah yes,' said Blasco with a smile. These dramatic Parisians! How seriously they took themselves and their differences one with the other!

The innkeeper had drawn his hand from behind his back, and Blasco stared with curiosity at the small white cross which he was holding in his hand. 'Monsieur,' he said earnestly, 'if you should go out tonight, wear this in your hat.'

'Wherefore?' asked Blasco

'It is necessary that you should, Monsieur. Nay, do not laugh at me. Wear this cross in your hat.' He had turned to the table on which lay Blasco's hat; deftly he attached the cross to it. 'And, Monsieur, a white scarf about the arm. Just about here. All will be well then.'

'I do not understand.'

'You will later, Monsieur.'

'But what is this mystery?'

'I can tell you no more. You are a foreigner, Monsieur. You speak our language, but with less facility than we do ourselves. There might not be time for you to explain, were you asked, that you are a good Catholic.'

'I have been thinking,' said Blasco, 'that I must soon be returning to my own country.'

'I shall be sorry to see you go, Monsieur.'

'I thought that tomorrow or the next day I should begin my journey.'

'Ah, tomorrow . . . and the next day,' murmured the innkeeper. Then he said that he had much with which to occupy himself. He was going to put up the barricades about the inn.

'You expect trouble again tonight!' asked Blasco.

'Oh, there is merrymaking in the streets since the wedding. Who knows what will happen? There have never been so many Huguenots in Paris as there are at this time. So many Huguenots . . . so many Catholics. At such times a wise innkeeper looks to his property.'

'Well, I will wish you good night,' said Blasco.

'A very good night, Monsieur.'

It was not easy to sleep. The heat was stifling. He dozed a little and dreamed, as he did so often, of Bianca.

Suddenly in the quiet of the night a tocsin rang out. The sound seemed to come from the direction of the Louvre and, starting up, Blasco decided it came from Saint-Germain l'Auxerrois. Almost immediately bells seemed to be ringing in every direction.

Then from below he heard the sounds of shouting and running feet.

He sat up in bed, listening to shouts, screams – bloodcurdling screams. Something terrible was happening in the streets below.

He ran to the window and looked out. He could see someone running in the direction of L'Ananas. It was a man, and he was brandishing a sword.

Blasco hurried into his clothes. He picked up his hat and saw the white cross in it which the innkeeper had fixed there earlier that night.

He remembered the furtive looks of the man, the urgent warning.

He saw then that the innkeeper had laid a white scarf by his coat. 'Tie it about your arm,' he had said, 'before you venture into the streets, because you are a foreigner and there might not be time to explain that you are a good Catholic.'

In that moment it was as though a great wall had been demolished and he could see clearly what lay beyond, what, had he not been so obsessed by his need of Bianca, he might have seen before. He understood the meaning of the message he had brought from his King to the Queen Mother of France. She was to go ahead with the wedding, the Catholic-Huguenot wedding, because only on such an occasion could she bring together, in Catholic Paris, without suspicion on their part, so many Huguenots.

It was clear to him what was about to happen in the streets below. This had been arranged by the flat-faced woman with the expressionless eyes; this had been arranged by the cold monk of El Escorial, who cared not how much blood was shed in the name of, what he believed to be, the true Faith.

They had been lured here – the jaunty bridegroom and his subjects and those who followed his faith – for this purpose, that they might be in Paris and handy for the assassin's knife on this night of August the 24th, which was the Eve of St Bartholomew. The Queen of Navarre had already met her death. The Admiral was recovering from his wounds, but he would not be allowed to live through the night. Two great leaders destroyed in a few days! And how many of their faithful followers would meet the same fate before this bloody night was over!

In his hat was the white cross; about his arm he had tied the scarf.

He thought then of the gentle family in the Rue Béthisy. Pierre and his father, Julie, the prim puritan.

He picked up his sword and it was as though some inner voice urged him: What has this to do with you? You are safe. You are a Spaniard and a good Catholic. None would molest you. You have your white cross, your white scarf. You are in no danger. Let them get on with their bloody work; your King and master would expect you to help them, for all that is done will be with the approval of Spain. Who knows, it may be for her very desire for friendship with Spain that the Queen Mother has decided that this shall happen. They say that she is without religion, that she favours neither Huguenot nor

Catholic, but either in turn when they can be of use to her.

Yes, it is your duty to take your sword and go into the streets, to stand beside the assassins.

And Pierre? And Julie? He thought of Julie – that fierce little puritan – in the hands of bloodthirsty fanatics!

Now the streets were full of noise. He was at his window again. Below he saw two bodies writhing in the death agony; they lay in pools of blood. A woman was running down the street; she had a child in her arms. There were two men with drawn swords in pursuit.

She had fallen to her knees; she was trying to protect the child.

Blasco heard her pitiable plea. 'Messieurs, Messieurs, have mercy.'

But the answer of those two was to pierce her body with their swords. The child rolled from her arms and swiftly one of the men cut off its head.

'In the name of the Saints!' cried one of the assassins. 'Come, friend. For the sake of Holy Church!'

They ran on, their white scarves gleaming, the blood dripping from their waving swords.

Blasco felt sickened. He stood for a while gazing in horror at the woman and the child.

Then, his sword in his hand, he ran down the stairs and out into the streets.

He made his way in the direction of the Rue Béthisy. Now the streets were filled with the agonised screams of the dying. Men, women, and children – none was to be spared. The smell of blood was everywhere. Men passed Blasco – men who looked like wild animals – with the blood lust on them.

Blasco was pale, his lips tightly compressed.

'Come, friend,' called two men to him, as their eyes alighted on the cross and scarf, 'there's much work to be done this night. There shall not be a heretic living in Paris by the morning.'

Blasco waved his sword and said: 'I go this way.'

'By the Saints, he's right!' said one of them. 'That's the way to the Rue Béthisy. There'll be work to be done there, I'll swear.'

They turned and ran with him. They killed an old man on the way. Blasco did not look; he ran on ahead of them. They followed, panting.

'There'll be one who with his own hand will wish to despatch the Admiral, I doubt not,' cried one of the men. 'That will be Monsieur de Guise! He'll want to avenge his father.'

Blasco saw that, about the house where the Admiral had his lodging, a crowd of people were gathered. He heard the shouts and screams and, as he drew near, he recognised the tall man surrounded by friends as Henri de Guise. He saw the murdered body of the Admiral thrown from a window, and Henri de Guise place his foot upon it.

Such a sight halted his two companions. They shouted: 'Death to the heretic! *Vive de Guise!*'

But Blasco did not pause. His eyes were on another house. He saw that several men were already trying to storm the entrance. He ran forward and joined them just as they had broken down the door.

He forced his way with them into the house. He saw Pierre and his father in their nightclothes. In one terrible second Pierre recognised him.

He cried: 'Blasco . . . So you . . . are on their side! You have come to kill!'

That was all he said before a sword was thrust through his body and he swayed and staggered to the ground.

Blasco felt sick with misery. He could feel the eyes of the dying man upon him as he leaped up the stairs ahead of those who had stayed below to kill Pierre's father and the servants who had gathered about him to weep and wring their hands.

'Julie!' he cried. 'Julie! Quickly! Where are you? It is Blasco.'

He found her in one of the bedrooms. She had hastily slipped a cloak about her, and beneath it she was naked, having risen straight from her bed.

She looked at him. She saw the white cross in his hat, the scarf on his arm. She had seen terrible things from her window, and she knew that the murderers were below.

'You . . . you with them! You . . . you devil!'

'Be silent, you fool!' he cried. He saw the ladder which led to the attics. 'There is a way to the roof,' he said. 'Get up there . . . quickly! Not a moment to lose!'

She obeyed. He followed. He had hardly let down the trap door when he heard loud tramping and shouts on the stairs.

They climbed through a window and scrambled on to the roof. 'Make for the chimney,' he whispered. 'With God's help, we may be able to hide ourselves there.'

She crawled towards it; he followed. They crouched behind the chimney stack.

Now the tumult was intense in all directions, and below them in the street the slaughter went on.

'Pierre,' she whispered to him. 'My father . . .?'

'We do not know.'

'But they are below. We should go to their aid.'

He shook his head.

'Too late?' she gasped.

He nodded.

Then she covered her face and began to weep silently. He was glad that she did so and even for those few moments shut out the terrible sights in the street below.

❧ ❧ ❧

For several hours they remained where they were. He was afraid to move, for he had heard shots fired at others who had tried to escape by way of the roofs. His mind was working quickly. He had to get Julie away from the house. If he could get her to his room in the inn, it might be that the innkeeper would help him to look after her until this madness had subsided.

It might well be that she was known by many as the young Huguenot who had come to Paris in the train of Jeanne of Navarre. It would not be safe for her to be seen in the streets.

Yet they could not stay long here on the roof. Now that the daylight had come they were in imminent danger of being seen.

He thought of a plan then; it was a desperate one, but he dared not stay here, and it was as likely to succeed as anything he could think of.

In the stables at the back of the house there would undoubtedly be stores of hay and some kind of sacks. What if he could procure a strong sack large enough to carry Julie back to his room? He would try it. He told her what he intended to do. She was terrified of being left alone; she clung to him. It was difficult to believe that this frightened girl was the Julie who had so reviled him for his beliefs. At any other time he would have been amused; he would have teased her; now he could feel only tenderness. He was sure that, having lived through this night, he would never be the same again – never the same lighthearted young man who had shrugged aside matters of state and concerned himself only with his immediate pleasure.

He made his way with the utmost care back to the attic; he crept down the stairs, stepping over the dead bodies which lay in his way. For a few seconds he paused to look at Pierre lying there, his eyes glazed and unseeing, and it was as though that face, so young and beautiful, was set in a mask of reproach which would haunt Blasco as long as he lived.

'Pierre,' he murmured, 'if you could only have known! Did you think that of me then, Pierre, my Huguenot friend!'

Now he was determined that he would look after Julie as long as she needed him; and he would never forget the look he had seen in the eyes of Pierre.

He found what he needed and went back for Julie. He brought her down to the stables without mishap; there he put her into a sack, packed hay round her and at the mouth of the sack, and humping his load onto his back set off for the inn.

The sweat poured from him, and as he staggered through the bloodstained streets of Paris on St Bartholomew's Day, he rejoiced that Julie could not see what he saw.

❧ ❧ ❧

He kept her in his room and for three days they lived there in hiding.

How could he explain what happened during those days?

He did not love Julie. He pitied her. She did not love him, but she was alone, desolate and robbed of her family; she was most fearful of terrible violent death, and he was her protector.

When he left her she was afraid, and her eyes would light up when he entered the room.

He could not have saved her but for his friend the inn-keeper. Blasco did not tell the man that she was a Huguenot, though perhaps he guessed. He was a Frenchman, that innkeeper, a Parisian, a good Catholic, but *l'amour* had always seemed to him the most beautiful thing in the world, and before it all else must bow the knee.

The gallant and so handsome Spaniard had fallen in love with a little Huguenot; he had brought her through the streets in a sack. That was love. That was romance. And even if she be a Huguenot he must help them to survive.

There was Matias, eager to serve them, Matias who seemed to have something on his conscience which made him long to see his master happy with a beautiful young girl.

So in his room she stayed, for she was afraid to go anywhere else. In the night she would wake and think of Pierre and her father, and she would cry like a child, for indeed she was little more.

'I have no one now,' she would sob. 'I am alone, all alone.'

So it was natural that Blasco should take her in his arms and soothe her, telling her that she should never be alone while he was there to comfort her.

Then she would cling to him and say that she had wronged him. She would weep and he would wipe her tears away.

It seemed strange that that in time of sadness they could become lovers. Blasco had not intended that they should; nor by any means had she.

Yet it had happened simply and naturally as she lay beside him on his bed, for she was afraid not to be with him within reach when night fell and there would be shouting and brawling in the streets.

He would always remember the occasion. Below them passed the procession on its way to the Cemetery of the Innocents. For it was declared that a hawthorn had blossomed there, and this was a sign that God and His saints gave their blessing to the massacre and were pleased with those who had shed the blood of heretics.

Priests led the procession, chanting praises to God and the Holy Virgin as they went; it halted for a while before the gibbet on which now hung the mutilated body of the great and noble Coligny which had been retrieved from the river after the mob had roasted it.

The chanting of the priests had filled the room, and Julie had cried, and he had soothed her, and kissed her, and held her in his arms.

It was then that there had come upon them both the need for that sad passion which was different from anything Blasco, that connoisseur of erotic adventure, had ever experienced before.

❧ ❧ ❧

It was quiet in the city when they slipped away.

Blasco looked at the girl beside him, whom he was taking to Spain. While they were in that stricken city, that had seemed what he desired above all things to do; but as they left the city behind them, he was filled with doubts.

He would marry her. He must marry her. She had lived with him in his room, and she, considering herself defiled, would also think herself damned for ever, if there were no marriage. She had talked of taking her life, for she had said that with her brother and her father murdered and herself 'unclean', she could no longer endure to live. It was then that he had talked of marriage; it was the only balm he had to offer, and in that small room in which he felt he had come to know more emotions than he had ever experienced in the whole of his life, there had seemed only one thing that mattered: to soothe Julie, to prevent her sinking into melancholy madness.

But as they moved from the bloodstained city, the events of those August days and nights seemed more and more fantastic. But for the fact that their lives had drastically changed because of what they had been through, they could not have believed in their reality; their minds could never have conceived anything so terrible as their eyes had witnessed.

They had escaped, and to Blasco it seemed that Reality now walked beside them, Reality with a hundred pressing problems. The cold, stern facts of everyday life had taken the place of fantastic devilries which belonged only to nightmare.

He was trying to see Julie in the Catholic household of the Carramadino, and he could imagine the continual and insurmountable problems her presence there would bring about.

He thought then: It would be better for her if she returned to her old home in Béarn. There she could forget what had befallen her. There she might marry with a man like Pierre, a Huguenot.

But she would not do that. In her rigid puritan code there was only one redemption for one who had committed the sin of fornication.

They were bound to each other. He saw that. He, the gay adventurer, was bound to the little puritan girl.

And in his home it would be necessary for her to worship in secret. He had warned her of that.

She had said: 'It is my cross, and I must carry it.'

How often had he thought of himself riding thus, a woman beside him!

How cruel was life! He had pictured a woman who would have laughed with him, sung with him, danced for him, and made love that was joyously lighthearted, adventurous love of which to be proud, not ashamed.

'Oh, Bianca, Bianca!' he murmured. 'Where are you now?'

PART THREE

DEVON
Summer, 1582

❧ Chapter III ❧

DEVON – SUMMER, 1582

In a house which overlooked Plymouth Sound, Isabella and Bianca were together. Isabella sat at the window, Bianca on the floor. Before Bianca the cards were spread out.

They were more than ten years older than when they had left Spain, and both had borne a child. It was so long since they had been in Spain that it seemed to them now that this house was as much their home as any other place could be.

Isabella's eyes were on the sea. It was sparkling today; it was as though thousands of diamonds had been cast over the blue waves; they danced and shimmered before her eyes. She often sat in this window seat looking over the sea. She had seen it black and angry, its great waves leaping and prancing like animals determined to trample the land under their feet and dash to their death any who tried to prevent them. She had seen it pellucid green in the early evening; she had seen it stained scarlet by the rising sun. And it never failed to fascinate her and her eyes would always search the horizon for a ship. She looked to the sea for what she wanted; Bianca looked to her cards.

'He will be coming soon,' said Bianca. 'It is written here.'

Isabella shivered slightly. She hated him, and he hated her. Yet he had married her. But that was because of Pilar, that strange child who was his and hers – a child born of rape and brutality. The dark eyes, the oval face were Isabella; the high and adventurous spirit, the recklessness, the quick temper, they were his. It was a strange combination.

It was at times like these that she thought of what had happened on that nightmare occasion. Perhaps that was why she gazed so often at the sea, hating to remember each vivid detail and yet, in some strange way, determined to remember.

Bianca was frowning at the cards; a brown finger pointing at one of them. Secretly Bianca was longing for his return. Bianca suited him better than she did, and Bianca was a gipsy accustomed to brutality, who could adjust herself; she could fight as Isabella never could.

Isabella remembered how he had emerged from his first encounter with Bianca, a great bruise below his eye and the marks of her nails on his cheeks. She remembered his gleaming eyes and his loud laughter. The rape of Bianca had delighted him as the rape of Isabella could not.

And after Bianca – Isabella. She had fainted and was thankful for that mercy.

There were six other women with them. One of them had leaped into the sea and had never been seen again. She had preferred death. How strange it was that the same circumstances should have different effects on different people. Another woman who was pregnant had had a miscarriage and died before they reached England; that left four. One, Carmentita, fat and jolly, yet lacking both good looks and the dowry which would have brought her a husband and was now a servant in this very house, had not been displeased at her treatment. She delighted in it; she talked of it continually; it was something she had thought would never happen to her. Two of those captured women had gone to other parts of England, and the last, Maria, was in service at the Manor House, which belonged to Sir Walter Hardy and which was but a mile or so from the house of Captain March. Maria had told her story and the Hardys, who were no friends of Captain March, had taken her in and treated her well. Maria had been seen now and then, neatly dressed, well cared for, a respectable maid-servant with employers who had her welfare at heart.

Isabella often thought of Carmentita and Maria and the woman who had jumped into the sea; she also compared herself with Bianca.

Now Isabella picked up her needlework. Into this house, which was so unlike that of her father, she had endeavoured to bring a peaceful domesticity. The Captain, by reason of his trade, was rarely in England, but it amused him to see this Spanish lady making a home for him. There were times when he would look at her and break into loud laughter.

'I did not do so badly,' he had said. 'Nay! I did not do so badly when I raided the Dons' country and got me a wife.'

But she would never have been his wife but for Pilar.

He had not cared about the child when she was born, any more than he cared about Bianca's Roberto. It was when she was four years old that he had seemed to see her for the first time.

Isabella remembered the occasion well. She had sat at the window, as she was sitting now, and she had seen his ship come in. She had trembled and the sharp-eyed little girl had noticed her trembling.

Pilar, all hate for those she hated, all love for those she

loved, had looked up into her mother's face and seen Isabella's fear.

She knew, of course, that it had something to do with the ship which was visible in the Sound.

Pilar did not remember him for he had been away two years. His voyages were long, for after his raid on the Spanish mainland he had received a certain amount of acclaim and it had not been difficult to find those who were ready to invest their money in a fine ship for such a daring captain. He sailed far away nowadays and came home with rich treasures. The Queen herself had received him and graciously taken her share of the booty.

So he had come, and in those days ashore he had sometimes turned to Isabella, but chiefly it was Bianca whom he wanted.

Isabella would dread lying in the ornate bed, the hangings of which were of silk and beautifully woven; there was Spanish workmanship in those silky hangings; they had been filched, he told her, from the Dons of Mexico, so it was fitting that they should form a setting for his Spanish woman.

How often had she lain in the bed listening for his arrival! How often had she heard the swish of the curtains and seen him laughing there! Then it would be as it had been on that first occasion. Bianca spared her what she could, but he was a man who needed many women. He had even turned to Carmentita for variety.

And so she had trembled, and the little four-year-old Pilar had noticed it; and when he stood on the threshold, the great man with the fair glistening hair and face tanned golden brown, he had seemed like an ogre to young Pilar. She knew no fear; in that she was his daughter; she knew great love; that was for her mother; and now she knew great hate, and that was for the big golden man who had changed the household by his coming.

So Pilar stood before him, barring his way, two small feet placed firmly on the floor.

He had seen her, but children did not interest him. He knew he had a daughter; if she had been a son he might have been more interested. He would have walked past her, but two small arms had caught his leg and Pilar cried: 'Go away, you bad man. You shall not come here!'

He stopped and looked at her. Isabella had risen to her feet. She had cried in terror: 'Pilar, come here.'

Pilar cried: 'Go away. Go away, man. You are not wanted here.'

'And who is this who would banish me from my own house?' he had demanded in his great rumbling voice. 'Who is this imp of Satan?'

'It is no imp of Satan,' said Pilar. 'It is a Pilar.'

Isabella had run forward and would have taken the child. But he forestalled her. He lifted Pilar up in his great hands and held her high above his head.

'Now what has this brave Piller to say?' He called her Piller; when he used a Spanish word or name he seemed to be striving to express all his hatred and contempt for Spaniards by making it English, as he would all their possessions.

'This is a Pilar, not Piller,' said Pilar boldly; 'and she says "Go away, man."'

Isabella had caught her breath in alarm. She had expected the child to be thrown across the room. But he continued to hold her with one hand, high above his head, and it was Isabella whom he pushed from him with the other.

'So,' he said, 'you would still tell me to go away?'

Pilar began to kick and cry: 'Yes, man. Yes, man. Go away! Go away!'

She spoke the English words with the accents of her mother, Bianca and Carmentita, and Isabella thought that would further enrage him. But his golden beard had begun to waggle, as it did when he was amused. His amusement could, however, often be the prelude to a display of brutality.

'Pilar, do not say such things,' cried Isabella.

Pilar's face was screwed up with anger. Perhaps she was beginning to be a little afraid of the big man with the strong arms. But it was typical of Pilar that when she was afraid she would be most defiant.

'I will, I will, I will,' she cried; and she continued to kick and struggle.

'I have no doubt, Miss Piller,' he said, 'that you are my daughter.'

'Let go, man. Let go!' screamed Pilar.

He lowered her a little so that her face was on a level with his.

He took one of her ears between his thumb and forefinger. Isabella shuddered; she knew the gesture and she knew how painful it could be. But Pilar made no protest.

He said: 'What'll you do if I put you down?'

'Kill you!' cried Pilar.

'With what?' he asked, and there was interest in his voice.

'With my hands.'

He took one of them and looked at it. 'Such weapons are indeed formidable!'

Then he held her in his two hands and threw her up to the ceiling. She held her breath. He caught her as she fell.

He began to laugh and Pilar, who had been momentarily frightened, now laughed aloud with relief.

For a few seconds he looked at her, at the great dark eyes with the long black lashes, at the flushed smooth skin.

He said nothing but: 'Piller. Miss Piller.'

'Pilar,' she corrected.

'Piller,' he said, 'my girl Piller.'

Then he set her down on her feet, burst out laughing and went away without so much as a word to Isabella.

And from then on he made a point of looking for the child, of talking to her. He gave her an ivory comb ornamented with rubies.

And the next time he came home from a voyage the first thing he did was to look for his girl Piller.

Then he had said to Isabella: 'We'll get married. My girl Piller will one day have all I've got, and I want it to be made ship-shape.'

So Isabella had married him. She believed it was a continual source of astonishment to him that Pilar was her daughter. If she had been Bianca's it would have been more understandable. But he was not dissatisfied. Isabella was a more suitable wife than Bianca would have been, and it was wise to conform with certain of the conventions of the neighbourhood. All voyages were not successful – a pirate's life was a hazardous one – and it was often necessary to raise money. People were more ready with a loan for a respectably married captain than one who kept a harem. So for expediency and for Pilar he married Isabella.

And now, when he came home, this girl would be the first to greet him and examine the treasures he had brought home. And it was Pilar who took her choice of these and, oddly enough, he could refuse the girl little.

So it was that in time Pilar had grown away from her mother

and closer to her father. She was more in tune with the wild English buccaneer than the gentle Spanish mother; and there were fresh fears for Isabella when he returned, though he visited her rarely now. He was, he said frankly – for he was always frank – sick of ladylike manners in the bedchamber, preferring a battle with Bianca or an hour or so with the ever-ready Carmentita, if his tastes ran to Spaniards.

It was this growing friendship, between her ten-year-old daughter and the ruthless man who was her father, which terrified Isabella.

For there was no doubt that the young Pilar had a great regard for this man. They would ride together; the sound of their laughter would ring through the courtyards. He had no restraint. He brought jewels for her; she possessed quite a hoard now. He was teaching her to be as coarse, as ruthless as he was himself, and it was indeed fortunate that he was rarely at home.

And soon, she supposed, he would be home again. It was two years since he had last been here, and the voyage should have been over by now. That was why every day, as she sat with her needlework, her eyes would often be on the horizon, watching for a ship; that was why Bianca consulted her cards.

❧ ❧ ❧

Bianca was sure that he was on the way home and she was glad. In her hatred of him she found great pleasure. Hatred and lust went well together. From their first encounter, when she had offered herself in place of Isabella yet had fought him with teeth and nails, she had recognised that pleasure which they could give each other.

She could hate him for taking her from Spain, where Blasco

would surely have one day sent for her; and she could be thankful to him, for in her encounters with him, she could for long periods forget her longing for Blasco.

She was a woman who could not live for long without a lover.

Now, as Isabella sat at the window and she made play with her cards, she knew that Isabella was thinking, as she did on such occasions, of that terrible time when their native land had slipped away from their sight and they had been in the power of the brutal English pirates.

He had chosen them both, and for that they had to be thankful. The others – apart from Carmentita – had suffered more.

It was a strange thing, Bianca told herself often. They had both loved Blasco and then they had both become the mistresses of the pirate. In Bianca's way of reasoning, clearly some fate bound them together.

She had felt strong even when he had overcome her resistance, and had quickly begun to make plans for returning to their home.

They were taken to a house near the sea, and she had believed that the sea would be their means of escape. Often on warm days it seemed that the south-west wind brought to them the scent of spices from Spain.

She was filled with wonder when she knew that she was to have a child and that this could only be Blasco's.

The house to which the pirate took them was not large like those of the de Ariz and the Carramadino families, but it was comfortable. The overhanging gables were pleasant to the eyes; the gardens were charming; there were many rooms, two staircases and odd little alcoves in unexpected places. The kitchens, the buttery, the bolting house and pantries were full of good food and good wine. The Captain lived well when he was at home, and his servants must be ready to receive him at any time.

In such a house her child could be born in the comfort due to it; so she shelved her plans for escape.

She had kept the secret from all until she knew that Isabella too was to have a child; but she had quickly made up her mind that she would never tell Isabella that her child was Blasco's. She knew that when Isabella sat in the window looking over the sea she dreamed that Blasco would come to rescue her, just as before, when the plans were going ahead for her marriage with Domingo, she had dreamed that Blasco would come and take her away.

Bianca could not therefore hurt Isabella more than she had already been hurt. Bianca's role was to protect Isabella from the world.

Isabella had said to her one day: 'Sometimes I think there is nothing left to do but kill myself. I would I had had the courage to leap overboard as one of our number did. She died before this shame could touch her.'

'To take life is an evil thing,' said Bianca, 'even if it is your own.'

'But to suffer this shame . . .'

'You would kill not only yourself but the baby.'

'His child, Bianca. Think of that.'

'I do think of it. Isabella, I too am to have a child.'

Isabella had stared at her. 'You . . . Bianca! Both of us . . . at the same time!'

Bianca nodded. Her child, she knew, would be born a month or mayhap two before Isabella's, but that was a matter she would deal with when it was necessary to do so.

'It is to be expected,' said Bianca.

Isabella had said then: 'I feel this to be the end of all hope. Now I do not wish any of my family to find me. I wish them never to know that this has happened to me.'

Bianca felt differently. It was easy for her to comfort Isabella. To have a baby was wonderful! In this child Blasco would live again.

Bianca was cunning. No one must know that the child was anyone's but the Captain's. She must ensure for it a comfortable birth. She sat for long hours with Isabella and they talked together of children, and Bianca was happy with a happiness which Isabella found it difficult to understand.

Roberto was born six weeks before Pilar.

'He is born before his time,' said Bianca. 'It is sometimes so.'

And, during the weeks that followed, Bianca was almost completely happy, for her baby – a beautiful healthy boy – had, it seemed to her, already a look of Blasco. She felt that with this child she had cheated the Captain. He had forced her, but he had not been able to force his child upon her. Here was Roberto, the fruit of true love. She loved the boy; she determined to make him the meaning of life to her.

Isabella's child was born after a long labour – a dark-eyed girl with light-coloured hair, and from the beginning it became clear that the little Pilar was unlike her mother in all except her appearance.

How like their fathers they were! Bianca often thought.

Roberto, growing handsome and with a natural charm which made it easy for him to extricate himself from trouble, was lazy, as Blasco must have been; he liked to lie in the sun and idle away the hours. Pilar was full of bounding energy, constantly urging Roberto to follow her in mischief, abusing him in her frank and fearless way if he displeased her, bullying, always leading the way. Roberto was all Spaniard; and there was more than a streak of her buccaneering father in Pilar.

It was a source of some anxiety to Bianca that Roberto had never found favour with the Captain.

She was often with him on the nights he spent in the house, and on these occasions she had opportunities of speaking to him; yet she had not been able to arouse his interest in Roberto.

She guessed the reason. It was due to that gossip, Carmentita. She must have told him when the child had been born.

One night she said to him: 'You show not the slightest interest in your son.'

'That gipsy boy!' he retorted. 'He's no son of mine.'

She had brought her hand smartly across his face which made him roar with laughter. He liked to arouse her to physical violence; it gave him an opportunity of showing her that, spitfire though she might be, she was no match for him.

'What do you mean by that?' she demanded.

'He was on the way before you met me.'

'That's a lie!'

He caught her by one of the rings in her ears and she squealed with the pain.

'Let go! Let go!'

'Don't tell me lies,' he said, 'or you'll be sorry.'

'Lies! What lies are these?'

'The child was born too soon,' he said. 'Do you think I don't know what goes on in my own household?'

'Some *are* born too soon.'

'They are small and sickly. Your brat was a sizeable one, I heard.'

'Who told you this?'

'Do not think I come here to be asked questions by gipsies.'

'I do not come here to be called a liar.'

She had walked to the door. He strode to her and effortlessly flung her back into the room. 'You come when you're told,' he said.

'You'll accept your son,' she cried.

His blue eyes blazed, and he caught her by the hair. He shook her so that her head was whirling. 'Stop your talk, gipsy. There is one thing I want of you, and it is not talk.'

She fought him, and he laughed at her efforts. She was bruised afterwards and she was almost sobbing with rage. But it was often thus between them, and it was during such scenes as these that she found the greatest satisfaction – as he did.

'It is Carmentita who has told you these tales,' she said afterwards.

'When I ask what happens in my household I can be harsh if the answers I get are not truthful.'

'So she has come to you with tales . . . the great elephant!'

'That is why you were so eager to please me,' he said. 'You thought, I'll have the Captain for the father of my child.'

'I . . . eager for you!'

'You have forgotten. You pushed poor Isabella aside to get at me.'

'What of that?' she said. 'The boy is yours. So you do not want a son. You are a strange man.'

'When I have a son I shall have to be sure he is my son.'

'You will see. As he grows up you will see he is yours.'

But he would not believe her; and he had scarcely a look for young Roberto. He had no objection to having the child in the house; but he would not accept him as his son, and he made that clear.

But she determined that one day he should accept Roberto as his son.

There was little she could do. She had been to the attic where Carmentita slept with the rest of the servants and, tearing the clothes off her, had heaved the great mountain of a woman over on to her face and belaboured her with a stick.

Carmentita had shrieked and sought to raise herself, but every time she did so, Bianca pushed her back. The other servants had gathered to laugh and, when Bianca had finished, Carmentita had sat up with tears of rage running down her cheeks declaring that she would never rest until she had had her revenge on the gipsy. Later she told the servants that Bianca was jealous because the Captain preferred a plump Spanish woman to a skinny gipsy, and this idea so pleased Carmentita that she seemed almost fond of Bianca again.

Bianca had talked to her son, stressing upon him the need to please the Captain, but Roberto could not do this; his solemn dark eyes would survey the Captain, but he always kept his distance; and when the Captain shouted: 'Hi, run away, gipsy!' Roberto would stand very still, poised for flight.

But Bianca believed that eventually she would make the Captain accept her son. It was for this reason that, as she spread her cards on the floor, she was hoping that one day, not far distant, the ship would appear in the Sound and the cry would go up through the house: 'The Captain has come home.'

It was early afternoon, and Isabella had called her daughter to her.

They had partaken of dinner an hour ago, and at this hour Pilar should be setting off for her daily instruction. For this she went to the house of the parson where she would sit in the big room overlooking the gravestones, with Roberto beside her, and they would both long for the hours to pass that they might be free again.

'Pilar, my *favorita*,' said Isabella, 'you must promise me to pay attention to Mr Power. You do not want him to think you are stupid, do you?'

'No, Mamma.'

'Then will you try to work a little harder? Roberto does better than you.'

'Roberto is lazy.'

'It is you who are lazy.'

'But no, Mamma. I am not lazy. I want to be out in the sun, and so does Roberto, but he is too lazy to want as badly as I do, so he just sits there and does what he is told. Roberto always does what he is told. He is too lazy to make a fuss, he says.'

'It is you who are the lazy one. You must work harder.'

'Yes, Mamma.'

Isabella kissed the young face. She thought then how different her life might have been had this house been the one to which she was to have gone in honourable marriage. She imagined her husband beside her talking to their daughter; and at such times she imagined Blasco, because she had continued to believe that Blasco would have come to carry her away before he would let her marry Domingo. But then this child of hers would never have been born. This was the daughter of Ennis March and could be no other.

She drew the child to her and kissed her warmly. Pilar wriggled free. Roberto liked to be fondled; if his mother kissed him he would put his arms about her neck. They were very different, Pilar and Roberto.

'So you will learn all that Mr Power has to teach you, and then I shall not be ashamed of you if . . .'

She paused. For the first time Pilar was interested. If! If what? she wanted to ask. But there were secrets in this house. There were things they kept from a ten-year-old girl.

If they thought they could long keep anything from her, Pilar, they were mistaken.

'I find out all I want,' she boasted to Roberto. She was a great boaster. If she was frightened she boasted the more; it gave her courage. She must never be afraid for her father would despise her if she were, and there was one thing she would not suffer and that was her father's contempt.

Her father was the greatest man in the world. No wonder Roberto's mother was always trying to pretend he was Roberto's father!

The things one could discover if one kept one's ears and eyes open! That was the greatest fun in the world – keeping one's ears and eyes open. Roberto never kept his open. Lazy Roberto. He just wanted to lie in the sun and listen to the sound of the tide's coming in, or stare endlessly at the sea. She asked continual questions. 'Roberto, who *is* your father, if the Captain is not?' 'Roberto, why does my mother always look out to sea as if she is waiting?' 'Roberto, who is my father's wife . . . my mother or yours?'

'Roberto, why is my mother sad and your mother glad when the Captain comes home?' But Roberto just shrugged his shoulders and laughed, saying: 'What does it matter?'

Then she would fly at him and shake him. Indifference, lassitude, were the last things she could bear.

'I want to know . . . I want to know.' She would open her arms wide as though to embrace the world and all knowledge. Roberto would laugh at her.

'What they keep from you you want to know. That which

they would teach you refuse to learn. That's just like women.'

Roberto repeated things he had heard others say. That was like Roberto. He was too lazy even to think his own thoughts.

But they were friends. Her energy and his laziness went well together. Each acted as a curb on the other. Besides, they were close, very close, and both would have felt their world to have been incomplete without the other.

Now Pilar said quickly: 'If what, Mamma?'

'What do you mean, my child?'

'You said you would be ashamed of me if something.'

'If you did not learn.'

'No . . . If something else. What were you going to say?' Pilar had put her face close to that of her mother. Her great dark eyes were alight with interest. Isabella had flushed slightly. She had pressed her lips firmly together, almost as though she feared, Pilar thought, that her daughter could charm words out of her mouth as a snake-charmer charmed his snakes. Pilar's heart beat fast, as it always did when she hoped to make discoveries.

'Run along,' said Isabella. 'You will be late. Find Roberto and go at once.'

Pilar went, lifting her skirts in her haste, lest she should trip over them.

Roberto was in the garden lying in the grass; he was watching ants crawl up a blade of grass. She flung herself down beside him.

'What's that?'

'Ants,' he said. 'Watch them, Pilar. Watch them. They do strange things.'

'People do stranger things,' she said. 'Roberto, do you think that some day our relations will come to see us?' Roberto did not answer. He often did not answer Pilar's questions. They were not meant to have answers. Pilar was really questioning herself. 'For,' she went on, 'we must have relations. The Captain has a brother, and he is my uncle. He is English and a sailor too. But our mothers are Spanish. We must have Spanish relations. Why do we never hear of them? How far away is Spain?'

'You ought to listen to Mr Power. He might tell you. Look! This one is carrying something. It's a piece of straw and almost as big as himself.'

'You ought not to be lying here,' said Pilar. 'It is time we went to Mr Power's. There are three Spanish women in the house. My mother, your mother and Carmentita. Have you noticed that they all have secrets that show on their faces sometimes?'

'If they are secrets, how can they show?' asked Roberto.

'You can see secrets,' she said. 'Like the things we try to hide in our pockets. Sometimes they bulge . . . but they are secrets all the same. There is Carmentita. She is coming out to feed the peacocks. Hello . . . hello there, 'Tita!'

Carmentita turned with the peas in her hand and looked round at Pilar.

'You should be at the lessons, you lazy ones,' she said.

'We are going now, 'Tita. 'Tita, do you ever think of Spain?'

'Of Spain? Why should I?'

'Because it is your native land, that's why, 'Tita.'

Carmentita's black eyes were embedded in layers of fat; she put her hands on her hips and laughed. She laughed often, for life seemed good to her.

'And I know why,' said Pilar, who often continued her conversations as though she had spoken her thoughts aloud.

'It's because you like England better than Spain, don't you, 'Tita?'

'I am one of those who find myself the pleasure wherever I should be.'

Carmentita's English was not very good; she had not been able to pick it up as Bianca and Isabella had; but that was no hindrance. Pilar knew that she could glean more information from Carmentita than from anyone else.

'I know why you like England, 'Tita,' said Pilar. 'It is the English men you like.'

Carmentita gave a titter of laughter. 'Oh, you are a wicked one . . . oh, you are a saucy one,' she cried.

'Oh yes, and so are you, 'Tita.' Pilar added diplomatically: 'When it comes to men . . . if they are English, of course.'

That made Carmentita laugh the more. Pilar studied her intently. It was almost as though Carmentita became drunk with laughter, and then it was easier to discover what you wished to know.

'They like you because you are Spanish, and you like them because they are English.'

More laughter. 'I shall die with the laughing,' declared Carmentita.

'That is why you came to England when you were a little girl. Did you come to England when you were a little girl?'

Carmentita's eyes glistened. 'Ah, Pilar, you ask too much of the questions.'

'You can't ask too many questions, 'Tita. Because it is only by asking questions that you learn, and we should all learn when we are little.'

'Oh, it is a sly one! Oh, it is a saucy one!' said Carmentita.

' 'Tita, what happened when you came to England?'

Carmentita shook her head; she was looking sad, but it was all a pretence. She could not deceive Pilar.

'Did you come with my mother and Bianca?'

Carmentita nodded slowly; her eyes had become slightly glazed as grown-up people's did when they looked into the past.

Pilar came close and looked up into her face.

'Ah!' Carmentita shuddered. 'Ah, that was a time. Never shall I forget . . . mine was a tall man, with dark eyes, but not dark as a Spaniard's . . .'

'Yes, 'Tita?' breathed Pilar.

But it was a mistake to have spoken.

'Oh, you are a sly one,' said Carmentita.

And there was Roberto coming up. It was useless now. She was angry with Roberto.

'You spoilt it,' she cried, when they had left Carmentita feeding the peacocks. 'I was just charming it out of her as the snake-charmers charm snakes. Soon I would have known, and you spoilt it.'

'Known what?' he asked.

But she had ceased to be interested. Her anger evaporated as rapidly as it came. She gave him a push which sent him backwards.

'You can't catch me,' she cried; and she ran all the way to the rectory.

Roberto made no attempt to catch her, though he ran. They were late, and it seemed less effort to hasten a little than to have to answer the questions, as to what had delayed them, which Mr Power would surely put.

When he reached the tombstones which marched up to the door of Mr Power's house, Pilar was waiting for him.

She had changed again; her eyes were dreamy. 'When I grow up,' she said, 'I'm going to discover things.'

'New countries?' he asked.

'Yes, those as well,' she told him. 'But mostly secrets . . . other people's secrets.'

❧ ❧ ❧

Mr Power had a colic, and there could be no lessons that day. Mrs Power said that if they would come in they might read their books, and Mr Power would question them on what they had read when he was recovered.

Pilar replied: 'We could not keep our minds on books, Mistress Power, while we were thinking of poor parson's colic. We will return tomorrow for the lessons.'

'And in the meantime we will pray for him,' added Roberto.

Mistress Power was clearly glad to be rid of them. She said with a smile: 'You are good children, both of you.'

So Pilar curtseyed and Roberto bowed and, within a few minutes of Mrs Power's shutting the door, Pilar was running among the gravestones. Roberto followed her more leisurely.

'You lied, Roberto,' she accused. 'You said we would pray for him.'

'Please God,' said Roberto, 'make Mr Power's colic better. There! I have not lied.'

'But not too soon better,' amended Pilar with fast-shut eyes. 'Better enough for him not to be sick, but not better enough to give lessons.'

'You are telling God what to do, and that is an impertinence,' said Roberto.

'Everybody tells God what to do. It's in all the prayers and hymns. They always tell Him.'

She dismissed the subject, for her darting mind had seized on another. 'Roberto, just think, under all these stones are dead people. Can they hear us, do you think?'

'Perhaps,' said Roberto.

'How quiet it is! Suppose they rose from under those stones and took us down there with them?'

'They couldn't. The dead are dead.'

'Let's go and look at the Hardys' vault.'

'Why?'

'Because it's like a real house – not just a grave – and because it's full of Hardys.'

'You're only trying to frighten yourself.'

'No,' she said, 'I'm trying not to frighten myself.'

She began to run again and he followed.

The Hardys' vault was an elaborately carved edifice, with a marble figure guarding the door. Pilar went to it and stood on tiptoe. 'He moves if you look long enough,' she said. 'He's not dead really, Roberto. When it's night he opens the door and all the dead Hardys come out into the graveyard.'

'The dead can't come to life.'

'What about on the resurrection day?'

'Every night is not resurrection night.'

'No, but perhaps that marble man thinks they ought to practise for when God calls them. They might be too stiff to move on resurrection day.' She went down the damp steps to the door of the vault. 'You can smell the dead,' she said. 'It's a cold smell, damp and earthy.'

'You'd smell damp and earthy if you'd been buried a hundred years; you'd be cold too.'

She shuddered. 'I don't want to be here any longer. I don't believe there's anything to be afraid of here. The dead are all locked away in there. It's much more brave to go to Hardyhall and climb the wall . . . and creep right up to the house . . .' She laughed suddenly, then started to run, and she did not stop running until she reached the lych-gate. There she stood waiting for Roberto.

There was a soft south-west breeze blowing, and Pilar sniffed it appreciatively.

'My mother says that when the wind blows this way she can smell Spain,' said Roberto.

'Spain! We both half belong there, Roberto.'

'I know.'

'Pilar. Roberto. Our very names belong to Spain. And yet we know nothing about it. Why will they never speak to us of Spain, Roberto? Where are our Spanish aunts and uncles and cousins?'

Roberto shook his head. 'One day we shall know.'

She stamped her foot. 'But I want to know now . . . now . . .'

'Why can't you ever wait for anything, Pilar?'

'Because if you wait you'd not want it any more. What is the good of waiting for something that you won't want when you get it?'

'You change too quickly.'

'Everything changes quickly . . . except the dead.' She laughed suddenly and started to run. He watched her, her skirts flying. He would not run; he would catch her, for at any moment she would stop short, her attention caught by something.

She had stopped now. She had come to the dark clump of trees which marked the beginning of the Hardys' land. They were conifers, sleekly green all the year round, always making a bushy screen for that wing of the house which could be seen from this part of the road.

'Come, Roberto,' she cried. 'We are going to Hardyhall.'

She darted through the conifers to pause before the grey stone wall which surrounded the parklands of the big house. When Roberto reached her she was scrambling to the top of it.

He climbed the wall and sat beside her.

They were silent contemplating the grey walls of Hardyhall. It was an ancient house, dating back to the thirteenth century, although the present Sir Walter Hardy had added a new wing. He had not tried to emulate the architecture of a past century: Sir Walter's wing was modern Elizabethan. The two towers at either end of the long building delighted Pilar. She peopled those towers with imaginary figures of the past. From the battlements soldiers had shot their arrows at their enemies, and from over the gateway they had poured boiling pitch and oil down on those who would have forced an entrance. Hardyhall was more like a castle than a house. It was the biggest residence for miles round. There were two young Hardys. She had seen them riding in the lanes, a girl and a boy, and they were of an age, she believed, with herself and Roberto. The village children bobbed a curtsey or pulled a forelock when they passed. Pilar and Roberto did no such thing. They stared haughtily past them as though they did not see them. They were, after all, the Captain's children and but for the Captain's strange mode of life they might have been accepted at Hardyhall.

Pilar had worked herself into a hatred against the two Hardy children. She invented all sorts of follies which they were alleged to have committed. She created adventures in which she and Roberto shared; they played the victors, the Hardy children the conquered simpletons. Roberto listened with an amused tolerance. There were times when he reminded Pilar that he was six weeks older than she was, which made him wiser. She laughed at him, and continued to lead.

The green lawns sloped from the house. There were old yew trees on the lawn and the box hedges had been cut into the shapes of cockerels and other birds. These enchanted Pilar. She said they were really people whom the wicked Hardys had turned into birds.

This day she was daring. She felt the need to display her courage, for she feared that Roberto believed – and perhaps he would have some reason for believing this – that in the graveyard she had been afraid. If she were afraid of dead Hardys she must show him that she was not afraid of living ones.

She said: 'I'm going over, Roberto.'

Roberto said: 'Do you remember the man we saw swinging from the gibbet? He was hanged because he had trespassed on land which belonged to the Hardys.'

'He stole a pheasant. He was hanged for that. Besides, I'm not afraid of Hardys.'

'Would you be afraid to hang on a gibbet?'

'I'd soon get down.'

'How could you, if you were dead?'

'I wouldn't die. Are you afraid, Roberto?'

She laughed at him as he would have seized her. She had already started to clamber down the other side.

'I'll hide,' she said. 'You shall find me.'

She had reached the grass and was looking up at him teasingly. 'Don't be afraid, Roberto. They daren't hang us.'

She ran swiftly across the grass. 'I'm trespassing, trespassing on Hardy land!' she cried; and she felt that whatever happened afterwards, this would be worth while.

Hardy grass was smoother than other grass, Hardy trees were bigger and they were alive. The yew there was an old lady – a very old one. The one beside it was a gentleman. He was her husband. He had two wives as her father had. She turned and saw that Roberto was making his way reluctantly towards her. She ran on.

Ahead of her lay a copse which might have been a nuttery. She had to explore. It was a nuttery. The trees were not large and it was easy to scramble up into one of them and hide herself there, waiting for Roberto. It was not long before he came. He would never find her, and he was going past, so she called to him.

'You are trespassing, boy. You will be taken to a gibbet and hanged there until you die.' Roberto stopped and looked up. 'Come up here,' she went on. 'There's plenty of room.'

She made way for him, and they sat there side by side.

'This is better than learning with Parson Power,' she said.

Roberto admitted that it was, although he supposed it was necessary for them to learn from books.

'I'd rather learn secrets than things from books,' she said.

They talked in whispers for some time; and suddenly Pilar said: 'Roberto, someone is coming. Listen!'

They were silent. Distinctly they could hear the sound of running footsteps.

'Coming this way,' whispered Roberto.

He was right, for a few minutes later a boy, perhaps a little older than Roberto, came running into the copse. He was panting as he came right under the tree in which they were perched. They saw that his hair was very fair – so fair that it looked almost white, and his face was pink with the exertion of running.

He moved swiftly away and throwing himself on the ground, he tore up great handfuls of grass and began to cover himself with this and the leaves which lay about him.

Pilar nudged Roberto, but there was no need to tell him to be silent. Breathlessly they waited, and it was not long before the girl came into the copse.

She said: 'You are there, Howard. I know you are there. Come out . . . Come out. You know I do not like to be alone in the wood.'

'Stupid!' murmured Pilar involuntarily.

Roberto nudged her so sharply that she almost fell out of the tree. The girl looked startled and stood very still as though poised for flight.

'Howard!' she called. 'Howard! I heard you then . . . I know I heard you . . .'

Pilar could not stop herself. She cried: 'Look for him. Look for him.'

For a few seconds there was a breathless silence in the nuttery; it was followed by a rustle from the bed of grass and leaves as the boy sat up.

'Who's that?' he called. 'Who's there?'

The girl ran to him.

'Someone spoke,' she said.

'I know, I heard.'

Pilar wriggled her arm free from Roberto's grip. She took a nut and threw it at the boy.

The girl screamed. The boy said: 'Don't be silly, Bess. We'll find them. They're somewhere near.'

'Somewhere near!' imitated Pilar; and her voice led the boy to the tree in which they were. He stood beneath it. He caught the gleam of Pilar's dress.

'Come down,' he said. 'You who are up there . . . come down.'

'You come up,' chanted Pilar.

Roberto was looking exasperated. Pilar was crazy. What did she think she was doing?

The boy shook the tree.

'Do not think we are nuts to fall into your hands,' said Pilar with an excited laugh.

The girl said: 'Howard, it is those strange children. Those Spaniards.'

'We are English and Spanish,' said Pilar. 'You are but English.'

'How long are you going to stay up there,' asked the boy, 'and what are you doing?'

'We are watching you.'

'But why did you get up there in the first place?'

'Because we wished to, and we do as we wish.'

'It was a bold thing to do. You trespass, you know.'

'Aye, we know it,' said Roberto.

'So there are two of you up there!'

'There are hundreds of us,' cried Pilar, her imagination afire. 'We shall come down and kill you; and it is no use thinking you can pour burning oil on us. We have already stormed the fortress.'

'You are strange people.'

That pleased Pilar. 'Yes, we are very strange,' she said. 'We do strange things while others play children's games like hide-and-seek.'

'We play hide-and-seek sometimes,' said Roberto, the placator.

'It is not very good with only two,' said the boy.

'It is better with three . . . or four,' said Roberto.

'And we have plenty of room to play here. There is the house and the gardens.'

Pilar was suddenly filled with the desire to play hide-and-seek in unknown territory. She began to scramble down from the tree. 'We will play hide-and-seek for four,' she said. 'Who shall hide?'

Roberto followed her down and the four children took each other's measure. The English boy was several inches taller than Roberto, but Pilar was as tall as he was.

The girl said: 'Howard, we should not. We should ask Mamma first.'

Howard hesitated but Pilar said: 'If you ask, she may say No. It is better not to ask.' She immediately assumed the leadership. 'There shall be two to hide and two to seek. I will go with you and we will hide, and she and Roberto can stay here and count a hundred. When they have counted they can come and look for us. May we hide in the house?'

'Not in the house,' said Howard. 'Not . . . you.'

'Would they hang us if they found us in the house?'

'Not if you were our guests.'

'We do not care,' said Pilar. 'They dare not hang us. We are half Spanish and Spaniards do not hang.'

'They do,' said the girl. 'My uncle has sailed the seas and hanged many.'

'Then one day he will be hanged himself, for no one is allowed to hang Spaniards and escape.'

'You talk treason,' said the boy.

She did not know what treason was, but she liked the sound of it. 'I often do,' she said. 'Now let's hide. You stay with her, Roberto, and count a hundred.'

The boy looked at his companion strangely as she started to run across the grass. He followed uneasily. He felt that he had been forced into something which was strange and which he did not understand. She did not stop running until she came to the grey wall of the house, and she was so fleet that it was all he could do to keep up with her.

There she paused and said: 'There is plenty of time. They will not find us until we want them to. Your Bess is rather silly, and Roberto is so lazy. What is this place?'

'It is the chapel.'

'We'll go in there and hide.'

He was startled. He said: 'A chapel is a holy place.'

'They'll never think to find us there.'

'We should be forbidden to go in there and hide. One goes in there to pray.'

'I'll pray when we are in there. Quickly! They'll be coming at any moment.'

She pushed open the door and went in. It was cool in the chapel. She looked about her eagerly; then she drew him in and shut the door after them. She said in a whisper: 'We have no chapel in our house. This is your house, isn't it?'

He nodded. He seemed somewhat bemused.

'What door is that?' she asked, indicating an iron-studded door on her right.

'It is the door we use. It opens on to the staircase which leads to the punch room.'

'You have your own chapel. You must be very good.'

He said: 'We should not be here.'

'You are worried about the prayers. Please God,' she said rapidly, 'don't mind our using this chapel to hide in. It's so quiet and they'll never find us here.'

'People mustn't talk to God like that.'

'I may.'

'Who are you?'

'I am Pilar.'

'Peelar. What an odd name!'

'Pilar!' she repeated. 'My mother came from Spain and my father is the greatest captain that ever sailed the seas. He brings back beautiful things.'

'I know.'

'How do you know?'

'People talk of you.'

'Of me,' she was clearly delighted. 'Listen! They are coming this way. We must find somewhere to hide. I know. There. Under that table there with the cloth over it. What a lovely cloth! It will hide us. I have never seen a chapel like this before.'

'You must not go up there. That is sacred . . .'

'Never mind. I'll ask God. Please God, this is the best place to hide, and you wouldn't like them to catch us, would you . . . not yet.'

'That is the altar. Did you not know that? Are you a heathen?'

'We have no chapel in our house. My mother prays in her own room. I pray with her, but I don't listen very much.'

'You are very wicked, I believe.'

She hunched her shoulders and laughed.

'It's a good place to hide,' she said, crawling under the cloth. Reluctantly he followed her. 'You are afraid. Why are you afraid, Howard?'

'I do not like to be in the chapel like this. And more especially in this spot. Let us go.'

'You ought to like being in the chapel. If you are good you should not be afraid of God.'

'Why don't you come away from there when I tell you? This is my house.'

'Then you should be more welcoming to your guests.' Her fingers moved over the flagstones as she spoke.

'I am not going to stay here,' said the boy. 'I am going out.'

'You may go, and you'll be caught. You must not tell them where I am. That is against the rules.'

'But you must come with me. You are touching the stones. You must not touch them.'

'Why?' Her eyes danced. 'Why? Why?' Now her interest was all on the stones. She lifted the cloth at the side so that she could see them better. 'Is there a secret about the stones? There's a space here by this one. I can put my hand down. Oh . . . Look, it moves.'

The boy remained very still, looking at her.

She had her hand down in the opening, and she found that she was able to raise the stone. It was not very easy for her because the stone was heavy, but she lifted it until it was at right angles to the floor. It rested there and she realised that it had been designed to do this.

She cried in delight: 'It is a cupboard down there. It is a little cupboard under the stone. Why, there are things in here . . .'

He said breathlessly: 'Do not touch them. Do not touch them.'

But her busy fingers were already exploring. 'Oh! A lovely cup. What a big one! It's silver, I believe. A lovely silver cup.'

He snatched it from her. 'You shall not. You shall not. I believe the devil sent you.'

The idea pleased her. 'Yes,' she said. 'The devil sent me. He told me that I should find a lovely silver cup.'

'Go away! Go away!' he cried. 'You have come here to betray us all.'

He was afraid, and she forgot the cup. She forgot that they were supposed to be hiding and should be talking in whispers. In that moment a certain tenderness came over her which she could not understand. He was a boy, as tall as herself, and he was frightened . . . frightened as, she had to admit, she would have been if she had found herself on the steps of the Hardy vault at midnight and alone.

She gave him the cup.

She said soothingly: 'Here. You have it. The devil did not send me here to steal it.'

He snatched it from her and put it back into its hiding place, and then replaced the stone.

'Is it a secret?' she asked.

He nodded. 'Swear that you won't tell. If you told, it would be better for me to kill you now.'

'You were very frightened,' she said. 'Only cowards are as frightened as that.'

'You can be frightened for others. That is not to be a coward.'

'So you were frightened for others? Is it a secret for grown-up people?'

'Yes, it is that sort of secret.'

'I'll not tell, Howard,' she said. 'I'll not tell anyone I found the cup in the cupboard.'

'I trust you, Pilar,' he said. 'You would never tell – not even if people did bad things to you to try to make you tell?'

'Never, never, never,' she said. 'Even Roberto shall not know this secret.'

'Let us go and find the others now.'

'We will go back to the nuttery. If we can reach it without being found, we have won.'

He brought a book and made her put her hands on it. He thrust a cross into her hands and made her say after him: 'I swear to keep this secret. I swear in the name of God and all His saints.'

She said it, wonderingly, her black eyes sparkling.

Then they went out into the sunlight.

They left the chapel behind them and were running across the grass to the nuttery when a woman's voice called: 'Howard! Howard!' The boy stopped still, and Pilar saw that he was pink to the tips of his ears.

'It is my mother,' he said. 'She has seen us.'

Now the woman came into view, and with her were Bess and Roberto. Lady Hardy was smiling; so was Roberto. It was evident that he had displayed his lazy charm and had attracted her.

'So you are Roberto's sister,' said Lady Hardy, looking at Pilar.

Pilar curtseyed.

'Roberto tells me that you children were playing hide-and-seek, and decided all to play together.'

Clever Roberto! He was so lazy, but he always found the right thing to say and the right way in which to say it.

'It is better for four to play than for two.'

'That is what Roberto told me.'

Lady Hardy turned to Howard: 'Would you not like to ask your friends into the house for some refreshment?'

'We should like to come,' said Pilar before anyone else could speak.

'It is something we should so much enjoy,' said the suave Roberto.

So they were taken into the house, through the great hall with stone-flagged floor like that of the chapel, up a flight of steps and into a small room which was hung with tapestry.

'This is the punch room,' said Lady Hardy. 'Now I shall have wine brought, and you can play host to your guests, Howard.'

'Yes, Mamma,' said Howard.

He was still uneasy, Pilar sensed; the adventure in the chapel was still with him. She herself had forgotten it except at odd moments.

They sat at the table and wine was served. There were pieces of pastry served with it, cut into odd and fantastic shapes. They were a delight to Pilar and, she saw, to Roberto also. But perhaps Roberto enjoyed most the opportunity of talking to Lady Hardy and charming her with his manners. Roberto was lazily being a gentleman – a courtier, as Isabella called him. Roberto basked in the admiration of women.

Pilar was asking herself – when she was not wondering where the door which was facing her led to, and whether there were any more secret cupboards under the stairs – why Lady Hardy, who had often passed them haughtily in the lanes of the neighbourhood, should now be so determined to be kind.

'So you are taught by Mr Power?' enquired Lady Hardy.

'Yes, we should be with him this day,' Roberto told her.

'But he has a colic,' said Pilar with delight.

'Poor man!' said Lady Hardy.

'We prayed,' continued Pilar, 'that he might not die but not be well too soon. His lessons are a little tiresome.'

'He instructs you in many subjects?' asked Lady Hardy.

'Oh yes,' said Pilar.

'We are not very good pupils,' said Roberto, with his charming smile.

'Roberto is better than I,' Pilar added.

'And does he instruct you in the Scriptures,' asked Lady Hardy, 'or does your mother do that?'

'We have not the same mother,' said Pilar. 'Our father has two wives.'

Howard and Bess looked at her in astonishment. Lady Hardy was staring hard at the tapestried walls so that Pilar turned sharply to follow her gaze, wondering what she saw there. Bess was about to speak, but Lady Hardy said quickly: 'Does your mother go with you to Mr Power's church?'

'No,' said Pilar. 'We don't go to the church either. We are Spaniards, you know – or half Spaniards. Our mothers come from Spain and our father is a great captain who is at sea and therefore far away.'

'Does your mother ever talk to you about going to church?'

Roberto spoke. 'My mother says prayers sometimes. She says them to the saints though.'

'My mother has a little prayer place all to herself,' said Pilar. 'It is in a little room. There are candles and she prays there. I have seen her. Carmentita prays there too. Sometimes they all pray together – my mother, Roberto's mother and Carmentita.'

'All those who came from Spain, you see,' said Roberto.

'Why did they come from Spain?' asked Bess.

Howard answered her: 'Because all Spaniards would come to England if they could.'

'Do your mothers tell you about their own country and the life they lived there?' asked Lady Hardy.

'Oh no,' said Pilar. 'They never talk about it. Carmentita talks though. When it rains here and the wind blows she makes faces at it and says: "Oh, you terrible English weather!" ' Pilar screwed up her face and delivered the words with a strong Spanish accent which made all the children laugh.

Pilar was drunk with success. She then began imitating Carmentita, and amid much laughter the children urged her to continue. So she went on, making up fantastic stories about Carmentita while Roberto looked on with mild amusement and the two Hardy children were almost choked with un-accustomed laughter.

When they left, Lady Hardy said to Roberto, for she had singled him out as the more reliable of the two children: 'I am going to give you a note which I hope you will deliver to Mistress March. It has been so pleasant for you four to play together that I am sure we should all be friends.'

So home they went, and in the pocket of Roberto's doublet was a note for Isabella.

Pilar snatched it from him when they arrived at the house, and ran breathlessly upstairs to present it to her mother.

❦ ❦ ❦

Bianca was with Isabella when she received Lady Hardy's note.

'She wishes to call on me,' said Isabella.

Bianca opened her eyes very wide. 'Why so? She has for years ignored you. You, the Captain's wife – at one time his mistress . . . at one time his plunder from Spain – to be called upon by the lady of the big house! What means this?'

'I do not know,' said Isabella. 'Pilar brings wild stories.'

'Pilar! She lives in her mind. One day she will suffer for it. What does Roberto say? You will more likely have the truth from him. I'll go and find him.'

He was in the small room where he and Pilar spent much of

their time together doing lessons which were set by the Reverend Arthur Power.

'Roberto?' said Bianca in that soft voice which she used towards her son.

He rose as she entered. His manners were gentlemanly, his grace was natural. He looked up at her, smiling, gracious, yet a little uneasy. His fiery mother worried him slightly; he was always afraid that she would get fiercely angry about something which it would be so much more pleasant to ignore.

'What happened this afternoon, Roberto?'

Pilar had skipped into the room. 'We climbed the wall and went into the nuttery. We climbed a tree . . . the tallest tree you ever saw, and . . .'

'I ask Roberto,' said Bianca.

'I can tell you better.'

'But not so truthfully, and it is truth I want.'

'Bianca, you dare to say I do not tell the truth!'

Roberto, the peacemaker, said: 'It is true, Mamma, what Pilar says – except that it was not a very big tree.'

'What did you say to Lady Hardy to make her wish to meet your mother, Pilar?'

'So she is coming here? So we are to go there again?' cried Pilar. She jumped high in the air. 'I shall go to the punch room. I shall drink and drink and then . . . and then . . . I shall go to the chapel . . .' She stopped suddenly.

'The chapel?' said Bianca. 'You went to the chapel?'

'I . . . I saw it when we were hiding. It is a grey place . . . and there is a door with iron on it. Then we went to hide among the trees near-by and, Bianca, they did not find us . . .'

'Roberto, my son, what did Lady Hardy say to you when you drank wine with her?'

'She asked us what we learned from Mr Power.'

'And we told her that he had a colic,' cried Pilar. 'And I said . . .'

Bianca firmly ignored the interruption. 'Was she pleased that you should play with her children?'

'Yes, she was very pleased about that,' said Roberto. 'She said it was better for four to play than two – at least someone said it.'

'I said it! I said it!' cried Pilar.

'So it is playmates for her children that she wants,' said Bianca.

She left the children and went back to Isabella.

'There are not many children hereabouts with whom hers could play,' said Isabella when Bianca was back with her and was sitting at her feet, looking at the cards to see if she could discover any reason for Lady Hardy's interest.

'And you will invite her here?'

'What else can I do?'

'What will *he* say?'

'He is far away,' said Isabella.

'It may be that he is not so far. Any day now his ship may appear on the horizon. But he need not know.'

'He might be pleased that Lady Hardy has called upon his wife.'

'Nay,' said Bianca. 'He'll not be pleased. He has always hated the Hardys. But, depend upon it, it is not merely because her children should have playmates that Lady Hardy is to call on you.'

Lady Hardy called next day.

She was soberly dressed and her ruff was of holland. Her

gown, split from the waist to form an inverted V, showed an undergown which was of richer material than her top gown. About her shoulders was a cape, and her French hood covered most of her hair, showing nothing beyond the beginning of the parting in the centre.

Isabella's manners were still those of her father's house, for she had never mingled with English ladies during her eleven years in the country. But these manners were gracious indeed, and they charmed Lady Hardy.

Bianca hovered, and seeing that her presence worried Lady Hardy, Isabella said: 'Bianca is my friend. We came from Spain together. She served me when I was in my father's house, but our adventures together have brought us very close.'

Lady Hardy was therefore somewhat unwillingly forced to accept Bianca.

'I thought the children charming,' said Lady Hardy. 'The little girl, and certainly the little boy.'

Bianca's eyes glowed warmly; Lady Hardy had immediately won her affection by her praise of Roberto.

'He is the best boy in the world,' said Bianca.

'So you are his mother?'

Bianca smiled proudly.

'I have heard rumours of the strange things which happened to you.'

'That we were brought here by force?' said Isabella.

Lady Hardy leaned forward and touched Isabella's hand. 'It was a terrible fate.'

'It is long ago,' said Isabella. 'It seems like something that happened in a nightmare. And now we have the children, we pray the saints that we shall be able to carry those burdens which have been placed on our shoulders.'

A faint colour glowed in Lady Hardy's face. 'You . . . you draw comfort from the saints?'

Isabella nodded, and Bianca, watching closely, had realised that Lady Hardy was approaching the reason for her visit. Now she continued very quietly, looking over her shoulder: 'You are both from Spain. You are here in a heretic country.' The word was enough to explain. Lady Hardy was a Catholic . . . a secret Catholic. It was for this reason that she had come to visit the women from Spain. 'You . . . you are able to worship as you wish?'

'I have only a little room which I call my chapel,' said Isabella.

'You have a . . . priest?'

'No, no. But we pray regularly to the saints.'

'It is years since you have heard Mass, years since you have confessed your sins?'

Isabella sighed. 'We shall be forgiven. We have no means of acquiring these blessings.'

'So you pray with . . .' Lady Hardy's eyes went to Bianca.

Bianca nodded. 'Yes,' she said, 'there are times when I pray. I was a gipsy in Spain. I am a good Catholic. And so is Carmentita.'

'Your . . .' Lady Hardy looked from one to the other. 'Your husband?'

'When he is expected we dismantle our little chapel. He knows nothing of our worship,' said Isabella.

'And if he knew?'

'We cannot say what he would do,' said Bianca. 'He might laugh; he might burn all which we set up in that little room to make it like a chapel. We do not know, and we dare not put this to the test. The Captain is a violent man.'

'I have heard the story. I remember the day you came here. There were wild stories in the village then. I must confess to you that Maria, who works for me and was one of your servants, has told me many things. Perhaps she should not have done so. But I have been filled with pity towards you, and it is for this reason – rather than out of curiosity – that I have asked those questions. I know of the terrible things which befell you at the hands of those . . . brutes.'

Isabella bowed her head. Bianca's bright eyes were fixed on Lady Hardy's face.

'And so,' went on Lady Hardy, 'at long last I am here; and I have a proposal to make. If you wish to receive the sacrament, I could make that possible for you. It will be necessary for you to come to Hardyhall and to have an excuse for coming. I would have you both come, and this other Spanish woman of whom you spoke. But do you know how matters stand in this land? To hear Mass and to enjoy the blessing of confession there must be a priest. Harsh laws have recently been made in this land. The Queen is afraid of the Catholics in this country, for it may be that she is aware she has no right to the throne. Her mother and father were never married, and there is a good Catholic Queen and rightful heir to England now a prisoner in the land. For this reason those about the Queen, fearing that there may be a righteous rising of Catholics, have brought in these harsh laws. It is said that the names of all those who are suspected of being Catholics or of harbouring priests are in the hands of the Queen's spies. There is little privacy in our homes, and at any time the pursuivants may descend upon us wrecking our houses in their search for priests and what they call Popish books. Therefore those of us who receive priests into our houses must do so in the utmost secrecy.'

Bianca's eyes were dancing. Here was excitement such as she loved. But Isabella seemed to cower into her seat.

'You have a priest in your house?' asked Bianca.

Lady Hardy looked wary. 'I might arrange for a priest to hear your confession and to say Mass. It came to me suddenly when I saw your children in our grounds. They are such foreign-looking children – so clearly not English, either of them. It occurred to me to wonder what religious instruction was being given to them, and when they volunteered the information that they should have been with the parson that afternoon I shuddered for I saw that they, who should have been brought up in the true Faith, were being trained by a heretic.'

Bianca said: 'I would not have my boy placed in any danger. It may be that these people who punish Catholics so harshly would punish children, should they find them with a priest.'

'Are you a Catholic to talk thus?' asked Lady Hardy.

'I am a Catholic woman,' cried Bianca, 'but I am a mother.'

'You would cosset your child's body at the expense of his soul?'

Bianca's eyes flashed. 'He is my boy. If any touched him I would kill them. I would take a knife and I would cut out their hearts. But what if they took him and harmed him . . . what good would the heart of my enemy be to me? I should have it, it is true; but then I should turn the knife on myself. For he is my boy and, since I came into this strange land, he has been with me – first unborn in my body and then my living son. I would never let harm touch him.'

'You speak not like a true Catholic.'

'Would you endanger the lives of your children, Señora?'

'If it were God's will that they should suffer I should pray that they would bear with fortitude all that their enemies meted out to them.'

'You are a good Catholic, I see,' said Bianca, 'but an indifferent mother.'

Lady Hardy had turned away from Bianca; she was now addressing herself to Isabella. 'You will come and meet the priest? We will arrange it. I suggest that the little girl and boy share not only my children's recreation but their tutor. How would that be? Then we should have them instructed in the truth.'

'So the tutor . . . he is a priest?' asked Isabella.

Lady Hardy smiled. 'These brave men who come to us . . . they must be very cautious. There are not so many of them that they can afford to be careless.'

Bianca had stood up. Her eyes were blazing. 'Isabella, no. I am afraid,' she said.

Lady Hardy's eyes were scornful.

But Bianca went on: 'Roberto shall not go. He shall not take lessons of a priest. It is forbidden here for priests to teach the children. In our country it is forbidden to be a heretic. Isabella, my lady, listen to me. Roberto shall not go. As you love Pilar, keep her by you.'

'So your supposed love of your children's welfare leads you to neglect their souls!'

'I do not know whether what I love in Roberto is his soul or his body,' said Bianca, 'but I will not let him be hurt.'

'Bianca's love is all for the boy,' said Isabella. 'Bianca speaks her mind. You must forgive her, Lady Hardy. But you need have no fear. Bianca would never betray you.'

'No,' said Bianca, 'I would not betray you. I would like to come and confess my sins and receive the absolution. But not for Roberto . . . No, no. I would not have that. I would not have him in danger.'

Lady Hardy did not look at Bianca. 'I had meant to offer this benefit to both children,' she said. 'And the little girl, would you like her to come and share my children's tutor?'

Isabella met Bianca's fearful eyes. No! No! No! Bianca was implying. Her hands were folded across her breast.

Isabella said: 'You have seen my daughter. Pilar is a child whom it is not easy to control. She has a wild imagination. She is irrepressible. I fear that to let her into such a secret would be to bring danger, not on herself only, but on everyone concerned.'

Bianca had relaxed; a sly smile came into her eyes. This was the difference between them; thus had it always been. Isabella was as alarmed for her child as Bianca was for hers. Bianca told all that was in her mind: Isabella couched her decision in diplomacy. That, thought Bianca, is the difference between a lady of high birth and a gipsy.

Lady Hardy's mouth had hardened. She was a convert to what she considered the only true Faith, and as such was more vehement than those who had been brought up in it. She had *chosen* it for her own; they had had it thrust upon them. Zeal was the essence of her Faith; passive acceptance the essence of theirs.

Isabella went on: 'We must be very careful what we say before Pilar. Moreover, when her father is home, he keeps her constantly with him. He is determined that she shall be *his* daughter. To betray such secrets to her could well prove disastrous. You have been most kind. If I might come myself and accept those blessings which you so graciously offer, most willingly would I do so.'

Lady Hardy smiled.

'It may be that in my enthusiasm to bring succour to you I have been a little incautious. You do, I know, realise that your children's souls are in danger of eternal damnation. The parson is instructing them in all the lies of this country's orthodox church. Their souls may be lost to God for ever.'

'Mr Power has not impressed either of them with his religious teaching,' said Isabella. 'I believe that they are both quietly inattentive; more so during religious teaching than any other.'

Lady Hardy's eyes shone suddenly. 'The saints are protecting them. Oh, I see that this is a miracle. I sensed it when I met them on the lawns yesterday. It is ordained that I shall save them. But you are right, of course. We must not endanger the lives of those who are doing so much for us and our Faith. We must go cautiously. Let the children continue with Mr Power, for if they came to take instruction at our house that might give rise to talk. First, you and I will be friends. You shall come to the house to return my call, and none shall know what happens while you are there. The two Spanish women shall come to carry messages or on some such pretext, and when they arrive they shall be equally blessed. As for the children, we must wait. Mr Power is ailing. This very day he has a colic. It may be that God in His mercy has decided to take him, that the way may be clear for your children to partake of that religious instruction which will lead them to the truth.'

'Yes,' said Isabella. 'That is what we must do. I am indeed grateful that you should have given me this opportunity.'

Lady Hardy rose and, coming to Isabella, put her arms about her.

'When I contemplate all that you have suffered my heart

bleeds for you. But God is good. He does not forget those in affliction. Who knows, at this moment He may have bidden the waters rise. It may be that just as He has given you the blessing of worshipping in the appropriate manner, He has decided to bring you relief from that great burden which, in His grace, He saw fit to place upon your shoulders. Come to me tomorrow. Come alone and it shall be a social call, a return visit.'

'I will come,' said Isabella. 'And I will come alone.'

❧ ❧ ❧

Pilar knew that there were secrets in the minds of the grown-up people. A subtle change had crept over the household. It touched her mother; it touched Bianca and Carmentita.

Her mother went often to Hardyhall. She never took Pilar with her, although Pilar went now and then to play with the children. Once or twice she had wanted to go into the chapel, but had found the door locked.

Pilar went by herself. Roberto would not come.

'Why? Why?' she had cried passionately. 'Why will you not come, Roberto?'

'Because I do not wish it,' said Roberto.

Roberto would lie, in his maddening way, in the grass, looking over the sea, and say: 'I like it better here.'

'Here! But we have always been here. There is so much I have not seen at Hardyhall.' She longed to tell him about the chapel and the secret cupboard under the stones. She stopped herself only just in time.

He answered: 'I like it here.'

'You are afraid, Roberto. You are afraid of something in Hardyhall.'

He only laughed. Sometimes she felt an impulse to shake him, to pull his hair, to try to goad him into anger.

'Why won't you go to Hardyhall, Roberto?' she pleaded. 'Do you hate Howard?'

'No.'

'Then that silly Bess!'

'No.'

'Why are you afraid of Hardyhall?'

'I'm not afraid.'

'You never go.' She wrinkled her brow and stood up slowly.

'Where are you going?' he asked.

She did not answer. She walked slowly away, lost in her thoughts. And this time he did not follow her.

⁂

Bianca had been washing clothes; she was hanging them on the hedge to dry.

Pilar stood watching her.

'Why are you not with Roberto?' asked Bianca.

'He is lying on the cliff. That is where I do not wish to be. I am going to see Howard and Bess. He won't come.' Pilar was watching closely. She saw the look of satisfaction cross Bianca's face. 'He never will come,' said Pilar. 'He doesn't like it there.'

Bianca said nothing – she who usually had so much to say.

'It is silly of him,' said Pilar. 'There are so many interesting things at Hardyhall.'

'What things?' asked Bianca, alert.

'Lots of rooms to play in . . . places to hide. They have a chapel there, too.'

Bianca said: 'You should be content with your own home.'

Pilar walked off.

She knew now. It was Bianca who did not wish Roberto to go to Hardyhall.

She went into the kitchens and there was Carmentita.

It was hot there, for the day was warm and Carmentita had made a big fire and the place was filled with the smell of *olla podrida*. Carmentita had brought some of her native dishes with her to England.

William, who worked in the gardens, was there, and Carmentita was arguing in her jocular way with him about the merits of *olla podrida* and brawn pudding.

Carmentita was another in this household who had changed, Pilar decided. She had grown gayer and more contented. Now she was clearly being very friendly with William, and was not very pleased that Pilar should present herself in the kitchens at this time.

William was saying: 'Ah, the smell of your olly! It lasts for days.'

'Then it has double merit,' said Carmentita with a laugh.

Carmentita pushed William, and William slapped Carmentita, and they seemed to find great pleasure in these pushings and slappings.

'One day,' said Carmentita, 'I will make you the *tortilla a la Española*. Ah, Williamo, there is a dish to make you smile. And if I like you very much I shall make you hot *churros*, eh? Dropped in boiling oil – and a feast you will so much like.'

'And what will you put in your *tortilla*, eh?'

'I will put the good herbs which you will find for me . . . and other things.'

'You must come and pick the herbs for yourself . . . eh? Eh, Carmentita?'

They had become aware of Pilar.

'Why do you stay here?' asked Carmentita. 'Do you like the smell of the onions?'

Pilar nodded. 'William,' she said, 'there are many weeds in your beds and Bianca has seen in the cards that the Captain will soon be home.'

William said: 'I work hard. Weeds grow, and where there was one there are two while a man's back is turned.'

'That,' said Pilar, 'may be because he likes better to slap Spanish ladies than to pluck the weeds from his master's garden.'

Carmentita gave her shriek of laughter. She was pleased that Pilar should recognise her great attractions which drew William from his weeding. William slouched off, muttering something about children who were too forward in their manners.

Pilar did not care. She wished to talk to Carmentita.

'Carmentita,' she said, 'you are a wicked woman, I believe. You lure the men from their work.'

'Oh, here is a saucy one!' said Carmentita. 'What next will she say?'

'She'll say that you will go out at dusk to look for herbs to put in the *tortilla a la Española* which you will make for William, and that you will be out there a long time, and when you come back you will bring no herbs.'

Carmentita picked up a cloth which lay on the table and threw it over her face, feigning to hide a confusion which did not exist.

'Who says such things?'

'All say them.'

'They will get to the Captain's ear,' said Carmentita.

'And when he returns he will be angry with you, 'Tita, and he'll not send for you when he is in his bedchamber, and you'll not go creeping up there and be so happy all next day and tell them all that 'twas no fault of yours if the Captain had a fancy for you.'

'Oh, you have the long ears.'

'They hear all, Carmentita.'

'And the clacking tongue!'

'And the eyes that see and the nose that smells evil . . .'

Pilar began to dance round Carmentita, sniffing. 'All those I have, Carmentita. You go to Hardyhall. I followed you. I saw you go in and I waited on the wall until you came out.'

'Why should I not be the messenger?'

'You take so long to deliver messages, Carmentita. What did you do at Hardyhall? What made you happy when you came out of Hardyhall? You went in afraid, and you came out pleased with yourself. You muttered to yourself when you went along the road as though you were praying. Were you praying?'

'I must speak to the Lady Isabella. I must tell her that you are the one who follows.'

'I shall tell her that you were in the outhouse a long time with William, and that you had put wood against the door so that none could get in. I shall tell her how you laughed when you came out, and how you looked wicked until you went to Hardyhall. Then you no longer felt wicked.'

'Is it my fault that these men will seek me?'

'Carmentita, it *is* your fault.'

'Go away with you!'

'Then tell me why you go to Hardyhall.'

'There is much you do not know, my little Señorita. One day you will know these things and then you will not be so hard on a woman.'

'Tell me about what I'll know one day.'

'Pilar, little Señorita, you are a wicked one. Why cannot you be like the good Roberto?'

'I want to know. Roberto does not care.'

'Ah, you must not. You must not. Should we, who were snatched from our land, not find a little of the comforts we knew when we were in that land?'

'Who snatched you, Carmentita?'

'The Captain . . . the Captain and his men.'

Pilar forgot Hardyhall. The Captain had snatched Carmentita. So that was what he was doing. Taking not only gold and precious treasure; he took women also.

She made Carmentita tell her of the wedding which was to have taken place between her mother and a great gentleman of Spain; she told of how, a few days before the wedding was to take place, the Captain and his men had descended on the house and taken away the women – 'all the women they fancied,' said Carmentita. 'Was it my fault that I was one of them? Aye, I was one of them. And what I suffered during that journey! There were so many of them . . . so few of us . . . But you have drawn these secrets from me. Go away . . . Miss Pilar. Go away.'

🌱 🌱 🌱

It was a few days later when she saw her mother leave the house. Previously Isabella had rarely gone beyond the gardens. Now she went, her cloak wrapped about her, her French hood hiding her dark hair; and Pilar knew that she was going to Hardyhall.

Pilar followed; she watched her mother cross the lawn. Pilar took her place on the wall on which she had sat with Roberto, for this wall commanded a good view of the house. When her mother had entered she intended to cross the lawn and pretend to be looking for Howard or Bess, to suggest a game. She was spying, but she made excuses for herself. She was her father's daughter. She had to discover what was going on about her.

Someone was running out of the house now, and she recognised Maria. Maria was agitated; she was waving her hands, and Pilar saw Isabella stand quite still. Maria ran to her and whispered something; then Isabella turned and hurried back the way she had come. Something was clearly wrong at Hardyhall. What now? wondered Pilar.

She watched her mother leave by the gate through which she had entered; then Pilar slid down on to the grass and went swiftly across the lawn, taking cover every now and then behind the trees. She came round to the chapel.

Now she could hear the sound of voices, the sound of men's gruff ones and women's high-pitched and protesting.

It was strange that Maria should have sent her mother away. What was going on in the house for that to happen?

She tried the door of the chapel. It was open as it had been on that day when she and Howard had gone there. She went inside. It was very still and quiet, but only for a few moments. Now she could hear the sound of voices again. A shrill scream and the sound of a man shouting orders, it seemed.

It was only the second time she had been in the chapel, and she ran swiftly to that slab beneath which she had found the silver cup. The table was still in its place but the beautiful cloth no longer covered it; there was something different about the slab. It seemed a little out of line with the rest of the flagstones; she slid her fingers into the gap she had noticed before, and she lifted the slab. The cup was not there.

She put in her hand. It went down and down. The cupboard was bigger than she had thought. She saw then that it was a ledge on which the cup had stood and which she had thought — for Howard had not let her look too closely — was the bottom of the cupboard. Now she could see that there were several of these ledges and they were really steps which led down to darkness. There was plenty of room in this cupboard for a girl of her size to hide herself if she wished. Pilar did not wish to hide; she wished to see how big the cupboard was.

She stepped through the hole and, as she set her feet on one step and felt for the next, she slipped; she lifted her hand to clutch at the slab. She touched it and it moved slowly down to form a dark roof over her head.

She had fallen a few feet and was in what seemed to be a small room. Pilar cried out in horror as a cobweb touched her face.

She stood where she was, staring into the darkness. She was so frozen with terror that she could not move for some seconds. It was cold in this dark place, but she felt the sweat trickling down her back. Something within her urged her to cry out for help, but her tongue and her lips would not obey her wishes.

Slowly her eyes became accustomed to the dark. She knew she must look about her, and yet she was afraid to; she was conscious of fear such as she had never known before.

Then the darkness in one corner took shape. It formed itself into a crouching figure — something out of a nightmare — as though ready to spring at this intruder on its peace. She caught her breath, and what might have been a scream was a gasp. Never in all her life had Pilar been so frightened. She turned and felt for the steps which would help her climb up to the slab.

Then a man's voice said: 'Who are you, and what are you doing here?'

Her teeth were chattering. She stammered: 'Let me go. I didn't want to come here.'

'Hush!' he said. 'Speak quietly. Who knows, we might be heard.'

'What is this place?' she asked.

'You are under the chapel,' he said. 'I don't know you. Who are you?'

She stared at the pale oval which was his face.

'I am Pilar,' she said.

'Why did you come down here?'

'I didn't mean to. I lifted the slab. I did not mean to come down here. I . . . just got inside and the stone fell back. Then I fell.'

'Speak quietly. You could betray us. Your voice might lead them to us.'

'I want to be found. I don't like it here.'

'You came here, my child,' he said, 'and here you will have to stay.'

'For ever! Am I dead, and is this hell?'

He said: 'You have an evil conscience.'

She cried in panic: 'I know what has happened to me. The slab fell on my head and killed me, and I descended into hell.'

'No, my child. You are not dead. Are you the little girl whose mother has visited Hardyhall these last few weeks?'

'Yes, I am,' said Pilar. 'And are we really under the chapel?'

'Yes, we are under the chapel.'

'Are you always here?'

'I had been here for about five minutes when you arrived.'

'Do . . . they know you are here?'

'I trust that those who are looking for me do not.'

'So you are hiding!'

'I pray you, speak more quietly. I believe the sound of our voices may be heard in the chapel.'

'If they heard us they would come and get us out.'

'Yes, my child. I fear they would.'

'But I want to get out. I don't like it down here. It's dark. It's cold . . . and there are things down here . . . creepy things. I want to go up.'

'Child,' he said, 'your curiosity led you here, and here you must stay. You must stay until those who are searching for me, search no longer.'

'How long?'

'They have been known to linger for a day and night.'

'I could not stay here all that time. My mother would be searching for me . . . and I should be hungry. Besides, I don't like it here.'

'How old are you? I know you are a child, but I cannot guess your age.'

'I am nearly ten years old.'

'I thought you were older. You are a brave child. You do not panic, as many would. You are inquisitive in the extreme. Such inquisitiveness often brings trouble. You see that it has brought trouble to you. You are nearly ten, and that is one lesson you have learned. I am thirty; three times your age. I too have lessons to learn.'

'But what are you doing here?'

'I am hiding.'

'Is it a game?'

'A grim game.'

'What will they do to you if they catch you?'

'You are a sharp-witted little girl. You know that I am as frightened as you are, don't you?'

'Grown-ups aren't frightened.'

'They can be as frightened as children. We are all children in a measure.'

Pilar was astonished at this revelation. For a moment she forgot she was in this dark and mysterious place with such a strange man. She was contemplating the fear of grown-up people.

She repeated: 'What will they do if they catch you?'

He said: 'They would hang me, mayhap. It might be that a more terrible death would be accorded me.'

'Have you stolen something?'

'They would say I had stolen members of their Faith. I would say I had led men and women to the truth.'

There was a sudden noise above them. Now they could hear voices distinctly.

She saw then that he was kneeling. She heard his faintly whispered words. 'Give me courage . . . If it be Thy will . . .'

Never had Pilar seen such a strange thing as a man kneeling in prayer – a prisoner with herself in a dark underground hole.

The noises stopped suddenly.

The man said: 'They have gone away. But they'll be back. They always search thoroughly in the chapel.'

'They were walking over our heads,' said Pilar.

'Yes,' he muttered.

'We heard *them*,' she said. 'They would hear *me* if I called.'

'Yes, my child; they would hear you. You could knock on these walls, on this dark roof above us, and they would hear you.'

'Would they find the right flagstone?'

'They would tear up all the flags, if need be, until they found the right one.'

'Who are they? Lady Hardy? Sir Walter?'

'Nay,' he said. 'Those two are my friends.'

'Who else would dare tear up the slabs in the chapel?'

'Those who seek me.'

'But if Sir Walter would not let them . . .'

'They do so in the name of the Queen, and they do so wheresoever it pleases them to.'

'I ought not to have lifted the slab, ought I?'

'Who knows, my child! You may be an instrument of God.'

'Do you mean God sent me here . . . made me lift the slab and fall down here?'

'It may be that He wishes to deliver me unto my enemy.'

'And He wants you to be hanged?'

'It may be that my time has come to prove beyond all doubt my devotion to His work. It may be that He has some work for you to do.'

Pilar drew her brows together; he could not see her, but he guessed that she was faintly worried at the prospect of God's eyes being upon her.

She said: 'I cannot see you clearly, but you talk like Mr Power.'

'I am a priest,' he said. 'Listen to me, my child. You have been sent here for a purpose. If those who seek me come back to the chapel, my life will be in your hands. If you call to them they will find you here and, if they find you, they must find me. It is for you to say what you will do. If you keep quiet they may not find us. They may go off and search for me in another part of the house. They may be in this house searching for many hours. In which case it will be necessary for you to stay here with me until they have gone.'

'But if I call they will hang you . . . or worse. What worse could they do to you?'

'I would rather not talk of that.'

She shivered. 'I do not like to see men hanging on the gibbets. They don't look like people any more. They frighten me. Is that how I shall look when I am dead?'

'The saints forbid it!'

'It is how you would look, should they hang you.' She paused and said suddenly: 'You could kill me. Then I should not be able to lead them to you.'

'What a strange child you are!'

'Would you kill me if I tried to let them know?'

'My child, this is a situation such as I have never been in before. You are right. I could silence you as easily as you could give me over to my enemies. In this small space we are beset with temptations – or we could be. The devil is never far off. If you attempted to betray me I could kill you, as you say. I could place my hand over your mouth to stifle your cries; I could put my hands about your throat . . . You see, your life is in my hands. I could say to myself: You are a priest, a man who has God's work to do; what is the life of one mischievous little girl compared with all the souls you hope to save before you die? As for you, you could scream aloud and lead my enemies to me. You see, there are devils in this little space with us. They are saying: "Save yourselves." If they remind me of the work I have to do, they remind you that I am a man who is wanted by the servants of the Queen. What will you do, child, if those men come back to the chapel?' He had stopped speaking and they both listened.

Pilar said in a whisper: 'I hear noises. They are coming back into the chapel.'

There were sounds above. They could hear the furniture of the chapel being roughly moved about. Breathlessly they looked at each other. Both were perfectly still.

For fifteen minutes or so the noise overhead went on. Now and then Pilar heard the faint murmuring of the priest's lips as he prayed.

'Be careful,' she whispered. 'They may hear you.'

As she spoke, the priest stopped praying and Pilar was aware that they both wanted the same thing: the men to go away that they might come safely out.

When the sounds died down, the priest said: 'You are a brave child.'

'Yes,' said Pilar proudly. 'I am brave. My father is brave. He says I must be like him. Do you think they will come back?'

'I think not now. They have searched the chapel, and have not found our hiding place. It may be that they will search the rest of the house for some time yet.'

'And we must not come out until then?'

'No.'

'My mother and Roberto will wonder what has become of me.'

'What were you doing in the chapel?'

She told him, and went on to explain how she had first come into the chapel with Howard. She did not mention that she had discovered the slab then, for she had sworn not to tell, and she was not sure whether this should still be kept a secret.

She asked him why the Queen's servants were after him, and he told her that it was because his Faith was that which the Queen's subjects were not allowed to hold.

'Why do you hold that Faith, if the Queen forbids it?' she wanted to know.

And he answered: 'Should a man or woman spurn the truth because lies are forced on them?'

He questioned her then on religious matters. He was shocked by her answers. He said her soul was in danger of eternal torment. He told her that the Queen had made a law in which it was high treason for any Jesuit to be in her dominions.

'What are Jesuits?' she wanted to know.

'They are priests, my child. They are members of the Society of Jesus. Many years ago a great man named Ignatius Loyola was born in the Basque Provinces of Spain. He formed this Society.'

'I am half Spaniard,' she told him.

'All the more reason why you should listen to God's truth.'

She said quickly: 'Tell me of this man who was born in Spain.'

'He was a member of a noble Spanish family. He was a soldier and, when he was wounded on the battlefield, God told him that it was not for him to kill men's bodies, but to save their souls. He rallied brave men about him: men who were ready to die for their Faith, as a soldier is ready to die for his country. So from far and wide he gathered together his own army. They were priests who were to carry God's war against the heathen into many countries where this scourge existed. In a chapel beneath the Abbey of Montserrat, his followers pledged themselves to work for God.'

'Did you pledge yourself?'

'Aye, I am pledged. But not on that occasion, which was just before I was born; but there have ever since been men to carry on with the work begun by Ignatius Loyola.'

'And if they caught you doing that work they would hang you?'

'If I were fortunate I should be hanged. In years to come you will remember that you held a priest's life in your hands, and you saved it. Tell me, what made you save it? It was some message from God, was it not? The saints were at your elbow.'

'No,' said Pilar. 'It was not God. It was not the saints. It was the man I saw hanging on a gibbet last week. I did not like it, and I did not wish that you should hang like that.'

'It was God prompting you, my child.'

'Was it God prompting you not to hurt me? You said you could kill me.'

'I would never have harmed you. I am a priest. That is not the way of a man of God. I did it to test you. If I emerge from this place in safety I shall know that it is God's will that your soul should be saved for Him.'

Pilar said: 'They will come soon for us, I hope. I am cold. I am hungry too.'

'I have no food. I had no time to bring any with me. The warning came suddenly. Wrap this about you.'

He held out something to her. It was his *soutane*.

'You will be cold,' she said.

'Nay,' he said. 'I fear not the cold. A priest learns to mortify the flesh.'

She wrapped the *soutane* about her; she sat on the floor and leaned against the wall.

'They will come for us,' he said, 'when it is safe for us to emerge.'

'Tell me about Spain,' she said. 'Do you know Jerez? That is where my mother and Bianca and Carmentita lived.'

'Yes,' he said. 'I have been there. It is a beautiful city sur-

214

rounded by vineyards and olive groves. It lies among the hills, and the sun is very warm there.'

She wanted to hear more of Jerez, but he did not wish to beguile her with his conversation; he wished to talk about God and the saints, and she found her attention wandering as it did with Mr Power.

There was very little air in this confined space and she was feeling drowsy. She grew warm in the *soutane* and after a while the droning of the priest's voice sounded like the waves as the tide slowly crept in.

❧ ❧ ❧

She awoke when she was being lifted out of the hole. It was dark in the chapel and she could not see the priest's face.

Lady Hardy was there with Sir Walter.

She heard the priest say: 'That is a brave child.'

They talked in whispers and, when she asked questions, Lady Hardy put her hand over her mouth and murmured: 'Not now, my dear.'

The *soutane* was taken from her and one of Lady Hardy's furred robes wrapped about her. She was taken to the punch room which was reached by going through the chapel door and up a short flight of steps; at the top of these steps was a door leading into the room.

Lady Hardy knelt at her feet and chafed her hands.

'You're frozen, child,' she said.

'It was cold in the dark hole,' said Pilar.

Lady Hardy herself poured something into a goblet and put it to her lips. It seemed fiery hot, yet it was comforting.

'I have asked your mother to come here with Bianca. She must have been very worried when you did not go home.'

'I did not mean to go into the dark hole . . .'

Lady Hardy put her finger to her lips. 'Do not speak of the hole. You were wrong to go into the chapel. You were wrong to touch the slab. We will forget that you did it; but you must forget too. We have heard of your bravery. At heart you are not a bad child; you are a good one. You did wrong, but when you saw that you had done wrong you decided to do all you could to put it right. You will not be punished. I will see to that.' Lady Hardy bent over her and kissed her cheek. 'My little Pilar,' she went on, 'I am glad of what happened. Great happiness awaits you. You shall see. But first promise me this: Speak to no one of your adventure. Tell all who ask that you were lost and that we found you. I shall tell your mother the truth . . . but none other. Pilar, will you do this? You must do this. Many lives depend upon it.'

Pilar's eyes glistened, and Lady Hardy hurried on: 'If you spoke of what you discovered, it might be that through your words much harm would come to many good people. It would be on your conscience then that you had brought this about. You would be a murderess, little Pilar, and that is a terrible thing to be.'

'I will tell no one,' cried Pilar. 'No one.'

'My good child. My good, good child.'

Lady Hardy was crying. She embraced Pilar and then began to chafe her hands again.

※ ※ ※

Bianca scolded when they took her home.

'You bad child! What anxiety you caused! We had searched everywhere. And with these ruffians in the neighbourhood, what could we think? You should be whipped. To lose your way . . .! And how did you lose your way? Where did you go?

Roberto did not know where you had gone. Why cannot you be good like Roberto?'

She did not answer. For once Pilar was subdued.

Her mother held her hand and pressed it. Her mother knew, and her mother was proud of her.

⚜ ⚜ ⚜

The next day, her mother said to her: 'Pilar, you are going to take lessons with Howard and Bess. Will you like that?'

'With Howard and Bess? But what of Roberto?'

'Roberto is still going to Mr Power.'

'But I have always been with Roberto.'

'You will like it better with Howard and Bess. They have a very good tutor. His name is Mr Peter Heath, and he is younger than Mr Power. He will make your work very interesting. Moreover, you are fond of Howard and Bess, are you not?'

'I like Roberto best.'

'But you will still spend much time with Roberto. It is only for a few hours each day that you will be working with Mr Heath.'

'Why does not Roberto come?'

'Someone must stay with Mr Power. It would not be kind for you both to desert him.'

'Is it kind for me to desert him?'

'His pupils must leave him from time to time. I thought you did not like Mr Power.'

'I think Roberto should be with me.'

'You cannot always be together.'

So she went to Hardyhall for her lessons, and Lady Hardy herself conducted her up a great staircase, through several rooms which she had not seen before, to an unfamiliar part of the house. In a long, low room at a table sat Howard and Bess already at work, and as she and Lady Hardy entered the room a man rose from the table and came forward to greet her.

'Here is your new pupil, Mr Heath,' said Lady Hardy. 'I trust she will be a credit to you.'

Pilar looked up into a pair of sombre dark eyes which were regarding her intently. The man's face was grave, but he smiled at her in a manner which was most friendly. He said: 'Welcome, my child. I trust you will be a good pupil.'

Lady Hardy said: 'Pilar will do her best, I know.'

Howard gave her the smile he always kept for her; it meant that they shared a great secret. She realised then that he did not know that she had spent hours in the dark with a man whom the Queen's servants were hunting, and she was glad, for she felt that she had in some way betrayed his trust in her. Bess looked at her in that deprecating way which meant that Bess was just a little afraid of the girl, who was about her own age but seemed so much more able to take care of herself.

'Now,' said Lady Hardy, 'I will leave you with the children, Mr Heath.'

So Pilar settled down to her first lesson. It was a strange lesson, she decided, although, like Mr Power, Mr Heath talked a great deal about the Church. There was a subtle difference though in Mr Heath's church; in his church there were many saints. She was taught to say something in Latin which was called an Ave Maria. And suddenly she knew that Mr Heath was not a stranger to her. She and he had met before.

The man with whom she had spent those hours in the dark, the priest whom the Queen's men would hang if they discovered him, was Mr Heath, the tutor.

One bright morning Pilar arose to the sound of bustle throughout the house. Something unusual was happening. Dreams were still upon her, dreams which came in the first moments of semi-consciousness. She thought she was hiding in a dark place, and those who sought her had found that hiding place. They were angry men with gleaming eyes and ropes in their hands.

Carmentita was at the window, pointing out to sea.

'Get up, and come and look here. Come and see what all the house looks at.'

She leaped out of bed, and saw the ship which was lying just outside the bay.

'It is the calmed ship!' said Carmentita. 'Ah, the Captain will be the angry one!'

'Are you sure?' cried Pilar.

'Williamo is sure. He says there is no mistaking. That is the Captain's ship.'

'How long has it been there?'

'Williamo saw it as soon as he rose. That was with the dawn. He woke the household with the news.'

Carmentita was giggling with anticipatory pleasure. She smoothed the folds of her dress. She had forgotten William at the prospect of a call from the Captain.

It was two years since the Captain had last been in the house. One grew up in two years, for all that time Pilar had scarcely been aware of the effect he had on all the inhabitants. She had merely realised that it seemed very quiet after he went away.

Carmentita was singing to herself; her plump face was vacant, her lips parted; Carmentita was lost in memory, and living in hope. Bianca was tense, seeming almost like a young girl, looking as Pilar had seen her look when she put a rose in her black hair and danced for them. But all the gaiety, which the prospect of the Captain's visit brought into the house, was spoilt by the attitude of Pilar's mother. Pilar discovered then that her mother was afraid of the Captain.

For the first time in her life she became intensely aware of conflict – of two desires which battled within her. Her desire to see the Captain in his house, and that other desire to see her mother happy and at peace.

She remembered now the great contentment she had some-times felt when she sat at her mother's feet, watching Isabella's long white fingers working on a piece of embroidery; the flash of the needle and the gentle voice of her mother filled her with quiet pleasure which she had appreciated more after her adventure in the dark hole; and she had made up her mind that she would protect her mother always.

And now the Captain would soon be home and although Pilar was overcome by the desire to laugh and sing, to run down to the shore that she might be the first to welcome him, she could not enjoy her pleasure in his return because she was aware of her mother's apprehension. She felt that her inclin-ations and desires were pulling her one way, and her duty to her mother another.

She thought of the Hardy children's feelings for their parents. They were a little afraid of their mother, and less so of their father; and when they feared they had committed some small sin it was often to their father they went that he might plead for them with their mother. That was a happy state of affairs, for although their mother was stern and their father less so, Pilar saw that they were as one; they reigned together at the head of the house. The Hardy children could talk of them in one breath: 'Our mother and father.'

But Pilar could not do that. They were apart, these two. One could not think of them together. She was becoming afraid that it would not be possible to love them both, that if she were to be true to her vow to protect her mother, she would be forced to hate her father.

They were as different, she was beginning to realise, as were Mr Heath and Mr Power. If you believed one, you could not believe the other. If Mr Heath was God's servant, Mr Power was on the side of the devil. Yet there were many – and they the Queen's servants – who declared that it was Mr Power who did God's work and Mr Heath who was the devil's man.

Life was full of problems. But the differences between Mr Heath and Mr Power seemed insignificant when compared with those which separated her own father and mother.

She realised this that very morning when her mother sent for her and said: 'Pilar, the Captain will soon be here, and when he comes you should not tell him that you are taking lessons with Mr Heath.'

'Why?' asked Pilar.

'Because, my little *favorita*, it is something I wish you to do, but he would not wish it.'

Pilar's eyes were round. 'I know,' she said. 'He would be for Mr Power, not Mr Heath.'

Her mother was frightened. 'Do . . . do not speak of these things.'

'What if he should ask?'

Isabella took Pilar into her arms and held her against her. 'For my sake, say nothing of this.'

'If I lie, would that be wrong, would that be wicked?'

'To lie in such a cause . . . I think not. The saints would not consider that a very great sin.'

'They assuredly would not, because they want me to take my lessons from Mr Heath.' Pilar laughed suddenly. She saw then how she could please both her mother and her father. She could lie to him for her mother's sake and, since she was doing this for her mother, she could ride with him, talk with him and make him laugh – as she remembered doing – because all the time she was remembering to do as her mother wished.

She touched her bodice. Beneath it was a little medallion which she wore on a riband. Mr Heath had given it to her. He called it her *Agnus Dei*, and both Howard and Bess possessed one each. On it was impressed a cross and the figure of a lamb.

This, Mr Heath had told her, had been blessed by His Holiness. His Holiness was another of those great figures of whom she was constantly hearing so much. 'It is the symbol of Christ,' Mr Heath had told her, 'and it has been the custom of our people for a thousand years to wear these about their necks. The lamb and the cross together will protect you from all evil, as the blood of the Pascal Lamb protected the Jews from the destroying angel of the Lord.'

So now, as her fingers touched the disc beneath her dress, which none could see – for it had been impressed upon her that the *Agnus Dei* should be worn in secret – she believed that through it she would be able to obey and protect her mother while at the same time she enjoyed her father's company.

❧ ❧ ❧

She was rowed out to the ship. She wanted to be the first to greet him.

She was seen by men on deck, and of course they knew who

she was. They roared a greeting to her. 'It's the Captain's girl – the Captain's Piller.'

They grinned. The man who drove them hard, whom they must all obey at his call or the lift of a hand, who had been known to flog a man to death for disobedience or with a careless word set one to walk the plank, had a softness in him for this fair-haired girl with the flashing dark eyes – the girl who was the result of one of the most spectacular, if not the most financially rewarding, exploits of the Captain's career, his girl Piller.

'You come to see the Captain, lady?' shouted the sailors.

'Yes,' said Pilar. 'Help me aboard.'

They did not hesitate. Her coming would put the Captain in a good mood. The Captain's girl, Piller, had always seemed part of the crew, for he was wont to say: 'Call yourself a sailor? Why, my girl Piller would do better than that.' He had been known to spare girls in the towns they ravaged because he admitted, when he was maudlin drunk, that they had a look of his girl Piller. He would take a particularly pretty ornament from the spoils and say: 'That'll be for my girl Piller.'

The Captain doted on the girl.

So they threw down the rope ladder and Pilar climbed aboard, and the cry went through the ship: 'The Captain's girl, Piller, has come to welcome him home.'

He heard it from the hold, where he was gathering together the more valuable of the jewels which he did not care to leave behind him even for a short while, and he came hurrying on to the deck.

'My girl Piller! My girl Piller here!'

And there she was – grown tall but still the same girl Piller

— long light-brown hair with the golden streaks in it that matched his own, and those big dark eyes which she had from her mother.

'By God!' cried the Captain. 'She's come aboard to greet her father. It's my girl Piller!'

She ran to him, laughing, as he always made her laugh. They did not embrace; there were rarely embraces between them. When she came within two paces of him she stopped, and they took each other's measure. His golden beard began to move in the way she remembered.

She said: 'Welcome home, Captain.'

'So you came aboard my ship, eh? You boarded her, eh? By God, no one boards my ship without the Captain's permission. Did you not know that?' He caught her ear. His hands were rough, but the gesture was one of infinite tenderness. 'My girl Piller!' he repeated. 'By God's sacred blood, I like the look of you.' His beard continued to shake. 'Come here,' he said. 'Come here! I'll show you something. I'll show you what we've brought home from the Dons' country, shall I? We've come home richer than we set out, girl. We've captured some pretty prizes.'

'Women?' she asked.

That made him roar with laughter. 'Listen to her! Listen to my girl Piller! Better than women,' he said. 'Gold. Riches. Did you hear that, men? My girl Piller wants to know if you've brought women home. Come with me, girl. I'll show you something. I'll show you jewels such as you've never seen before.' He pinched her ear and then her cheeks. 'You've grown up, girl. And didn't forget the Captain, eh?'

'No, I'd never forget the Captain.'

His eyes were misted suddenly. 'Here!' he roared. 'Down

with you. Come on, girl. I'll show you some of the treasures we're bringing back to England.'

He pushed her before him. A strong wind had sprung up suddenly to break the calm, and the ship rocked beneath her. She staggered, and he caught her; she felt his fingers strong on her arm. She thought how different he was from any man she had ever known, and how happy she was to be in his company.

A young man was in the hold. He was tall and as fair as her father; his eyes seemed even more blue than the Captain's, and they had the same alert, long-sighted expression.

'Hey fellow!' cried the Captain. 'What do you here?'

'Making sure none of the men slip a trinket into their pockets before they go ashore, sir. It would be easy.'

'It would be more than their lives are worth, and they know it. By God, if I found any man of mine pilfering from me I'd string him up and make him a feast for the buzzards. They all know it; that'll keep pilfering fingers from my spoils.'

'Men will fall into the temptation, sir. There are women ashore . . .'

'Ah, women! My girl Piller here wants to know if we've brought any with us?'

The young man laughed with the Captain.

'We met plenty on our travels,' he said.

'But none we liked well enough to bring with us,' said the Captain. He turned to Pilar. 'Here's a young man I want you to know. He'll be staying with us at the house for a while. He's my second-in-command. Petroc Pellering's the name.'

The young man bowed over-courteously. 'We've met before,' he said.

'I have never seen you before,' said Pilar.

The Captain laughed. Everything Pilar said seemed to make him laugh.

'All men who sail under the Captain know his girl Piller. We say she comes with us on our voyages.'

Pilar looked puzzled. 'This Captain doesn't forget his daughter,' said the Captain, 'and he sees that no others do. Now get on deck, young man, and see the men ashore. Leave Jed and Little Tom to guard her; and when they've all left but the guards, come back and we'll take my girl ashore.'

'Aye, sir,' said the young man and left them.

Now the Captain was alone with Pilar, and he allowed himself to touch her. He took her face in his hands and looked long into it. 'My girl,' he said. 'My little girl. And so she's glad to see the Captain back, eh?' Then he seemed afraid of his emotion; for he dropped his hands abruptly. 'Now you shall see what we've brought home, girl. And this is not all. We called on the Queen on the way home. There's a woman, eh? She reminded me of my girl. Not that she's got this long fair hair and dark, flashing eyes – oh no! She's a ginger woman and, to tell you the truth, Piller girl, she wasn't the sort I'd sack a town for. But, by God, what a woman! She's pleased with me, Piller. She gave me a welcome to compare with your own. And what do you think, Piller – she laid a sword on my shoulder and made me Sir Ennis. She honours such as I am, my girl. She knows we're the ones to fight the Dons – and she hates 'em. The Queen hates 'em, as do all good English men.'

'Why?' said Pilar.

'Why, girl? Because they're Dons. Because they've sailed the seas and robbed the lands they visited of what they should have left for us. That's why. Ah, I've got something for you, girl. You shall wear it about your neck. I'll tell you something.

It was on the neck of a princess – a black princess. That's what she calls herself. I took it from her. What's good enough for a princess might just about do for my girl Piller, I said.'

'I don't want the necklace,' she said. 'I care less for such things than seeing you again.'

Then he seized her suddenly and held her against him. He would not have released her if they had not heard the steps of young Petroc Pellering coming down to the hold.

🌿 🌿 🌿

The Captain bellowed through the house. There were big meals to be prepared now, and the cooks were busy in the kitchen. Carmentita worked until the sweat ran down her face.

'By God!' he cried, for almost every sentence he uttered began in this way. 'Bake me pies filled with those meats I love, and give me good clotted cream to garnish them. By God, it's English food I've been dreaming of these last months, and if I don't get it I'll lay the whip about you in the kitchen with my own hands, by God I will!'

The young man, Petroc, was a guest in the house. It was clear that the Captain was fond of him; Pilar noticed how his beard waggled when he watched him swaggering about the house. He was like another Captain, for it seemed that he imitated him in all he did. His voice could be heard roaring through the house – by God this, and by God that!

Pilar knew that her mother kept away from her father as much as possible. He did not seem to mind. He would sit at the table, Bianca on one side of him, her mother on the other, and often he would put a hand on Bianca's shoulder and pull at the heavy rings in her ears until she screamed and fought.

But Bianca seemed to like that treatment. Roberto would

watch without any expression on his face, but Pilar, who knew him well, knew he did not like to see his mother thus with the Captain.

Often the two men would talk of the new voyage they would soon be making; for now it was understood that this visit of the Captain's would not be a long one. He had sold some of the jewels he had brought home to provide money to refit his ship, and was to set off on new adventures; he was to bring back more treasures of which the Queen would take a goodly share.

At such times he liked Pilar to stand beside him and fill his goblet with wine or the ale he sometimes preferred to drink. He liked to keep her with him, and often his hand would rest on her head while he talked.

His moods were various, and he often sat at the table drinking until he could not stand. At such times he would pass through his several moods. He could be angry, ready to pick a quarrel with anyone except Pilar. Then everyone kept out of his way as much as possible. He could be jocular; then everyone laughed with him; he could fall into his affectionate mood, when his eyes grew glazed and would come to rest on one of the servants who happened to be near, but Carmentita tried hard to see that she was the one who should come within his range, and at such times he did not stay at the table until he slumped forward into a drunken sleep. There was an occasional maudlin mood when he complained that he was a man whose home was on the sea, and that meant that he missed the comfort of a warm bed at night and his own family about him.

It was on one occasion when the anger was upon him that he made known his dislike of Roberto. They had all been sitting at table, and none realised that the angry mood had come upon him, so quickly had it descended.

Suddenly he roared: 'You boy there! At what do you stare with those great Don's eyes, eh? You insolent pig! Why do you stare there, eh? I'll take the insolence out of you. By God I will!'

Roberto had risen to his feet. Bianca, who was sitting beside the Captain, said: 'Roberto, go away. Quickly go away.'

But the Captain had risen also. He took the goblet from which he was drinking and threw it at Roberto. Roberto ducked and the ale splashed the wall.

Pilar, who was standing beside the Captain's chair, felt her heart begin to hammer.

'Come here!' roared the Captain. 'Come here, you bastard!'

'You touch him and I will kill you,' cried Bianca.

He turned to her and his eyes were like bits of blue glass, thought Pilar.

'You foisted your bastard on me,' he said. 'That's no son of mine. He eats my substance, he lives under my roof, that bastard . . . and he looks at me with his insolent Don's eyes. By God, I'll cut the heart out of him, and you can send it to his father.'

Roberto stood quite still.

'Come here,' roared the Captain. Bianca had moved back a pace or two. The Captain looked at her. Pilar saw his beard begin to move and great relief swept over her. He was laughing inwardly; he was not angry any more. But suddenly his great hand shot forth, and, pushing Bianca aside, he strode towards Roberto.

Roberto stood, miraculously calm. His dark eyes were alert, but he did not move.

Pilar dashed round the table and reached Roberto's side.

'No!' she cried. 'No! You shall not cut out his heart.' She had placed herself in front of Roberto. Roberto tried to seize her and pull her aside. But now Bianca was beside them, and gleaming in Bianca's hand was a knife.

The Captain began to laugh suddenly. He forgot Pilar; he forgot Roberto; he forgot all but Bianca. He went to her and seized her arms. She screamed, and the knife dropped to the floor. Then he picked it up and threw it at the wall. It pierced the tapestry and stayed there quivering. Now he gripped Bianca by the shoulders and shook her as he laughed aloud.

'Gipsy!' he said. 'Spanish gipsy! Come on. I've something to say to you.' And he pushed her towards the door. She looked over her shoulder, laughing. She ran and he followed.

Pilar had seen on Bianca's face a look of mingled pleasure and triumph.

Her gaze went to Roberto who had quietly sat down at the table, and from him to her mother who sat still and white-faced, staring ahead of her.

Later Pilar followed Roberto out to the cliffs and they lay on the grass, looking out to where the Captain's ship lay.

'Roberto,' she said, 'you hate him. Ought I to hate him too? I can't, Roberto, because he is kind to me, and he is big and strong and I like to be with him. When I thought he was going to cut out your heart, I didn't hate him even then. I only wanted to stop him.'

'Yes,' said Roberto, 'he hates me.'

'And you hate him.'

'No, I don't hate him. He hates me because he loves my mother.'

Pilar did not understand.

She went riding with her father.

He liked to see her in the saddle. He was happy on this day, and not only because he enjoyed riding with her. Something else had occurred to please him.

She asked him what it was.

He sniffed the air. 'Our Devon lanes,' he said. 'The smell of the sea and the damp on the grass. Do you know, girl, there's nowhere in the world where the grass is as green as Devon grass. Smell the air. 'Tis good to be in the Queen's country. And this is a morning to gladden the hearts of all her true subjects.'

'Why so, Captain?'

'Because news has come to me this day that in London Town those who plotted against the life of our Queen have met their just reward. Hanged by the neck, but not till they be dead . . . taken down alive and slit up the middle. That shocks you,' he added sadly. 'They are indeed making a ninny of you.'

'Captain, what did these men do when they plotted against the Queen's life?'

'Sought to set the Scottish whore upon the throne in place of good Queen Bessie.'

'What is the Scottish whore?'

'The woman from Scotland who plotted with her lover to kill her husband and, because of this, was turned from her own country. She became our Queen's prisoner and has been these many years . . . and, by God, she should have lost her head ere this. There'll be no safety for Queen Bess while the Scottish harlot lives.'

'Tell me about it, Captain.'

She was trembling, for she knew that what the Captain would tell her would be quite different from that which her mother wished her to learn from Mr Heath.

Mr Heath had talked of the Scottish Queen – the royal martyr, he called her. He told of a gracious and beautiful lady who had been deeply wronged and was in truth the lawful Queen of England. She was not to speak of this to any outside the schoolroom; it was a secret she shared with Howard, Bess and Mr Heath. She whom they called the Queen of England was a bastard, which meant that she had no right to the throne – just as, in the Captain's eyes, Roberto was a bastard and had no right to live in their house.

Her mother believed what Mr Heath believed, as did Sir Walter and Lady Hardy. But who was right? Her mother who was gentle and kind? Her father, who was harsh to many but soft to her, and who had travelled far and wide?

Who was right? How could she know? And to whom could she give her loyalty until she knew the truth? Who was right – Mr Power or Mr Heath?

Her father told her his story. She must know that there was a wicked King who lived in the country to which she half belonged. He was the Queen's greatest enemy. He was called Philip of Spain. He saw her father's Philip – a small loathsome man, pale-faced and cruel; his hands were stained with blood, and he called aloud for more victims whom he might torture. Mr Heath's Philip was pale too, with golden hair; he had the face of a saint, and he so loved the world that he wished to bring to all that which would do them the greatest good; and if to bring them this good they must be hurt, this saintly Philip prayed for them in a palace which was like a monastery and which he had built because of a vow he had made on the battlefield of Saint Quentin.

But her father's Philip trained men whom he sent into England to work for the downfall of that country.

'By God, they come with their rosaries and their prayers, in their *birettas* and *soutanes*. By God! I'd string them up and cut their hearts out. I'd roast them in Smithfield Square. I'd cut them into pieces and send those pieces back to their priests' colleges.'

'They come as priests?' asked Pilar.

'Aye . . . spies in priests' robes. This was their plan: They come here . . . they are sheltered in the houses of English Catholics. Their task is to turn good English subjects into bad ones. They tell them tales of God and his saints, and this glory and that . . . and then, when they have bemused them with religion, they pour the poison of treason into their ears. They say: "Work for the downfall of Protestant Elizabeth, and put the Catholic whore on the English throne." '

'And . . . those who say they will do this . . .'

'Should surely die. Aye, and will. As Throckmorton shall die and the priests they hold with him.'

'Tell me about this Throckmorton, Captain.'

'What is there to tell but that he was a young fool? He had been seduced by priests and was ready to work for traitors. This plot of theirs was to bring a Frenchman into the country – a kinsman of this harlot Scot – the Duke of Guise, a man who would have landed his armies here with the Pope's help.'

'The Pope! He whom they call the Holy Father?'

'Holy Father! Let me not hear such words upon your lips, girl. Holy Father indeed! Rascally Pope! They were to land here . . . to take our Queen's throne and give it to the harlot of Scotland, turn England into a Catholic land. By God, and it might have happened. But we were too smart for them. We had our spies too. Ha! I hear they searched the Hardys' place, and found nothing. More's the pity. They were searching all suspected houses in the south of England. By God, if the

Hardys harboured such devils I'd like to see them caught, I would.' She was silent for a while. She was back there in the hole beneath the chapel. Then Mr Heath was more than a priest; he was a spy. He had said nothing to her about spying. Had she then been guilty of treason? Had she saved the life, not of a holy man, but of one who would work against the Queen?

She was afraid; she was ignorant; and she felt impatient with her youth. When one was young one could have the emotions of an adult, all the power of feeling; all one lacked was experience. But what a real lack that was!

And yet these grown-up people lacked much too. Otherwise why should her mother look, as it were, through one door and her father through another, so that what seemed good to her mother was treason in her father's eyes and what seemed virtue to her father was black sin in her mother's eyes?

'In London,' said the Captain, 'there was great rejoicing. Bonfires blazed in every open space. The plotters were discovered. The Scots harlot is safe in her prison. And good Queen Bess is on the throne. But I'll tell you this, girl, there are still spies in our country, for we did not find them all. But we'll get them, and then shall be done to them what has been done to those whom we discovered.'

'Hanged!' she said. 'But not till they are dead. Cut down alive and slit . . .'

He turned to her and laughed aloud.

'By God, girl! You're pale and trembling. They're making a ninny of you here at home.' He slapped his thigh. 'Mayhap I'll take you away with me when I go. Shall I leave my girl Piller behind, for ninnies to make a ninny of!'

The idea amused him. He put his horse into a gallop and she heard his laughter above the thudding of their horses' hoofs.

‘Here, girl,’ said the Captain, ‘come up to the attic. I’ve got a necklace for you. It’s the one I told you of. I want to see you wear it.’

She went with him, and he unlocked the door. There was a strange smell in the attic, of spices, perfumes and salt sea spray. Goods were piled from floor to ceiling; among them were gold plate and jewels, as well as rich cloth and furnishings. The Captain’s eyes glinted as he looked about him.

‘Feast your eyes on it, Piller,’ he said. ‘Mayhap one day it’ll be yours.’

‘Was it all stolen?’ she asked.

‘Stolen? It was *taken*, if that’s what you mean. What we take from the Dons is not stolen, for they took it from others before that. All legitimate spoil, my girl.’

She said: ‘There’s blood on that cloth.’

‘Aye, girl, that’s the coin we buy with. Is that my girl . . . turning pale at the sight of blood? Not you, Piller! You’re going to sail with me one day. It’s what I wanted my son to do. I have no son, but you’re better than a son to me.’

‘To sail with you and Petroc Pellering?’

‘He’ll make a captain one day. And that day not far distant. He’s a born buccaneer. We’re born to it, Piller. You’ve got it in you – and we’ll keep it in you. We’ll not let them make a ninny of you. See what riches are here . . . bought with blood and daring on the high seas. There’s the life for a man, and mayhap a woman . . . a woman with my blood in her veins . . . a woman you might one day be.’ He took her cheek between his fingers and pressed it tenderly. ‘You’re a child yet. But you’re my girl, and by God you’re better than any boy. Now, where's that necklace I promised you? It's worth a fortune. You must guard it well. Here it is. I keep it in this box. Those are emeralds and rubies. I thought when I saw them, they'll suit my girl Piller. Here! Try them on.' He put them about her neck. He laughed aloud. 'They seem odd on that prim bodice. You'll wear them when you're a beautiful young woman, Piller. You'll need your shoulders bare to show them. Here! Let's try them.' He unfastened the linen ruff at her throat. She saw his face change. He was staring at something. He put out a hand and pulled at the ribbon about her throat. She had temporarily forgotten it. It was the *Agnus Dei*.

She watched the blood rush into his face; she saw the veins knot themselves in his temples.

He cried: 'By God! By God! What means this?'

She lifted her hands to take it, but he dashed them aside. 'You . . . with this thing!' He threw it to the floor and ground it with his heel. 'You . . . my girl . . . *my* girl, with that sign of the devil about your neck! How came you by it?' He took her by the shoulders and shook her. 'How came you by it, girl? I know. 'Twas that simpering woman. It was that Spanish mother of yours. So she would make a Catholic of you when my back's turned. By God! She'd make an idolatrous traitor of my girl.'

He seized her by the arm and dragged her out of the attic. He had never been so fierce with her before. He paused for a second at the top of the stairs and, tucking her under his arm, started down them.

Her impulse was to kick, to protest, to scream that if she wished to wear an *Agnus Dei* she would do so. But she remembered that life had become suddenly complicated, and that she had become deeply involved in the secrets of others.

Her mother was sitting at the window. A thought flashed into Pilar's head that she was looking at the ship which she could see from that window, and longing for the day when she would be able to look out and see it no more.

She started to her feet with a cry when she saw the Captain and their daughter.

'Ah, my lady March,' he cried. 'You may well look alarmed. I have uncovered secrets which could send you to the gallows. I might have expected treachery from Spaniards. I have seen the devil's charm this child has been wearing about her neck. What do you say to that? Madam, what do you say to that?'

Isabella replied as calmly as she could: 'Why should she not wear the *Agnus Dei*? It is a sacred charm in my country, which is in part her own.'

'Your country! Your country, Madam? Your country is this country, and, by God, if I should discover you to be a traitor I'll have you lodged in the Tower of London and sent thence to the block. By God, this is my daughter. My daughter to be taught to deceive me!'

Pilar said: 'It was not my mother's fault. It was not she who gave me . . .'

But Isabella said quickly: 'Pilar, I am not afraid of this man. Nor must you be.'

'Must she not, by God, and must you not be either? I tell you, Madam, I'll have obedience in my own house or I'll make everyone in it wish they had never been born.'

'You should not blame the child,' said Isabella. 'She obeys her mother and has no idea what the *Agnus Dei* signifies. To her it was just a pretty ornament.'

'An odd state of affairs, Madam, when pretty ornaments must be worn out of sight.'

'I take the blame . . . all the blame. I beg of you, leave the child alone.'

'She is my daughter,' he said, 'and she shall obey me. I see you would sow the seeds of idolatry in her mind. But that shall not be so.' He turned to Pilar. 'Of what does your mother talk when you are alone, eh? What lies does she pour into your ears?'

'She does not tell lies,' said Pilar.

'And that thing about your neck . . . that thing you were at such pains to hide, what of that?'

'It . . . is as my mother said.'

'By God! I'll be hearing next that you entertain priests in this house.'

'We have never done that,' said Isabella quickly.

He stepped to her threateningly. 'If you had, Madam, I'd make you regret it to the end of your days.'

Isabella had turned from him; her head was held high. She said: 'You took me from my country, from the man I was to marry, from my home and all the happiness I might have known. Is not that enough? Must you make me your abject slave as well?'

The Captain had lifted his hand and Pilar rushed forward. She clung to his leg, trying to hold him back. For a second it seemed as though he were about to kick her angrily away from him, but he stopped short and looking down at her, clinging there, her fair hair falling back from her little face and those enormous dark eyes looking up at him appealingly, he laughed suddenly. He said: 'You are the only one in this house with any spirit, girl, you . . . and Bianca. Would to God she were your mother instead of this one! But what matters it? You are my girl. You belong to me. No one shall come between me and you and what I've planned for you.'

He looked at Isabella. 'Now, Madam, I'll leave you to snivel in private. And know this: this girl of mine stays not here with you. When I leave she comes with me.'

Then he disengaged himself and, turning, walked out of the room. When he had gone Pilar rushed to her mother.

Isabella seized her and held her firmly; her tears began to flow fast and she murmured, as she used to murmur when Pilar was a baby: '*Niña* . . . *Favorita* . . . my good brave Pilar. On no account must he know that Mr Heath gave you your *Agnus Dei*. On no account must he know that you go to Mr Heath to learn. If he knew, it would bring disaster to brave good people. Always remember that, my *niña* . . . Be brave and never tell, little *favorita*.'

Pilar took the kerchief from her mother's belt and wiped her mother's eyes. She could not bear to see this distress, yet her heart was beating fast because he had said he would take her away with him. That would make her mother sad, and yet she longed to go. Once more she felt that she was being drawn in opposite directions at the same time.

She loved her mother and longed to please her; but how she wanted to lead an adventurous life with her father!

'You'll not go away, Pilar,' Isabella was saying. 'Do not be afraid. He did not mean that. He could not take you. There is nothing to fear. And when he is gone you shall resume your lessons, and I doubt not that Mr Heath will find another *Agnus Dei* for you, my child.'

Pilar put her arms about her mother's neck and kissed her, but all the time she could not shut out of her mind the hope that when the Captain went away he would take her with him.

Pilar could not sleep at night. What the future held for her she could not guess. She was forced to make a choice; there were two ways open to her; her mother urged her upon one road, her father on the other.

Isabella said to her: 'Little *niña* . . . you must not go with the Captain. It would be a terrible life . . . so terrible that I sometimes cannot believe that he really means he will take you away with him. When the ship is ready to sail you must creep out of the house and go to Lady Hardy. She will hide you until all the danger is past.'

She would hide me in the hole, thought Pilar; I should crouch there and listen to the sound of his footsteps in the chapel as he searched for me. But he would never find me, for he would not think to lift a slab and come down into the dark hole.

The other road was to go with him. To have her hair cut off, to wear the clothes of a boy, to stand on deck and watch the land slowly slip away. To do so would be, so her mother said, to break her heart.

Which way?

She knew what she wanted. She wanted adventure. She wanted to sail with him. That was why she kept telling herself that this was the right way to go.

Mr Heath is a traitor, she told herself. He would betray the Queen. I was wrong to keep quiet in the hole. I should have led them to him.

Then she thought of Mr Heath taken by those men, and she knew that had she been in the hole at that moment she would have kept silent as she had done on that previous occasion.

But I want to go with the Captain, she thought. I want to sail the seas and find treasure and fight the Queen's enemies.

One night, as she lay wondering about the future, she heard

the sound of footsteps below her window, and the rumble of men's voices.

She slipped out of bed to see who was below, and in the faint moonlight she picked out the unmistakable figures of the Captain and Petroc Pellering. They were arguing fiercely. The Captain was angry; but she could hear from Petroc's tone that he was determined. When she realised that they were talking about her, she strained to hear more.

They stood right beneath her window, and she heard Petroc say: 'It's impossible, sir. I know she's a spirited girl, but it's impossible.'

'Nothing's impossible for me, man.'

'Not impossible, sir. The wrong word. It's inadvisable.'

'Are you seeking to give me advice?'

'Yes, sir.'

'Then keep it to yourself.'

'It's the child I am thinking of. What would you do with her if there was a running fight aboard?'

'By God, she'd not be afraid!'

'I should . . . for her. What if she fell into their hands?'

'She's but a child.'

'She is ten, you say. There have been children . . .'

The Captain was silent.

Pilar heard them walk into the house. She knelt on the window seat, clenching her hands together. She knew then that she wished to go with her father and that she hated Petroc Pellering for trying to prevent her doing so.

❧ ❧ ❧

So she was not to go. He had decided. His decision made him sad, but he was adamant. He engaged a tutor who should concern himself rigidly with her education; she was to swear to him never to wear one of those graven images round her neck again. She was to learn all her tutor told her and not listen to anything her mother might wish to teach her. She was to wait for his return and, perhaps in a year or so when she was old enough, he would take her with him.

She protested. He laughed and liked her protests.

'Nay, girl,' he said, ''tis a life of too much danger as yet.'

'I'd not be afraid.'

'Nay, my girl Piller's afraid of nothing. Why, she's not afraid of me!'

'Captain,' she implored, 'take me with you, please.'

'Ah! Now you think to plead with me, you scheming wench. Would to God you could sail out of the bay with me, Piller girl . . . but not this time. Why, time'll soon pass. Soon I'll be sailing in again and then, by God, you'll be ready for me.'

She said: 'It's this man . . . this Petroc who has turned you against taking me.'

'He's right, Piller girl. He's right enough. I tried not to see it, but he made me. Ah yes, he's right.'

She said: 'I could hate him for this.'

'Don't hate him too much,' said the Captain, and his smile was enigmatic.

'I do,' she said. 'And I shall always do so.'

The Captain went off into roars of laughter. 'That's right,' he said. 'He's an arrogant fellow. He'll want keeping in order, Piller. I reckon you could do that very well. By God, I do!'

Then he went into more laughter, secretly enjoying his joke. But she was angry and she would not speak to Petroc.

They were amused at this – both Petroc and the Captain.

She thought: I will teach them to laugh at me. And she began to plan.

It was growing dark.

Soon the tide would turn and the ship would sail.

In the hold under a heap of sacking Pilar lay. She was laughing to herself to think what they would say when she made her presence known. It would not be until they were a long way out at sea. She would make sure of that. Then the Captain would laugh and slap his thigh; he would roll about with merriment and tell her that it was just what he expected of her; it was what he had done when he was a boy, he had told her, so he would surely expect her to do this, since she was a buccaneer's daughter and a buccaneer herself, just as he was. He was always telling her that.

She would show Petroc that he could not order her life. She might, in his eyes, be only a little girl, but he should see that she was a little girl accustomed to having her own way.

She believed she had managed this very cleverly. She had come out to the ship to say a last farewell to her father. She had wept a few angry tears because he was not taking her with him. She had gone to his cabin, and they had all started to drink there. She had said good-bye and pretended that old Joe from the house would row her back, when she had previously told old Joe that one of the others was to do so.

It was well that her father had already drunk a great deal.

She believed that he did so because he was sad at the parting. He need not be sad, she told herself gleefully.

She heard voices suddenly. There were footsteps. Someone was coming down into the hold.

She crouched further under her sacks.

'She must be here somewhere,' said a voice, and she shivered, for the voice belonged to Petroc.

'Hiding herself, the young devil,' said another voice.

'That child's in need of a good whipping,' came Petroc's voice. 'One thing is certain. We're finding her before we raise anchor.'

Pilar felt sick with disappointment. She had thought they were already at sea.

At that moment Petroc had lifted the sacking and she was exposed. He burst out laughing. 'So the search is ended.'

'By all that's holy, so you were right, sir!'

'Of course I was right. I've seen it in her eyes these last few days. Get up,' he ordered Pilar.

'I will not.'

His answer was to seize her in two strong arms and plant her firmly on her feet.

'I'll have you put in irons,' she said.

'You're not the Captain yet,' he answered. The two men laughed together.

She flew at him and began thumping him with her fists. It was difficult to hold back her tears.

He tucked her under his arm.

'What now, sir?'

'We'll get her ashore, most certainly.'

'Take me to the Captain,' screamed Pilar. 'I demand to see the Captain. Where is the Captain? He'll let me stay. He wants me to stay.'

The two men looked at each other.

'Stand away,' said Petroc, 'and I'll get her out of here.'

'Put me down. Put me down, you great oaf! How dare you? I shall have you put in irons.'

He laughed, and she declared she would never forgive him for that laughter.

'I'll kill you,' she said.

'She is but a child,' said Petroc to the other with a wink, 'otherwise we could mete out the usual punishment we give to stowaways.'

Her curiosity got the better of her suddenly. 'What is that?' she wanted to know.

'Fifty strokes of the lash and a month on bread and water. Do you still want to stay aboard, Madam Piller?'

He dragged her out of the hold. She kicked, but he only laughed at her. But she saw her opportunity and suddenly broke free from him, calling, 'Captain! Captain! Take me to the Captain.' She ran headlong towards his cabin, Petroc close behind her.

She saw her father then. He was in his cabin, his eyes glazed; and he was half asleep. He was quite drunk.

She shook his arm. 'Captain! Captain, I am here.' But he did not quite recognise her, and Petroc was beside her; he picked her up in his arms and carried her struggling away.

'When the Captain is indisposed, Madam Piller,' he said, 'I am in command of the ship.'

She felt spent with misery and emotion; she could only sob: 'I hate you! I hate you! One day . . . I . . . I will kill you.'

But her voice lacked conviction and she knew, before he had her in the small boat, before he himself rowed her ashore, that she was beaten.

PART FOUR

SPAIN
1585

❧ Chapter IV ❧

SPAIN, 1585

When Blasco had arrived at his father's house and the news had been broken to him, he had at first been too bewildered to do anything but demand to hear the story again, to fire questions at his parents, to demand why this had been done and that left undone. Then he turned to Matias, Matias trembling before him. 'You lied to me then. You told me she had run away.' '*Si, señor* . . . *si, señor* . . . And it was so; gipsies always run away. They cannot live under a roof as we do. It has always been so.' Had he not felt so helpless, so melancholy in his bitter and frustrated grief, he would have struck him down there and then.

'You could have done nothing that we did not do,' his mother told him. 'Señor de Ariz lost his life because he did not stop to think and, as a result, Señora de Ariz has lost not only her daughter but her husband as well.'

'Something could have been done!' cried Blasco. 'It should have been done.'

But they shook their heads and, turning to Matias, he said very quietly: 'Go away from here. Never let me see your face again. One day it might arouse such wrath within me that I should kill you.' And sadly, Matias had ridden away.

There was Julie with him, Julie who was now his wife. They had been married *en plein prêche* in one of the Huguenot strongholds through which they had passed. It was only after that ceremony that she had seemed able to hold up her head again.

As soon as they had crossed the border into Spain he had realised that Julie was going to present one of the greatest problems he had ever had to face. Julie did not belong to Spain; she never would; all her life she would be an outsider. A Parisian could have fitted into life at Carramadino more easily than a simple girl from Béarn.

A terrible melancholy had come to him then, for he was realising that it is a comparatively easy thing to make a noble gesture, to be a brave deliverer, to face death on the rooftops, to walk through a blood-crazed city with one, whom many sought to make a victim, cowering in a sack upon his back. All daring deeds, worthy of great praise. But how much more bravery, skill and patience is required to live one's life with that noble gesture!

He was not in love with Julie; nor was Julie with him. Yet chance had thrown them so irrevocably together that they were fast bound for the rest of their lives. He had talked very seriously to Julie as they came into Seville.

To him never had the town which he looked upon as his native one – although he had spent his childhood in the house some miles south of it – looked so beautiful.

Riding through the narrow Moorish streets, past the houses which never failed to remind him that Spain was free, when once she had been in thrall, past beautiful pimienta and orange trees, he had felt his spirits lifted. He had felt the joy of being home again and it was, in the first moments in Seville, as though the man he had become was supplanted by the irresponsible boy to whom life had been full of pleasure.

But there was Julie beside him, Julie on whom the beauty of Seville was lost. There was pleasure in the hot sun, in air scented with orange blossom, but Julie did not sense these things because her senses were shut to pleasure.

He had said: 'Julie, very soon now you will enter my father's house. They must not know your Faith is not our own. How will it be possible to keep this from them?'

She said: 'It is my cross. I must bear it.'

'Julie, do not forget what we saw in Paris.'

She shivered. 'Do you think I shall ever forget?'

'It happens here . . . It happens all over the world. There is no real peace anywhere. Can you imagine something even more terrible than the massacre in Paris?'

'There could be nothing more terrible. I think we tasted hell in those few days and nights.'

'But it was over quickly, Julie. The torture can be prolonged. Here you would seem to be in a peaceful land. Do not be deceived. Terrible things happen in this country. Terrible things are happening all over the world. I beg of you, Julie, do not let any know that you are not of the Catholic Faith.'

She said: 'I see the cross I must carry. I see my folly. My father did not wish me to accompany him and Pierre to Paris. I was foolish. I longed to see strange places. I longed for gaiety. What gaiety we saw! Those bloodstained streets . . .'

'I beg of you, do not think of it. It is a part of our lives which is done with.'

'It is not done with. It is something we must live with all our lives. But for that we should not be here at this moment.'

'I beg of you, Julie, remember my words. Let us live in peace. No more horrors.'

And so they had ridden south to the house.

His mother and his father greeted him warmly.

He said the words which he had rehearsed for many days. 'Father, Mother, I bring you not only myself but my wife.'

They were astounded, and yet so glad to see him that they were ready to welcome Julie. It was a strange thing that a man in his position should marry without the knowledge of his parents, but strange things were happening all about them, and the deed was done, Blasco was home with them; he had already a wife, and Señor and Señora Carramadino had said that only when Blasco married and filled the house with children could they be happy again.

He asked for Isabella, and his eyes were alert, searching for Bianca.

It was then they told him; and it was then that he had been struck dumb with horror, with frustration and a terrible melancholy because he knew that his longing for Bianca would haunt him all his life.

It was good that there should be responsibilities. He saw that now. It was good that there were others of whom he must think. He must devote himself to Julie now. He must forget Bianca in the accusation in Pierre's dying eyes.

⚜ ⚜ ⚜

Blasco had left Jerez behind him now and was approaching the de Ariz vineyards. They were as grand as they had ever been, even in the days when Señor de Ariz was alive.

He could see the new house which had been built on the ruins of the old one. He spurred on his horse and was soon in the courtyard, where a groom ran to take his horse and lead it away. He went into the hall.

Isabella's mother had seen his approach and was there

waiting to greet him. There was always a welcome for the Carramadinos. She remembered all they had done for her when she had lost everything, when she had felt an intense longing to die.

'Come, my dear Blasco,' she said. 'Come into the cool of my little room. Behind the sun-blinds we will drink a glass of wine together and you shall tell me news of your family.'

'There is little news. I rode over as I often do, not to bring news, but merely to see you.'

'Ah Blasco, what should I have done without you and your family through these long years! I do not know. And the little Luis?'

'He is well, praise be to the saints. I had thought to bring him with me, but his mother thinks he should not have too many holidays.'

She clapped her hands and a servant appeared, silent-footed, a pretty girl. Blasco's eyes lightened momentarily. The swaying of her hips reminded him of Bianca. What foolish preoccupation was this? Bianca must be a middle-aged woman by now. What had become of Bianca? Was he to die without ever knowing?

'He was most eager to come,' went on Blasco.

She laughed indulgently. How the elderly doted on the young . . . and how impatient the young could be of such dotage! He thought of his mother's continual preoccupation with young Luis. She could scarcely bear the boy to be out of her sight. He was the grandson for whom she had always longed. He was sorry that she had no more than one. He remembered the occasion of the boy's conception – a reluctant Julie, and himself a little flushed with more Jerez wine than it was his custom to drink. He could be sure of the occasion for there were not many such between them. It had been Julie's desire that it should be so, and now it was his.

'Leave me alone,' she had said. 'Leave me to bear my cross.'

Julie's life was made up of crosses; no sooner did she stop carrying one than fate placed another on her shoulders. He was tempted sometimes to tell her that those shoulders were far from unwilling, and that she derived great pleasure from her crosses. It was so easy to quarrel; so difficult to live with the noble gesture.

Blasco went on to talk of Luis. 'His grandmother cannot bear to let him out of her sight,' he said.

'How old is he now?' She knew, but was waiting for the servant to pour the wine and leave them.

'He is five years old. You should see him sit his horse. In the vineyards they look for him when he is out riding; they send up a cheer for young Don Luis.'

The servant had gone and they were alone. Doña Marina leaned her elbows on the table and looked at him.

She said slowly: 'You remember, every time you ride over. I see it. I see it in your eyes. I know you loved Isabella. I was aware of it, you know. And I was sad because of it. You would have made her a good husband, Blasco, if she had not been taken.'

'Don't speak of it,' he said. 'It is too painful even now.'

'I never speak of it to any other but you, Blasco. We used to say that you were the careless one. We used to say that Domingo would make the better husband for her. But it was he who found consolation more quickly than you did.'

Blasco looked into his wine. He could not tell her that the love she had seen in his face was not for Isabella.

'Oh,' he said lightly, 'I have my home, you know . . . my little family.'

'There is compensation,' she agreed. 'You have your sweet Luis. It is in these little ones that we find such joy. They are born, and there are new lives to watch over. They grow like grapes . . . so tender, so beautiful.'

'You are brave, Doña Marina. Shall I tell you now that I come here often to draw courage from you? Out of the ruins of your home you built a new one; you lost daughter and husband, and yet you are not lonely here.'

She said: 'I have Gabriel and his Sabina. They have been as children to me. I have tried to look upon Alonso's nephew as my son, and his wife Sabina as my daughter. They have worked well for me. They have tried very hard to replace those I lost.'

'But nothing could do that. I know it. I see it in your eyes.'

'So I thought., Blasco, but now Sabina is with child. I pray the saints that all may go well with her; I believe that when I hold the baby in my arms he will be as my own grandson, the boy my Isabella might have had. I think he will mean much to me. I shall have him as a baby. I shall see him grow as I saw my Isabella grow.'

'I rejoice for you.'

'And Sabina is young. She is healthy. They have been married but a year, and it will not be long before the baby is born. I see many children, a house full of them. I shall be so busy watching them that I shall not have time to think. Oh Blasco, if I knew that she was dead . . . as Alonso is . . . I could know some peace, I think. It is what may be happening to her that gives me evil dreams.'

'Bianca was with her. Bianca would take care of her.'

'Oh yes . . . the gipsy girl. I remember so well the day she came. A strange girl. Bold and insolent. I did not greatly care to have her in the house and that she should be the constant companion of my daughter. But I am glad now that she was here. She was a brave girl and she loved Isabella truly.'

'I think,' said Blasco, 'that she could not live long in that land. I have heard that there is nothing but rain and fog; and the cold damp seeps into the bones and kills those who were not born to endure it.'

'I would I knew, Blasco, I would I knew. I shall never be at peace until I hold my daughter in my arms again or am sure that her suffering is over.'

'It is so long since it happened.'

'So long,' she answered. 'Sabina has said that if the child is a girl she will call her Isabella, and if it is a boy, Alonso. But I talk too much of my affairs. I am glad you came today. There is something I have to say to you, and it is for your ears alone. Blasco, go to the door and make sure we are not overheard.'

He obeyed. There was no one in the great hall on to which the door opened.

Doña Marina had lifted her eyes to his. She said in a whisper: 'I have heard talk. It concerns Julie . . . and the way she worships.'

His heart began to beat a little faster. 'How . . . heard you this?'

'It was servants talking. A servant from your house says a word to a servant here.'

'The servants are our friends. We have always treated them well.'

'And they would be faithful on all matters save one. There is one subject on which it might be considered wrong not to inform if questions were asked.'

'Yes,' said Blasco.

'She has lived in that house all these years, and I have never heard a whisper of this before.'

'No. It is a great secret which we have all kept.'

'Oh Blasco, Blasco, terrible things can happen. We know that.'

'Yes, we know. And none knows it better than I. What I saw in Paris I hope never to see again.'

'Julie is Spanish now,' said Doña Marina. 'For all these years she has lived among us. Her child is Spanish. He is a Carramadino. He cannot be a heretic.'

'Terrible trouble looms ahead of us, I fear. My mother will never let him be brought up as a heretic. Julie will never let him be brought up as a Catholic. He will soon be of an age when something must be done about his religious instruction. And now they are talking of Julie! What would happen if this got beyond our servants . . . if it got to the ears of those who would be interested?'

'You should never have married the Huguenot girl, Blasco.'

'No,' he said. 'I should never have married Julie. But I must protect her with my life.'

'You will best do that by keeping watch on her actions. You have seen terrible things in Paris. They were done in the streets. In this country similar things are done in underground prisons . . . things as terrible as were done in the open streets of Paris. Remember it, Blasco. Remember it and take warning.'

Soon after that he went out with her into the vineyards to see the vines and talk with Gabriel. He took a meal with them and rested with them during the hot afternoon and, when the siesta was over, he took his leave and rode back towards Seville.

It had been a happy day apart from the warning about Julie — and he had need of such days. But as he came nearer to his home he grew more melancholy.

Between his wife and his mother there was continual discord. And he would have to pass on Doña Marina's warning – but not to his mother. He must not give her another rod with which to beat poor Julie.

He would talk to Julie, he would beg her to take care. They had kept her secret well over these many years. She never attended Mass in their chapel. Father Garcia knew that they harboured a heretic in their house. It was necessary that he should know; but he was uneasy, and if he should ever leave them they would feel most unsafe.

In her room Julie said her prayers. She declared often that she did not need the trappings of the Catholic Church. Hers was a religion of simplicity. Huguenots did not believe it was necessary to chant in Latin, to have priests in ceremonial robes to say Mass; they did not pray to images in magnificent cloaks. 'We appeal direct to God,' she said.

So Julie followed her religion in the Catholic household, and the servants thought her strange, a foreigner with foreign ways; and none, so they had hoped, understood the meaning of those strange prayers of hers, none knew that she was one of those heretics whom their King and the dignitaries of their Church had determined to eliminate with torture and fire.

It was a situation filled with a hundred dangers, not only for Julie but for the whole household.

And *he* had done this. He had brought this upon his family, he who had had no great desire but to bask in the sun and enjoy his life.

Riding home now he thought of Julie, grown tight-lipped and sterner with the years, bearing her crosses all through the days. He thought of the smouldering passion of his mother, who adored her grandson but could never love her daughter-in-law; and how, since the coming of the boy, that feeling his mother had for the intruder within their walls was mounting to little short of hatred.

As he came near to the house he was aware of a dark-clad figure riding a mule a short distance ahead of him.

A priest! From his attire he recognised the man as a member of the Society of Jesus. He did not ride up to him, for if he did so, he could but invite the priest into his home for food and shelter. Times had changed. He dared not ask a priest into their home now. Doña Marina's warning was timely. There was a secret in their house which a priest might discover.

So he slowed down his horse to keep the distance between them, hoping that the Jesuit would turn off so that he might gallop the rest of the way home. But the man kept steadily on, and it became clear that the house was his destination.

Why was this? What was the meaning of such a visit? Could it be that others had heard the servants' gossip? Was it possible that this man had some purpose in coming this way, in seeking admission to the house?

If that were so, the sooner he faced it the better. He must be at hand to warn Julie of what could happen if she were not very careful. He must make her see that she was putting the whole household in danger.

He dug his heels into his horse's flanks, rode swiftly forward, and overtook the priest as they came to the gates of the house.

'A good evening to you, Father.'

The priest turned his head and looked straight at Blasco. Blasco stared, and his fears fell away from him.

'Domingo!' he cried.

They sat at table. The servants were running back and forth, anxious to put a good meal before Father Domingo.

He was at the right hand of his father, and his mother was on the other side of him. It was a long time since they had had their two sons together at their table.

Domingo had come, he said, to stay for a few days before he passed on.

He was paler than he had been when they last saw him; he was very thin, and his mother yearned over him. She believed he submitted himself to all sorts of hardships. She should be proud of him for this, and in a way she was; but she could not see him as other than her boy Domingo, and she wished that she could keep him home with her and look after him for a little while at least. She was disappointed in her sons – Domingo a celibate priest, and Blasco married to the French woman. The only good thing which had come out of that marriage was their son, her beloved Luis.

Luis was now eyeing his uncle with great interest. He was asking questions in his high piping voice. Domingo answered them gravely. Domingo told them of the cities in which he had been living. He had been to Paris and Rome to study, and had recently come from Rheims.

'Soon,' he said, 'I shall be going across the seas. That is why I wished to see you all before I go away again.'

'Will you go in a big ship?' asked Luis.

'It may well be,' said Domingo.

'I wish I could go in a ship with you,' Luis told him.

His mother bade him be silent.

'Your uncle wishes to talk to his mother and father, not to little boys,' she told him. 'Come, finish your food. It is time you were in bed.'

'I pray you,' said Doña Theresa, 'let the child eat in peace. It is bad for him to hurry over his food.'

'I think I know when it is good for him to hurry,' said Julie.

'That should not be over meals. Come, my love, do not gulp down your food. Do not forget to chew well as your grandfather told you to.'

Luis looked from his mother to his grandmother; he was accustomed to the strife between them, and he felt proud to be the cause of it. Now he began to eat very slowly because he wished to stay and listen to what his new uncle had to say.

Julie took him by the hand and said: 'Come along, Luis.'

The boy looked at his grandmother. Blasco thought: If we are not careful we shall have one of those scenes between them. They fight over the boy like two starving dogs over a bone.

But it might have been that his mother wished to be alone with her sons, for she made no further protest and, although he looked at her hopefully, Luis was hurried away from the table by his mother.

Domingo talked of his life in various colleges, not only those of Spain but also of France; he told how he had been ordained and had joined the Society of Jesus.

Blasco knew what this meant. Because he had joined this society of missionaries he would eventually be sent abroad to carry the Faith into those countries where it did not flourish as it did in Spain.

Now there was some reason why Domingo had come home. Blasco wondered what it was; he wondered what was the meaning of that tortured look in Domingo's eyes. Had he, after all, failed to find the peace he sought in his vocation?

When the meal was over he suggested that Domingo should walk with him in the gardens about the house. There had been some changes and he would like to show them to his brother.

Domingo was glad to fall in with his brother's suggestion, and in a short time they were strolling through the scented gardens.

'I fancy your wife does not like me,' said Domingo. 'Have I done aught to displease her?'

'You have done nothing. It is the cloth you wear. I must tell you for, as a member of the family, you should not be kept in the dark. Julie is a Huguenot. All the years she has been under this roof she has never accepted our religion,'

'But this is a very grave matter. A Huguenot! And living in this house!'

'What would you have me do, Domingo? Hand her over to the Inquisition? She has been very cautious. We all have. There is little danger of its coming to light. We never all go to the chapel together. That means that no one can be sure that she does not go. You see, Domingo, we have had to be careful . . .'

'You talk as though this were some slight inconvenience in the house. But this woman is a heretic! Terrible things can happen to those who shelter heretics beneath their roofs.'

'And what of those who marry them?'

'Why did you marry this woman, Blasco?'

'Because she was homeless and friendless, and I had seen her brother die.'

'Strange reasons for marriage.'

'Not so strange. Her brother reproached me as he was dying. It was a scene I shall never forget.'

'And on the strength of a death-bed reproach from a stranger . . .'

'Yes, on the strength of that. You see, it was not as you think. The death-bed was the hard floor of his father's house, and his death came about through the swords of his enemies. It was on the Eve of St Bartholomew that it became necessary for me to protect Julie. Her brother made me feel this as he lay dying.'

'But a heretic, Blasco!'

'I try to forget that.'

'You try to forget! How like you this is, Blasco. I remember you of old. You pushed out of sight anything you found troublesome. What of your son? What of young Luis?'

'Our mother will look after him.'

'Ah yes, she is a good Catholic. But I cannot understand how our parents can harbour a heretic in their house.'

'She is their daughter now and the mother of their grandson.'

'You lay a heavy burden on my conscience, brother, by harbouring a heretic.'

'Do you mean you might think it your duty to betray her?'

'As a son of Holy Church . . .'

Blasco clenched his fists and cried: 'No, Domingo. No! You could not do that.'

'Sometimes,' said Domingo, 'our duty is painful.'

Blasco had stopped in his walk and looked incredulously at his brother.

'I did not think . . . I could not believe that such a thought would enter your mind.'

'You see me before you. I am a priest. Should I not do my duty?'

'Domingo, you know what is done to heretics.'

'They are persuaded to follow the true Faith.'

'Persuaded!' cried Blasco. 'I have witnessed scenes of terrible slaughter. In Paris on the Eve of St Bartholomew I saw the like of which I hope never to see again. Yet in my heart I know that Spanish persuasion is more cruel than French massacre.'

'What has come over you, Blasco? You are not the brother I used to know.'

'No. I have changed. Shall I tell you what changed me? It was that night in Paris – that night and the days that followed. Sometimes I think that I should give my life to sheltering heretics – not only one, and she my wife – but all heretics, in order to expiate the terrible sin of Catholics on that night.'

'Are you mad, Blasco?'

'I am saying strange things. I have never said them before. I never even knew I thought them. It is seeing you stand before me there, in your priest's robes, and your face grown cold and ascetic. Oh, Holy Mother, why cannot we live in peace one with another? Why must our mother fight with my wife for our son? Why do our *alguazils* come at dead of night to take heretics to . . . I dare not think where? Why did the French Catholics rise on that most bloody of all nights and slaughter innocent children in their streets? Why . . . why . . . I ask you why?'

'Blasco, you are beside yourself.'

'Forgive me, brother. I know not what has come over me. I betray myself. You see, if there is one person in this house whom you should inform against, that one is your own brother Blasco.'

'It is your duty to turn her from heresy,' said Domingo earnestly.

'I shall look after her, Domingo,' Blasco answered. 'I shall see that she is saved.'

Domingo put his own interpretation on the words and nodded. But he, Blasco, must be careful. It was a long time since he had seen his brother, and people changed. He must remember that *he* had changed. Yet, he thought, I would never let them take her. I would kill her first and kill myself, rather than that she should fall into their hands. I will keep her with me, all night I shall keep her with me – for they come at night – and at the first sign I will press a pillow over her face or strangle her with my own hands; then I will turn the knife on myself. They shall never take her.

They had walked to the chapel.

Domingo said: 'I should like to stay in here a while and pray.'

Blasco nodded and left him.

He was frightened now. This man who had come home was a stranger.

❧　❧　❧

Blasco said to Julie: 'I must talk to you.'

She turned to look at him. He thought that the years had been unkind to her. All that youthful charm had gone, and life had given her nothing with which to replace it. Poor Julie! She had lost her father and brother, and she had nothing left but a husband whom she did not love, a child whom her mother-in-law sought to take from her, and beliefs which could at any moment place her in danger of torture and violent death.

'Julie,' he said tenderly, 'it will be necessary for you to go very carefully in future. There has been talk.'

'What talk?'

'Gossip among the servants. I rode over to see Doña Marina today, as you know. She warned me. She had heard talk.'

'I see,' said Julie. 'You think someone has betrayed me?'

'Not yet. But we must be more careful than ever.'

'I should never give up my Faith. If they take me, that would be but another cross to carry.'

'Julie, they must never take you. Never!'

'It would be better for you if they did. If they took me and killed me you would be free. You would be free of me and your sense of responsibility.'

'If they took you, the rest of the household would be suspect.'

She laughed bitterly. She had grown very bitter. She did not love him herself, and yet with jealous eyes she watched his love affairs with others. He had tried to explain: 'I do what I can. I cannot be other than what I am.'

She liked to enumerate her sufferings; she liked to cherish them.

'Ah, you are concerned about the rest of the household, not me.'

'We have rich vineyards, Julie. My father is wealthy, and if we were taken our lands and riches would go to them . . .'

'So that is your Holy Church! Full of iniquities. I thank God for my Faith, and I will never give it up.'

'Julie, could we not try to understand each other a little more?'

'How can we? You are of a different Faith. What could be more of a barrier?'

'Yet it is almost the same Faith. Are these differences so great? Do we not all believe in Jesus, and did not Jesus say "Love one another"?'

She said: 'You believe that the bread is the body of Christ.'

'What matters that? It seems of small account. If we but love and try to understand each other, is that not enough?'

'You are not even a good Catholic,' she said. 'You talk of love . . . love all the time. What has love to do with religion? What is your religion? What is a religion which permits you to commit adultery again and again, and all you need do afterwards is go to your priest and say: "Father, I have sinned." "Very well, my son, say so many Hail Marys and that will wipe away your sin." '

'It is useless to discuss these things. All I can do is beg of you to take great care.'

Doña Theresa came into the room.

'Is the child in bed already?' she demanded. 'It is early.'

'I thought it well that he should go early . . . with his uncle in the house.'

'Do you suggest that his uncle could harm him?'

'There are others in this house who would seek to harm him.'

'So this is how our affection is repaid!'

Blasco could bear no more.

He left them and went out of the house.

His steps led him, as they so often did, towards the chapel. If he were only young again! If he were but emerging from the pepper trees to see a dark-skinned gipsy standing on the ledge there looking through the window. If he could but go back!

But he was foolish to dream. She would be middle-aged now. She would be quite changed. If he could but find her, see her once, then perhaps she would be so different from his dreams of her, no longer young and beautiful, that he might replace the Bianca of his dreams with a wrinkled old gipsy. So much for your beautiful Bianca! he could tell himself. That is what she has come to.

But how could he ever see her again?

He started, for Domingo had come to the door of the chapel. For a few seconds Domingo did not see his brother. Blasco was shocked. Domingo's face was distorted with emotion, and he was muttering to himself.

He is torturing himself, thought Blasco. He has been praying in there. Holy Mother, can it be that he is turning over in his mind whether or not it is his duty to betray Julie?

'Domingo!' He spoke his name aloud. 'Domingo . . . brother!'

'You, Blasco?'

'Domingo, you are in trouble.'

Domingo did not answer.

'You have been praying in the chapel. You have been asking guidance. You often did that in the old days. I do not think you have changed very much, Domingo.'

'You are right,' said Domingo. 'I have not changed. I am . . . as I was. That is my tragedy. I am the same sad 'Mingo. You scorned me often when we were boys.'

'I was a brute – a careless brute. I never stopped to think. It was you who should have scorned me.'

'Nay, Blasco. You were right to scorn me. You were impious often. You were full of boyish wickedness. You lied, you made promises which you did not keep, mayhap you stole. I know you did these things. It was easy enough for me not to do them. I had no wish to go where I was bidden not to. I had no wish to plague our tutors, to hide myself when I should be at lessons, to copy the work my brother had done and pretend it was my own.'

'That would have brought you little praise,' said Blasco with a laugh.

'It was easy for me to be the one who obeyed, the good one,

so they thought. But I envied you, Blasco. There was one trait of yours for which I would have given everything I had in exchange: Courage, Blasco. You were fearless – quite fearless – and I was always afraid.'

'That was because you were wiser, more thoughtful. Often I nearly broke my neck. I didn't stop to be afraid. If I had I should have been less foolish.'

'No, Blasco. It was not that heedlessness of which I speak. Fear . . . I see it as a monster. It comes in many guises. It has many faces and every one of them fills me with terror. I am a coward, Blasco. That is what I know after all these years of prayer. I knew it before I became a priest. I know that I shall always be a coward. There is no escape from ourselves.'

'You are afraid of physical pain. Is that it, Domingo?'

'I am afraid of life,' he said. 'Yes, I am afraid of physical pain, too. I am very much afraid of that. I am afraid of torture and death; but perhaps most of all I am afraid that I shall betray my fear. I tell you this thing, Fear, which walks beside me, has many faces. I know now that I became a priest because I was afraid of life. I became a priest because I believed that I could spend my days shut away in a monastery, that I need never face the world.'

'But why did you not become a monk? Why did you not join some brotherhood? Why did you join the Society? If you are afraid . . .'

'I was marked for this work. I did not know, but all I have learned has been to lead me to this. I see it clearly. I was invited to join the Society and . . . I lacked the courage to tell of my fear. If I had been a brave man I should have said: "No. I joined to escape from life. I joined to live in peace, not in danger." But then, had I been a brave man I should not have needed to say it.'

'It is not too late, Domingo. Go to your confessor. Tell him what is in your mind.'

'My confessor is Father de Cartagena. He has told me that I have been selected for this work; that it is the wish of the King that I should undertake it. He has heard that I was to have married before I joined the priesthood. I have been trained with this object in view. I knew it, and I always believed that by the time I was ready to set out on my journeys I should be ready. And now I know that I am no more ready than I was all those years ago when I could not make up my mind.'

'You are to make a journey across the sea? You are to bring succour to Catholics in a foreign land?'

'Yes. I shall be leaving very soon for England. I know what you are thinking. You are thinking that it may well be that Isabella is there.'

'Isabella . . . Bianca . . . and all those women whom those scoundrels took.'

'Let me tell you, Blasco. When Isabella was taken her father wished me to go with him. It was a fool's chase but it was what every man in my place would have wished to do – had he not been a coward. But I ran away. And when I ran away I told myself that one day I would do this thing. I would go to England, but I would go when I was ready.'

'Thirteen years after it had happened!' said Blasco.

'Don't you see? I have been putting it off . . . putting it off . . . making excuses. There comes a time when excuses are no longer valid. Now I must face my fear. I can no longer shut my eyes to it!'

'You will go from house to house. You will meet many people. You will be able to speak of them. You remember his

270

name? It was Mash . . . something of that sound. Domingo, if you find her . . .'

'I shall find some way of bringing her home. I believe that this is the will of God. I shall bring her home. She will be able to go into a convent and there make reparations for what has doubtless been a life of sin.'

A grim smile touched Blasco's lips. 'Our gentle Isabella living a life of sin! I cannot believe that.'

'She would assuredly have been forced to it.'

'Would that be sin then?'

'You have strange ideas, Blasco. You used not to have such ideas.'

'No. I have changed. More than you, Domingo, I have changed. I see two Blascos. A bridge separates them. One crossed it on a night in Paris and left the other behind. He saw Catholics behave in such a way that he hated them and saw them as his enemies.'

'You have become a heretic.'

'Nay . . . nay. For do I not see you now, trembling before me because you are in fear of what should happen to you in a heretic land? Nay, I am not a heretic. I know not what I am. I go to confession. I go to Mass. But I can no longer accept what I once accepted. I know not what I am. I see two Blascos. Perhaps one day there will be a third.'

'You talk in riddles. Blasco, I beg of you, take care.'

'Would I could come with you to England!'

'What would you do there?'

'Look for Isabella and Bianca and the rest.'

'It would give me great comfort to have you with me. But your life is here.'

'Yes,' said Blasco, 'my life is here. Domingo, I wronged

you. For a moment I thought you might betray Julie. I know you never would.'

'Then, Blasco, you know me better than I know myself.'

They turned and went into the house.

☙ ☙ ☙

'Blasco,' said his mother, 'this cannot go on. The child asks questions. He is five years old. It is an age when his religious instruction should begin. How can he be brought up in this land as a heretic?'

'He is young yet; leave it awhile,' said Blasco.

'Leave it! Leave it! You are always for leaving what is unpleasant. I tell you this cannot endure. We have kept it secret that we harbour a heretic in this house. But children cannot keep secrets. It will become known that we are bringing up a child in a way contrary to the laws of Holy Church. What will become of us then, Blasco? What will become of us all then?'

'Mother, I implore you, be patient a little longer.'

'What monster is this you have brought among us, my son? What viper is this we nurse in the bosom of our family?'

'Nay, she is no monster; she is no viper. She has different views on a few subjects. We have managed to live all these years, turning our eyes from what we did not like in each other. Why cannot we continue?'

'It is because of the child.'

'You love him dearly, Mother.'

'I always wanted children in the house. I hoped that both my sons would give us grandchildren.'

'I know. It is a sad disappointment to you. One becomes a priest, and the other marries a heretic.'

'How could you have done this to us, Blasco?'

272

'You asked me that years ago. I have told you. I have made a vow. I made it on that night in Paris. It is not merely myself looking after one Huguenot girl, lost and bewildered in an alien city. I took her and cared for her on behalf of all Catholics. It was a penance, shall we say, for our sins on that night.'

'She has impregnated you with her doctrines. Our sins on that night! It is a night glorious in our history. Did not our King congratulate the Queen Mother of France on her work that night? Was not the whole of Rome illumined to show the people the need for rejoicing? I heard how the Te Deums were sung and the cannons of Castel St Angelo were fired, and how the Pope and the Cardinals went in procession to the Church of St Mark, calling on God to see how French Catholics loved Him.'

'Mother, you need not tell me these things. I know of them.'

'Then should you not, as a true Catholic, rejoice with those who are the leaders of the Catholic world?'

'Mother, there are two points of view. In Holland it was said that the French nation would be plunged into trouble for what it started on that night. It was said that the slaughter of the unsuspecting was not the way in which religious differences should be settled.'

'Settled! How can they be settled? Only by these heretics coming to the Truth.'

'Ah, the words of a good Catholic. Mother, Lord Burleigh in England declared that the massacre of the St Bartholomew was the worst crime since the Crucifixion.'

'Crime! When the Holy Father lauded it! Nay, Blasco, you frighten me. She has sown evil seeds in your mind. Take care! Take care!'

'Mother, I pray you, put your mind at rest. Try to understand Julie. Luis is her son.'

'He is my grandson. Blasco, I tell you this. There is very little I would not do to save his soul. He has become more to me than my own sons. You two have grown so far away, but in Luis I see the fruition of all my hopes. Your father feels the same.'

'Be patient a little longer, Mother. I will speak to Julie.'

❧ ❧ ❧

'Julie,' he said, 'this is a subject most painful to both of us, but it must be faced. Our son is of an age when religious teaching is necessary to him.'

'I shall take care of that,' said Julie.

'Julie, you dare not.'

'Dare not! You say that to me? There is much I would dare.'

'You have courage, I know. You have followed your own Faith during these difficult years. You should never have come here. You should never have married me.'

'Marriage was necessary. Only marriage could cleanse me.'

'Julie, a happy, peaceful life in your own country would have been more cleansing than this sad life we lead.'

'You took advantage of my weakness.'

'Which of us was the weak one? Mayhap your weakness took advantage of the weakness in me.'

'This is foolish talk. The thing is done. I was afraid. I should have been bold. I should never have escaped from that house. I see it now. I should boldly have walked down and let the murderous Catholics do to me what they had done to my father and brother.'

'But you longed to live, Julie. I sensed that, as we cowered together on the roof. You clung to life, as I think we all do when we face death. It is easy to talk of death when it is not near us. But let us not talk of that now. Let us face life and all the difficulties with which it presents us. What of our son?'

'I will never let your mother have her way. He shall be taught the truth.'

'In Spain we are harsh with those who do not hold the Catholic Faith.'

'You have no need to tell me of the cruelties which are perpetrated in the name of the Catholic Faith.'

'Cruelties are perpetrated on both sides, Julie. Catholics persecute Huguenots, and Huguenots Catholics.'

'Have we ever lured Catholics to one of our great cities, there to murder them? Have we any system as cruel as that which persists in this country?'

'No, you have not. But it may be because we are stronger, because we are more certain . . .'

'None could be more certain than I am. Nay, Blasco. Luis must take his chance. He shall be taught the truth no matter at what cost.'

He turned wearily away.

Through the window he could see the child with his nurse. He was high-spirited and already a little spoilt, already aware of the enmity existing between his mother and his grand-parents.

What will become of us all? wondered Blasco.

It was almost midnight.

Blasco lay in his bed sleepless. He knew that in his bed Domingo also would be lying awake.

Julie occupied the room adjoining Blasco's. But was she sleeping or was she thinking bitterly, angrily, of the antagonism which existed between herself and her mother-in-law?

He was glad her room was close to his. He had felt uneasy ever since the day he had talked with Doña Marina. That discussion had brought the danger of this situation home to him. And then on the way back he had met Domingo and that meeting had emphasised the danger.

Blasco was alert suddenly. In the distance he could hear the sound of horses' hoofs.

A traveller travelling late? What else? Why was it that such sounds could fill him with misgiving? His hand closed about the hilt of his sword. Ever since he had ridden back that day from Doña Marina he had kept it beside him night and day.

Would he have the courage to use it, to turn it first on Julie and then on himself? How could he be sure until the moment came?

But he must have that courage. She must never fall into their hands, for if she did he would have broken his vow to protect her.

His ears were strained. The sound of horses' hoofs was more distinct and he knew that there was more than one rider.

He thought of stories he had heard, of how the officials of the dreaded Inquisition called on houses which were suspected of harbouring heretics. They came at night; they came almost in silence.

Sweat had broken out all over his body. Nearer . . . nearer they came. Now there was no doubt that they were coming to the house. They must be. Who had betrayed them? Servants' chatter? Domingo!

He looked up. The door had opened and Julie was standing there.

In that moment he could have believed she was a girl again. Her long hair was free; it fell about her shoulders. She wore a wrap which she had picked up in haste, as she had on that other night of fear.

He heard her voice, young, frightened, devoid of all bitterness. 'Blasco . . . they come . . . they are coming for me.'

Then she ran to him, and he caught her in his arms. He drew her into the bed beside him. She saw the sword and she shuddered.

How different she was from the woman he resented in his daily life – how young, how defenceless! Julie, who had talked so boldly of her courage, was as frightened as a child. She was trembling. He held her very close to him; he could feel her fluttering heart against his own.

'Julie . . . Julie . . .' he said, and he kissed her hair.

Her voice was so faint that he could scarcely hear it.

'They will take me,' she whispered. 'They will shut me away and they will do terrible things to me.'

'They never shall,' he answered.

'How can you prevent it, Blasco?'

'As I did before.'

'There was safety there, in the room at the inn. What safety for me would there be in Spain?'

'Not in Spain,' he said. 'There is . . . somewhere else.'

She began to shiver again. She said: 'If you sent me thither you must needs come with me.'

'Aye,' he said. 'You shall not go alone.'

'I am so frightened, Blasco . . . so very frightened.'

'It is easy to *talk* of facing death,' he said. 'You are no exception, Julie. We are bold and brave with words. It is the deed which makes cowards of us all.'

'Blasco . . . Blasco . . . forgive me.'

'It is not for me to forgive. You should forgive me.'

'You saved my life.'

'For what? Years of dissatisfaction with an unfaithful husband?'

'You did not want to marry me.'

'I wanted to take care of you. Marriage was the only answer.'

'Blasco, I wish I had been kinder.'

'You did your best. We are not much alike, Julie. You are fierce and determined. I am casual, wanting only peace. Two such natures might have mingled well. But our Faiths – our different Faiths – came always between us.'

'Sometimes I have thought you clung but listlessly to yours.'

'Ah, Julie, if others had clung as listlessly there might have been less suffering in the world.'

'Suffering is of no account, Blasco. It is the truth that we must find and cling to.'

'Truth has many faces, Julie. It may be that you have a little and we have a little. That is not to say that either of us is the sole possessor of truth.'

'You talk to distract me from what is to come. Shall we hear them coming up the stairs?'

'Yes.'

'What if it is too late then?'

'It will not be. The door is locked. They will have to break it down to get at us.'

They could hear the thumping of their hearts in the silence.

'I am praying,' she said.

'I also am praying. Oh, Julie, we pray to the same God, do

we not? What does He think, I wonder, of these differences between us? Does He laugh at us? Does He mock us, think you, for the fools we are? Such little differences – of what account are they? Does He say, "You both worship me. You both accept me as your true God. But you disagree as to the manner of your worship, and for such reasons you are cruel and hate each other when I have commanded you to love one another." Might He not say that in wrangling over how we shall come to His presence we break His greatest commandment?'

'Blasco, you blaspheme, and at such a moment! Blasco, I beg of you do not.'

'Julie . . . it cannot be long now.'

'Not long now.'

'Listen! Footsteps on the stairs. It is now . . . Julie. It must be now.'

She had risen and was kneeling on the bed. Her hands were clasped in prayer and her eyes were shut.

He took the sword in his hands.

'Oh Holy Mother, help me,' he murmured.

'Blasco! I must wake you . . .' It was his mother's voice. 'Such news . . . news from Doña Marina! Sabina has given birth to her child. It is a boy. Doña Marina has sent a messenger over with the news. He was delayed; that is why he arrives so late.'

Blasco had knelt on the bed; he had clasped Julie in his arms; he held her against him and began to laugh.

He heard his mother trying to open the door.

He called out: 'What is this? We are half asleep. Sabina has a boy, did you say? Then give the messenger refreshment and a bed. We'll drink the baby's health in the morning.'

'Tomorrow you must ride over to Doña Marina.'

Blasco gave a good imitation of a yawn.

'Aye, tomorrow,' he said. 'Tomorrow.'

🌹 🌹 🌹

They lay close together.

She whispered: 'It was thus on that night . . . do you remember?'

'Yes. Beneath our window the procession passed on the way to the Cemetery of the Holy Innocents. It was as though the angel of death had passed by. The shadow still darkened our faces, but the angel had passed on. Julie, we lived through that. Could we not try to live in harmony when fear is not there to drive us into each other's arms?'

'It might be that we could, Blasco.'

He kissed her. He knew that he asked for the impossible. The fear of this night had not settled their insoluble problems.

But that night they were lovers, as they had been in the Paris *auberge*.

🌹 🌹 🌹

The harmony between them was lost during the next day. Julie was subdued. She had had nothing to fear during that night, but fear had been none the less real for all that, and she was ashamed.

When Julie was ashamed her lips grew tighter. Blasco began to understand that her sharp tongue with which she flayed others was a defence against their discovering the weakness in herself. He felt more tender towards her than ever before.

But the differences in the household did not diminish. Julie seemed more determined than ever to keep young Luis from the influence of his grandmother.

Domingo would shortly be leaving for Madrid. The brothers were often together. Both talked of their problems.

'Domingo,' said Blasco, 'it is good to have you here. I could almost believe that we are young again. And when shall I see you next?'

'Only God can know,' answered Domingo.

'Domingo, when you leave here I shall ride with you to Madrid. It will be pleasant riding together, talking together, solving each other's problems. What think you?'

'I should find great pleasure in your company.'

'It will be some short respite for me. This house, with two women wrangling over my son, grows intolerable at times. But I must not speak of it. We have talked enough of my troubles . . . Then it is settled, I shall ride with you to Madrid. And mayhap, Domingo, if it is not forbidden, I may accompany you to the coast. I should like to wish you Godspeed on your journey across the sea to England.'

'Nothing could please me more. To no one else have I spoken of myself, except to my Confessor. Blasco, we are as different as two men can be, but we are brothers . . . we shall always be that.'

A few days later they set off together for Madrid.

II

It was many years since Blasco had been in Madrid, but he remembered the occasion clearly. It was from Madrid that he had travelled to El Escorial, and his brief visit to that monastic palace was something he would never forget as long as he lived.

He saw little of Domingo while he was in the city. Domingo was busy preparing to leave for England. He was in conference with members of the Society. There were many preparations to be made.

There was little to do in Madrid. It was not a city to be compared with Valladolid or Salamanca. Only recently had it become of any importance. That had happened when Philip had declared it to be *única corte* and capital of Las Españas. The climate was trying, for the city was set high above sea-level in the middle of a plateau which was swept by the winds, and was in turn fiercely hot and cruelly cold. The large forests which surrounded the city afforded some protection though, and Philip had rebuilt it to some extent. He found it within easy reach – it was some thirty miles – of his retreat at El Escorial.

Blasco wandered through the town, wondering how long before Domingo would set out on his journey. It was almost evening and the people were coming out into the streets after the heat of the day. On the balconies the women were sitting; their fans were brightly coloured, and in their dark clothes they looked more enticing than he knew closer inspection would prove them to be.

He strolled through the Plaza, where a water-seller cried: '*Agua quién . . . quiere agua? Agua. Agua fresca?*' This reminded Blasco that he was thirsty, and he turned in at one of the taverns, took a seat, and ordered wine. As he sat drinking the gipsies came in. Gipsies always excited him. He studied them eagerly, always hoping that among them he might find Bianca. There was one young girl with long black hair in which she wore a rose. She might have been a young Bianca.

Someone was calling to the gipsies to dance. Blasco turned his head to look at the man, who sat back, dark-haired, somewhat gross, his heavy lids and hooked nose giving him the appearance of a bird; his full lips were sensual.

The music began, and the gipsies danced the *sardaña* – the ancient Catalonian dance in which they all joined on the tavern floor, turning and twisting this way and that, seeming to weave strange patterns. The music made by the flageolet and tambourine reminded Blasco of Bianca, and it seemed that the young gipsy girl, as she danced, grew more like Bianca.

There was another who had his eyes on the gipsy girl; this was the fat man with the heavy-lidded eyes.

He called to the girl: 'Hi, gipsy, here! Come . . . drink with me.'

But the girl snapped her castanets in mockery it seemed, and the glances she threw over her shoulder were contemptuous.

'You . . . gipsy!' growled the man.

Still the girl did not heed him. She was proud and bold – as Bianca had been. But as she danced close to him, the man shot out an arm and seized her. Lithe as a cat, the girl turned and dug her teeth into his hand.

Blasco was on his feet.

'Release the girl,' he demanded.

The fat man's face filled with purple anger. 'Why so?' he said.

'She wishes it, and so do I.'

'Señor, I wish otherwise.'

'Your wishes, Señor, are of no account.'

Now the music had abruptly stopped. All eyes in the tavern were on the gentleman from the South and the man who was a well-known figure in Madrid.

'Who are you, Señor?' asked the fat man, his face growing a deeper purple every moment. 'Who are you from the country who would invade the peace of our city and bring your country manners to Madrid?'

'If these be your manners,' said Blasco, 'it is well that I show you how noblemen behave in my part of the country.' Blasco's hand was on his sword. The man threw the girl from him and drew his own.

'Señores, Señores,' cried the innkeeper, 'I beg of you . . . not here!'

The fat man waved him aside. He raised his sword, but before he could use it, Blasco's had flashed up and, by a trick which he had learned from his fencing master in his father's house, he flicked the weapon out of his opponent's hand, and pricked his arm. Then, sheathing his sword and turning away, he found two men beside him.

'You are under arrest, Señor,' said one of them.

❧ ❧ ❧

Domingo was received in the private room of Father de Cartagena at the college of Valladolid.

'Welcome, Father Carramadino,' said Father de Cartagena. 'It is long since I saw you.'

'Father, I am happy to see you again.'

'Pray you sit down. I will send for wine. And while we refresh ourselves, I will tell you what plans have been made for you. Are you prepared to leave Spain very shortly?'

'Yes, Father.'

'May God's grace go with you. You will leave in three days' time and make your way through France to the town of Calais. Thence you will take boat to England. The captain will know where you are to land. It is at a lonely spot on the coast of England. There will be some of our friends waiting there to conduct you to a house where you will spend the night. Then you will make your way to London.'

'I understand, Father,' said Domingo.

'You will find many of our Faith there, ready to give you shelter, but once on English soil you must employ the utmost caution. You must always remember that if you are caught you bring disaster, not only to yourself, but to those who have helped you.'

'I realise that.'

'Therefore – caution. You know what your task is to be?'

'Yes, Father. I shall rest in the houses of those of our Faith. I shall give the Sacrament to those who need it. I shall do my best to spread the truth throughout the heretic land.'

'That is what is required of you, Father Carramadino. But there is more besides.'

'More . . . besides?'

'Although, of course, it is the same task. It is merely this: There are sometimes duties other than giving the Sacrament to those of our Faith and seeking to turn all others from their evil ways.'

'Yes, Father?' said Domingo breathlessly.

'In England . . . in London you will meet fellow-Jesuits; many are English gentlemen, some of whom have studied in this very town; they are men whom I trust and know. There is living in England at this time an Englishman of noble family and some fortune who has sworn to fight for our cause with lands, goods and life if need be.'

'As all good Catholics should,' murmured Domingo.

'Indeed it is so. Six years ago this gentleman founded a secret society. Its aim was to protect and maintain Jesuit missionaries in England. You will go to his house, and there you will meet many faithful missionaries like yourself. This gentleman will tell you which houses will be ready to receive you.'

'Yes, Father.'

'I will give you instructions but you must memorise them. This is a matter of such importance that we dare not commit it to paper. The gentleman I told you of once served as a page to the true Queen of England, Mary Stuart, who is now a prisoner, as you know, of the woman who wrongly wears the crown of England. Father Carramadino, I give you now orders from your King.'

'From the King!'

'The King and the Church, they are as one. We are blessed in our monarch. Listen carefully, Father Carramadino. Your task will be to travel from Catholic house to Catholic house and not only administer to the daily needs of our friends. You must prepare them to rise against the Queen. You must tell them that our King has said that nothing shall be spared, in money or troops, to bring the reign of the heretic Elizabeth to an end and set the true Queen on the throne. I can tell you no more. You will meet Anthony Babington in London, where he will be expecting you, and he will tell you what he wishes you to do. Obey him. He is a good Catholic. Your duty will be clear to you.'

Domingo was silent, and Father de Cartagena went on: 'You seem surprised.'

'I had not thought to take part in matters of state.'

'Matters of State and Church are one in Spain.'

'But it would seem to me that I shall act, not as a priest, but as an agent for my country.'

'It is the desire of King Philip to see a Catholic England. Could you wish otherwise?'

'No, indeed I could not. I would the whole world were a Catholic world. But this is a plot to assassinate the Queen of England.'

'The Queen of England! The Queen of England is a prisoner of this usurper. Once we have destroyed her and the heretics who surround her – Leicester, Walsingham, Burleigh and the rest – there will be no obstacle to establishing the true Faith in that sad land.'

'I see, Father.'

'Now, my dear Father Carramadino, make your preparations. Be ready to leave within a few days. I will see that all is made easy for you. May God give you His blessing.'

Father de Cartagena had risen. He grasped Domingo's hand and felt that it was clammy with sweat.

When Domingo had left him he pulled a bell rope, and the young man who had brought the wine reappeared.

'My son,' said Father de Cartagena, 'I pray you find Father Sanchez and bring him to me as soon as you do so.'

'Yes, Father,' said the young man and went out leaving Father de Cartagena alone with uneasy thoughts.

Domingo Carramadino was an unhappy man. He was afraid of what he had been called upon to do. Father de Cartagena knew Domingo well. A good, religious, conscientious man, a worthy priest in less troublous times, a man who could be trusted to give conscientious consideration to all problems which might be presented to him. But the times *were* troublous.

He wondered if it were wise to employ such a man on such a mission.

These were great days for Spain. At the head of the list of prayers, which Philip said in his Escorial, was one for the conquest of England. And Philip – although he spent so much time on his knees – was not a man to leave all to Divine aid. In the harbours Spaniards were working day and night; all their efforts were preparing their country for the great day to come. Then would Philip set on the seas a fleet of ships such as none had ever seen before – an invincible Armada. It would sail to the shores of that proud island, so long ruled over by an insolent woman who was now deemed the hope of the Protestant world.

It would be a mighty fleet, and in command of it would be the great sailors of Spain – the soldiers too – and with it would go the *chevelet* and the bilboes, those instruments of torture, those friends of the Holy Inquisition, which would firmly place the Holy Office there on English soil.

But Philip wished to avoid war if he could obtain what he desired by peaceful means. He hoped his Armada would sail to an already conquered land, where Burleigh, Leicester, Walsingham and their kind had been either slain or made prisoner, Elizabeth murdered, and Mary on the throne waiting to receive the great ruler who had been the means of placing her there, ready to accept his help in ruling the country he had won for her.

But a priest who was afraid of intrigue, a priest who merely wanted to be a priest, was he the man to send to England at such a time? But Philip was asking for priests. He wanted as many as could be found to do the work for which the Society trained them.

Father Sanchez came to him.

'Sit down, my friend,' said Father de Cartagena. 'It is of Father Carramadino that I wish to speak. I am uneasy. I wonder whether it is wise to send him to England. He is beset by fears.'

''Twas always so. I was at the house of the Carramadinos for some time. There was a brother who was quite a different type. By the way, this brother . . .'

'Yes, yes,' interrupted Father de Cartagena, 'but it is Father Carramadino whom we must discuss. The King is anxious that as many Jesuits who can be sent should go at once to England.'

Father Sanchez nodded. 'Another plot?'

'One which many believe is certain to succeed. His Majesty has had word from Don Bernardino de Mendoza, his ambassador in Paris, that he is certain that this time the plot cannot fail.'

'It was thus, I remember, with the Ridolfi plot.'

'That? Oh, that went wrong from the start. This is a different matter. Babington is an earnest young man, a man who, it is said, is not only in love with the Catholic Faith but with Mary of Scotland as well. He was her page, and became enamoured of her at Sheffield, I believe. There are some who say he even hopes to marry her.'

'There will always be those to say such things.'

'If there is truth in it, it means that the plot has greater hopes of success. But I am more than a little worried about Father Carramadino.'

'It is a pity,' said Father Sanchez, 'that it is not the other brother who is our priest. *There* is a man who would do our work well. Mind you, he might err on the side of recklessness. I have news of him. He's in a Madrid jail at the moment.'

'For what reason?'

'A brawl in a tavern. He was apparently defending a gipsy girl from the attentions of one of the King's ministers.'

'And for this he has been put into jail?'

'It seems he twisted the man's sword out of his hand and

wounded him in the arm. This high official is furious with him and demands that he shall be severely punished. Now you are worried about Domingo. I have an idea: What if this brother were sent to England with him? He was employed in the King's service once, and I hear that although the task allotted to him was a small one he performed it with zeal. I know these brothers well. They have been brought up together. Domingo would not quail if Blasco were beside him. Blasco could go with his brother and do the King's work, and Domingo would have his brother beside him.'

'I see. I wonder. I will see the brother. I will talk with him mayhap. Then I will make this proposition. The man could go as his brother's servant. Then he could travel with him, live with him in the houses to which he goes.'

'And put courage into him,' said Father Sanchez. 'I have seen him do it many times, Father; and he would do it again.'

'I will look closely into this matter. It seems to me a good thing that there should be two brothers Carramadino going to England to work for Spain.'

❧ ❧ ❧

It was Father Sanchez, with Domingo, who came to Blasco in his Madrid prison.

Blasco was passing alternately from anger to depression. He was kept locked up; his jailer was not a bad fellow, but he could get no satisfaction from anyone as to how long he was to remain in prison. He cursed himself for going to the tavern. He called himself a fool for seeking to protect a gipsy girl who doubtless did not need or wish for his protection. He had been bemused because she had a look of Bianca, and he had doubtless endowed her with qualities she did not possess.

His jailer was at his door, the keys jangling in his hand. 'Visitors for you, Señor!' Was it fancy or was there a note of respect in the jailer's voice which had not been there before? The door was opening.

'Domingo!' cried Blasco. He looked at the two priests and murmured: 'Why, and 'tis Father Sanchez!'

Father Sanchez embraced him. 'I am sad to see you thus, my son.' He waved to the jailer to leave and close the door on them.

'You are surprised,' continued Father Sanchez. 'We heard what had happened and came to your help.'

'I am right glad to see you,' answered Blasco. 'Domingo, when do you leave? It would seem as though, shut up in this place, I shall be unable to accompany you to the coast.'

'It is concerning your detention that we have come,' said Domingo.

'We have a proposition to make,' said Father Sanchez. 'I could procure your release in a few hours if you would consent to do as I ask.'

'I would do much to leave this foul place.'

'Accompany your brother to England?'

Blasco was astounded. He did not speak, and Father Sanchez went on: 'Indeed, you would have little alternative but to do so, were I to suggest it in certain quarters. This could come, not as a choice, but as a command from the King.'

'To go to England . . .' Blasco was looking about his dark prison cell. To go to England would be more than release from this prison. To leave his home and the continual battle between his wife and mother which he felt to be coming to a head; to go to England where it might well be he would find Bianca. This priest was opening the door of a more constricting prison than this narrow cell.

But almost immediately that memory came back to him, the vision which had haunted him for many years. Pierre, looking at him accusingly, and the unspoken vow he had made as he had mounted the stairs to defend Julie with his life. He had discovered that that was not merely the easy gesture to be made by a reckless man with a sword in his hand; it carried him over many weary years. He had to fight depression, boredom, continual strife, and they could be more formidable than a murderer with a bloodstained sword in his hand. How could he go to England with Domingo and leave Julie in Spain, at the mercy of his mother – and worse!

'Well?' said Father Sanchez.

Domingo was looking at him eagerly.

'You wish it, Domingo?' he asked.

'Greatly,' answered Domingo. And he saw in Domingo's eyes an appeal which had been there years ago when they were very young and Domingo's great enemy, Fear, had first begun to plague him. In those days he had often wanted his brother beside him. Domingo was afraid now; he was begging Blasco to go with him.

'There are my wife and son,' said Blasco.

'Your wife? Your son?' cried Father Sanchez. 'What have they to do with the King's mission?'

Blasco looked from his brother to the other priest. How could he explain? How dared he explain: Julie is a heretic! I fear to leave her alone and unprotected in Catholic Spain.

Domingo said: 'Blasco, you must come with me. There is work to do for Spain, and you have been chosen to do it.'

'It is the price of my release?' asked Blasco.

'It has not yet come to that,' said Father Sanchez. 'But it could do so. If you agree to leave for England with your brother within the next few days I am sure there would be no difficulty in procuring your immediate release.'

'I must first return to my home. There are certain matters which must be put in order.'

Father Sanchez was thoughtful. There was a recklessness about this man. It was the quality which was needed for the tasks which lay ahead of him; but at the same time it meant that he was the sort of man who would make his own decisions. It was clear that Blasco's family ties held him firmly to his home. He would insist on making the arrangements he considered necessary, and it would be wiser therefore to put no obstacle in his way.

'It might be arranged,' said Father Sanchez. 'If I procure your release you could start for your home immediately. If you could be back in Madrid within ten days, you could then start for England. When you reach England our friends will tell you what the King requires of you.'

'I will do it,' said Blasco.

🌿 🌿 🌿

Those at home were surprised to see him back so soon. They were at a meal when he arrived at the house.

One of the servants, seeing him, ran into the hall where they sat at table, crying: 'It is Don Blasco who has come home.'

His father had risen; his mother was running to him; Julie watched him without moving, and young Luis was wriggling down from his stool to run to his father. 'It is good to have you back, Blasco,' said his mother.

'I have news for you,' he said. 'I have come for a very brief stay. I am to go away again on the King's business.'

His son, tugging at his doublet, said: 'I am here, Papa. Luis is here.'

He lifted the boy in his arms. Luis smiled. Luis must be the centre of attraction. He was sharp-witted, and he had quickly learned that all the disturbing currents circulated about his small but important person.

'And how is my son?'

Luis stared wonderingly at his father. 'Welcome home, Papa,' he piped. 'Did you see the King?'

'No. I did not. He is rarely seen, my son. He was not in Madrid while I was there.'

'He is His Most Catholic Majesty,' said Luis. 'He is the best King in the world.'

That was what his grandmother told him. His mother did not like him to refer to His Most Catholic Majesty. He wanted to remind them that although his father had just come home and all eyes were upon him, they must not forget that he, Luis, was here and that he was the one they were really concerned about.

'What does this mean?' asked Doña Theresa.

'You had better tell us quietly,' said his father. He was looking about, always anxious that nothing should be overheard by the servants which might give rise to discomfort. A furtiveness had come to the house since it had harboured a heretic.

'Sit down and have something to eat,' said Doña Theresa. 'We will wait for your news.'

Blasco sat next to Julie. Her eyes were on him. They were fearful. He was going away, he had said. That meant that she would be in this household without his protection.

She did not love him; the thought of love between them filled her with shame; yet she relied on him and he was her protector; it was during those times when danger threatened that she turned to him.

No one could eat very heartily at such a time.

They left the table and followed Blasco to the small room.

His mother, father and Julie watched him. Julie had called to the nurse to take Luis away. The child had gone, protesting.

'I am to go to England with Domingo.'

'For what purpose?' asked his father.

'That I shall learn when I arrive. I go on the King's business.'

'But we need you here. There are the estates to manage.'

'You can manage them, Father, until I return.'

'When do you leave?' asked Julie, and the tremor in her voice reminded him poignantly of the girl she had been in Paris.

'Tomorrow. I dare not delay.'

'How . . . how long will this mission last?' asked Julie.

'I do not know.'

Her eyes were wide. 'It might be for years . . .'

He did not answer her; but he knew in that moment that he could not leave Julie behind him.

He said: 'There is much to be done in a short time. I propose to take Julie to Béarn. We are riding through France, Domingo and myself. In Béarn, Julie, you would be with your own people. You could stay there until I return.'

'What of the child?' asked Doña Theresa quickly. 'What of Luis?'

'He should go with his mother,' said Blasco.

'And be brought up as a Huguenot? My grandson!'

'It is perhaps well that he should follow his mother's Faith.'

'Blasco, are you mad? Would you condemn the child to heresy?'

'He would be a happy heretic in Béarn among other heretics.'

'Do you care nothing for your son, then, that you would condemn him to this?'

'I care for him,' said Blasco, 'and I like not to see him growing more conscious each day of the strife he causes.'

Gregorio said: 'France is a troubled country. There is continual strife there. The wars of religion have never ceased since that man Luther pinned his theses on the door of a Wittenberg Church. France is not a happy country now, Blasco.'

'Is any country happy?'

'Here in Spain we are united.'

'We have our rebels.'

'And we have those who know how to deal with them.'

Blasco shuddered. He said slowly: 'Here we Catholics reign; in England the Protestants reign; and in France there is continual strife, one against the other.'

'My son, what talk is this?' said Don Gregorio. 'You speak dangerously at times.'

'And what of Luis?' said Doña Theresa. 'What of my grandson? He shall not leave this house.'

'When I go,' said Julie, 'I must take him with me.'

'You shall not,' cried Doña Theresa. 'He is my grandson, and I'll not see him led along the road to damnation.'

Blasco looked at his mother and he was alarmed. He said: 'I have a great deal to do. I must leave tomorrow. Let me talk to Julie alone. We must make up our minds quickly what is the best for us all.' He took Julie's hand and led her away.

In their bedchamber she covered her face with her hands.

'If you leave me here,' she said, 'they will betray me. I see it in their faces.'

'You think my parents would do that? You are my wife, Julie. I am their son, and they love me.'

'People do strange things for love, Blasco. They would tell themselves that what they did was best for you.'

'You really think they would betray you if you stayed?'

'I cannot stay!' she cried. 'I dare not stay if you are not with me.'

'Julie! So I mean as much to you as that?'

'I am afraid every time you are not in the house.'

'I thought you so brave. You defied them all. You told them openly that you would follow your way of life and that nothing would change you. You came here to Spain. You have heard of the harshness of our religious laws. You – of Béarn – knew of them. I thought you brave to come.'

'I was brave because you were here. I did not believe that any harm could come to me while you were near. It is when you are away that I am afraid. It is not death I fear; that would be easy. One step to glory, and then peace for evermore. But it is many steps that I should have to take if they were to seize me. Perhaps I should wait for years for death; some have, in those underground prisons. And I should be afraid, Blasco, that I should lose my soul for the sake of my miserable body's comfort.'

He put his arms about her. In fear she was the defenceless girl again, the girl whom he had vowed to protect.

He said: 'I had planned to take you and Luis to Béarn and leave you there until I returned. I could have felt you might have enjoyed some measure of safety there . . . you and the child. But my mother will never let Luis go. She is a strong woman, Julie. It is she who rules the household. It is she who has safeguarded you all these years in our house. Our servants

297

fear her anger; so does my father; so did I and Domingo. It was always so. And she has determined never to let Luis go.'

'There is something I must tell you, Blasco. I am going to have another child.'

'Can this be true?'

'It was the night when they came to tell us that Sabina's baby was born. Do you remember? I was so frightened, because I thought it was the *alguazils* come to take me away. You comforted me; you had your sword ready to kill me. You would have done that for me which I could not do myself. That was the night, Blasco. And now there is to be another child.'

There was a slight frown between his eyes. Another child to cause dissension – another such as Luis for his mother to claim.

She went on: 'When you said that you would take me to Béarn, I thought of living there in peace with my son, waiting for my child to be born.'

'There is not much peace anywhere in France, Julie. Queen Catherine rules, although her son is King, for he is weak and she is wily. She is neither Catholic nor Protestant; she favours either for the sake of expediency. France is not a happy place at this time.'

Julie said: 'Take us to England with you, Blasco. I have heard that it is a country ruled by a great Queen who is the leader of the Protestant world. There we could find some peace, with our son and the child who is yet to be born.'

'It would be impossible. I go in the service of the King. Could I take a family with me?'

'Then what shall we do?'

'Prepare for the journey to Béarn. I shall not leave you here. Prepare yourself and the child. We set out tomorrow.'

It was dark in the *patio*.

The blinds were drawn back to let in the cool night air. Two candles burned in the bedchamber. In his room Luis was sleeping. He had been told nothing of the journey he was to undertake the next day.

Julie was gathering together a few of her possessions which she would take with her. A smile played about her mouth, and her face was soft in the candlelight.

How she must have hated this house! thought Blasco. How delighted she is to leave it!

The door opened suddenly and silently, and Doña Theresa came in. She shut the door and leaned against it. Her face was pale and her eyes were brilliant.

She said very quietly: 'I have something to say to you. You two are leaving this house tomorrow, but Luis will remain here.'

Julie uttered a cry of protest.

'He will remain,' repeated Doña Theresa firmly.

'No,' cried Julie. 'It shall not be.'

'Mother, please understand,' said Blasco. 'Julie is his mother. There has been too much dissension and he is aware of it. It is ruining his character. What are you doing to him, Mother?'

'What am I doing! I am bringing him up in a manner befitting a Spanish nobleman. I am saving the child from the disaster which will surely overtake him if he is left to his mother's care.'

'What are you saying?' cried Julie.

'I should have taken you to see Maria Lopez and her

299

husband,' said Doña Theresa. 'They were once servants of heretics. They were taken with the rest of the household. But they were released because their offence was not great. They had merely listened to the teaching of those who employed them. Maria can just move about the hovel in which they live. She could show you her scars. Her husband? He cannot walk at all. He has lost all power of his limbs; that was the *chevelet* . . .'

'Stop,' said Julie. 'Stop, I pray you.'

'They escaped lightly,' said Doña Theresa. 'They were after all only servants of heretics and mildly contaminated.'

'Mother, why do you say this?' asked Blasco. 'Why do you seek to upset Julie?'

'I want her to know what she is doing to that child, what she is doing to herself.'

'No,' said Julie. 'No. Please do not go on. I am going away from here tomorrow. I am taking my son away.'

'If you attempt to take him away,' said Doña Theresa, 'you will not ride very far.'

'What do you mean, Mother?' asked Blasco, on a note of alarm.

'I mean what I say. I mean that if that child is taken from this house he shall soon be brought back to me. I will do that which mayhap I should have done long ago. Aye, and would, had I not feared for my own son. But now I see the way clear to me. The saints have shown me the way.'

'You mean you would betray us!'

'Yes, my son, I would betray you. The saints command it.'

There was silence in the room. Blasco's eyes were fixed on the guttering candles.

Then Doña Theresa said slowly: 'Go tomorrow. Ride away from here in peace. I will look after Luis until Blasco's return.'

'Mother!' protested Blasco.

But she silenced him. 'My elder son is a priest and he is all but lost to me. My other son married a heretic. I will have Luis. Luis is mine. I had thought to see this house full of children. I had thought to see both my sons happily married to women whom their father and I could have welcomed to our house. It was not to be. But at least I shall have Luis.'

'It is not for you to decide, Mother,' said Blasco.

'Is it not? I tell you the child shall be mine. Take him with you if you wish. He will be given back to me when she is arrested. And arrest her they will, before she is many miles along the road to Madrid! I have evidence, have I not? I tell you she only lives in freedom at my will – and has these many years. So . . . go if you will. It matters not; Luis will be mine in either case.'

❧ ❧ ❧

They rode north to Madrid next day.

Luis stayed behind with his grandmother.

As he had watched her with the child and seen her triumphant, Blasco wondered that this could be the mother who had once seemed tender to him. Her Faith had hardened her feelings; her belief in a doctrine had made her indifferent to the sufferings she inflicted on others.

Sometimes it seemed to Blasco that, although both she and Julie had watched carefully over Luis, neither of them had truly loved him. They had seen his soul as something to be fought for.

He had argued with Julie throughout the night. What purpose would be served, he demanded, by taking the child? They would never escape from Spain if Doña Theresa informed against them.

Domingo was waiting in Madrid, and they set out without delay.

❧ ❧ ❧

They rested at an inn near Bayonne. The innkeeper's wife was interested in them. Strange company, she thought; the woman who was so quiet, the Jesuit in his *soutane* and *biretta* and the handsome man whom it would have been so amusing to welcome had he been alone. She brought them food and wine and promised them beds for the night.

'You travel far, Messieurs?' she asked.

'Yes, we have far to go,' said Blasco.

'It is long since you have been in France?'

'It is many years since I was last here,' Blasco told her.

'Ah, Monsieur, you will find many changes.'

'There are always changes.'

The woman lifted her shoulders.

'It will not do for the priest to venture into Béarn.'

'Ah, no, I suppose not,' said Blasco.

The woman shook her head.

'Monsieur, these are terrible days for France. How does one know from one day to the next what will happen?'

'Terrible days!' said Julie.

The woman looked at her sharply, for she recognised the French accent of the district. She began to speak volubly and addressed herself to Julie.

'It is more than fourteen years since I was in Béarn,' Julie told her.

'Fourteen years! Why, that would be before the wedding. *Les noces vermeilles!* There was never such a time for France. It will never be forgotten.'

302

'I was in Paris,' said Julie.

'*Mon Dieu!* And Paris was not all. What we suffered! All through France there was the bloody massacre. Dijon, Rouen, Saumur, Angers, Blois. The bodies lay piled one on the other in every town in France. But we in Bayonne, Madame, we were slow to follow. We said we would not put the Huguenots to the sword until we had express orders from the King to do so. Nor should we have done so had not a Jesuit priest – like yourself, Monsieur – come expressly to us to tell us that it was St Michael himself who ordered us to do so. We must obey St Michael, but it was with misgiving that we did so. And did you hear, Messieurs, Madame, of the ravens which flew about the Palace of the Louvre for so many hours . . . cawing . . . resting on the ledges, throwing themselves against the windows? It was said that they were the souls of the slaughtered ones.'

Julie shivered. 'I pray you,' she said. 'Do not speak of it.'

'And will it happen again, think you?' asked the woman. 'How do we know? There is trouble in France. In Béarn the Catholics are despised. In Rochelle it is the same. In Paris the Catholics reign. Messieurs, Madame, we are a nation divided against itself.'

'That is most unhappy,' said Blasco. 'Now may we eat? We are hungry after our journey.'

When they were alone, Blasco said: 'How much longer will these troubles last? Is there to be strife for ever throughout the world because people wish to worship God in different ways?'

Domingo looked at him sadly. 'Blasco, there was so much you never understood. There is only one truth, only one road to the Kingdom of Heaven.'

'He is right,' said Julie. 'There is only one – and it is not his!'

They returned to their rooms, for it was true that they were worn out with the journey; but Blasco could not rest. It seemed to him that Pierre came between him and peace. It was as though Pierre were reminding him that he had promised to look after Julie, and that he was preparing to leave her in a land which was almost as dangerous to her as Spain.

He went down and sought the innkeeper's wife.

She was not averse to a little talk, and she looked tolerably handsome in the dim candlelight, with the red flower in her hair and the black lace head-dress.

'Monsieur travels in strange company,' she said coquettishly. 'A priest and a woman! Strange company, indeed!'

'Yes,' he said, 'we are strange companions.'

'The lady is French. And from these parts. I knew at once that she came from the south. I knew too that she was a Huguenot.'

'Is it so obvious?'

'To us who see many of them, yes. Ah, Monsieur, she has come from abroad back to her home; that is so, is it not? She would have done better to have stayed where she was. France is no place for Huguenots these days.'

'Why do you say that?'

She came and sat at the table. She was inviting him to talk of other things, her own charms, for instance, which he was prepared to admit existed – by candlelight. Fourteen years ago he would have acted differently. At that time he would have taken what was offered, and passed gaily on.

Now he was beset with responsibilities. He could not stop thinking of Pierre, for the young and earnest men whom he had seen on the way reminded him of Pierre.

'It is nothing but war following war in France,' she said. 'And when it is not one civil war it is the small wars. And the King of

Navarre, he sets new fashions. He has forgotten, it would seem, that many of his friends were massacred on that tragic night. He comes back to his kingdom, and his bride is with him – ah, La Reine Margot – she sets the Huguenots by the ears with her wigs and flaunting gowns and her lovers. One after another, Monsieur. There was never one like our Margot, and it is said she still has a craving for Monsieur de Guise. And now there is this League – the Catholic League, at the head of which Monsieur de Guise has set himself. We know what that means. It means that at any time there may be another St Bartholomew. Ah, these gloomy things we speak of! There are happier things, eh? Will Monsieur drink a glass of wine with me?'

He sat drinking wine. He told her she was beautiful; he paid the compliments expected of a Spanish courtier, and all the time he was making up his mind. He could not leave Julie in France. She must go with him to England.

❧ ❧ ❧

Fearful memories returned to them as they rode into Paris. Julie held her head high, and colour burned in her cheeks. Neither could bear to look at those streets in which they had seen such cruel sights.

'Let us see if the old inn is still there,' said Blasco, when Domingo had left them to go to the college where he had been told to report, and Julie nodded.

The innkeeper was still there. He remembered them at once and tears of emotion appeared in his eyes. He said they must have the best room and that he must set his cooks to cook a special meal.

They would have the old room, said Blasco, and the innkeeper nodded sagely, believing he understood.

305

It was theirs and no others'. By the blessings of the saints it was vacant, but it should have been theirs no matter who had occupied it. Even if La Reine Margot had engaged it as a cosy place to entertain a lover, still they should have had it.

So they were in the room together; and they were as close as they had been during those tortured days and nights. Julie told him then that she was sorry that their life together had not been happier. She cried a little for Luis. 'For I fear,' she said, 'I shall never see him again. I fear that I have thrown him to the devil to save myself.'

He soothed her; he told her that his mother, for all her seeming harshness, was a good woman. She had taken the child because she believed she had been right in doing so. They would have another child ere long; that child should be born in England, and England was a Protestant country. If she would promise not to grieve for Luis, he would promise that he would never interfere with the upbringing of the child who was yet to be born.

She wept and clung to him. And when he slept he dreamed that Pierre was with them in the room, well pleased.

※　※　※

Domingo came to the inn next day. He said that he wished Blasco to accompany him to the house of a friend where there was business to discuss.

Julie stayed behind at the inn.

When they were in the street Domingo said: 'We are going to the residence of the King's ambassador in France, Don Bernadino de Mendoza. He has something to say to us.'

'To both of us?'

'Yes. From now on, you are engaged in this matter even as I am.'

They had come to a tall house, and on entering were taken to a room where the ambassador was waiting for them. He greeted them with warmth and spoke to them in low and earnest tones.

'I am glad to see you here. I have had news of your coming. You will have many to help you in your task. All is going according to plan, and we have the greatest hopes of success. I have asked you to come here that I may assure you that, when you obey the orders of those to whom we shall send you, although they be Englishmen they are our friends and their orders come direct from His Most Catholic Majesty.'

'Yes, Your Excellency,' said Domingo.

'Señor Carramadino, when you go from here, which you will do in exactly five minutes from now, call at the inn at the corner of the Rue St Paul. There you will be greeted by a man whose name is Charles Monk. He is an Englishman. He will speak to you, of casual things, and you will appear friendly. You will tell him that you are a stranger to Paris, and he will offer to direct you to your inn. When you arrive there you will give him hospitality, asking your landlord for a room in which you can be undisturbed. Your brother, Father Carramadino, will meet you there later. And, Father, it would be as well if you did not wear your priest's robes from now on. I would warn you now that the English have their spies everywhere, and they are suspicious of all Jesuits. Therefore it would be wise if all communication with Charles Monk in France takes place through you, Señor Carramadino, and not through your brother.'

'I begin to see of what use I may be,' said Blasco with a smile. 'I have been wondering.'

'You will do great service to His Majesty, I doubt not.

There is little else I have to say to you. I wished to see you in order to impress on your minds the importance of this enterprise, and that you might understand that it has the approval of many in high places. You came together. Perhaps it would be better if you left separately. And — make your way out of Paris as soon as possible. The sooner you are safely in England, the better for us all.'

They took their leave, and Blasco left the house first.

He made his way to the tavern mentioned, in the Rue St Paul, and it was not long before a man with a merry face, a pug nose and wide-set blue eyes was jogging his elbow, apologising for upsetting his wine, offering to get more and informing him most casually that he was an Englishman whose name was Charles Monk.

PART FIVE

LONDON
1586

⚘ Chapter V ⚘

LONDON, 1586

They arrived on the coast of England feeling battered and exhausted for the crossing had been a boisterous one in the small ship which, Charles Monk assured them, it was necessary for them to use. It was necessary also to land after dark for, although the spot to which they were taken was isolated, it was very important that they should not be seen landing.

It was Charles Monk who kept their spirits high during the perilous voyage. Domingo had found it difficult to understand his speech in the first place. It was unlike that which he had learned during the last years, for Monk's tongue was that of the London streets. Blasco seemed to understand the merry man as easily as Domingo, although Blasco's English was poor in comparison with that of his brother. Even Julie fell under the spell of Charles Monk – Charlie as he called himself – who seemed to make it one of his especial duties to bring a smile to her face.

He was, he told them, in the service of a gentleman who had a large house in the village of Chelsea not very far from the City of London. It was to this house that he was taking them.

'Ah, my lady and gentlemen,' he told them, 'there'll be a ready welcome for you there. They're eagerly awaiting the arrival of the Father here. You'll be made comfortable, sir, in my master's house, you will. Charlie tells you that, and Charlie well knows what he's talking of!'

His master, he told them at another time, was a schismatic, a gentleman who was at heart a Catholic, but who for reasons of expediency attended the Protestant church.

'Ah, my lady and gentlemen, a man with a family, such as my master, Sir Eric Aldersly, has to consider his family. There is his lady, who wavers. She likes to hear her husband talk, but she is not yet won over. That will be your first task, Father – to win her for the Faith.'

Blasco asked questions about the house to which they were going.

'It's a sweet place, master,' said Monk, 'a sweet house indeed. Why, I've been with my master these two years and more. He chose me because of my Faith. He wants to have as many of us in the house as possible. He's dead set on the mistress's conversion.'

Blasco said: 'What of my presence in the house?'

'Lord bless you, sir, my master would be ready to welcome any servant of the Father's.'

'And my wife?'

Monk shook his head. 'Now that's a different matter. It wouldn't do for the lady to be in the house. I've listened to her talk, and though I don't speak the language as well as I'd like to, there's a look in her eyes that tells me she's all for this heresy. The master won't want such opinions aired in his house, you see.'

'I should have to be with her,' said Blasco quickly.

'Now what if I could assure you she was being well looked after, eh? I know of a family in the village of Kensington. They're like her. She might be one of them. Just the same way of holding their heads, just the same look in their eyes and the same way of talking. They got out of France in '72. Came here. Oh, there was lots of them and a good welcome they got from our Queen and country. What tales they had to tell, and how the people lapped 'em up! They settled here – some of 'em in London and round about. Quiet, industrious people they were. All they wanted to do was their weaving or their lace making – just to give them a living – and to be able to say their prayers quietly. Our Queen was all for helping them, and she did.'

'They were Huguenots?' said Blasco.

Monk nodded and winked. 'Now I'd say that if I could find one of these families to take her in . . . We'll let on that she's a Huguenot who can't stand living in France no more. They'll take her in, giving her board and lodging for a trifle, and teach her their trade. When she's had the baby . . . well then, sir, you can look after her. We wouldn't want the little 'un to be brought up in the dark, would we? As for the lady, no amount of preaching would save her soul, I fear. She's one for the devil.'

Blasco said: 'I'll think about it. I will consult her wishes.'

So when they landed on that dark night Blasco was uneasy. He realised that in the haste to get Julie out of Spain, in his determination not to leave her in France, he had failed to consider what difficulties might await him in England.

The dinghy, in which they had been brought ashore from the ship, struck the sandy beach and Monk leaped out. He was smiling. Nothing seemed to disturb his merry humour.

'That's it, sir. Now, lady. You're safe enough. Ah, worn out by that rough crossing, eh? Now you're on dry land . . . the soil of old England.'

He gave a loud call in imitation of the hoot of an owl. The call was answered by a similar one.

'We'll get the books and your bits of things out of the boat,' said Monk. 'Then Jacques here can row back to the ship.'

'How can we carry all those things?'

Monk touched his nose slyly. 'Leave it to Charlie,' he said.

And before they had finished taking the things from the dinghy they heard the sound of horses approaching. Two men emerged from the shadowy night and stood at some little distance from the party.

'Leave everything there,' said Monk, 'and follow me.'

He led them over to the pair.

'You've got horses for the lady and gentlemen?' said Monk. 'Ah, I see, and pack horses for the books and robes and baggage. Good men!'

'You're late, Charlie,' said one of the men. 'We've been waiting here at this hour the last two nights.'

'Oh, the sea's unaccountable,' said Monk with a laugh. 'She even plays tricks on Charlie. Get the baggage loaded as quick as you can and get it clear of this place.'

'It shall be done,' said the man.

'And be quick,' said Monk. 'If any see you . . . ride for all you're worth. Don't let any of the books fall into the hands they're not intended for.'

They rode away from the sea, and, after a journey of half an hour or so, they came to a lonely house well hidden among the trees, and there they were given a warm welcome, hot food and beds for the night.

🌿 🌿 🌿

They stayed that night and the next day at the house near the coast and the next night they travelled north towards London. Monk rode beside Blasco.

'As I told you,' he said, 'I can't take the lady to my master's house. If she had seen the light it would be another matter. She hasn't, poor lost soul, and like all those who are lost she seeks to drag others down to perdition with her. Won't do! Are we going to watch other lost souls sliding down to perdition?'

Blasco had never heard anyone talk so merrily of those things. Catholics, Huguenots, had all been so serious in their discourse. Charles Monk made the path to damnation sound like a merry skating party.

Charles went on: 'I would say that the lady should be put safely in the care of those Huguenots. There she will be at peace, and so shall we. She is your wife, sir, and she loves you well; and when a woman loves mayhap it is safe to trust her – in most things. But these heretics, sir, there is a fierceness about them, and you cannot be sure when their heresy will become the most important thing in their lives for which they are prepared to sacrifice all. Charlie has met that sort.'

Blasco was silent. He was thinking of his mother as she had stood in the candlelit bedchamber demanding Luis.

'You'll feel safer, sir. See?' said Monk. 'There are searches made in the houses of the schismatics, and many of them are known to the Queen's searchers. These pursuivants will tear a house to pieces if they suspect a priest to be hiding there. And what do they do when they've found them? Take them off to the Counter in the Poultry or the Clink just by Blackfriars, and there they have to answer for themselves. They wouldn't take into consideration, sir, that one of the suspects was a woman, and a woman with child. Oh, dear me, no, sir. Whereas in that quiet little house, busy with her lace or her weaving, taking little walks, praying with her friends, she'd be as safe as Charlie could make her. The Queen's got a soft spot for the

Huguenots. Industrious, quiet, good citizens, she calls them; and they worship in the way she likes her subjects to, and she feels pleased because she can snap her fingers at old Philip – I mean great Philip, you understand – across the sea there. And that's one of the old lady's favourite tricks, snapping her fingers at King Philip. She's full of scorn for His Most Catholic Majesty, I might tell you. And the reason? Charlie could tell you. She's afraid of him, she's frightened to the marrow. Got it on her mind, they say, that one day he'll come over here with his Inquisition – the Holy Office, I mean – and set it up and make true Christians of her people. She's got some notion that he's building ships, big ships – bigger ships have never been seen before – and what for, the old lady wants to know. To come after me and my subjects, she tells herself. You've been recently in Spain, sir. Would there be any truth in all this talk of ships being built?'

'Aye, there's truth in it,' said Blasco. 'I've seen the work that goes on in our harbours. In Cadiz – not very far from my home – they have been working hard for months. They work by the light of cressets when it's dark . . . day and night they work.'

Monk nodded and winked. 'Ah, it won't be long then, you reckon. One day great Philip will purge this land of every single heretic, eh? And what fate has he in store for the old lady? A not very happy one, I'll warrant.' That seemed to amuse Monk. He went off into roars of laughter.

Blasco said: 'And my wife? You can assure me that this house to which you propose to take her is all that you say it is?'

'You know these Huguenots, sir. Quiet, sober folk, thinking of nothing but their industry and their prayers. She'll be one of 'em, sir; and we can't risk having her near us with the things we have to talk about. Couldn't find a safer spot on earth!'

316

'What if there was a rising here . . . a rising such as there was in Paris?'

'The Bloody Bartholomew, sir? Why, Lord bless you, it couldn't happen here in London. More like to be the other way round. It's the Catholics who have to take care in England. The gentlemen who surround the Queen see to that. As to the old lady, I don't think she minds 'em . . . Catholic or Protestant. She's a heretic all right. But that's to please her friends, Master Leicester, Master Walsingham, Master Cecil – or Burleigh as he calls himself now.' Monk screwed up his face in an expression of mock respect. 'But the old lady, all she wants is to live in peace, to have the people shout to her in the streets that she's the best Queen in the world, while the gentlemen about her tell her she's the most beautiful. The old lady would smile on a Catholic if he did that. Believe me, she's all for peace and flattery!'

'I think,' said Blasco, 'that you are right. I think my wife should be living a peaceful life with her own people.'

So Julie had gone to the Huguenot family of lace-makers in Kensington and, through the following night, Domingo and Blasco with Charles Monk to guide them, set out for the home of Monk's master in Chelsea. The stars were bright in the sky that night. They could smell the river and feel the damp from it as they approached the house.

'A good place this,' Monk told them. 'We can leave the house by water or by road. See, the river flows at the bottom of the garden.'

It was too dark to see the house clearly, but they were aware of pleasant gardens, a large building with gables – the home of a man of substance.

Charlie said: 'This way to the stables.' And he led the way.

The door of the house was opened and a man hurried out to

greet them. He was tall, grey-haired and his beard showed a glistening silver in the dim light.

'Welcome, Father, welcome,' he said; and it was Blasco's hand he seized.

Blasco said in his slow uncertain English: 'It is my brother who is Father Carramadino.'

'You are welcome none the less,' said the man, and turned to Domingo. 'Father, I have long waited for this.'

'Bless you, my son,' said Domingo. 'I have heard much of you from your faithful servant, and it is with great pleasure that I enter your house.'

'It is brave of you to come to this land of ours, Father.'

'It is our duty to come, my son,' said Domingo.

Monk had joined them. 'Now, sir,' he said, 'better get inside. No whispering out of doors to attract the servants, eh?'

'You are right, Charlie,' said Sir Eric Aldersly. 'What we should do without you, Charlie, I cannot imagine.'

'You can always trust Charlie, sir.'

'This good man of mine,' said Sir Eric, laying his hand on Monk's arm, 'has risked much for the Faith. He has been with me but two years, and during that time he has well proved his worth.'

Charlie was clearly delighted with the compliments.

'Now,' said Sir Eric, 'we will show Father Carramadino to the room we have prepared for him. It is not the best room in the house which I should have liked you to have, Father. But there is a reason why you should have this one. It is apart from the others and there is no access from any other room. Charles, bring candles and light them. I will conduct our friends to their room. Then bring refreshment also, Charlie, and join us.' He turned to Blasco and Domingo. 'As you will know, Charlie is no

318

ordinary serving-man. He is a trusted friend. He has shown me good service and made it possible for me to do much which, without him, would have been impossible. But I pray you come in. My family is asleep now. I shall tell them of your arrival in the morning. In the meantime let us make as little noise as possible.'

He took them into the hall which was dimly lighted by a candle or two, and they mounted a staircase at the top of which was a gallery with several doors. He opened one of the doors and they found themselves in a small chamber, the walls of which were panelled, and the floor covered with a carpet. There were bookshelves, a table and several stools.

'Pray sit here,' said their host, 'and Charlie will bring you food and drink. I have been waiting these several nights to receive you. Through this door is the room where you will sleep. You see that there is no way of entry to it except through this door. No one can enter the bedchamber except through this room. There are two small beds in there, one for each of you. But before we talk I will show what preparation I have made for you and the priests who stay here. But you must be worn out. I pray you, sit down, and when you have refreshed yourselves I will show you the hole I have made in this room. But that shall be when we are alone, for not even Charlie knows of its existence. I trust him. He is one of us. But he is an open and honest fellow, and it might be that were the house searched, he would betray us by a gesture or glance – perhaps of anxiety that there was something to hide in this room; and then those men would tear apart every floor and wall until they found what they sought.'

Charlie came in with meat pies, cakes and ale, cider, perry and methyglin.

He set it all out on the table, talking as he did so. 'Did I not tell you gentlemen that you would find a right good welcome at this house? Did I not tell you, eh? My master's store-cupboard is always full of good food. Ah! But it makes the mouth water to see food such as I dreamed of these last weeks while I have been away from home.'

'Charlie is a true man of London,' said Sir Eric. 'He pines for home when he is obliged to leave it. Come, Charlie, draw up and eat with us. You are one of us tonight. You have done good work, and there is still more dangerous and difficult work to be done.'

Domingo said: 'There is a chapel attached to this house?'

'Oh yes, we have our chapel. I must tell you, Father, that my family are not all of the Faith. My son has a place at Court and rarely comes home. When he does he must know you as plain Señor Carramadino, a merchant travelling in England for business reasons. These little subterfuges are necessary. My wife and daughter are both wavering; they cannot bring themselves to renounce the orthodox faith of this country. But I trust, Father, that you will bring forward such arguments that they will be unable to resist them.'

'That is what I am here for,' said Domingo.

'I trust that you will be able to stay with us for a long time.'

Charlie said: 'Well, sir, once he has brought the ladies to the light, it'll be his duty to pass on and save other souls.'

'That's so, my son,' said Domingo.

'In the morning I shall show you the Chapel. We have some rich and beautiful vestments and such articles as you will require such as wafer irons for making altar bread.'

'I rejoice to hear it,' said Domingo.

Blasco said: 'Do many in the household hear Mass?'

'Oh no. It will have to be conducted in some secrecy. I want my wife and daughter to attend the ceremony. I am sure that, now we have a priest in the house, it will not be long before they will most willingly join us.'

Sir Eric went on then to describe the house. 'It was built by my father some twenty years ago. There are many rooms on this floor. You noticed the gallery mayhap as we came up. There is the big chamber into which all the bedrooms, except this one and the adjoining chamber, lead. You will be in complete privacy here, and that is how you would wish it, I have no doubt. Your books and vestments arrived here yesterday, and I have had them put out in the next room. I trust you will be most comfortable here.'

'We'll see to that, sir,' said Charlie. 'We want the Father and his brother – I mean his servant – to be comfortable while he is with us.'

While they ate, Sir Eric talked to his guests of the new decree which declared it to be high treason for a Jesuit to be discovered in England.

'You run great risks in coming here, Father,' said Sir Eric. 'You are brave men, you priests who leave the security of your native land to come to us. There are many Jesuits here – Englishmen who have heard the call, who have gone to Spain and France to study and have returned here to do the work for which they feel themselves to be fitted. But that is different. Although they run the same risks, they are English and owe a duty to their countrymen. But you who are not English . . . to come here . . . That is a brave act to which I would do homage.'

'Do not speak of our bravery,' said Domingo quickly, 'until you are certain that we possess it.'

'But, Father, how can you say such a thing?' said Sir Eric. 'You know what dangers you face, and yet you have come among us.'

Blasco was watching his brother intently. Domingo had turned pale, as he went on: 'It does not require a great deal of courage to sail across the sea, to journey thus to a friend's house. The test will come if I am called upon to stand before my enemies as their prisoner.'

'It may never come,' said Blasco quickly. 'It need not, if we are careful.'

'Oh, the Father will face it bravely when it comes,' said Charlie. 'All Fathers do. They've got the Faith to help them. I believe it rarely fails.'

Charlie was chuckling as he drained his goblet.

'It will be necessary to go carefully, very carefully indeed,' said Sir Eric. 'But you are tired. You have eaten, I trust, to your satisfaction, and you should go to your rest. Charlie, take away the remains of the food and I will conduct our guests to their bedchamber.'

He took them through the connecting door and showed them the cabinet in which he had placed the books which had arrived before them. Here in the drawers were Domingo's *soutane* and his *biretta*. Here, too, were surplices, the chalice, wafer irons and such articles as he would need for Mass.

Sir Eric went to the door and opening it looked into the room they had left.

'Charlie has now gone,' he said. 'A good servant, but, as I say, we must not forget that he is but a servant, and as such may have less control over his demeanour. Come through with me and I will show you how solicitous I am for your safety.'

They followed him into the room in which they had eaten. He went to the door and bolted it.

'Now,' he said, 'I can show you that which will be known to none other in the house but myself and you two.' He went to the wall and, pressing firmly on one of the panels, moved it slowly aside.

'A hole!' said Blasco.

'A priest's hole,' said Sir Eric with pride. 'There is room in here for several people to hide. It is necessary to bend slightly, for it was not possible to make the hole as high as I would have wished. You see, the whole point is that its existence must on no account be betrayed to people who are looking for it. In almost every Catholic house throughout this country these holes are being made; and rightly so, for how could we ask you brave gentlemen to stay with us if you were in constant fear of the terrible death which would be yours if you were caught?'

Blasco did not look at Domingo. He was keenly aware of his brother's emotions. Domingo's imagination was too vivid. Blasco knew that at this moment his brother felt he was already on the hurdle being dragged along to the scaffold.

'Pray step inside,' said Sir Eric, 'and you will see for yourself that, although it may not be comfortable, it is adequate. And you can slide back the panel from the other side as neatly as you can from this. I had put some food in there, but the mice took most of it. However, I have secreted away some bottles of quince juice and some ale so that, should the pursuivants come to this house and you be forced to remain there for any length of time, you would not go without sustenance altogether. Is it not a neat contrivance? I pray you, try it for yourself.'

Blasco did so. He knew that Domingo was trembling too much to work the panel. Blasco's one desire now was to prevent Sir Eric from noticing his brother's fear. This was how he had protected Domingo in the days of their childhood; and it was for this reason that he had come to England with him.

'It will be excellent for the Father and myself if it is needed,' said Blasco.

Sir Eric seemed a little disappointed at Domingo's lack of admiration.

'My brother is sad that such a device should be necessary,' said Blasco.

'I learned how it was done from a friend of mine,' went on Sir Eric. 'He has a house in Kent. He made the place himself and then did this for me. You see, it is a safe secret.'

'Let us hope,' said Blasco, 'that it will never be necessary to use it.'

'Amen,' said Sir Eric. 'But they say the Counter and the Clink are full of Jesuits and Papist priests.'

'Awaiting . . . death?' murmured Domingo.

'Oh no, they don't all suffer death. Elizabeth is all for tolerance. She hates an execution, they say. She's never sure how the people are going to take it. She likes to play the loving sovereign. She would never execute our priests but for the fact that some of her ministers have set the rumours abroad that they are agents of the King of Spain, come over to plot against her.'

Domingo was visibly shivering.

'My brother is very tired,' said Blasco. 'I think he needs sleep. The journey was rough and we were long at sea.'

'Forgive me. I keep you from your rest. I hope you will find all to your satisfaction. I shall leave you now. Sleep as long as you like. Charlie shall wait on you, and Charlie only. I shall tell the household that you are a merchant from abroad and his servant, to whom I am offering hospitality. We might say that you are a wine merchant. And if any ask questions which you prefer not to answer it will always be possible to pretend that you do not understand.'

He laughed, bade them good night and left them.

Blasco looked about the room in which they were to sleep, and yawned.

'I could sleep for days and nights, I am sure,' he said.

Domingo was silent.

Blasco laid a hand on his brother's shoulder.

'All will be well,' he said. 'What a quiet house this is! We'll bolt the door and we'll be safe. We have our little hole should any come disturbing us. Forget it not.'

'You are right,' said Domingo.

Each lay still, listening. Nor did they speak. Both were trying to pretend that they were fast asleep. But Domingo was thinking of the future, and Blasco was thinking of Domingo.

A few days passed in the house in Chelsea. It was June, and the gardens were beautiful. Peacocks strutted in the sun and the little dogs in whom the family delighted played about the lawns. White butterflies danced above the flower-beds and the bees were busy on the lavender bushes.

The peace in these gardens, thought Domingo, is like that of a monastery cell.

Who could have believed that danger lurked behind the gables of the charming house, from which he could now hear the laughter of one of the serving-maids in the pantry on the lower floor, as she exchanged banter with one of the men-servants. There flowed the river at the end of the garden with the privy steps leading down to the water. All day the barges floated by; sometimes there was music coming from them. Often the river danced in the sunshine, and now and then it was overhung by a grey mist which turned blue as the twilight touched it.

I could be happy here, thought Domingo. Here seemingly there is perfect peace.

But he knew that he must be ever alert, that if a barge should slow down as it came towards the privy steps, then he must make for his room with all speed; he must slide open the panel and get into the hole.

He thought regretfully of the life he might have had. He loved the quiet family life, the sound of young voices, the good table, Sir Eric's booming laughter, his wife's gentle manners. He was winning Lady Aldersly. She was veering towards the Faith. She liked to sit in the garden with him, talking. She knew, of course, that he was a priest, but she never mentioned this fact. Like himself she was afraid, since it was a crime in England to harbour a Jesuit priest.

Now he heard footsteps and felt the familiar hammering of his heart, the sweat trickling down his back. But it was only Blasco.

'A beautiful day,' said Blasco. 'This is a beautiful country. What a warm benevolent sun! It does not scorch you. You let it play upon you here. You do not have to find a place in the shade.'

'They say it is not always kind, and often hides itself for long periods in the winter.'

They both thought of the England they had imagined. Domingo had thought of a land where cruel pirates abounded. Blasco had thought of a land which contained Bianca.

'So it was to this country that they came,' said Blasco. 'Isabella and Bianca! I wonder if they looked on that river.'

'So you still think of them, Blasco?'

'Aye,' said Blasco, 'I still think of them. I have asked many if they ever heard of a pirate named Mash, but no one has.'

'It is so long ago now, Blasco. It might be that it would be better if we never found them again.'

'I cannot accept that point of view, Domingo. I shall continue to enquire. If they are to be found, I shall find them.'

'If it be God's will, Blasco.' Domingo turned to his brother. 'Blasco, I once had a dream. I dreamed that I would come to England, find Isabella, and take her back that she might spend the rest of her days in a convent. I thought that there was some purpose in everything that happened, that Isabella had a cross to carry, as I had.'

'Like Julie you talk of crosses. Should we not look for happiness in place of these crosses?'

'We are not here to be happy.'

'I am not sure of that. If God created happiness and pleasure, was it not for man to enjoy? Perhaps we should seek to bring that happiness, that pleasure, to our fellows, Domingo. Perhaps that is the purpose.'

'We are here to worship God.'

'Does He want worship? Who are we to praise Him? Surely He does not want our fulsome flattery. It may be that all that is expected of us is to love each other, to bring pleasure to each other, pleasure and happiness. Man is God's work. Let us love and help one another. That is what our Lord Jesus said was the greatest commandment.'

'Brother, you say strange things.'

'I talk as I feel, without thinking. It may be that I like to hear my own voice. Here comes Charlie. He looks secretive. The fellow has something to say, and it is for our ears alone, I'll warrant.'

Charlie's somewhat comic face expanded in a wide grin.

'Ah, gentlemen, I am glad to find you together. That is good. I must speak with you. I have had orders that we are to go to the house of a Catholic gentleman in the City who has heard of your arrival and greatly desires to meet you. Gentlemen, this evening I will take you to him.'

'Is Sir Eric to accompany us?'

'No, gentlemen, no. He is to know nothing of this as yet. If he should ask where you are going, tell him that you have had orders from the Superior of the Society to visit certain members of the Society who are in London. That will suffice. He will ask no more questions. Be ready at dusk, gentlemen, and we will ride towards the city. I shall be waiting for you in the stables with your horses.'

'We shall be there,' said Blasco.

Charlie gave them his familiar nod and hurried off. Blasco and Domingo stood where they were, looking at the river. The sound of a young girl's laughter from the kitchen quarters floated towards them; someone on a passing barge was playing a lute. The sun was warm and benevolent; the butterflies danced and the bees were working on the lavender; but the peace of the afternoon had been destroyed.

🌹 🌹 🌹

It was not quite dark when they rode towards the city.

Ahead of them lay the houses with their gardens which ran down to the river; beyond these were the towers and steeples of the city itself, the huddle of houses and there, dominating the twilight scene, stood the great grey fortress, its weather-washed towers grim and forbidding, guarding the city, threatening death to the Queen's enemies.

Charlie led them away from the river. They crossed the Fleet bridge, entered a maze of narrow streets and eventually came to St Martin's Lane, thence proceeding through Aldersgate Street to Long Lane and Barbican.

Here before a house they halted. Two men came to take their horses as they dismounted.

They were then conducted into the house, where a young man in his middle twenties, handsome, richly dressed, vivacious and clearly pleased to see them, extended a very warm welcome.

'My friends, you are late,' said the man. 'I feared something might have happened to detain you. But come along in. My friends are eager to make your acquaintance.'

He led them out of the main hall into a small room which he called the winter parlour. There, ranged about a table, on which food and wine were set out, were some seven or eight men dressed similarly to himself. The man who had first welcomed them made the introductions.

'My name is Babington, Anthony Babington. These are my friends: Charles Tilney, Edward Abingdon, Edward Jones, John Charnock, Jerome Bellamy, John Travers, Robert Gage and John Savage. We are all gathered here to perfect our arrangements for the great plan, the Holy Enterprise. Come, drink with us, and then we will talk of what must be done. Come, John there, fill glasses for our friends from Spain.'

The glasses were filled as Blasco and Domingo took their places at the table.

Babington rose. 'To the true Queen of England!' he cried. 'To Queen Mary, now wrongfully held the prisoner of the Bastard at Chartley!'

'To Queen Mary!' echoed those about the table.

'To the Holy Enterprise!' cried Babington, when they had drunk the first toast.

And afterwards another was drunk: 'To our new friends and all those friends of ours across the seas who have done so much to make this venture possible!'

When the toasts had been drunk they sat down, and Babington began to speak.

'My friends, you may not as yet have heard details of our plans. We have had news from Spain that you would come to help further our Enterprise. All goes well. There are many in sympathy with us, I rejoice to say, and we can be sure of their rallying to our aid once we declare ourselves ready to strike. I do not know how much you have been told by those from whom you come and who, from their high places, have given their blessing to our enterprise. But we trust you. Charlie Monk is one in whom we have learned, through long experience, to put our trust. My friends, how much of this matter have you learned?'

'Little as yet.' Charlie spoke for them. 'It was considered well, sir, that you should be the first to put before them the plans of the Holy Enterprise. Father Carramadino speaks good English and his brother, who comes on instructions from the King of Spain himself, speaks less well. But if you will tell them in simple words what the plan is, sir, they will understand.'

'I see. I see. We are indeed grateful to your King and country, gentlemen. Without the backing of the King of Spain we should feel less happy in what we are about to do. Once the Bastard Elizabeth is dead and her ministers either imprisoned or dead themselves, he has promised all the aid we shall need. Money and troops will be at our disposal.'

'We cannot fail,' cried he who had been introduced as John Savage. 'I, as one who has served in the army, tell you this. Destroy the Queen and those men who are constantly about her – her chief ministers who uphold her in her heresy – and England is ours to hand over to our lawful Queen Mary.'

'It cannot fail,' said Babington. 'Now I will briefly acquaint you gentlemen with what has gone so far. The assassination of

Elizabeth is to be performed by some among us who already have instructions. Walsingham, Burleigh and Leicester will then be seized. If they should resist capture and be killed in the attempt, so much the better. Once this has been effected, all shipping in the Thames will then be seized. Within a matter of hours we shall be in command of London – and when London is safe, gentlemen, the rest of England will follow.' He looked significantly at the company. 'I have had a letter from Queen Mary.'

There was silence round the table.

Blasco was looking at Domingo, who could understand so much more of the conversation than he could. Domingo was pale. His eyes were half closed, but Blasco knew he was tense, and that the blank expression on his brother's face veiled his fear. Blasco was torn with pity.

One of the conspirators broke the silence. 'So Queen Mary has actually written in her own hand?'

'In her own hand,' said Babington. 'There is no mistake about it. I have the letter here.'

'But how was it possible to send such a letter from the stronghold of Chartley? Is she not closely guarded?'

'We have been ingenious, my friend,' said Babington. 'We could not, of course, send our letters to the Queen by ordinary routes. We have done this by means of the barrels of beer which have been taken into Chartley full and brought out empty. Good Gilbert Gifford, our staunch friend and supporter, has been most helpful. He secured the friendship of the brewer – himself a good friend to Queen Mary. He had the idea of making a corked tube which could be put through the bung-hole into the barrel of beer. Inside the tube were our letters to the Queen; and, when the barrels came out empty, inside the same tube were her replies to us. Thus she has been kept well informed of all that we plan; and, my friends, I rejoice to tell you that we have her approval. I have informed her that ere long she will be free and Queen, not only of the Scots, but of the English, as is her right. The Holy Catholic Faith will be restored to our country, and heretics persuaded, as they are persuaded in the country of our friends here, to come to the true Faith. I will show you Her Majesty's letter. It is long, and you may each peruse it at your leisure. You will see that the Queen asks what forces we can raise, and what towns will be open to receive succour from our friends abroad. She enquires what plans we have made for bringing her out of her prison. As you will see, she is most grateful to have such friends. When Mary is on the throne, not only will you rejoice that the true Queen reigns over our country, that the true Faith prevails, but you will grow rich in your honours; for Mary, I must tell you, is not the woman to forget those who were her friends in adversity.'

Blasco had risen. He said: 'I pray you tell me what part my brother and I shall be called upon to play in this.'

'We need supporters,' said Babington. 'We need the entire Catholic community to be ready to rise when the right moment comes. It is necessary to prepare all those gentlemen who could be of use to us. Some of these would be willing to come into the open and fight. Others are more cautious. This is particularly so in the case of the schismatics. They have their families, and they are afraid on their account. It is understandable. Therefore, it is necessary for such as these to be persuaded to give that help which is necessary. Your task is to persuade Catholic gentlemen whose houses you visit to join with us, and to be ready when the moment comes, with all the firearms they possess, in case it should be necessary to use them, and all the

332

men they can muster, ready for action. Father Carramadino will persuade them that this is their duty, and you, Señor, will look to the practical side; you will see that the weapons each house contains are ready for use. To you are left the practical duties. To your brother the spiritual ones.'

'And,' said Domingo, rising and standing with Blasco, 'I understand that the first gentleman whom I must persuade is Sir Eric Aldersly.'

'That is so. His house is in a good position on the river there. When you have made him realise his duty, Charlie will conduct you to the next man's house. He is a Catholic in secret but reluctant to help us on account of his family, and will need to be persuaded. I must tell you that there are many Jesuits in this country at this time who are working with us. When we are successful we shall have other tasks for you. You can see that in a society such as ours there will be much work to be done. The English are a stubborn people, as you may have noticed. They are not over-zealous in their religion, but once try to change their opinions and they'll cling with all their might to old ideas. It is a national trait. They say they will not be driven. Gentlemen, if we are successful, there will be some who *must* be driven.'

Charlie, who had been standing in the background, coming forward now and then to fill the glasses, said: 'And we shall do it. King Philip is ready, waiting for the day. These gentlemen from Spain have seen the great work that is going on in Spanish harbours. They'll give you gentlemen all the details you want, I doubt not, if you ask them.'

'This is wonderful news,' said Babington.

He questioned them as to the ships which were being built.

'As we passed through coast towns on our way north, we

saw men at work,' said Domingo. 'We saw great galleons in the process of construction. They were bigger than anything I ever saw before.'

'They will come to our aid, the minute Elizabeth's head is severed from her shoulders, and we have those ministers of hers powerless,' cried Babington. 'They will come, with their priests and the Holy Inquisition. In a few years England will be as Catholic as Spain.'

Charles Tilney said: 'It is true, I believe, that Queen Mary's relations, the powerful Guises, are waiting to spring.'

' 'Tis true indeed,' said Babington. 'Gentlemen, success beckons us. In a few short weeks we shall be meeting here to congratulate ourselves on bringing the Holy Enterprise to a satisfactory conclusion. We shall no longer be insignificant gentlemen of England. The whole world will be ringing with our names. Come, let us once more drink the toast to the Holy Enterprise, and then let us go to Fetter Lane and hear Mass. Our new friend, Father Carramadino, will officiate. Come, my friends. To the Holy Enterprise! We stand together, one and all, and we cannot fail, gentlemen. We cannot fail.'

It was a few days later – a quiet afternoon. Domingo sat in the room which had been set apart for them. On the table before him were his books, and he was reading. He was conscious of perfect peace; the sun was shining warmly into the room – comfortingly, and not too hot; through his open window he could hear the sound of the servants' voices; he could hear the splash of oars in the river.

His work was progressing well. Lady Aldersly was being won over to the Faith. In a little while he would go down to the chapel which he had made ready for her. There for the first time she would hear Mass. All the beautiful vestments were laid out there. The altar breads were made, the wine was waiting. All was ready in the locked chapel.

He had talked to Sir Eric of his duty, and Sir Eric was eager that the true Queen should be restored to her throne, but he was afraid of becoming involved in a plot which might fail. There had been many plots, he pointed out, ever since Queen Mary had become Elizabeth's prisoner; and not one of them had succeeded. It had always seemed that Elizabeth was one move ahead of her enemies.

Might this not be, Domingo had argued, because there were many men in England who, in their hearts supporting Mary, were afraid to do so openly. He had talked of Fear, that arch-enemy of many would-be martyrs. It was not Elizabeth's greater cunning which had preserved her and strengthened heresy; it was Fear which had held back those who should have gone forward to establish the truth.

So with Sir Eric wavering on the point of surrender, and Lady Aldersly about to hear Mass this very day, it was clear that Domingo's and Blasco's days in this pleasant house were numbered.

Blasco wandered in the city by day, entering taverns, talking to men who frequented such places. He asked all whom he met whether they had ever heard of a sea-rover, who had raided the coast of Spain and brought a Spanish woman to England. Several had raided the coast of Spain, he was told, but no one had ever heard of a man named Mash or Marsh.

Now Domingo was conscious of footsteps below and the sound of many voices. He started to his feet for he must always be careful when there were strangers in the house; but even as he rose the door was burst open and Blasco hurried into the room.

He whispered: 'The house is being searched. Quick,

Domingo! Quick! Nay, do not stop for anything. They are already in the hall. They will be up the stairs in a few minutes.'

He pressed the panel, pushed Domingo into the hole and was about to close it.

'You too,' stammered Domingo. 'Quickly, Blasco!' Blasco said urgently: 'Impossible. The chapel is prepared. There is not time to hide all the books in this room. They'll know a priest is in the house, and they'll pull down every wall until they find him.'

'Then Blasco . . . you . . .'

Blasco's answer was to pull the panel across and Domingo was alone in darkness. The palms of his hands were sweating. So the moment was at hand. They had come for him. There was possible escape for only one of them, and Blasco had forced him to seize the chance.

But this was ridiculous. It was the priest they were after, and he was the priest. Blasco could easily have escaped. It was Blasco who should have got into the hiding-place. But they must know there was a priest in the house, and Blasco was going to take on the role of priest.

'There is yet time,' a voice whispered within him. 'Open the panel and step out. Force Blasco to hide in your place. One of you must be discovered. You are the priest. It is you whom they seek.'

Then that other voice, the voice he knew so well, the voice to which it was such balm to listen: 'God has arranged this. It is for this reason that He sent Blasco with you. This is God's will. There are many souls for you to save. Blasco is uncertain, wavering in his Faith. Perhaps God has chosen to show him the light through the suffering which will follow his arrest. Stay where you are. God means to preserve you.'

It was like a refreshing drink to a man parched with thirst, food to the hungry, that voice. He took it ravenously. ''Tis true,' he whispered. ''Tis right. God has chosen to preserve me.'

He was on his knees. 'Holy Mother of God, show me the way,' he whispered. 'Show me the way.'

And as he knelt he heard them in the room beyond the wall. He could hear distinctly, for the panel was thin and there was nothing but that between him and his enemies.

A man shouted: 'Here he is! Here is the Jesuit. Seize him.'

Blasco's voice came to him, cold and cool in his English with the Spanish flavour: 'What do you wish of me?'

'He's a foreigner,' said a voice. 'Take him. He's the man we want. You are a priest, are you not?'

'That,' said Blasco, 'is for you to discover.'

Now Domingo could hear the sound of furniture being moved. They must already have discovered the books.

'What is this?'

'It looks like a robe of some sort,' said Blasco.

'A robe? It's a *soutane*. A priest's *soutane*.'

'Since you know what it is, why do you ask me?'

'Come, take him. He'll not be so saucy when we have talked with him awhile. You take those books, and you the *soutane* and *biretta*. We've caught our priest this time. You, fellow, go down to the chapel and fetch all those specimens of idolatry. We shall want them. This was a quick one, eh, my friends? Come, let us be going. No point in staying, since we have found him we sought.'

Domingo, leaning against the panel, straining his ears, heard them moving about the room. They were gathering the books together. This took them ten minutes or so. It seemed like hours to Domingo.

Then there was silence. He was on his knees, praying.

An hour passed; he remained where he was, sick and hurt, loathing himself, longing to live the last two hours of his life over again that he might live them more nobly. What of Blasco? What would they do to Blasco? Would they discover that he was not a priest? Would they come back? He must give himself up.

But for what purpose? So that they should both fall into the hands of their enemies? No, the deed was done. Whatever happened to Blasco, he could do no good by exposing himself to danger. His moment had passed; and he had failed.

Someone had entered the room. Charlie whispered: 'All's well, Father. If you are hiding you may come out now.'

Domingo drew back the panel and stepped out.

Charlie's grin greeted him. 'Well, that was neat enough. So there wasn't time for you both to get in.'

'My brother reminded me that it was clear that a priest was in the house. He insisted . . .'

'Ah, a brave man, Señor Blasco. A very brave man. But listen, Father. They'll soon discover he's not their man. They'll put a few questions to him, and he'll answer in a way no priest would. They've had experience of priests. They'll be back. You must get away from here at once.'

'What of Sir Eric?'

'They've taken him along for questioning.'

'And Lady Aldersly?'

'They have not taken her. Only Sir Eric. They won't keep him long, I'll warrant. You see, it's priests the law is against. The Queen does not care to interfere with her subjects' religion. It's just you priests she won't have about the place. She thinks you come from old Philip – His Most Catholic Majesty, that is – and that is why she's so set against you. It's an offence to harbour priests, but that's not treason. It's you who are the one who's in danger, Father. Now listen. I was ready for this. There's a horse saddled in the stables now. Go down there and ride out . . . as quick as you like. I don't like you being abroad in daylight, but there's no help for it. I'll follow you. We'll meet along by the river, taking the road away from the city. There's a gentleman just beyond Richmond who'll be right glad to give you shelter. Go straight down now, Father. Your horse is ready. Don't wait another minute.'

'Charlie, my son,' said Domingo, 'I thank God for you.'

Domingo took one last look round the room – the scene of my cowardice, he thought.

Blasco must not remain their captive. But of course he would not. Soon their friends would have completed their plans; soon those men who held Blasco prisoner would themselves be prisoners. All would be well. This was God's will. God had tested him.

Now he began to see his cowardice as his love for God. He had thrown away his self-respect because God had commanded him to work for Him. It was the braggarts such as Blasco who could lightheartedly throw away freedom, who could look defiantly into Death's face. This was because they had no Faith. They had never believed that they had been put on earth to do God's work.

He entered the stables. There was the horse ready saddled, as Charlie had said. But as he went to it, two men came out of the shadows, and laid their hands upon him.

'You are Father Carramadino,' they said, and it was a statement, not a question. 'You will leave with us immediately. We have a barge waiting. We are arresting you in the name of Her Majesty the Queen.'

※ ※ ※

As he was rowed to the shore and taken to the Counter in the Poultry, a comfortless prison composed of four houses situated in Bread Street in the parish of St Mildred's, Domingo was like a man in a coma. He was immediately conducted to a room where irons were placed on his legs. They were heavy, and the iron immediately began to cut into his skin.

One of the men who had brought him to the prison told him: 'We know who you are, Father Carramadino, and we determined to bring you here. You will be taken before an examiner, and it would be advisable for you to speak the truth.'

The close air of the place, the fetid atmosphere, made Domingo want to retch. He believed that he was about to face his great test, and he was full of remorse for his cowardice which had been responsible for betraying Blasco. Had they found him, they might have been satisfied to take the priest and Blasco might be safe at this moment. He saw himself now as a wretched coward, for his soothing balm had been snatched from him.

He said: 'Where . . . oh, where is my brother? Where have you taken him?'

'Have no fear, Master Carramadino, your brother is being taken care of.'

There was a grim smile on the man's face, which struck terror into Domingo's heart.

He cried out: 'He has done nothing. It is I who am the priest.'

'He is a wise man, this one,' said one man to another. 'He's going to talk. He's going to make our task easy. Bring him along now. The examiner is waiting.'

He was taken down a flight of stairs to a dank cellar where he saw two men hanging by their arms from the ceiling, their bodies suspended in mid-air. Their faces were the colour of bad cheese and Domingo saw that they were glistening with sweat. One called: 'Have pity! Have pity!' as they passed. The other could only moan.

'Priests!' said one of Domingo's captors. 'Priests who sought to tamper with the Queen's justice. Who came as spies in *soutane* and *biretta*.'

Domingo was shivering. His legs seemed as though they would refuse to carry him. But the men were beside him, jostling him, hurrying him forward.

He was taken up another flight of stairs and into a room where a man was sitting at a table.

Those who had brought him thither stood on either side of him, led him to the table, and halted there.

He who was at the table looked up at him and said: 'I am the Queen's examiner. You are Domingo Carramadino arrived from Spain. Is that so?'

Domingo licked his lips. He tried to speak and just managed to mutter: 'Yes.'

'Bring a stool for Domingo Carramadino,' said the examiner. 'I see he is feeling faint. Now, Domingo Carramadino, you will answer my questions. Who sent you to England?'

'The Superiors of the Society of Jesus.'

'For what purpose?'

'To bring back lost souls to their Maker.'

'You were sent to seduce people from the Queen's allegiance to the Pope's, and to meddle in matters of state.'

'Matters of state are no concern of mine.'

'How long have you been here?'

'But a few weeks.'

'How did you land? And where have you lived since?'

'Since I came to England I have lived at the house in which you found me.'

'Whom have you met since coming to England?'

'I have met the servants in the house. I have also met members of the family.'

'Have you ever been to a house in Fetter Lane and there said Mass?'

'I do not understand. What is Fetter Lane? I am not English, and there is sometimes difficulty with the language.'

'It is a convenient difficulty. I will ask you another question. Have you a friend who owns a house in Barbican?'

'There again you defeat me. What is this Barbican?'

'You belong to that company who are known here and abroad as the "Pope's White Sons", and you are responsible for divers pieces of service which have been done for Rome against this realm. What would your action be if the Pope declared war with the avowed object of establishing the Catholic Faith in England?'

'I am a priest,' said Domingo. 'You talk of matters of state.'

The examiner rapped with his knuckles on the table.

'You Jesuits come here with your talk of piety, with your talk of Faith, but do not imagine we are deceived. We know you for the spies you are. Take him to his cell. Go back the way you have come. Let him be reminded of the way we have with those who come to spy among us. It may be that when I next desire to question him, he will be in a more communicative mood.'

The two men were laying their hands on his shoulders. Domingo rose. He was almost fainting with nausea and fear as they led him away.

In the streets of London there was great rejoicing. Processions were marching through Cheapside, London's main thoroughfare. Held high were effigies of those conspirators who had plotted against the Queen's life. The people were going to throw them on the bonfires which were already burning in every open space.

The bells were ringing. Every merchant and his wife, every apprentice and scrivener had come out into the streets to make merry.

Later an ox would be roasted, and there would be a slice of tasty meat for all who could fight their way to the carver – the gift of a loyal merchant who rejoiced that once more a foul plot had been discovered and the Queen's life saved.

All London was talking of those men who had sought to bring Popery back to England. There were many alive who remembered the days of Bloody Mary, when the smoke from the Smithfield fires had hung over London, and the roasted flesh they smelt was not that of oxen.

From Aldgate and Bishopsgate, from Cripplegate and Aldersgate, Newgate and Ludgate, came the demand: 'Death to the traitors! Death to the Scottish murderess!' Drapers from Gornhill and grocers from Soper Lane, cooks of East Chepe and poulterers from the Poultry, had come to demand that justice be done. The noise and the revelry had extended to the village of Kensington. Julie heard and was afraid, for she had had word that Blasco had been taken, and that Domingo was also in prison. She had spent hours on her knees, praying that Blasco might be saved.

This family, with whom she had lived and who had treated

her as though she were their daughter, caring for her, teaching her their trade and best of all perhaps talking to her in the language she had spoken as a girl, worshipping with her in the way she had been taught as a girl, had made her feel that she was one of them. She was fond of them, but Blasco was never far from her thoughts.

There seemed so little now to remind her of him, and yet she could never forget. She awakened sometimes in the night and felt the sweat upon her. Then she would start up, calling his name; and she remembered that it was in times of such danger that her first thought was of Blasco.

Often she would recall that occasion when they had been on the roof together, and only Blasco was between her and violent death. She would remember with equal vividness that day when he had held his sword at her throat, because they had thought the *alguazils* had come for her.

In times of danger it was Blasco she wanted. And no matter to what peace she came, what pleasure she found in the simple companionship which was hers in this house of people like herself, she would always think of Blasco.

And now Blasco and Domingo were prisoners and they would of a surety die the deaths of traitors.

She did not love Blasco, as he understood love. She had no need of his embraces. Yet she had need of his presence; the need to know that he was still in the world and not too far away, so that she might call upon him if she wanted him. No one could help her as Blasco could; no one but Blasco could make her feel safe and happy in a world where men hated each other and tortured each other because they could not all think alike.

She must find her way to the Clink. She must see Blasco for

herself. She left the house and following the river made her way towards the seething city. There were many to invite her to share their barge. She accepted one invitation gratefully, and as the barge went along the river she stared about her without seeing the noisy crowds, without hearing the shouts and the sound of music on the water.

'There are seven of them to die today,' said the man who had invited her into his barge.

'I hear they're to be drawn on hurdles from Tower Hill through the city,' added his woman companion. ''Tis to take place at a field at the upper end of Holborn, hard by St Giles's.'

'And not one, mark you,' said her companion, 'but seven of them.'

'Seven,' murmured Julie. Was Blasco one of them? Could that be so? 'What are their names?' she asked.

'Oh, 'twill be Babington for sure, and Ballard with him. But there'll be the five others to go with them. They're such young men. 'Tis a pity they should plot against the Queen.'

'So perish all traitors,' said the man.

She asked them to take her over to the south bank and set her down there. They looked at her in some amazement, but there was no time on such a day to be bothered with mournful strangers. They had to make their way to Holborn and be sure of a good place.

There were crowds on the south bank. They were all going in one direction – the opposite of Julie's. She was caught in the crowd; it pressed about her. The smell of cooked meats, which the traders were trying to sell to the crowds, made her feel ill. It was impossible to escape from the press of people. The child moved within her, and for a moment she was dizzy. The blue sky seemed to be descending on her and turning dark; she felt the hot breath of those close to her, and she sank to the ground.

Pain shot through her as the crowds surged on and over her prostrate body.

☙ ☙ ☙

A man had entered the cell. Domingo had lost count of the time he had spent there. He had prayed much and eaten little of the bread and water which was his prison diet.

He could discover nothing. He had no idea what had happened to Blasco. His jailer would tell him nothing, but the man looked at him in a strange way whenever he entered the cell.

Each time he came, Domingo would start, believing that they had come to take him away to torture him. When he slept, his dreams were haunted by images which resembled those of the two men he had seen hanging by their wrists in the cellar. He had dreamed that one of them was Blasco, and that Blasco's dark eyes accused him as he passed; and Blasco's parched lips cried: 'I suffer here for you. *You* have tortured me thus.' Sometimes he dreamed that Blasco was crucified. He would awake and stare at the cross which he wore beneath his shirt, and it would seem that the holy figure changed subtly until those features were Blasco's and it was Blasco who suffered there.

Then half-delirious he would imagine that he had betrayed Christ; that he himself was the world which had spurned his Master. He felt himself to be heavy with sin, and that there were no means of casting off his burden.

He believed he ought to go to the examiner and say, 'I am to blame for anything my brother and I have done. He is innocent of everything of which you accuse him. I am the priest. I came to work against the Queen. Take me, torture me, but let my brother go free, for he merely came for my sake. He is a man who has no great love of our Faith.'

But he could not bring himself to ask to see the examiner. He was afraid, afraid of those dark cellars and what might befall him there.

Even now he was trembling as the man entered his cell. He came to him and said: 'You are to prepare to go out. A man will come for you. You must be ready when he comes.'

'I am to be freed?'

'I did not say so. You are to go out. That is all. It is not to be freed, for I am to keep your cell in readiness for you on your return.'

Domingo thought the man was mocking him. But shortly afterwards a tall man, whom he had never seen before, came into his cell and said: 'Are you ready to leave? Follow me, Señor Carramadino.'

They left the prison, and no one sought to stop them. They went to the river's edge where a barge was waiting for them and they were rowed across the river.

'Where do we go?' asked Domingo.

'We go to the upper end of Holborn. Our destination is a field there. You will see, when we reach it.'

He stood close to the scaffold, and he who had brought him stood close and not once did he release his hold on his captive's arm. Domingo could feel the fingers, strong as steel, holding him lest he should attempt to escape.

He saw those young men. How different they looked from those confident conspirators about whose table he had sat in the house in the Barbican. Now they were afraid for they knew of the terrible fate which was in store for them. Domingo turned away.

'You are not allowed to look away,' said the man.

'I do not wish to see.'

'You are not allowed to do as you wish. You are the Queen's prisoner. You must miss nothing of this ceremony. It is important.'

Domingo stared before him; vaguely he heard the shouts of the crowd. He saw those barbarous things which were done to the man Ballard; saw him hanged and taken down alive. He was forced to look on at the butcher's ugly work, for he was commanded to do so, and he must not forget that he was the Queen's prisoner.

And then Babington – that young man who had sat at the head of the table, that young man whose eyes had gleamed with ambition.

He had plotted against the life of the Queen, and this was the traitor's death; this was the law of the land.

He saw the once handsome young man writhing on the ground. He saw the butcher's knife raised. He heard the agonised shriek from the young man's lips: '*Parce mihi, Domine Jesu!*'

And as Babington lay dying, Domingo fell fainting to the ground.

❧ ❧ ❧

Charlie Monk made his way with great haste to a certain house in Seething Lane. This was an honour. It was not often that Charlie was received in Seething Lane. The pages looked askance at him.

'Do not fret,' said Charlie grandly. 'I have an appointment with your master.'

'And who are you?' asked the haughty flunkey.

'Just tell your master that Mr Charles Monk waits below.'

He bestowed a coin on the man; the flunkey looked at it in astonishment and went to inform his master who, very much to the flunkey's surprise and Charles Monk's satisfaction, asked for Charlie to be brought to him. Charlie was then taken to a large imposing room hung with rich arras; there was an air of quiet in this room which communicated itself to Charlie who walked on tiptoe and stood before the man seated at the table, and when he spoke it was in a whisper.

'You sent for me, sir?'

The man looked up; he was elderly and swarthy. 'You have done well,' he said.

The man picked up papers which lay before him. On the top sheet was written 'The Carramadino Brothers'.

'Yes,' murmured the older man, tapping it. 'Good work.'

'Thank you, Sir Francis.'

'You may be leaving Sir Eric shortly.'

'At your service, sir.'

'I think I shall have work for you in the West Country.'

'Very good, Sir Francis.'

'It may be – and I very much hope it will be – with these brothers.'

'Ah, yes, sir.'

'But I cannot tell you immediately. I have sent for you that you may prepare a story to pass on to Sir Eric, which will explain why you can no longer stay with him. And you must be at hand when the brothers leave their prison – if leave it they do. I will give you more details later. But I wish you to know that I am well pleased with you. I have been able to add considerably to my knowledge of these young men because you have discovered much concerning them. You have told me that the priest is a man who is much afraid and is deeply perturbed by his fear. That was useful information – all knowledge is good. Every particular, however small, however seemingly insignificant – for it may well be that the small piece, which seemed of no importance, adds that bit to the whole which gives meaning to the puzzle – should be gathered and passed to me.'

'Yes, Sir Francis.'

'I want you to keep closely in touch with these Spaniards. I want all the information you can get for me concerning the Armada which is being constructed in Spain. Remember, no information is to be considered too insignificant. You understand me, I know. Tell me, did either of these brothers ever mention in your hearing a man named March?'

'March, sir? Not March. But Mash or Marsh – some such name. Why, the younger brother continually mentioned the name, sir. He's been asking almost everyone he met if they had ever heard of a sailor by that name.'

'Very good, very good. Now I cannot give you instructions as yet.' He looked at the elaborate timepiece which he kept on the table. 'But shortly I shall do so. Meanwhile I wish you to wait in another part of this house, for I am expecting visitors. I do not wish these visitors to see you. On no account must they do so, or your services will be useless to me. You will wait in a room in another part of the house where you will partake of refreshment. And by the time I send for you again I hope to have your instructions ready.'

'I shall be waiting, sir. Waiting and ready to continue priest-hunting.'

'Priests and spies. They are often one and the same. Pull the bell-rope, and I will have you conducted to your refreshment. And on no account stray from that room until I send for you.'

'I am always at your service, Sir Francis,' said Charlie Monk.

When Charlie had left, Sir Francis Walsingham picked up the papers on his desk and studied them. Thanks to his efficient secret service, which was the best in the world, and which was responsible for the employment of hundreds of men in England and on the Continent, he was better informed of world events than any man living.

But for him, many a plot to assassinate the Queen might have succeeded; but as with the Ridolfi Plot many years ago, so with the Babington Plot; by means of his intricate system he was enabled to have full knowledge of these plots almost from the moment of their inception, and to follow their progress until he decided that the best moment had come for drawing all the conspirators into his net. Now he had brought Babington and his conspirators to their deserved fate; and this time even the Queen herself could not save the life of Mary Stuart, for Walsingham was going to show Elizabeth how deeply involved was the Scottish Queen in this conspiracy. His main concern now was to convince her how acute was the danger from Spain. He must force her to spend more money on the refitting of ships. Every day he was laying before her information concerning the progress of the Spanish Armada, which, it was clear, Philip was building to send against England.

He glanced through the dossier once more. It told him that Domingo Carramadino had entered the Seminary at Valladolid in the year 1572, and that he had done so after the woman who was to have been his bride had been captured by an English buccaneer. How he delighted in piecing the evidence together! About this time there had arrived in Plymouth Captain Ennis March, with his ship and a cargo of Spanish women to prove he had successfully raided Spain. He had since married one of the Spanish women. The Queen had favoured him after he had arrived home from Mexico with a very rich cargo into which her greedy hands had delved deeply; he was now Sir Ennis March, and he was living in Devon close to a house which, it was suspected, priests were using as a *pied-à-terre* on their arrival from the Continent.

Did it not show how every little piece of information could be useful!

Domingo stood before him.

Sir Francis said to the man who had brought him: 'You may leave us.' And when he had done so: 'You look ill, Señor. Pray sit down.'

Domingo sat. He was scarcely aware of his surroundings. He had no notion who this man was who was sitting opposite him, surveying him with calm yet alert dark eyes. He could still see nothing but the horrors he had witnessed. He could feel the hangman's rope about his neck, the butcher's hands on his body.

'It was a distressing sight,' said Sir Francis slowly, 'and I heard that it affected you deeply. And I do not wonder at that. It is the death which has been accorded to traitors for many years. One would think it would prove a deterrent. But each man thinks he will be victorious. That is one of the tricks of human nature. You know, do you not, that we are in full possession of details of your own activities since you came to this country.'

Domingo nodded.

'You and your brother are our prisoners. We know that you consorted with these traitors who have this day died in St Giles's Field. More will die there shortly. There are many in our prisons who may follow them.'

The sweat had broken out on Domingo's brow. He thought: It has come now. Oh Jesus, save me! I cannot endure such suffering. It is greater than the agony on the cross.

Sir Francis saw the man's lips move. He recognised his terror. Charlie Monk was right. The man should never have been sent on such a dangerous mission. He had not the courage for it. Sir Francis felt a twinge of pity. Here was a man of gentle character, a man of peace. Poor fool, to have been seduced into the life of espionage, which went with that of these men who called themselves the missionaries of Jesus! Missionaries of Philip would be more apt. But how like the monk-king of the Escorial to combine religious fervour with the work of his spies.

Walsingham had one great passion in his life – the service of his country through his Queen. If he were to let his pity for one fearful priest interfere with his duty, he would not have been the man who had spent his great fortune in the service of his country. He was not likely to forget that his country was in acute danger. The great shadow of the Armada hung over the land and, since he could not impress on the Queen the need to build ships, he must gather every scrap of information concerning the enemy's manoeuvres – and in this every man on whom he could lay his hands must help him, no matter what means he used to press them into service.

He leaned across the table. 'You have seen today men suffer a fate which you and your brother have merited. I offer you your freedom, and his, at a price.'

Domingo raised his head. It was pitiful to see the hope which shone in his eyes.

'From henceforth you become my servant . . . you and your brother with you.'

'My brother,' said Domingo; and his voice was high-pitched with emotion.

He heard the familiar voices within him. It is not only to save yourself, it is for Blasco too.

He will do it, thought Sir Francis. A Jesuit priest! Another Gilbert Gifford! The best sort of spy; such confidence they inspire! How could I have gathered the information which enabled me to expose the Babington plot, but for Gilbert Gifford, Jesuit turned spy to save his life as this man will?

Sir Francis began to speak quietly, persuasively. 'It is so very simple. I want you to go to a house in Devon where I suspect priests, such as yourself, are arriving in secret. I want every bit of information concerning the fleet of ships which are being built in Spain. Do not think that you can deceive me – you in your turn will be watched – and if you should ever think to do so, remember what you have seen this day. I offer you a pardon in exchange for your services. It will only hold good while you work for me. What is it to be?'

Domingo said nothing.

Sir Francis thought: There he will meet the woman he was to have married. A Spaniard. There are Spaniards in the Captain's house, and Spaniards in the Hardy house. A hot-bed of traitors. And Charlie Monk will be there at Hardyhall to keep me informed.

Still Domingo said nothing. He sensed the voices arguing one with another within him. He could not shut out of his mind the barbarous scene he had witnessed that day in St Giles's Field. He tried to picture that happening to Blasco, but it was always himself whom he saw in the hands of the executioners.

354

PART SIX

DEVON
1586

✣ Chapter VI ✣

DEVON, 1586

For many weeks after Petroc Pellering had put her ashore, Pilar nursed her resentment against him. She had taken to spending long hours lying on the cliffs gazing over the Sound, her eyes fixed on the horizon. Roberto would be beside her, watching her, a sheen of amusement clouding his eyes.

Roberto was happy. The Captain had sailed away and there was peace in the house once more. No longer did he have to consider the relationship between the Captain and his mother; and Roberto was not one to worry about that which was not immediately before him. The Captain's large, blaspheming, disturbing presence was removed, and he was only a memory. That was how Roberto wished it to be.

They both took lessons from Mr West, the tutor whom the Captain had engaged to undertake the education of Pilar. Mr West was easy-going; he was a victim of Roberto's casual charm and Pilar's fiery temperament. Both children delighted in turning the tutor from the subject on hand to tell tales of his travels through the country and his residence in the various houses where he had taught children such as themselves. Pilar invented exciting adventures for these children; in her imagination she and Roberto shared those adventures, and were always successful. It was an amusing pastime and one in which Roberto encouraged her. He did not like to see her looking out to sea with brooding eyes.

She had told Roberto of her desire to stow away on board the Captain's ship, and how she would have succeeded in doing so but for the odious Petroc Pellering. She exaggerated the adventure, and stressed the brutality of Petroc until her eyes flashed with hatred; then she would swear to be revenged on him.

Often, when she lay on the cliffs looking out to sea and imagining that she and Roberto were sailing the high seas, boarding Spanish galleons, taking the treasure from those ships which were carrying it to Spain and diverting it to England, her eyes would shine and she would communicate her excitement to Roberto. Pilar could never keep anything to herself unless she had promised to do so. She was generous. She liked to share. Whatever the treat, it would lose half of its value unless she had someone to share it with her.

But into these adventures the enemy would come; and the enemy, Roberto had begun to realise, was not the Spaniards so much as Petroc Pellering. Roberto, who understood Pilar better than anyone else, knew that this was not entirely due to their Spanish blood and that lurking loyalty she must feel towards all Spaniards because her mother was one of them; it was due to the fact that this man Petroc Pellering had not only foiled her attempt to sail with her father, but had humiliated her deeply, and that was something she would never forgive.

So into their peaceful hours when they lay looking out over

the sea, living in that world of imagination which Roberto believed was more satisfying than reality, there would come, to shatter the peace, that violent feeling against this man. Pilar would grow restless. The adventure would be spoilt. She could not forget that moment when he had discovered her in the hold and had lifted her, kicking, from beneath the sacking. He had wounded her deeply and she could not forget him.

Roberto sensed something disturbing in her continual pre-occupation with the sea. He was afraid of something which was in the future; and suddenly he realised that what he feared was the end of childhood. It occurred to Roberto as they lay there and she talked once more of how she might have sailed away on her father's ship but for the hated Petroc, that one day he would lose Pilar. Others might come between them; others might share her stormy companionship, those adventures of the imagination, the scorn and the tenderness.

Already, but for Petroc Pellering, he might have lost her. He knew then that he wanted them always to be together.

🥀 🥀 🥀

When Pilar went to Hardyhall she rarely entered by way of the drive and front porch. Often she climbed the wall. She liked to remind herself of the first time she and Roberto had trespassed and gone into the nuttery and surprised Bess and Howard.

She often climbed that very tree, hoping they would come there and she could frighten them.

Now she ran across the lawns. There was not the same thrill, there was not the fear of discovery. If anyone saw her they would smile and say, 'Oh, it is Pilar again.'

But the chapel had always held a fascination for her. Every time she saw its grey walls she felt an excitement, because she believed that she could never be sure what she might find within those walls. So now, as she started running towards the nuttery, she made a sudden swerve and changed her course. She paused outside the chapel and trying the door found it locked. She shrugged her shoulders and went round to the front of the house.

She had reached the porch. The door had been left open so she went in. The hall was deserted. It always fascinated her when there was no one in it, because then she had the feeling that in it she might be secretly watched. She knew that in the solarium on the next floor there was an alcove hidden behind rich velvet hangings. In the wall was a star-shaped aperture through which it was possible to look down into the hall. When one looked up from below, even though one knew where the hole was, it was difficult to find it and it was not possible to see if anyone stood there watching.

Pilar turned her gaze up to that spot where she knew the peephole to be. She fancied that she saw a shadow there. But she always fancied that.

At the end of the room, on the dais near the great open fireplace, the large oak refectory table stood on its baluster legs which were joined by stretchers. It was laid as for a meal. On the walls hung daggers and pikes, the Hardy banner, and helmets, breastplates and shields.

It seemed to Pilar that there was an expectancy about the hall, as though it were waiting for the arrival of some important people.

She crossed the hall, glancing over her shoulder again and again at that star-shaped hole high in the wall.

She went through the opening on the left of the great fireplace, and up two steps into a room in which she had

360

often been when she visited the house. Tapestries covered all the walls; through the window she could see the deserted courtyard.

She knew that if she passed through the door on the far side and mounted two more steps, she would come to the door of the chapel. It was the chapel, which, she felt, held all the mystery of this house. That was natural. It was in the chapel that she had first become aware of its secrets. Never would she, on entering the place, fail to remember that moment when she stepped down and had fallen into the dark hole and found she was not alone.

Quickly she crossed the room and mounted the two steps. The chapel door was open and she went in. She caught her breath, for that which she had previously thought was a table was covered with a beautiful cloth, and on it stood the silver chalice. Two candles were burning on the altar.

She knew that she had no right to be there, but she could not resist going forward on tiptoe towards the altar. She knew that the guests, for whom the house seemed to be waiting, were probably her mother and others of the same Faith come to perform the sacred rites which took place in the chapel, and in which her father had forbidden her to participate.

And as she stood there she heard a step on the stairs. It was too late to hide, for Mr Heath was coming into the chapel. He was dressed as a priest.

He started when he saw her. 'Why . . . Pilar?' he said.

'Good day to you, Mr Heath.'

'What are you doing here?'

'I came to see Howard and Bess. The door was open.'

'You are drawn to the chapel, my child, are you not?' he said.

'Yes, Mr Heath.'

'Why? Can you tell me that?'

She said: 'It was what happened . . .'

'An unforgettable experience for us both.'

'And the chapel itself. It's as though something is going to happen, and everything's waiting for it.'

'You sense the Divine presence. My child, I greatly regret that you no longer come to me for instruction.'

'My father forbids it.'

'And your desire is to obey him?'

She said: 'Should not one obey one's father?'

'You have two fathers, Pilar. An earthly one and a heavenly one. Are you to fear the earthly one more than your Father which is in Heaven?'

'Why yes,' she said. 'He was very angry when he saw the *Agnus Dei*. He ground it under his foot. He made me swear never to wear such a thing again.'

'And you promised to obey him. You did not feel the desire to defy him?'

'Everybody obeys the Captain,' she said. 'He would be very angry if they did not.'

'I hope that one day you will come under my care again. I have felt great interest in you since that meeting of ours. You speak of it to no one, do you, Pilar?'

'I promised Lady Hardy not to.'

'You are a good child, and you have a strong character. It is a great pity that you have been forbidden to come here for instruction. It is a source of great sorrow to your mother.'

'She would wish me to learn all you have to teach. She would have you make a Catholic of me.'

'Pilar, if you feel strongly that you wish to continue with

your instruction, if you feel that by doing so you would be pleasing God, I do not think, in that case, you should feel it is necessary to obey your earthly father.'

'I have promised the Captain not to come here,' she said. 'Not to be taught, I mean. I may come to see Howard and Bess.'

'And you feel you must keep that promise?'

'Yes, of course.'

He laid his hand on her head. 'I am grieved at your decision. But I feel this, and I feel it very strongly: one day you will be one of us.'

'No,' she said firmly. 'I am the Captain's daughter, as well as my mother's, but being the Captain he made me take a bigger share of him than of my mother.'

'Go now,' he said. 'You will find Howard and Bess in the schoolroom.'

As she went out of the chapel, she heard Mr Heath lock the door behind her. She made her way to the schoolroom, where Bess and Howard sat at the table completing the lessons Mr Heath had set them.

The children looked up eagerly. As soon as Pilar appeared, life became unexpected, sometimes dangerously uncomfortable, but they could not be bored.

'I am going to hide,' she cried, 'and you two can find me. I'm a buccaneer who has landed from Spain, and I'm in your house and you're hunting for me. All my men have run away. If you find me you'll try to string me up on a tree where from the house you can watch my body rot. You're looking everywhere for me. Come on!'

Howard had risen from the table, but she did not wait to hear what he had to say. She entered into all her self-appointed roles wholeheartedly. At this moment she was a Spanish raider. She thought: By God, I'll not be caught. I'll hide myself until the coast is clear, and I'll take a few of their women with me and all the treasure of the house before I escape to my ship waiting in the bay.

She ran breathlessly out of the schoolroom, up a short twist of stairs and through two of the bedrooms until she came to the solar. Behind the hangings, which covered the star-shaped hole, was a good place to hide. She crept behind it. She was not really hiding; she was enjoying the pleasure of looking down on the hall.

How quiet it seemed down there! It looked different from up here. So very far down. She imagined that the suit of armour, standing in the corner beneath the banner – which, Sir Walter had told her, all the Hardys carried into battle – sprang into place and became just a suit of armour because it knew she was looking down on it. She believed that all those things on which she now looked had a life of their own which they could only pursue when they were unobserved. The sword, she believed, had been in the iron man's hand and only just managed to leap into the accustomed place on the wall. All the figures in the piece of tapestry, which depicted the battle of Flodden Field, had stepped back and become silk stitches just in time.

That was the delicious excitement she experienced in this house. One of her most enjoyable games when she was quite alone – for it was a game she could only play when she was alone – was to shut her eyes and open them quickly, hoping to catch on the move all those seemingly inanimate things.

One day I shall, she told herself. I shall catch one of them who hasn't been quite quick enough.

She was tired of looking at the hall. And she thought: The others will soon be coming. They'll find me. I have hidden here so many times.

She emerged from behind the hangings and stood in the solar, looking about her for a fresh place to hide. She was reluctant to leave this room.

She heard Bess's voice then. They were in one of the bedrooms; they would be upon her in less than a minute.

Bess said in an audible whisper: 'She's in the solar. She always goes to the solar. She's at the peep, looking down on the hall.'

Pilar looked about her quickly and her eyes rested on an escritoire in the form of a chest – a massive piece of furniture. To her delight she could see that there was room for her to crawl behind it. There were hangings on this wall and, by getting behind these, she could stand upright; and she was sure that she was completely hidden.

She stood still, breathlessly waiting for Bess and Howard to go past.

'You look at the peep,' said Bess. 'She's there, Howard. She's there!'

Howard went to the hiding-place Pilar had recently vacated. 'No,' he said, 'no, she's not here.'

'She always goes there,' said Bess obstinately. 'She must have heard us coming and knew we'd look there first.'

Pilar closed her eyes. She was the English sea-rover now. 'What do you see on the horizon, sir? That! By God, she's a Spaniard and bearing straight for us. By God, have all guns manned. She's one of the treasure ships from Cadiz.'

She had turned and was looking at the wall. The light was dim behind the hangings, but she was attracted by a faint shaft of brightness just above her head, and she saw that it came from the edge of a picture. It was a small picture of one of the Hardys of the previous century – a smiling lady in a wimple. As Pilar looked at it, a shiver ran down her spine. The lady's eyes seemed to be looking straight at her, and a smile seemed to curve the mouth. She was almost certain that the face moved as she watched it.

Her impulse was to slip out from behind the hangings and into the room. But determined not to be afraid she stood firm and stared back at the painted face.

'Nothing but a picture,' she said. 'You're dead. You can't come out of that frame. Besides, you've got no body. You're only the face and shoulders of a woman. Where's the rest of you? How could you walk about? Even ghosts have to have legs, surely.'

Her eyes were then directed to the ridge of light on the lower part of the frame; it showed up quite clearly in the gloom.

She put out her hand gingerly and touched the spot, never taking her eyes from those of the woman in the picture.

She dropped her hand, for the picture had moved to one side and the woman's face had changed suddenly. She seemed to be daring Pilar to do more. But of course it was merely because Pilar was seeing the painting from a different angle.

Because she could not take her eyes from the woman, feeling that, if she did so, life, horrible, uncanny life would spring from the canvas, she had not noticed what she had uncovered. But as her eyes slowly took in the space which had been revealed by the movement of the picture she saw the pointed tip of a star which was similar to that on the other side of the room, through which it was possible to look down on the hall. Now she understood and almost every trace of fear left her.

The picture was there for the purpose of hiding the hole.

The hangings were there for the same purpose, and so was the escritoire. Truly this was a house for a great explorer such as herself. She put up her hand and pushed the picture aside. Now the complete star was revealed. By standing on tiptoe she could look through it.

There was the chapel. It was the same barrel-vaulted ceiling with its wooden ribs decorated with Tudor roses; there was the Flemish triptych with the Adoration in the centre panel and the figures kneeling in those at the sides.

But it was the people in the chapel who caught her attention. They were ranged about the altar, which was covered with a beautifully embroidered cloth. Her mother was among these people and they were celebrating Mass, she knew. It was what her father forbade her to hear and which had to be done in secret. It was because he did this that Mr Heath had found it necessary to hide under the chapel floor. She could not hear what was said, although she was straining her ears. She saw the beautiful silver cup which contained the wine. She wanted to see more of this ceremony; she wanted to see whether the wine really turned into blood and the bread into a body.

Her father had forbidden her to hear Mass, but he had not forbidden her to look down on it. She had often found it necessary to make such fine distinctions. She looked round the chapel and her eyes fell on an opening in one wall which she had not noticed on her short visits to the chapel.

She stared at this opening for she was sure she detected a movement there. Someone was watching; she was not the only one who was peeping at what was happening in the chapel.

She was suddenly horrified, for she remembered afresh that day when she had hidden under the floor of the chapel with Mr Heath. She remembered – for she would never forget – his words about grown people being as frightened as children. These people, including her mother, were doing something the Queen did not want them to do – and someone was spying on them.

She must warn them in some way. But as she stood there wondering how to do this, she heard a movement beside her; she started and the picture moved back into place.

'Pilar, what are you doing?'

Relief made her laugh lightly as she looked into Howard's scared face. 'I was hiding,' she said. 'This is a good place.'

'I knew it. I saw your feet when we passed through.'

'Where's Bess?'

'I made her go into the courtyard to seek. I didn't want her to know you were here. Pilar, why do you always go where you are not supposed to?'

She looked pleased. She was an explorer again – but only briefly. She remembered what she had seen in the chapel.

'Howard,' she said, 'we must warn all those people who are hearing Mass in the chapel. Someone's spying on them.'

'You are the spy!'

'I'm a good spy. I shan't tell the Queen. But that other one might.'

'What are you talking about, Pilar?'

'Look through there.'

'No,' he said. 'No! It's sacred. You shouldn't spy on those things.'

'Then what is the peep there for?'

'So that those who . . . who should not go into the chapel may share in the ceremony.'

'Why shouldn't they go into the chapel?'

'Perhaps because they're too young. Perhaps because they're sick.'

She nodded. 'What is that little room behind that long hole in the wall of the chapel?'

'You mean the squint?'

'The squint! You didn't show it to me.'

'I didn't want to show you anything in the chapel. You're not supposed to pry. A chapel isn't a place to play games in. It's a place to worship in.'

She gripped his arm and shook him. 'Howard, you must tell them. Someone is spying. They'll all be caught. And my mother is there.'

'You saw someone in the squint?' he said.

'Yes.'

Howard looked suddenly bewildered and, in this bewilderment, very young. He said: 'There are things I have to explain to you, Pilar. You find out things. You found the hole under the chapel flags. And now you've found this.'

She cried: 'I find everything. It's no use trying to hide anything from me.'

'You'll have to swear not to say anything about this peep you've found.'

'I'll swear.'

'The person you saw in the squint was not a spy. It was someone who wished to share in what was going on in the chapel, but who did not want to do so openly.'

'A spy?'

'No, no. You always think of spies. Perhaps a friend of my parents . . . someone who didn't want to show himself to others who were in the chapel.'

She said: 'There were two strange men in the chapel.'

'You could not see properly from here. It's too high up.'

'I could see. I could see clearly.'

'Nobody's eyes are good enough for that.'

'Mine are. Howard, do you look through this peep up here on to the chapel?'

'No,' he said.

'Do you go into the chapel to hear Mass?'

'Sometimes.'

'Does Bess go?'

'No, Bess looks through the peep. My mother does not wish her to go into the chapel yet. She is always afraid.'

'That men will come to search for the cups and altar cloths, and the people who use them?'

'How do you know of these things?'

'I know everything. Besides, people often talk of it. The Queen does not like people to use these things. That's why my father forbids me to.'

'Let's go away from here,' said Howard. 'Bess will be coming back. She must not know that you have found the peep and seen the squint.'

She led the way down the stairs, through the rooms and out into the courtyard.

Bess said: 'Oh, you found the Spaniard, then. What shall we do, string him up to the nearest tree?'

'I'm not a Spaniard any more.' Pilar's eyes were scornful. She wanted to be a member of the Queen's pursuivants who, having discovered a family indulging in idolatry, forgave them all and rode away pretending she had seen nothing.

❧ ❧ ❧

In Pilar's opinion Hardyhall was only second to the Spanish Main in the excitement it offered.

'I'd like to live at Hardyhall,' she declared one day. 'I think it's the most wonderful house in the world.'

'You couldn't live there,' Bess retorted. 'It's our home.'

'I *could* come and live there . . . I know. I'll marry Howard.'

'He might not want to,' said Bess.

'He would have little choice, once Pilar decided,' suggested Roberto.

'Have you decided?' asked Bess, turning to Pilar.

'Yes . . . no. Yes, I think so. I can't marry Roberto because he's my brother. I think I'll marry Howard. I like him next best. Besides, we'd have such fun there. Seeing all the people who came there . . . all the strange people.' She was aware of Howard, willing her to silence, and she added: 'Sharing secrets and keeping them. No matter how they tried to prise them from us.'

'What about Howard?' said Roberto.

'Yes,' said Howard. 'I'd marry Pilar.'

Pilar opened her mouth, and put her hand over it suddenly.

'You're a Catholic though, and I'm a Protestant.'

'One of you could change,' suggested Roberto.

'I couldn't,' said Pilar. 'The Captain would say no. You'll have to be a Protestant, Howard. Oh, but if you were, there wouldn't be . . .' She looked at Howard again. She saw the worried frown on his face. Poor Howard! He was continually worried. First when they had gone into the chapel; then when she had discovered the peep behind the escritoire; and now because she was going to marry him. A tenderness came to her then, a softness quite novel in her emotions. She determined to protect Howard, to make him see that he need not worry, no matter what adventures they had; she would look after him, she would make him see that in all her exploits, she, Pilar, was victorious.

She said now quickly: 'And Roberto shall marry Bess. We shall all live together at Hardyhall. There's plenty of room.'

'Oh, yes,' said Bess.

Roberto looked at her and smiled.

❧ ❧ ❧

Pilar was turned thirteen when the Captain next came home. She had grown up suddenly. Her dreams were less wild, though she still had them. She would still look longingly at the sea. She still wished to sail to unknown latitudes and discover new lands; that dream had remained; and was it such a dream? she often asked herself. The Captain would have taken her the last time, had she been older. And she would have gone then but for Petroc Pellering.

She kept alive her hatred for that man. He was one she would never forgive. He had impaired her dignity, and Pilar's dignity was not to be ignored.

She no longer prowled about the grounds of Hardyhall; she no longer desired to play hide-and-seek through the house.

She knew what happened there. It was the continual strife between Catholic and Protestant. The country was Protestant, but there were many people like the Hardys who were fiercely Catholic, and they were determined to worship in the way they wished; and for this worship it was necessary for them to have a priest. The Queen had made a law which declared that it was high treason for any Catholic priest to be on English soil, and an offence for any householder to harbour them. Still these priests came to England, and still people like the Hardys continued to receive them.

She and Roberto were being brought up by Mr West to be Protestants and true subjects of the Queen, whom such as the

Hardys considered to be in wrongful possession of the throne. It was all very dangerous, and it was this tension which she had sensed in Hardyhall as a child which had made the house so attractive to her.

She was different from Roberto and Howard. They wanted peace; she wanted adventure.

But now she was a sober young woman, growing up quickly.

Carmentita said: 'It is now we see that you are a belonger of Spain.'

That meant that she had matured earlier than Bess who, although but a few months younger, looked many years her junior.

'It is a woman you will be in a year or two,' said Carmentita, simpering, congratulating, hinting of the wonderful things which could happen to a girl when she became a woman.

She had made up her mind that she was going to marry Howard. Hardyhall was to be her home. Instead of those fantastic dreams which used to occupy her mind, she saw herself now as the mistress of Hardyhall. There would be danger at Hardyhall, Howard would continue to hear Mass; there would be a priest in the house. It would be for her to make sure that Howard, with his priests and his ceremonies in the chapel, was never discovered. She would remain a Protestant because she had promised the Captain; she would be a true subject of Queen Elizabeth; but Howard must remain a Catholic, and thus it would be her very first task to protect him.

She and Roberto would be the Protestants, Bess and Howard the Catholics.

She realised that if they all conformed to one religion a great deal of the zest would be taken out of her life.

It occurred to her then that there were some people — herself, the Captain, Bianca and Roberto — to whom religion was merely an accessory to life; there were others, like the Hardys, her mother and Mr Heath, to whom it was all-important.

And now in the bay lay the ship, and the Captain was home.

She went out to meet him as was her custom.

There he was, a little older, a little more wind-scored, burned with the sun, with a scar on his cheek where he had been slashed in a fight. His eyes were even more deeply embedded in their wrinkles, so that they were almost hidden. They were like little pieces of brilliant blue glass, tiny windows looking out of his brown wall of a face.

'It's my girl Piller!' The greeting was the same.

'Welcome to you, Captain!'

'By God, you grow up, Piller. You grow up fast.'

And there was Petroc Pellering to come and look at her. His eyes were as blue as the Captain's, the same sort of eyes; but his skin was golden-brown instead of walnut-brown and his hair bleached yellow by the hot sun.

'Well, Piller,' he said, 'how's the Captain's girl?'

She gave him the haughtiest stare she could muster.

'I am well.' She turned her back. 'Captain, shall we go ashore?'

A hand gripped her shoulder; that grip hurt.

'You did not ask how I am.' he said.

'There is no need. I see your health is as rude as your manners.'

The Captain roared with laughter. His eyes gleamed appreciation. Trust his girl Piller to amuse him as soon as he clapped eyes on her!

'That's your answer,' he said to Petroc. 'You've got to mind your manners now when you speak to our young lady.'

'There was naught wrong with my manners,' said Petroc, grinning. 'It's my person she does not like.'

'She's a lady now, who won't have rough sailors' manners shown her. That's so, eh, Piller girl?'

'It's his manners, his person, and everything about him that I won't have.'

'She has not forgiven me for taking her ashore last time,' said Petroc. 'By God, if she had seen what we have seen this voyage she'd be down on her knees thanking me for having such care for her.'

'Aye, that's so,' said the Captain. 'Come, Piller, smile at the man. He had naught but your good at heart.'

'I smile only when I wish to,' said Pilar. 'Come, let us go now. They are cooking such a feast for you. They started as soon as they saw the ship on the horizon.'

'Ah, you see what it is, Petroc fellow, to have a home and a family waiting for you at the end of a trip. It'll be good to have our feet on land again ... English fresh-cooked food to eat, and our own women about us.'

'Aye, sir, good indeed,' said Petroc.

'Then come. Piller will take us ashore.'

Pilar said: '*He* is to come with us?'

'Where else should he go?'

'There are places round about. There is Plymouth with its inns.'

'Here's hospitality!' said the Captain.

'She holds it against me, I fear. I had naught but her good at heart, and she holds it against me.'

The Captain turned to grin at Petroc, and they all followed Pilar to the boat.

He was to stay with them as he had on that other occasion.

There were some in the house who wondered at the Captain's affection for Petroc Pellering. There were some who hinted that the young man might be his son.

Pilar would not have that. 'My brother! That oaf!' she cried. 'Don't dare say such things!'

Carmentita giggled. 'I would not wish such a one to be my brother, no. Oh, no! Oh, what a man! What a man he will be, and I doubt not already is.'

Pilar's answer to that was to slap Carmentita's fat cheek, and it was not a playful slap either. Whenever Petroc's name was mentioned, Pilar could be aroused to fury. She found that she was comparing him, even during that first evening, with Howard.

They all sat at the table; even those servants who were not required to serve were there in the old fashion. It was the occasion of the Captain's homecoming, and he would have everyone in the house there to welcome him.

The table was loaded, for the Captain's appetite was always at its sharpest on his first night at home, and he wished to savour all those good roast dishes which he had missed on board. Mutton and beef had been roasting on the spits from the moment the ship was sighted; and a great pie had been made, containing chicken and pork, all highly flavoured with cloves and pepper and the spices the Captain loved; the shape of the pie was that of a ship, and it stood in the centre of the table. There were wines and ale, cider and mead.

Pilar sat next to the Captain, at his right hand as he had insisted. On the other side of him was Isabella. Bianca was further down the table next to Roberto. Pilar saw that she was half pleased, half apprehensive, because the Captain was home – pleased for herself, apprehensive for Roberto.

Carmentita was there, plump cheeks glowing, very happy on account of the Captain's return, glancing now and then along the table at him and the handsome young man whom he had brought ashore with him.

Pilar was angry, for the young man had sat next to her. The Captain had signed for him to do so and for once she had been too taken aback to protest. Then she had been glad, for it would be easy to show her hatred of him if he was near her, and that was what she wanted to do.

'Captain,' said Pilar, 'tell us where you have been this trip.'

The Captain pointed to her with the bone from which he was tearing the flesh with his strong teeth. 'She wants to know,' he said. 'She wants to know what she missed when she didn't come with us. My girl, we've all but circled the world. 'Tis so, eh, Petroc fellow? Mexico . . . and south of Mexico and north, too . . . as far north as any ship has sailed.'

'And what treasure did you bring back, Captain?'

'Hark to her! Hark to her! What treasure? she says.' He turned to look into her face. Clear skin, clear eyes, brilliant, flashing eyes full of interest. His own grew a little misty. He thought: By God, she surprises me every time I see her, this girl. 'What treasure, eh? You shall see. There'll be a trinket or two for you. We've had a good trip, but it's nothing . . . nothing to what the next will be.' He glanced at Petroc who nodded in agreement.

Now his eyes had gone back to the girl who sat beside him; his blue eyes were a little bluer; his beard moved uncontrollably. She was better than a son, better than five sons. His girl Piller. She'd not try to take his place. Not that she couldn't!

He was lucky. It wasn't only the good English ale that made him feel so; it was here at his table, with his wife and mistresses about him, that he felt like a King come home, with good food to eat and wine to drink, and his girl – his beautiful Piller – beside him, and on her left hand young Petroc, who was going to take his place one day; who would be a rover just as himself, full of oaths and courage, a man who could make a decision in less than a second and make it the right one – the only sort of man he'd trust his ship with – aye, his ship and his girl Piller. For that was what he was going to do; his girl was going to have everything he'd got. But what could a girl do with a crew like his? He'd seen them in Cuba, in Porto Rico, mad with the drink after months at sea . . . mad for the women. How could a girl – even his girl Piller – rule men like that! No! It had to be a man – a man who was a head taller than most of them, a man who could roar and blaspheme and apply the lash himself. A man like Petroc.

He had marked him for his own. He took sudden fancies. The boy had come to him. Run away from home because he wanted to sail the Spanish Main. Came from a good family, though from the other side of the Tamar. Somewhere inland – a fine old estate not far over the border. The boy had come to him and he had taken him on board; nor had he made life too easy for him on that first voyage. He didn't believe in being soft. But there was the boy, still aboard on the second trip, and because they were so much alike, they understood each other.

Yes, one day he'd see that his girl was in good hands. She and Petroc would be together, and she'd have this house, and when Petroc came home with his booty, she'd be there at the table beside him, and the servants round the board just as it was today. Petroc would have a lovely wife waiting for him. And mistresses? Not he! Piller would see to that. Not on English soil at any rate. The thought made him almost choke with amusement.

'No,' said the Captain slowly, looking round the board, 'this is naught to what the next trip will be. The countries we have seen are rich, and the people who live there are brown-skinned and friendly. There are many people here in this country of ours who might make good lives for themselves there. Soon you will see, sailing out of Plymouth, ships which will carry many of our people to the shores of that new country which the Queen has graciously called Virginia – to remind all who settle there, and all who come after, that it was discovered when she was Queen, and by the men to whose adventures she was pleased to give her blessing. When we have our settlers there living in that wonderful land, growing rich there, our ships will ply back and forth and make much trade. The settlers there will discover the good things of that fair country, and we shall bring many of those good things back to England.'

Pilar was watching him, her eyes shining.

'Tell her, Petroc fellow,' said the Captain. 'Tell her what we found in the Queen's new land.'

Pilar did not look at Petroc though he had leaned closer to her as he said: 'The climate is more delightful than any we have ever known. If the country were but inhabited by Englishmen, and they had horses and cattle, there would not be a place in Christendom to compare with it. The people there are gentle and friendly – a strange people who live in wigwams under one chief. The walls of their wigwams are made of bark fastened to stakes, and they live in small groups so that there are rarely more than thirty or forty together. They are dressed in mantles made from the skins of animals, and they wear aprons of the same skins. Their swords are of wood, their arrows are made of reeds, and their bows of witch hazel. They looked on us as gods.'

Pilar threw him a scornful look over her shoulder.

'It is easy,' she said, 'to seem godlike before such simple people.'

'We found them wherever we went, these simple people,' went on Petroc, smiling at her. 'They welcomed us and we gave them gifts. Such little things pleased them. They showed us the land, and seemed happy to act as guides for us. We found the same attitude all along the coast. And the forests are quite beautiful. I have never seen anything so rich; they are just as nature made them; everywhere are wild fruits and flowers, beautiful coloured flowers. The smell of the honeysuckle almost made us drunk, did it not, Captain? The tansy grew in profusion with the young sassafras, and all about these forests were strawberries and raspberries and massive grape vines.'

'Ah,' said the Captain, 'they listen intently to you, fellow. They'll think you're urging them to leave our own Devon and settle in Virginia.'

'I'd go,' said Pilar.

'I'd take you,' said Petroc.

'I'd go alone.'

The Captain laughed. 'I trust my girl has been taking her education from Mr West,' he said.

Mr West spoke up. 'Indeed she has, sir; and also Master Roberto. They are good pupils – as good as can be expected.'

'That's well. That's what I like to hear. Here, fill my goblet.'

Isabella did so. Then he asked for music. 'Who can play for us, eh?'

Mr West played the virginals and Bianca the flageolet.

It was a pleasant homecoming.

Isabella asked if he would come to her little sitting-room, as she had something to say to him.

Come to her sitting-room? he demanded. Why should he? He was not one for sitting-rooms. If she had aught to say, let her say it now.

She answered with dignity: 'What I have to say is for your ear alone. My sitting-room would supply the necessary privacy.'

Her dignity could defeat him at times; it took him unawares. She was a Spanish lady of high standing; he knew that. It had delighted him in their relationship, given it something which all the pleasure he took in Bianca could not give. She disliked his attentions but perforce must suffer them. When he was with her he felt that he triumphed not only over her, but over Spain.

He went to her sitting-room, but he had kept her waiting there an hour.

She was sitting at her needlework. There again he was defeated. The sight of the needle, going in and out, exasperated him. She looked so graceful sitting there with the light from the window behind her, that he felt at a disadvantage, clumsy, a coarse sailor in the presence of gentility.

He felt the blood rushing to his face. He had kept Bianca with him all last night, and they had slept late. It was an insult to the lady of the house. Everyone knew whom he had chosen on his first night home. What should he care? He had always taken what he wanted when he wanted it, and last night – as it always was – it had been Bianca.

'Well?' he said brusquely.

'I pray you sit down,' she said.

But he did not sit. He stood, legs apart, like an angry bull ready to charge.

She did not look up from her needlework. 'It concerns Pilar. She is growing up. She will soon be fourteen. That is an age when we should be thinking of finding her a husband.'

'Madam,' he said, 'you may safely leave my daughter's future in my hands.'

'I would wish to have a say in her future also.'

'You mean you've found a husband for her?'

'I mean that may be possible.'

'You need not bother, Madam. I already have a husband for my daughter.'

'I believe he could not be as advantageous to her as the man I have in mind.'

'And who is this man who, in your greater wisdom, you have picked for our daughter?'

'Howard Hardy.'

'What!'

'I said Howard Hardy. He is the heir to the Hardy estates. A considerable fortune will be his.'

'Considerable fortune! That's if the Queen hasn't confiscated it by the time it should come to him. And let me remind you, Madam, my daughter will have a considerable fortune of her own.'

'You mean that you would not give your consent to a match between Pilar and Howard Hardy.'

'You have taken my meaning exactly. I would not. By God, I would not! Dost think I would let my girl go into that hot-bed of Popery? That I'd let her link my fortune with that of a Papist?'

'You forget that I have my own religion.'

'Bah! You, a feeble woman! If you had any spirit I'd have put an end to your flirtation with Popery long ago. No! Go and make your genuflexions. Go and worship your graven images if you must. But leave that girl alone.'

'Do you mean you will not even consider what a very good match this is? It is the best our daughter could hope for!'

'Our daughter could hope for the best in the land, Madam. And I've got a husband for her. She's going to marry Petroc Pellering, that's who. And that's my last word.'

'That . . . buccaneer!'

'Buccaneer, did you say, Madam? Let me tell you that those you call buccaneers are accorded greater respect – aye and freedom – than any lily-livered Papist who hides a priest in his house and is afraid to receive the fellow openly.'

'I did not mean . . .'

'You did not mean! Madam, do you know what you mean? I tell you this: My girl will marry where I wish, and it shall be with no lily-livered Papist.'

He turned and strode out of the room. She infuriated him with her silly bits of embroidery and her Spanish dignity.

It was disturbing to have Petroc in the house. There was no avoiding him, and even when Pilar went out on to the cliffs, she would often meet him. She tried always to take Roberto with her. The man inspired her, not only with hatred, but with some unaccountable fear. She was afraid now to be out after dark alone, lest she should come upon him. His brilliant blue eyes followed her; during meal-times she would look up and find them fixed upon her. She knew that he was plotting something, and that she figured largely in his plots.

She thought in those first days that she understood. He believed she was planning to stow away again, and he was determined to catch her if she did this a second time, as he had on the first occasion.

That amused her. She was not planning to stow away. To sail with her father was not the same exciting proposition as it had been, for the reason that *he* would be there.

Her vivid imagination was at work. She pictured the silent ship; everyone but the watch asleep. And herself perhaps in the hold, with him suddenly coming towards her.

No! She did not think she wanted to sail with her father if Petroc Pellering was also sailing with him.

Bess and Howard did not come over to the house at all, now that the Captain's ship was in the harbour. It was as well, they had evidently decided, that he knew nothing of the great friendship which existed between the two houses. Those secret visits which the women had paid to Hardyhall were suspended. They were saving up their confessions until the Captain sailed away, thought Pilar.

Sir Ennis went to London and, to Pilar's disgust, Petroc did not accompany him. Strangely enough she felt more in fear of Petroc when her father was not at hand.

Petroc was busy, superintending the work which was being done to the ship; he would row out to it every day; and that was good, thought Pilar, for it meant that he was absent from the house for long periods at a time. But it also meant that he made a habit of turning up at unexpected moments, and she could never be sure when she would come face to face with him.

On several occasions he had tried to persuade her to go to the ship with him. There was this, that, and the other he wanted to show to her.

She always declined. He expressed himself disappointed at her refusals.

'You should take more interest, Miss Piller,' he said. 'Your father tells me it will be yours one day.'

'While he's alive it will be his,' she said, 'and he is not going to die.'

He bent down to bring his face on a level with hers. 'The sea's a hard life, Miss Piller. And a dangerous one. We never know from one dawn to the next whether it's the last time we'll see the sun rise.'

'Yes,' she said. 'It is like that, I know.'

'Therefore,' he said, 'we make our preparations. We make the most of life.'

His eyes had taken on that intense look which made them glow a deep blue, like the blue flames from the firewood which had been washed up by the tide.

'That is why we do not like to waste our time. We like to enjoy every moment as it comes along.'

'That's wise,' she said. 'You should enjoy your moments lest they should prove to be your last.'

He took her by the shoulders suddenly, and his hands were as hot as the look in his eyes.

'A sound philosophy, Miss Piller,' he said. 'I'm glad you applaud it.' He drew her to him and kissed her.

She was hot with shame and anger, and she obeyed her immediate impulse to kick him.

He released her. 'I remember,' he said, 'you cling to old methods. One day you will learn to use your lips as readily as you now use your feet.'

Her inclination then was to run, but she feared that would be cowardly; it was also undignified, and she had great need to remind him of her dignity.

'I cannot think why you should do such silly things,' she said.

'Can you not? Shall I tell you?'

'I have no wish to hear, so I shut my ears.'

'Never shut your ears, Piller. Keep them open and alert. It's the way to learn and, until you've learned what life has to offer you, how can you take it and enjoy it?'

'How dare you! Do you imagine I am a serving-girl to be kissed as you think fit?'

'I did not imagine that for a moment.'

'I know what your manners are with serving-girls. When my father returns, I shall tell him how you have treated me. You will, I doubt not, spend your first weeks at sea in irons.'

'I doubt it,' he said. 'I doubt it very much.'

She did not wait for more. She turned sharply and walked away.

※ ※ ※

Roberto and Pilar lay near the edge of the cliffs. There was such activity in the bay. Seven vessels lay there, and there was much corning and going between them and the shore. Stores were being loaded; workmen were testing the ships to make sure that they would stand up to the hazards of the long sea crossing. In the streets of Plymouth the leaders of the expedition could often be seen. There was Sir Richard Grenville who was to command it, and Ralph Lane who was to act for Sir Walter Raleigh as governor of the new colony which these people were founding. There were the emigrants too – one hundred and eight of them – men and women with dreams in their eyes and immense courage in their hearts.

'Roberto,' said Pilar, 'do you wish you were going to sail with all those men and women to Virginia?'

'Nay,' said Roberto. 'I'd rather stay here.'

'You are without the spirit of adventure.'

Roberto fell silent. Nor did Pilar speak; she was sailing on one of those emigrant ships; she was landing in the beautiful foreign country; she was saving the life of Sir Richard Grenville, and being made governor of the colony.

'A bay full of ships. By God, they're a brave sight!' said a voice behind them; and they both turned, startled to see Petroc standing over them.

He threw himself down beside them and went on: 'It'll be a hard life for those settlers. I wonder if they'll stay the course.'

'Of course they'll stay the course,' said Pilar.

'Do not forget they are leaving their homes. They are starting a new life in a new land. Homesickness can amount to a disease. Men even die of it.'

Roberto nodded slowly. 'I can understand that,' he said.

'*You* left *your* home,' Pilar reminded Petroc. 'I expect you have wounded your parents deeply by leaving them. Do you never think of that?'

'Often,' he said, moving nearer. 'But I tell myself that I should have wounded them more deeply had I stayed.'

'I see you are one of those who will always find excuses for their shameful conduct.'

Petroc laughed. 'This girl has never forgiven me for refusing to allow her to accompany us last trip,' he said. 'Miss Piller, you should not bear such grudges. It was solely out of my consideration for you, I do assure you, that I carried you ashore.'

'I could most happily do without your consideration.'

Petroc had turned his face to hers and was looking at her earnestly. 'I see dreams in your eyes,' he said. 'You look at the ships below, and you think of those people going to a land of beauty and plenty; you think of a friendly brown-skinned people. My child, your dreams do not encompass the true picture. These lands we visit are rich. Vast tracts remain undiscovered. There is great rivalry for them. The country really belongs to the Indians. The French have already settled in the North; the Spaniards are in possession of great tracts in the South. And we English have staked our claims. Our greatest enemies are the Spaniards, because their strength matches ours. There are many battles fought on land and on sea; and let me tell you this – the cruellest people in the world are the Spaniards.'

'And you,' said Pilar haughtily, 'you are so kind, so gentle?'

'I am a buccaneer. I sail the sea in search of booty. This I bring back to England, and I take a goodly share of what I plunder. But it is not all for plunder, not all for riches that are quickly come by – *quickly*, you understand, not *easily* so, for all is fought for, and we buy our treasures with our blood. There are those among us who visualise an expanding England, lands populated with our people working in friendship with the Indians and making trade and prosperity here at home. But the Spaniards want more than treasure and trade. They are fanatics. They want to spread the Catholic Faith throughout the world, and those who do not hold that Faith are less, in their eyes, than the lowest animals. I have seen them burn whole villages; I have seen terrible things. That is why I could not let you travel with us. You are too young, and you are not a man, who can defend himself. You would be at the mercy of blood-crazed men, men whose petty desires of the moment are more important to them than the lives of their victims.'

'You make long speeches,' said Pilar.

'Aye! I make long speeches. We have a war to fight, my girl. And wherever we look we see our enemies. They are rich and they are strong. They build their ships to sail against us. They are in possession of half the world. In the Caribbean, from the remote south-east along the shore to Florida and beyond . . . these rich lands are all in the possession of Spain. But it shall not remain so. Forget your Spanish blood. Soon you will marry, and in your children that blood will be diluted still further.'

'We shall marry,' said Roberto soothingly, for the fire of the man disturbed him. 'And we shall marry into a good English family. I am to have Bess, and Pilar will marry Howard.'

'What is this?' asked Petroc, frowning.

'We have planned our marriages, have we not, Pilar?'

'Yes,' said Pilar. 'It is all settled. But you know, Roberto, we should not talk of it to those to whom it cannot be in the least interesting.'

Petroc looked at her earnestly. 'It is of great interest to me,' he said firmly.

❧ ❧ ❧

The ship was ready. In a few days it would sail out of the bay. The expedition led by Sir Richard Grenville had already left.

The Captain was uneasy. He was going to be away for two years. Pilar grew up astonishingly fast, and he did not forget her Spanish blood. She would be a woman in two years' time. What if he were delayed? What if this marriage, on which he had set his heart, should not take place because Isabella forestalled him?

The Hardys? Sir Howard, as he'd one day be. What of that? He himself was Sir Ennis. And his title had been won, won with blood and booty on the high seas – not handed down from lily-livered parent to lily-livered son.

They could keep their title. He did not doubt that Petroc would receive his one day from the Queen. The Queen loved all handsome men, and Petroc was handsome enough; she loved adventurers. Sir Ennis reckoned that when the Queen saw blue-eyed Captain Petroc from the West Country, she'd be captivated. 'My Piller will be Lady Pellering one day, I'll warrant,' he assured himself. 'And she shall be! By God, she shall be! Lady Pellering – no fancy Lady Hardy.'

But he was perturbed, for he was going away, and two years was a long time.

He said to Pilar: 'When I come back you'll be a woman, girl. It'll be time we found a husband for you then.'

'I'll find my own,' she answered.

'I'll warrant you will, but I'd want him to be worthy of my girl.'

'I'll make my own choice, Captain,' she said.

It was all very well for him to throw back his head and guffaw. It was all very well to pretend she was but a child. But he knew himself, and he knew that he was afraid of her, afraid of that spirit in her which would cross his will if she thought fit to do so.

He sought out his wife.

He said: 'I shall be away mayhap two years or more. When I'm back we'll get the girl married.'

She did not answer. She was still at that accursed needle-work. She went on with it as though her life depended on it. He felt an impulse to snatch it from her and stamp on it. He could do that, he knew, and she would still sit regarding him imperturbably. Therefore he restrained himself.

'What are you thinking there, eh? Are you thinking to get the girl married to that lump of pap up at the hall there?'

'I was not thinking that,' she said.

'You would do well to refrain from such thoughts. I'll come back to find my girl unmarried, and then I'll arrange her marriage for her. Forget you not, woman, that she is my girl.'

'She is also mine,' retorted Isabella with unwonted spirit.

'Yours! You bore the girl, yes. That's all. She's mine . . . all mine. What were you doing all the time you carried her, eh? Shuddering and weeping, muking, puking . . . telling yourself you were shamed. Shamed! By carrying my girl Piller. No wonder when she was born she was all mine!'

'You were not interested in her, as I remember, when she was born. No more interested than you were in Roberto.'

' 'Tis true enough. I thought her yours then. 'Twas not till she began to strut about . . .' His beard wiggled at the memory of her, and his voice grew a little harsh with emotion as he recalled the small sturdy figure looking up at him with fiercely belligerent eyes — 'Not till she began to show her spirit and whose child she was. But then I knew her for mine, and I'll not have her life ruined by your traitor friends. Woman, listen to me! If aught ill befall that girl, I'll kill you: for I shall lay the blame at your door.'

He was enraged at the thought. He watched the white hands with the needle. She cared little for his threats. She had suffered, she was telling herself, so acutely at his hands, that she was indifferent to what further suffering he would inflict. She was like one of those martyrs who would die willingly for the sake of someone they loved, and for something they believed to be right.

He was frustrated. If Death could not terrify her, what could?

❧ ❧ ❧

On the day he sailed, Pilar rowed out to the ship with him.

He bade her a warm farewell.

'It's the last I'll see of my girl Piller,' he said. 'When I come back she'll be a woman.'

'It will be at least two years, Captain?' she asked.

'And likely to be more. By God, I'll bring you something back. I'll bring you jewellery such as you've never seen before. It shall be my wedding present to you.'

He hesitated and looked into her face, but her expression was non-committal. He was afraid to mention Petroc. He knew that, by refusing to allow her to stow away, the young man had aroused a resentment which he had been unable to eliminate.

'Mayhap,' he said, 'your husband will take you to sea one day. It's what you want, is it not? There's nothing like it, girl. You must marry a man who's a sailor like the Captain. There's none other that would be right for you.'

Then Petroc came and stood beside the Captain.

'I look forward to the day we return,' he said.

But Pilar did not look at him.

When she was rowed ashore, the Captain and Petroc stood side by side watching the boat. The Captain was realising that when he had made his plans he had not taken one factor into consideration; the will of his girl Piller.

He turned to Petroc and was about to say that he hoped they would be able to carry out their plan regarding his girl, but he saw that Petroc had no doubt that they would. The smile on his

392

lips was one of complete confidence. The Captain gave him a rough pat on the back.

Petroc was as he himself had been twenty years before. He knew that, to such as they were, all things were possible.

Isabella called on Sir Walter and Lady Hardy, and was received in the punch room because it was small and intimate and there they could speak undisturbed.

Isabella was saying: 'In two or three years he will be back again, and then I fear he will insist on Pilar's marrying the man of his choice. This is his young second, who sails with him, so like himself that if he did not wish Pilar to marry the young man I should believe he was his natural son.'

Lady Hardy shivered.

'I fear,' went on Isabella, 'that if Pilar marries him she will have such a life as I have had. He will coarsen with the years, and mayhap one day he will raid my country's coast and bring women into the house to live with her . . . as has been done before. I cannot endure the thought of such a future for my child.'

Lady Hardy said: 'It is a pity that his ship is not swallowed in the storms. I wonder such a man is allowed to go on living. But it will not always be so. Nay, there is change in the air. I feel it. I was told . . .'

Her husband silenced her with a look. 'My dear,' he said, 'it is Pilar's future which Lady March has come here to discuss.'

'I have told him that you would have no objection to a marriage between Pilar and Howard,' went on Isabella. 'He was . . . quite abusive.'

'And why so?' demanded Lady Hardy.

'He has heard rumours, I fear. He talks of Papists . . .'

Sir Walter looked alarmed.

393

'How dare he . . .' began Lady Hardy, but she was too angry to continue.

Isabella hurried on: 'I feel I must defy him. I would like to see my daughter safely married before he can interfere.'

Sir Walter looked grave, but Lady Hardy said: 'Why should it not be so? She is fourteen. A good age for marriage. Indeed, if we concluded they were too young for the consummation, she could come here and live in the nurseries, as so many young brides do in their future homes. Then she could share Bess's lessons with Mr Heath.'

'That would please me greatly,' said Isabella. 'If I could feel that she was safely married and receiving the religious instruction I wanted for her, I could be contented. I should not care what happened when he came home. He would be too late to do anything to prevent a marriage which had already taken place. He could kill me if he wished. I should not care, if I knew that Pilar was in safe hands, far away from the life he would force upon her, receiving instruction in our Faith.'

'It must be done,' said Lady Hardy.

Sir Walter said: 'He is her father. This matter requires some thought.'

'Some thought!' cried Lady Hardy. 'When the child's whole future is at stake — and not only her earthly future! Her soul is in danger.'

'I greatly wish that this could come to pass,' said Isabella.

'I have talked to Howard,' said Sir Walter. 'He is certain that he wants to marry Pilar when they are old enough. He loves her dearly.'

'And she loves him,' said Isabella. 'I can see no reason why they should not be very happily married. But I think her father may have spoken to her. She is very fond of him, and I fear he may have prevailed on her to give a promise to remain unmarried until he returns.'

'Could he have done such a thing – and Pilar so young yet?'

'I fear he might.'

Lady Hardy pulled the bell-rope, and a servant appeared.

She said: 'Go to the schoolroom and tell Mr Heath I would speak to him here in the punch room.'

'My dear Lady March,' went on Lady Hardy when the servant had gone, 'I can see that this matter gives you anxiety. I am going to ask Father Heath to give us his opinion. He has a special fondness for Pilar.'

Father Heath came hurriedly into the room.

'Father, this concerns Pilar,' said Lady Hardy. 'The Captain wishes her to marry one of his sailors – a coarse, crude creature – and dear Lady March is alarmed. As you know, we have often thought that a match between Pilar and Howard would be an excellent thing. They are so fond of each other. Father, do you believe it is God's will that Lady March should oppose the wishes of her husband in this case?'

'I feel convinced of this,' said Father Heath fervently. 'I shall never forget the occasion when Pilar and I were together beneath the chapel. I knew then that she was meant to be one of us. I was desolate when she no longer came for instruction.'

'The Captain is away for two years, possibly more,' said Lady Hardy. 'God has surely given us this time to do His work. If the children were married and Pilar brought here to receive instruction from you, by the time the Captain returned it might be that she had become not only a bride but a good Catholic.'

'I see in this the hand of God,' said Father Heath. 'I see this clearly. Not only shall we save Pilar's soul but those of many others. I have been uneasy since my first meeting with Pilar. She is a good child and has kept her promise to be silent, but she is young and, if she were cunningly questioned, who knows, it might be difficult for her not to betray us. If she were here with us – if she were one of us – ah, then I think we could feel more secure. Yes, clearly I see in this the hand of God.'

Lady Hardy was excited.

'We must prepare the children's minds for marriage,' she said. 'We must let them realise they are no longer young. I will give a ball – a ball and a banquet – and we will use the occasion to let both Howard and Pilar see that they are fast approaching an age which is ripe for marriage.'

❧ ❧ ❧

The great hall was decorated for the occasion. Festoons of leaves were hanging on the walls among the weapons and banners. Flowers from the gardens had been set about the room. In the centre of the hall a long table had been set up, and on it were great joints of meat and pies of many shapes, and in the centre a replica in golden pastry of Hardyhall itself. The great boar's head, which had been in pickle for days, graced the centre of the table; legs of mutton, chines of beef, sucking pigs, pheasants, peacocks, hares, and fish of all kinds were displayed there.

After the banquet the servants came hurrying in to remove the table and all its contents; then some of the guests, who came from the Court itself, led the dancers in a *branle*, which had been introduced to the Court from France, it was said, and was very fashionable. The local people joined in as well as they could, and made it into something of a romp. Pilar was there dancing with Howard, flushed, excited, declaring that this was the happiest night of her life.

'I would we could have a ball every night,' she told Howard.

'You would tire of them.'

'Not I! I would dance all through the night and never be tired.'

'You would find there were other things to interest you. It is because you are so young.'

She looked at Howard, with his delicate features and that air of being perpetually worried, and she felt a great longing then to comfort him.

He said: 'Pilar, you want to marry me, don't you?'

'Why, of course!'

'We could be betrothed. It would be a betrothal with a formal ceremony, and you could come here and live in this house.'

She looked about her at the great hall which seemed so different now that it was full of people. She glanced up at the peep. It seemed nothing on this night but a star-shaped aperture.

She had a great desire then to be up there, in the solarium, looking down on the crowded hall.

'Howard,' she said, 'let's go up there. They won't miss us. I want to see all the dancers through the peep.'

'Come then,' said Howard, and they slipped beneath the arras, up the staircase and through the rooms which led to the solarium.

Pilar looked round her and shivered. The solarium, touched by moonlight which shone through the several windows of the big room, was more ghostly than it had looked by daylight on the other occasions when she had seen it.

'It's quiet up here,' she whispered.

He put his arm about her and she clung to him, pretending to be afraid and enjoying that fear.

'This is a wonderful house,' she whispered. 'You never know what's going to happen in it.'

'Pilar,' he said, 'I'm glad you love this house, because it's going to be your home, you know. Pilar, sweet Pilar, how fortunate we are! So many have marriages made for them; they often do not see those whom they are to marry, until everything is arranged. I should have hated such a marriage. But now that I know you are to be my wife, I can be very happy about that part of my future.'

'And not about another part? You mean you're not happy because I'm a Protestant and you're a Catholic?'

'Don't let's think of that tonight. Let's enjoy this, shall we?'

'Oh yes, let's enjoy it.' She began to dance through the great room, twirling round and round, not the dances she had seen in the hall below, but those she had learned from Bianca. 'This is the *farraca*, Howard. I am fighting a bull now. See! I am teasing him . . . he is coming straight for me . . . I leap aside . . . and he has rushed past me. He thinks to kill me. I intend to kill him.'

'Don't talk of killing on a night like this,' said Howard. 'Come here. I thought you wanted to look down on the dancers.'

'Oh yes, I did. Indeed I do.' She was at his side. 'Oh, how beautiful they look! How different! I have always thought the hall seemed different through this peep. Isn't it exciting? It's like looking on at other people's lives. I think one of the most exciting things is watching people when they don't know they're being watched. I wonder if that's what God does. Just imagine Him, watching all the time . . . seeing everything we do, and writing it down in the big book. But that's the recording-angel, isn't it? I wonder how many recording-angels there are. There must be rows and rows of them, all with their special books. Look! Who is that talking to your father? They are going over to your mother now. Howard, they look afraid. Howard, you're trembling. What's wrong?'

'Trembling? I'm not.' He was staring at his parents who were making their way out of the room through the arras-covered doorway leading to the two stairs which, in their turn, led to that room from which it was possible to reach the chapel. 'You imagine things that don't exist. You always did, Pilar.'

'If I'm going to marry you, Howard, I shall have to know what is going on. I shall have to comfort you.'

He turned to her and took her face in his hands. 'Pilar, I love you dearly.'

'Yes, yes,' she said impatiently. 'But I want to know about what is going on. People come here. They're Catholics, aren't they? They come here to hide.'

'When you are one of us, Pilar, you will share our secrets. They will be safe with you.'

'I want to know them now . . . now.'

'It would seem that you do. Let us go back to the hall. They will miss us and wonder where we are.'

She was silent for a few seconds; then her eyes went to the escritoire, and she remembered that other peep. She was filled with a desire to look into the chapel because she believed that Sir Walter and Lady Hardy had gone there in great haste.

She drew herself away from him. 'Where are you going, Pilar?' he asked. But she was already squeezing herself and her elaborate dress behind the escritoire and the hangings; she was moving the picture and looking down into the chapel.

'No, Pilar,' said Howard.

He was beside her, but she had already seen, by the light of the candles, Sir Walter and Lady Hardy. With them were two men — strangers, their mud-spattered clothes suggesting that they had just made a long journey.

They were talking quietly and earnestly. Pilar could not see their faces, but she knew by their demeanour that they had brought bad news.

'Come away, Pilar,' Howard insisted. 'You must not peep at the chapel. It is a sacred place.'

He was beside her looking down as they heard one of the men say: 'The whole plot is discovered. Gifford was a spy, Walsingham's spy!'

'Holy Mother of God,' said Sir Walter, 'that means that every letter that went into the place and every one that came out by way of those beer barrels would have been seen by Walsingham before they fell into the hands for which they were intended? What villainy! What rascality! To pose as a priest! And that it should be Gifford! What will be the outcome, think you?'

'What indeed,' said one of the strangers. 'We await that with trepidation. There have already been many arrests.'

Howard had succeeded in pulling her away, and dragged her into the middle of the room.

'What does it mean?' cried Pilar. 'What has happened? Who is Gifford?'

'You know, do you not, who Walsingham is.'

'Of course I know. He is the Queen's Secretary of State.'

'He is the greatest enemy of all Catholics.'

'And he has discovered something . . . in which people in this house are engaged?'

'Pilar . . . Pilar, for the love of God do not say a word about what you have seen and heard.'

'I can keep secrets,' she said.

'If you did not keep this one you could bring great disaster to us. Your loyalty belongs to us. You are going to marry me. You are one of us already.'

'You are more frightened than you have ever been, Howard. You must not be frightened. I'll not let anything harm you.'

He put his arm about her and held her fast to him, and she was filled with a tenderness she had never before experienced. This was being in love, she supposed.

❧ ❧ ❧

Pilar could not sleep. It had been the most exciting night of her life – a different sort of excitement this, from that adventure in the priest's hole with Mr Heath.

When she saw the first sign of dawn in the sky she got out of bed and went to the window. The sea, reflecting the scarlet clouds, was faintly pink in the morning light. Even as she watched, the colour changed, growing deeper; away to the east the sea looked like mother-of-pearl; and as she watched the pink stain spread across the water, she saw a ship limping out of the morning mist and immediately recognised it, in spite of its crippled appearance, as the Captain's.

❧ ❧ ❧

There was tumult throughout the house. The Captain had been away only a few weeks and he had already returned.

They brought him ashore; he was as battered as his ship; but a ship could be repaired. One of his legs had been shot away and there was a malignant sword wound in his side. He had aged ten years since he had left his home a few weeks before. Pilar, Isabella, and Bianca dressed his wounds, but he refused to stay in bed. He demanded a feast such as they had always prepared for him on such occasions, and sat propped up at the head of the table, Pilar on his right hand. His voice was as loud as ever, his oaths as frequent, his expressions as fierce and at times terrifying.

He would have them all at table, the entire household, including the servants.

'So I'm back,' he roared at them. 'And you didn't think to see me so soon, by God! But here I am, and you see I met bad weather. We were sighted by two Spaniards. They're growing saucier, these Spaniards. They came into the attack, and we were one against two. We sank one of them but men from the other boarded us — at least one or two of them did. I'd lost my leg by that time, but we made short work of them; not before they'd done some damage to us though. One of them sunk, and the other beaten off! It was not bad, but it wasn't good enough. I shouldn't be here to tell the tale but for that fellow there. He was beside me when I was all but spent. By God, it was a sight to see him run that fellow through. I got his blood on my jacket, and I'll keep it as long as I live. Yes! you see me here by the grace of Petroc Pellering, who is my good friend from now on, and the good friend of you all. You, Pilar — just take his hand and say a word of thanks on behalf of my household.'

Pilar had risen to her feet. Petroc rose with her.

He said: 'Nay! Nay! What need is there of thanks? I did what had to be done. I curse myself because I did not do it sooner.'

The Captain's eyes were glazed with emotion. Bianca, watching, thought: His adventurous life is over but he's going to cling to it; he's going to live it through those two.

Pilar said quietly: 'We all thank you for saving the Captain's life and bringing him home to us.'

Petroc took her hand in his. He held it firmly.

She would not lift her eyes to his face. She was ashamed because there were tears in them. She tried to withdraw her hand but he would not let her.

Then suddenly she could not control her emotion. She burst into tears and, wrenching herself free, threw herself at the Captain, flung her arms about his neck and sobbed before them all: 'You might have been killed. You might have been killed!'

All those about the table remained motionless. Only the Captain moved. He put up his weather-beaten hand to stroke her hair.

And all those watching had the strange experience of seeing the tears roll down his cheeks.

🌹 🌹 🌹

The Captain's sentimental mood did not last long. He hobbled about the house on a crutch. He wheezed and roared as he suffered the pain in his side; it was as though a tempest had struck the house.

He was making plans. That became clear. The old routine was over for ever and life had changed drastically.

With dread Isabella realised that the Captain could not go to sea again. He planned that Petroc should captain the ship and carry on the Captain's work; yet it would still be the Captain who was in command. Petroc should bring home the treasure. He should have his share and it would be a big one. But the treasure which was carried in the Captain's ship was the Captain's treasure.

He trusted Petroc. He was giving him command of the ship, and he was making him his heir. He was doing more than that. He was going to make him his son through marriage with his daughter.

On the third day after his return he told Pilar of his plans. He was lying on his bed – for to his disgust he was forced to spend many hours resting – and Pilar was sitting beside him. 'Piller,' he said, 'I want to talk to you.' She turned her face to his expectantly and he marvelled afresh at her beauty and youth.

'Piller,' he went on, 'I'm a man who has had most of his own way. I've lived the life I wanted to live, and the sea has been my life. I'll never go to sea again. No, I won't! What use would I be? I'm a battered and waterlogged old bucket – that's what I am. No good to anyone. You've got to be hard and strong to sail the seas in these great days. My life's done with, Piller. By God, I'd have cursed young Petroc for saving my life, but for one thing. That one thing's you, Piller. You're going to make my life worth living, you are. I'm going to see you have all that I want for you. I'm going to see you the master of my treasure ship . . . you, Piller, no one but you.'

'You mean . . . you want me to go to sea?'

'Ah, no! The sea's no place for you . . . Look at me. Look at my ugly face. Look at this stump. Look at this that has happened to me. It could happen to you, Piller, if you went to sea. Oh, I won't say I haven't thought of you, standing there beside me with the wind in your hair, and you dressed like a boy. I've thought of it often. By God, I've said to myself, she's got the spirit. She ought to be with me, my girl Piller. But that wouldn't do, Piller. I want you to be beautiful, rich, to live in comfort. I want you to marry and have sons. That's the woman's job, and you – even you, my Piller – are but a woman. To produce sons . . . by God, to bring them safe into port, that's as good a job as bringing in the treasure. And that's what I want from you, Piller. I want us to be together. I'm a sick man, Piller. I went away hale and healthy, and came back a wreck. It's what happens to many a vessel that puts to sea – but it's only when it happens to yourself that you understand what it means. Piller, do you know what I'd do if it wasn't for you? I'd take my sword and run it right through this old hulk of a body, because, Piller, I've got no use for the sort of life that's left to me.'

'Don't say it! Don't say it!' she cried. And she shook her head vigorously, as though she could shake the tears away from her eyes.

He put his arms about her and held her close to him.

'I won't do it, Piller. I'll live, my girl. And life will be good, for you'll make it so for me. You're my girl, and by God, while I've got you that's good enough for me or any man. We're going to be partners, girl. We're going to be together. We're going to send out our ships. We'll fit 'em up and we'll send 'em out and we'll watch for 'em to come in. And if we lose one, there'll be two others to take its place. We're together in this, and when I die . . . you'll go and do the same, and your sons will learn to do it. By God, Piller, we're goingto drive the Spaniards off the seas, and we're going to pull in for ourselves all the booty they're taking from their colonies to Spain. We're going to do it for England and the Queen – but there'll be a pretty profit in it for ourselves.'

Her eyes were gleaming. He saw it and laughed triumphantly.

'I knew you wouldn't disappoint me, Piller. You wouldn't

disappoint the Captain. Now listen here. In four weeks our ship will be ready to face the sea again. Thank God we brought her back. I never lost a ship yet, I'm thankful to say. I'd never have wanted to make port if I had. Petroc will sail her when she's ready. And when he comes back — less than two years from now — I want you to do something for me. I want you to take Petroc for your husband.'

'No, Captain! Not Petroc.'

'Why are you so set against him?'

'I like him not.'

'Like him! Petroc's not the sort for liking. He's for loving or for hating. That's Petroc. He wants you, Piller. He'll give you sons worthy of you. Tell me now what's been happening here while I've been away. Your mother has not been telling you that tittering ninny of Hardy's would make a good husband, has she?'

'If you mean Howard,' she said boldly, 'I'm going to marry him.'

'No!' The Captain threw back his head and laughed. 'That's child's talk, Piller. You marry him! Not you, Piller. You see, what's happened is this — you're but a little girl and you've not yet learned what men there are in the world. You mustn't go fancying the first you see, for the odds are that he won't be good enough for my girl Piller.'

'He is good enough, Captain. He's very good, and we have decided we'll marry.'

'Nay, girl,' said the Captain. 'It's Petroc for you.'

'It shall not be Petroc,' she said. 'I hate him.'

'That's well enough. You begin by hating him. I tell you, in a year or two you'll see there are few men in the world to compare with Petroc. As for that Papist over at the Hall! Nay, girl, do you know we've just discovered Papists plotting to murder the Queen?'

'Gifford betrayed them,' she said. 'Yes, I knew.'

'Yes,' he said. And he laughed. His face grew purple with laughter and then constricted with pain. He put his hand to his side and grimaced. 'We have our spies right in their midst. What do you think of that, eh? A spy disguised as a Jesuit priest! I call that cunning of the first order.'

'Will they search the houses?'

'Aye, they'll search the houses. They'll drag out the priests. The prisons in London are swarming with 'em. A pox on them all! Nay, girl, steer clear of Catholics. Turn your back on this pretty boy, and turn your face towards a real man.'

'Captain, I must tell you I will never marry Petroc.'

He laughed. He refused to take her seriously.

❧ ❧ ❧

There was tension throughout the house. Pilar knew that the old life was over. The Captain dominated the house. He spent long hours in his chair on the lawn, looking broodingly at the sea. His anger was terrible; he would throw his crutch at whoever annoyed him, and his aim was sure. Only was he contented when Pilar was beside him; then he would talk of the future and the ships they would have. He never tired of telling her how to deal with the spoils of a treasure ship, what portion must go to the Queen, what to the Captain, what to the men. He talked of his adventures, and Pilar would sit beside him dreaming that with him she sailed the seas.

Bess and Howard never came to the house and on those rare occasions when she visited Hardyhall she must go there stealthily, for she knew that if the Captain became aware of her visits he would be bitterly hurt, even if he did not forbid her to go.

The whole world seemed to be full of plots. The news of the one which had failed in London was talked of in Devon. It was said that this would be the end of the Queen of Scotland; the chief of the conspirators had already suffered, and Mary would be next.

The Captain raged against the Scottish whore. He liked to do so in the presence of Isabella; he seemed to enjoy seeing her flinch.

He is badly hurt, thought Pilar, and he likes to hurt others too, because he wants them all to be hurt as badly as himself.

She longed to soothe the Captain, for just as Howard's fear moved her, so did the Captain's rages. Her voice would be very tender when she spoke to him; and when she was by his side she begged him to tell her of the actions at sea in which he had taken part, because she knew that she could make him live in those adventurous days and forget he was sitting in an English garden – a Captain who would never go to sea. He was so like herself that she understood him.

But all the time she was with him she was aware that one day she must hurt him, because she would never marry Petroc, and she had decided that she would marry Howard.

Petroc himself was continually near her. He knew that she hated him. She had made that clear. He did not seem to mind. He made no attempt to placate her. He was quite certain that when he came back from his next voyage she would marry him. It was the Captain's wish. All men at sea had obeyed the Captain. He expected all in the Captain's household to do the same.

He would watch her with brooding eyes. He frightened her.

He set new thoughts circulating in her brain. She thought often of the stories she had heard of how her mother, Bianca and Carmentita had been taken from their homes and brought to that of the Captain. She was beginning to understand for what purpose, and that the Captain in his youth must have been very like Petroc Pellering.

She was afraid to be out after dusk lest she should come upon him and there should be no one near to help her if need be.

She asked Bianca if when she had lived the roving life she had been afraid of men.

'Yes,' said Bianca. 'Many times.'

'What did you do?'

Bianca's eyes narrowed. 'I took care that I should preserve myself, that I might be bestowed as I wished and never forced.'

Pilar nodded. 'How so, Bianca?'

'We gipsies carried a knife under our skirts, a little knife, but sharp enough to pierce the heart of any who might attack us. It was a *faja*. When I went to your mother's house it was taken from me. I thought I should no longer need it there. Then a day came when I did need it, and I no longer had it.'

'Did you leave it in Spain?'

'Yes, but I found another. I took it from the Captain's cabin when we sailed to England.'

'Show me, Bianca.'

Bianca took her to the room near Isabella's in which she slept. There she showed her the knife.

'Often,' she said, 'it is enough to show it. Men do not care to fight with women.'

She went out, leaving Pilar with the knife in her hands.

Tomorrow the ship would sail and he would be gone. Pilar lay in her bed and told herself she was glad. When he had gone, when he was no longer a malevolent presence in the house, she would feel bold again. Then she would tell the Captain that she was going to marry Howard, because she had promised to do so. She would be his girl who watched with him for the ships to come home, and she would be Howard's wife as well.

She would feel strong and ready for those tasks, once Petroc Pellering was on the high seas.

Then suddenly her heart leaped in terror. She was not sure afterwards whether she sensed evil or whether she had heard that creak of the stairs and had guessed. In any case she was out of bed and had a robe to cover her nakedness before the door was opened and he stood there looking at her.

He shut the door and laughed at her.

'You!' she cried. 'How dare you come here? Go away at once!'

'I've only just arrived,' he said.

'Go away! Go away!' she panted.

She realised then that she had expected this. She was not unprepared.

He still stood at the door. He had a leisured air. It was as though, enjoying this glimpse of her straight from her bed, ruffled and perturbed, he wanted to go on savouring the scene a little longer.

'What do you want?'

'To be with you,' he said.

'Here?'

'What better place?'

'Go at once. I shall never marry you. Understand that, now and for ever.'

'You've promised yourself to that praying mantis at the Hall,' he said. 'You think you're going to marry him!'

'My marriage is no concern of yours.'

'It is my greatest concern, since it will be mine also.'

'That shall never be. I hate you. I hate you every minute of the day.'

'So I am constantly in your thoughts?'

'Only to be hated.'

'I'd rather you hated me than forgot me.'

'I do forget you. I never think of you.'

'Contradictions, my dear Piller.'

He had started to come towards her. Her heart seemed to leap to her throat.

'Go away . . . go away!' She had thought to shout, but she found she was speaking in a whisper. 'Go, you pirate . . . you buccaneer!'

'It is a waste of energy to fight a buccaneer, Piller. They always take what they want, whether it's prettily given or has to be fought for.'

'The Captain would kill you,' she said.

'The Captain understands.'

She picked up Bianca's knife which was by her bedside. Now she knew that this was the materialisation of one of her greatest fears. She had imagined its happening just like this. That was why she had appropriated Bianca's knife.

'Then I will kill you,' she said.

He was staring at the knife in her hand.

He laughed. He opened his arms wide. His smile was mocking. 'Come, strike me!' he said.

He was looking at the hand which held the knife; it was trembling.

She lifted her arm, and it seemed that slowly he caught it. She cried out as the knife fell to the ground.

'You see, Piller,' he said, ''twas useless . . . even as I said.'

He lifted her in his arms then. His face was close to hers. She saw the gleam of his eyes and the flash of his teeth.

'Did you hate me so much?' he said.

She could not understand the emotion which swept over her. She felt the tears in her eyes, and she was ashamed of them. This was the second time that others had seen her cry – she, Pilar, who for as long as she could remember had been proud never to let any see her shed a tear.

There was silence which seemed to go on for a long time.

Then he laid her gently on the bed, leaned over her and kissed her with tenderness.

He said: 'There, Piller, little Piller, do not be afraid. There is nothing to fear. You are just a child after all. Wait for me. That is all I ask of you.'

Then he had gone; and she lay for a long time crying quietly, though she knew not for what reason.

And the next morning his ship sailed away.

PART SEVEN

DEVON
1572 AND 1588

Chapter VII

DEVON, 1587 AND 1588

It was late spring when Domingo and Blasco with Charlie Monk rode into Devon. The banks were starred with the white stitchwort flowers, and the meadows were golden with cowslips. The lush greenness of the grass seemed very refreshing to them after their long stay in the Clink and the Counter.

They had not been immediately released. Domingo had asked for time to make his decision, and it had been given.

He would never forget the long weeks when the weather grew colder and colder, and the discomfort of prison more pronounced, when he had spent long hours on his knees praying for guidance.

His two voices were stronger than ever. One demanding that he should not in any circumstances deny his Faith and betray his country; the other reminding him of the souls he could save if he but lied to do so. 'It is God's will.' Again and again he heard that voice. 'What use are you to God . . . a dead man? You must live and bring many to Him; there are souls drowning in the seas of heresy. It is for you to throw them the lifeline. God does not mean you to die as

Babington and the others died. What good would that do?'

But he had delayed his decision, pleading for more time. Yet on every occasion when the key was turned in the lock of his cell he would start up in a sweat. He was afraid that they would put him on the rack and, in the extreme torture when they cried to him 'Deny your Faith', he would. He feared he would die a coward, denying all that he believed to be good and right, and all because he could not endure the torture. He feared he would barter eternity for a release from pain.

Charlie Monk had come to see him while he was in prison. He told him he had left Sir Eric's service, for Lady Aldersly had considered it wise that he should do so. Sir Eric was detained in prison; Charlie was doing odd jobs, holding horses, working for a week or two in various houses. It was the best he could get. He hoped that when Father Carramadino was released he might again be his servant.

Domingo had blessed him and told him that he would be glad to employ him if ever he left his prison.

'I pray the saints you will, Father,' Charlie had declared vehemently. 'I pray that you will ere long be released so that you and Charlie and the Señor, your brave brother, may travel the roads together snatching souls from the devil.'

Charlie had spoken with his customary jocularity but Domingo had believed he saw the fear that was in the man. He needs me. So many need me, thought Domingo. Could I not serve God better in life than in death?

And in the end he had made his decision.

The instructions he had received had been brief.

'There is a house in Devon. It is Hardyhall, and we believe it to be a house at which very many Jesuits are calling when they first arrive in England. Those places on the south-east coast are becoming dangerous for them and they seek to go further afield, so they make a longer sea voyage and strike our coast in Devon where they think we are less watchful. These priests, many of them coming direct from Spain, may have information which will be useful to us. We want it immediately conveyed to us. There is a house on the moors to which messages may be sent by Charles Monk, a poor simple fellow, a convert to Catholicism. You may wonder why we do not arrest him since he is a traitor; but he is of such small account that we let him go free. What we are most interested in is news from Spain, particularly that which concerns the Armada. Any hints as to when an attack may be made, any chance word overheard in a tavern – that is all-important.'

'You are asking me to betray my country and my cloth!' Domingo had cried.

'We are asking you to save your life,' he was told.

In this house to which he was going there had been a resident priest, who was to be called to the English college in Rome, and Domingo was to take his place. There were young people in the family to whom he would act as a tutor. That would be his nominal position in the house. His brother might go with him in the role of secretary and very personal servant, with Charlie as a menial servant.

If he had any doubt as to the efficiency of those who would now be his employers, he need only consider what had taken place. He could ask himself how it was that every movement he had made since he had been in England had been noted, how it was that Mr Heath could be recalled to Rome when it was expedient for this to take place. Sir Francis Walsingham himself had said: 'I hold that no price is too high to pay for knowledge and that no knowledge, however slight, can be ignored.' This was his policy; and it was for this reason that his tentacles stretched all over England and the Continent. 'If you ever think to betray us,' Domingo was told, 'remember St Giles's Field. Then I believe that you, being a wise man, will consider long before you commit such a foolish act. It may be that you will find some comfort in the fact that there are many – most of them where you would least expect it – in the employ of the English Secretary of State.'

There were many preparations to make. Those who worked for Sir Francis Walsingham must be as thorough as they were secret. There was a code to be learned. He must always employ it in his correspondence. All persons concerned must never be referred to by their names. There were code words for all people of high standing.

Charlie was allowed to visit him frequently in prison and when he was released was waiting for him, bustling and efficient.

'Oh, you can trust Charlie!' Never had Domingo seen Charlie in such high spirits. 'I made it my business to be ready for you . . . and for Señor Blasco when you came out.'

'So Blasco is out too?'

'To be released tomorrow. Don't you worry, Father. Leave it to Charlie.'

Charlie had taken a humble room over a tavern.

'Not quite right for your reverence, but the best I could find. And you did tell me you'd be travelling soon.'

'Very soon,' said Domingo.

The room Monk had found for them was in Lad's Lane and hither he carried cooked meat which he bought in Thames Street, and wine from the Vintry by the river.

Blasco joined them in the room next day – pale from his

418

long imprisonment, his features seeming more sharply cut, and lines of suffering about his mouth. They had not tortured Blasco; Blasco had been the victim of his own thoughts, for it was while he was in the Poultry that news had been brought to him of Julie's death. But to be reunited gave them great pleasure. Yet Blasco was puzzled. 'I understand them not,' he said. 'What manner of people are those we have come among? They capture us, hold us prisoner, and then . . . release us.'

'We are not of enough importance to be worth keeping,' said Domingo.

'Yet we were worth searching for.'

'Perhaps it was for others they sought.' Domingo's gaze had shifted. 'But let us not concern ourselves with their methods. There is work for us to do. There are houses waiting to receive us.'

'How do you know of these houses?'

'There were priests in the Clink when I was there. There were two in the cell next to mine. I heard them praying. We knocked on the walls of our cells and had conversation together. Our jailer was not a bad fellow. He shrugged his shoulders and said that he did not see what harm could be done if we spoke together. There were times when he would unlock my cell and I would visit the priests in the next one. They talked of all the good work I could be doing if I were free. We confessed our sins to each other and together we received the Blessed Sacrament. But more than this – they told the names of people who would be willing to give me shelter should I ever leave the prison, and I have now heard of a family in the West Country who wish me to spend some time with them as their resident priest is called away.'

Blasco said: 'We are most extraordinarily fortunate. I would not have believed it possible that two people could be so fortunate. I think the English must be a little mad to have captured us and then to release us in this way.'

'Let us thank God for their madness,' said Charlie.

At length they rode to the West, through the counties of Hampshire and Somerset into Devon, and the fresh beauty of all they saw might have lifted up their hearts had not both Blasco's and Domingo's been heavy with guilt.

Only Charlie was happy. He lifted his voice and he sang as they passed along the steep and winding lanes.

❧ ❧ ❧

Blasco could not sing. She died, he told himself, as they came across the stretches of moorland, she died coming to see me. Why had she so desired to see him?

He pictured the peaceful scene – the quiet house, the home of the Huguenots in which Julie had lived during those weeks since they had been in England. Why had she felt that she must come to his prison and endanger her own liberty by doing so? Foolish Julie! Careless, reckless, Julie! He had never thought her so before.

She had not loved him. There had never been love between them. Pity on his side, duty on hers.

Where was I wrong with Julie? he asked himself. What could I have done that was different? Should I have left her to the murderers of the Rue Béthisy? Would she then have been spared much pain? Should I never have made my way into the house? Should I have stayed in my room at the inn on that night, like a good Catholic? But no good Catholic was indoors on that night. Good Catholics were striding through the streets of Paris, blood dripping from their swords.

Had I been a good Catholic, how different my life would have been! I should have returned to my home, married a suitable wife – a Catholic, of course. We should have lived together in harmony as my parents did, and many years of suffering would have been avoided.

He would be haunted by Julie all through his life. Julie on the rooftops; Julie in his arms in the inn while the procession on its way to the Cemetery of Holy Innocents passed below; Julie kneeling on the bed listening to the footsteps on the stairs; and, lastly, Julie trampled underfoot by the crowds rushing to see the execution of Babington.

Now riding across the moorlands he gazed at the gorse bushes golden in pale sunshine, and the little streams trickling over the rocks, shining silver, and asked himself: What are we doing here? Domingo is doing work for which over many years he has been training, and I . . . I am a spy for my country.

Charlie spoke. 'We'll be in sight of Plymouth shortly. The house we're making for, you said, Father, was just outside the town.'

'Yes,' said Domingo, 'so our journey is nearly over.'

'Can you be sure that we shall stay there?' asked Blasco.

'There is work to be done at Hardyhall,' said Domingo.

'Work indeed, my gentlemen,' said Charlie. 'The good work. Souls to be saved, eh? Souls to be snatched from the devil.'

'We shall be very near the sea,' said Blasco. And he thought: Domingo has been instructed to come to this house. It is a Catholic house in a position of great advantage. Expeditions to the Pacific, to Mexico and the Americas set out from Plymouth. Now he was beginning to understand. Domingo's work was to make people change their Faith; his own would be to gather information about the shipping which came into the Sound.

He was expected to work against these English who had been so foolish as to release him; he was to work for the return of England to the Catholic Faith, he was to prepare the way for the setting up of the Holy Inquisition on this soil.

He shuddered. He had no zest for the task. He had felt himself aloof on that night in Paris. He could not endure the cruelty which was practised by that sect to which, because he had been born into it, he belonged. He was no longer a good Catholic; he was no nearer to Protestantism than to Catholicism. He was merely aloof; he was a man who had come to hate cruelty and wished to have no part in it.

At the same time he was conscious of a great lethargy within him. He was like the blades of grass which he could see blowing this way and that in the wind.

He had loved Bianca and he had lost her; he had felt it was his great task in life to protect Julie, and now he no longer had need to do that, and it seemed to him that nothing was of any great importance. He would do what was expected of him, he supposed; he would do it listlessly. He would live from one day to another, without greatly caring what became of him.

So Domingo and Blasco came to Hardyhall.

When they arrived at the house they were met by Sir Walter and Lady Hardy who greeted them warmly. Their horses were taken by grooms, and they were conducted to a winter parlour where food was laid out for them.

Charlie was given his in the buttery – good roast beef and tankards of Devon cider. He lost no time in making himself very friendly with the servants, telling them that he had ridden far with his master who had come to tutor the young people. He had never lived so near the sea before. He came from London, where many big ships sailed up the river. He reckoned they were as big as anything they saw in the Sound. The servants were indignant, and said they would show him what sort of ships sailed into the Sound, great ships bound on great adventures. Charlie was jocularly sceptical, and he soon had them talking away merrily.

Meanwhile Lady Hardy and Sir Walter sat down with their guests and told them how very pleased they were to see them.

'We had a great regard for Father Heath,' Lady Hardy told them. 'He has been with us so long. It was a great blow that he should have been recalled to Rome.'

'We priests are frequently recalled to our colleges,' said Domingo. 'It is natural that he should be, after such long service.'

'It was a sad blow,' said Sir Walter, 'when we heard that the Holy Enterprise had failed. And we were filled with alarm when we heard that there were traitors right at the centre. A terrible discovery.'

'You had heard that?' said Domingo.

'Indeed, yes. We are kept informed. We were warned soon after Babington was called to see Walsingham, and, as you know, the arrest immediately followed that. It was a terrible blow to know that it was Gilbert Gifford – he whom we had believed to be a Jesuit and a holy man – who was the traitor. How could he have done this, and he a priest! We know now that Walsingham had captured him and made him work for him in exchange for his life. Who would believe that a priest could behave thus?'

423

Domingo thought then that they must hear the violent beating of his heart. He managed to mutter: 'Men are weak.'

'But priests!' said Lady Hardy. 'Priests! And because of this our Queen is dead. I have heard that she met her death bravely and that, although the executioner made three attempts to sever her head from her body, she was unflinching to the end. And to think that we may not wear mourning for her!'

'We can mourn her in our hearts,' said Sir Walter.

'We have many visitors to the house,' put in Lady Hardy. 'They stay only for a little while, and we like their presence to be unnoticed. We leave the door of the chapel open. They come through that way. The chapel is particularly suited to these arrangements. There is the little room – we call it the squint – which can be reached through an ivy-covered door. In this squint it is possible for a man to lie hidden and unseen by any in the chapel. He can therefore choose a moment when all is clear to come through the chapel and up a short staircase to the punch room. We do not want the servants to know too much of what goes on. One always has to be careful, and after this Gifford affair I shall trust very few. You must understand, Father, that we have a hole, too, under the floor of the chapel. Father Heath was once saved by making use of it. We must show it to you this very night. One never knows when it may be necessary to put it into use.'

'I trust that may never come to pass.'

'We also,' said Sir Walter. 'But we have enjoyed a long period of immunity from the attentions of pursuivants.'

'It may be,' said Blasco, 'that now the Queen of Scots is dead there will be fewer of these plots, for it seems she was always the centre of them.'

Lady Hardy's eyes burned with a fierce fanaticism. 'We

will find another centre, never fear! Our task is to bring Catholicism back into England.'

'I doubt not that Father Carramadino will want to meet the children,' said Sir Walter.

'Indeed yes,' said Domingo, 'for they are to be my ostensible reasons for being here.'

'They are not such children,' said Lady Hardy. 'Howard is nearly eighteen, Bess well past fourteen. I will have them come here.'

She went to the bell-rope, and stood at the door until a servant came and took her instructions. She returned to the table and said in a low voice: 'Howard hears Mass. Howard is a good Catholic. He is discreet. But I have always been a little afraid of my daughter's taking too much part in these ceremonies. I am a coward, I know, but I fear for her and I have tried to keep her from partaking too much, until I feel it would be safer for her to do so. Father, you must forgive my cowardice. She is my daughter and . . .'

Domingo said: 'I understand. I beg of you do not excuse yourself. Your fears are reasonable. We all have our fears.'

Howard and Bess came into the punch room then.

'Here is Father Carramadino and his brother,' said Lady Hardy. 'My two children – Howard and Bess.'

Bess curtseyed; Howard bowed.

'Welcome,' said Howard.

'We are glad to see you, Father,' said Bess.

'I think,' said Lady Hardy, 'that now we have Father Carramadino with us we shall not regret so much the departure of Father Heath. But remember, call him Father Carramadino only when we are together thus. He is Mr Carramadino on all other occasions. And his brother is Mr Blasco. Now, come and sit down and talk to our guests. Later you can show them what they wish to see of the house. And do not forget, my children, to show them that you are good Catholics.'

Blasco was reminded of his mother's fierce fight for Luis. Lady Hardy was another fanatic. He felt uneasy.

$$\text{❧ ❧ ❧}$$

Pilar and Roberto met Howard and Bess as often as they could on that spot on the cliffs where they could overlook the sea. No arrangements were made for meeting; since the Captain had been home they had all secretly thought it wiser not to make such arrangements. They merely wandered out to the clearing among the gorse and bracken – sometimes alone, sometimes not so – and waited there hoping that one of the others would arrive.

The Captain had always disliked the Hardys. He disliked them more than ever now. He had made a bonfire in the home field when he had heard the news of the execution at Fotheringay. He had the servants make a figure stuffed with rags and wearing a tartan skirt, and this they had thrown on to the bonfire, joining hands and making a ring about the fire as they danced.

The Captain had hobbled among them urging them to call curses on the Scottish whore. He knew that in the big house there was deep mourning for that over which he rejoiced.

He and the Hall would always be enemies. It did not make him feel any more kindly towards them because he knew that his wife had planned to marry his daughter to the son of that house, and it inflamed his resentment against them to reflect that his daughter was by no means averse to the match.

He had said nothing of this to Pilar, fearing to arouse her

resentment. It was a new role for him to consider what he said; to try to mould a young girl – and she his own daughter – to his way of thinking. He would never have believed it possible, until it happened. He would have thought he would have commanded obedience from a shivering girl, and there would end the matter.

So the young people met in secret, and on this afternoon as they lay on the grass looking over the sea and talking as they invariably did on such occasions, Blasco came upon them.

He saw Howard and Bess and, not being particularly interested in them, would have called a greeting and turned away; but as he was about to do so he saw the other two and he was immediately attracted by them. The girl was unusual in appearance with her light brown hair and enormous dark eyes; her face was animated, and she was chattering away while all the others were silent. The boy, too, was attractive. He was as dark as a Spaniard and perhaps it was that hint of gipsy blood in him which made Blasco decide to stop.

'Why! 'Tis Mr Blasco,' said Bess.

Howard scrambled to his feet. Roberto followed his lead in his leisurely way. Pilar lay still, looking up at the stranger.

'He is staying with us,' Bess explained. 'He is Mr Blasco Carramadino, but we call him Mr Blasco because he has an elder brother.'

'A merry day to you all,' said Blasco. 'I pray you sit down, and introduce me to your friends.'

The girl spoke. She said: 'I'm Pilar, the Captain's daughter, and this is my brother Roberto.'

'Pilar! Roberto! But they are not English names.'

'Indeed, no,' said Pilar, eyeing the newcomer with great

interest as she wondered whether he was a priest and whether he had landed on the coast by night and whether it was safe for him to wander abroad by daylight. 'They are Spanish names.'

'So you are Spanish! I am also.'

'Blasco — that's Spanish, is it?'

'As Spanish as Pilar.'

Pilar noticed that Howard was uneasy. This man was one of those secret guests; she was sure of it.

'Have you been long in England, Mr Blasco?' she asked.

'Many months.'

'And you came from Spain? I know a great deal about Spain. It's through being half Spanish.'

'Pilar's mother,' said Howard, 'often comes to Hardyhall to . . . the chapel.'

Bess said: 'And so does Roberto's mother — sometimes. Only not as often as Pilar's mother.'

'I see,' said Blasco. 'And do you two come?'

Pilar and Roberto looked at each other. Pilar was about to speak, but Howard was clearly imploring her to be silent. She pressed her lips together as though forcing herself not to speak. It was a habit of Pilar's childhood, out of which she had not yet grown.

'We call sometimes,' said Pilar demurely. 'It was due to a call we paid in the first place that we all came to know each other.' Pilar laughed. 'We trespassed and hid in the nuttery. Then we all played together. Lady Hardy was charming. She said we could come when we liked. But we don't come now because the Captain's home.'

'You said you were the Captain's daughter, did you not?'

'Oh yes. I am. He is the greatest captain that ever sailed the seas. His ships used to come home laden with treasure . . . more

428

treasure than any had ever brought home before; we would see them glittering in the bay.'

'Pilar exaggerates a little,' said Roberto, with an apologetic smile which seemed very charming to Blasco. 'We feel we must warn strangers that they must divide and subtract and diminish by at least one half all that she tells.'

'Roberto! I hate you!'

Blasco was amused. He said: 'Are you not desolate to be hated by such a pretty young lady?'

Pilar was delighted at being called pretty, but Roberto said: 'Oh, she doesn't mean it. Pilar always hates and loves, and tells you about it. She changes a great deal too.'

'It's her Spanish blood, mayhap.'

'Roberto is half Spanish too. He is not in the least fiery,' said Pilar. 'The Captain is English, and he *is*. Roberto is so calm that he makes me angry. I feel I would go to great lengths to rouse him.'

'Roberto is calm because he is kind,' said Bess. 'He would not say he hated people, for fear of hurting them.'

'Why do you not come to visit Howard and Bess now the Captain is home? Does he object to your coming?'

'He does indeed!' cried Pilar, and added: 'Oh, Howard, don't make faces at me like that! He'll have to know. He's staying at the Hall, so he'll hear. You see, Mr Blasco, Howard and I are going to be married and, although Sir Walter and Lady Hardy want us to, the Captain doesn't.'

Blasco said: 'You make such a charming pair, such pleasantly contrasting personalities, that I wonder why the Captain is against the match.'

'He has other plans for me.' Pilar rocked on her heels and her eyes seemed to grow darker as she looked back over the past.

She was seeing Petroc in the hold, Petroc in her bedchamber. She shivered slightly, but her mood changed almost immediately. 'But I shall marry whom I choose,' she added. 'Even the Captain can't stop me.'

'I should think no one could stop you doing what you want.'

'You have sharp eyes, Mr Blasco,' said Roberto.

'Are you a sailor?' asked Pilar.

'No. I am a landsman.'

'What part of Spain do you come from?' asked Pilar.

Roberto said: 'Mr Blasco, do not be surprised. Pilar does all the talking; she always has. We know that if we start she will talk too, and that is rather an effort – so we let her talk by herself.'

'They tease you,' said Blasco to Pilar.

'They tease me! No, it is I who tease them. I used to make them play all sorts of games, when we were little, of course. But you were telling us where you came from.'

'My home is not very far from Seville.'

'Seville!' said Roberto suddenly. 'That's what the people call *la tierra de Maria Santisima*.'

'That's so. Who told you that?'

'My mother.'

'So your mother comes from those parts?'

'She comes from many parts.'

'My mother lived in a big house near the town of Jerez. Do you know Jerez, Mr Blasco? There are vineyards there and the wine they make is the best in the world.'

'You are speaking of country which I know very well. When was your mother last in Jerez? I should know her family.'

An air of solemnity had fallen on the little group. Pilar was silent, staring ahead of her. Howard was uneasy because he felt that Mr Blasco should not have stopped to talk to them thus; and Bess as usual took her cue from Howard. Even Roberto's interest was aroused.

It was he who answered: 'They do not speak of it much, Mr Blasco.'

'They do not talk of Spain? Was I wrong to ask?'

'You couldn't be wrong,' said Pilar, 'for how were you to know that the Captain burned my mother's house and brought her and Bianca and Carmentita to England?'

The silence was brief, but to Blasco it seemed to last a very long time. He felt the blood drumming in his ears. Overhead the gulls shrieked as they swooped and rose again.

He did not believe he could have heard correctly. It was just a thought which had come into his head, as it had so many times. It could not, after all these years, happen as casually as this, surely!

He heard himself speaking rapidly in Spanish. He was saying: 'Who is your mother? What is the Captain's name? When did all this happen? For the love of God, do not keep me in suspense.'

They were all watching him.

It was Roberto who spoke. 'We do not speak much Spanish,' he said. 'We have learned a little from our mothers, but the Captain will not have anything but English spoken in the house.'

Blasco said: 'What is the Captain's name?'

'He is Captain Sir Ennis March.'

'And he raided the coast of Spain sixteen years ago?'

'It would be about that,' said Pilar.

'And he . . . he brought your mother back with him?'

'Both our mothers — mine and Roberto's. And Carmentita too, and Maria who is at the Hall . . .'

'Your mother's name was . . .'

'Isabella . . . Isabella de Ariz.'

Blasco said: 'Holy Mother! Santa Maria! So it is true! And . . . Bianca . . .?'

The boy's dark eyes were fixed upon him. 'She is my mother,' he said.

He stared at the boy. I might have known it, he thought. The boy is beautiful. The boy has Bianca in him. I have found Bianca. I have found her at last.

'Mr Blasco,' said Pilar, 'you look very strange. You are not ill, are you?'

He passed his hand over his brow. He stood up quickly and said: 'I knew your mothers. Take me to them . . . take me to Bianca . . . at once.'

Pilar had leaped to her feet. 'You knew them? You knew them in Spain?'

'I knew them both,' he said. 'Isabella and Bianca. I must see them at once.' He caught the boy's arm. He wanted to go on looking at him. 'Come,' he said. 'Take me to your mother.'

Pilar was dancing on ahead.

'Pilar!' called Roberto. 'Pilar! Remember the Captain!'

Pilar stood still then. The Captain would be on the lawn looking out to sea. He might not be pleased to see a Spanish gentleman from Hardyhall, particularly as he had turned out to be a friend of her mother's many years ago.

'Let us go to the back of the house,' she cried.

Howard had taken Bess by the arm. Howard was older than the others; he had sensed something in Blasco's face which the others had missed. He knew that the Captain had abducted

432

Isabella, Bianca and the others; he knew, too, that Isabella was a lady of noble birth. He thought there might be trouble when Blasco and the Captain met, and Howard disliked trouble, particularly when it threatened to be violent.

So he kept Bess with him while Pilar and Roberto went running on with the man from Spain.

🌹 🌹 🌹

Bianca was at the back of the house hanging clothes on the bushes.

'Bianca!' called Pilar. 'Bianca, here is a man who knew you long ago!'

'Mother,' cried Roberto. 'Mother, a friend has come.'

'Bianca . . . Bianca!' said a voice. 'I am here.'

Bianca turned sharply. For a few seconds she stood very still; then the blood seemed to be drained away from her face and rush back to it. She tried to say something but the words did not come through.

Then they both moved forward – Bianca and Blasco. They leaped, it seemed to Pilar; and their arms were about each other.

They did not say anything; they just clung to each other, then held each other at arm's length and looked into each other's face; they laughed and they cried; they felt each other's arms and shoulders and hands and faces, as though they wanted to be sure they were indeed flesh and blood.

This was love, thought Pilar. This was more than affection. This was love which was a hunger, a thirst, a need; it was the most important thing in the lives of those who knew it. So much she learned as she stood there watching Bianca and Blasco.

They were oblivious of the young people who were

watching them. Pilar knew that they were unaware of anything but each other. For him there was only Bianca, and for Bianca this man from Spain.

Oddly enough she was reminded of Petroc, Petroc coming towards her in the bedroom. That was hate she felt for him, and this was love; so it could only be their fierceness which they had in common.

They spoke at last. He said her name over and over again. 'Bianca . . . Bianca . . .'

And she said: 'Yes, Blasco. My Blasco!' And they spoke in Spanish then . . . quickly, so that it was not easy for Pilar to understand.

Roberto understood more.

'So you were here . . . all the time . . . Bianca, my Bianca!'

'Here, Blasco, thinking of you . . . all day . . . each day. I thought you would come.'

'Things happened there in Paris . . . in Spain.'

'Things happened here.'

'There is much to tell.'

'Much . . . much. . . . But there is one you must meet. It is Roberto. Roberto, our son . . .'

Roberto went forward. Blasco looked at him and Roberto looked at Blasco.

'Is it so?' he said. 'Can it really be so?'

'It is so indeed,' said Bianca.

Then Blasco embraced Roberto, calling him *hijo* . . . his own dear *hijo*.

They saw nothing but each other, those three. Pilar stood apart, watching.

Pilar slipped past them and went into the house and up to her mother's room. Isabella was resting.

Pilar went to the bed and said: 'Mother, Blasco is here.'

'What did you say?' said Isabella.

'It is a man who has come from Spain. He used to know you all. He is below with Bianca. Should I ask him into the house? They are standing outside. His name is Blasco.'

Isabella sat up; her face was flushed and her eyes brilliant. 'What are you saying, Pilar? Is this some game of yours?'

'It is no game,' answered Pilar. 'He is staying at Hardyhall, and we met him on the cliffs. He said he knew you . . . but mostly Bianca, when he lived near Seville.'

Isabella was trembling; she put her hand to her head. 'Pilar . . . Pilar . . . you have heard us talk. You have imagined this.'

'No, Mother, it is true. Why, how you are shaking! Stay where you are. I will bring them to you.'

Pilar ran downstairs. Roberto, Blasco and Bianca were still standing where she had left them, looking into each other's faces, as though they discovered something new there with every second.

She said: 'I have told my mother you are here. She begs you to go and see her.'

They followed her into the house. He had his arm about Bianca; he gripped Roberto's arm. Pilar led them to her mother's bedchamber. Her thoughts were busy. She remembered that the Captain was sitting in his accustomed place at the front of the house, and it might hurt him to meet this man. He was a man not quite so tall as the Captain, but he could, she suspected, be fierce. He was in possession of his full strength while the Captain was, as he said, a battered unseaworthy old bucket now. Her busy mind was working. It was the Captain who needed her protection. Bianca and this man would need no one in the future but each other. And the Captain had raided the coast; he had abducted her mother and Bianca. When this man stopped thinking about love, he would start thinking about hate.

She threw open the door. Her mother was standing in the middle of the room, her hand to her heart.

'Blasco!' she cried.

He strode towards her. He took her hands and kissed them. Isabella began to weep silently; she threw herself into Blasco's arms and he held her tenderly, but oh! how differently from the way in which he had held Bianca!

Blasco said: 'It is the most amazing chance. It had to be though. I knew it had to be. The pity is it took so long to find you all.'

'Blasco,' sobbed Isabella. 'You came at last. We waited; we watched the sea and waited. And now . . . it is so long . . .'

'He is here,' cried Bianca fiercely. 'What matters aught else? The past is as nothing now that he has come.'

Pilar watched her mother. She thought: She loves him too. But it is Bianca he loves – Bianca and Roberto.

He had called Roberto – son. She had heard Bianca call Roberto *hijo* when they were young. She had said, 'What does it mean, Bianca?' and Bianca had said, 'My little one, my baby, my son.'

And he had said that – my son.

Everything was changing. First the Captain had come home; then Petroc had frightened her as no one ever had before, and now Roberto was not her brother.

She thought of the Captain. What would he say when he saw this man? And what would Blasco say and do when he saw the man who had taken Bianca from him all those years ago, when she was going to have a child, his son Roberto? He was charming, that man, but his eyes flashed in love as they would flash in hate. And the Captain, who had been invincible, was no longer so; he had been beaten by Spanish guns and Spanish swords. Was he now to meet his death by another Spanish sword?

They must not meet. She had a quick vision of her life without the Captain. It was something she could not bear to contemplate. Whatever he had done, however cruel he had been to her mother and Bianca, could not alter this, for she reasoned to herself: it is what people are to *us* which makes us love them.

She must keep the Captain away from this man. She sensed that. She believed Blasco's hate would mount as fiercely as his love had done, and when she thought of the hungry way in which he had embraced Bianca, she could imagine the angry way in which he would attack her father.

She ran from the room and down the staircase to the great hall. The Captain was just coming into the house.

'Ahoy there, Piller,' he roared. 'Why, girl, what's happened? You look as though you've sighted trouble.'

'I was coming to look for you,' she said, and she started to descend the stairs.

'What is going on up there?' he asked.

'Nothing of importance. I have just left my mother.'

He was watching her closely.

'Hey, girl,' he roared suddenly, and his voice had lost none of its volume, 'what ails you?'

Pilar paused on the stairs. The Captain stood very still, looking up. Pilar saw his bewildered face.

She heard him cry: 'By God, who's that?'

Blasco, who was leaning over the rail, said: 'I am Blasco Carramadino, recently come from Spain. My brother was to have married Isabella de Ariz, and Bianca was my mistress.'

'What!' said the Captain. 'A Spanish Don to enter my house and stand in my gallery and shout at me! Come down, you dog. Come down! Piller girl, a sword. That on the wall there. Mayhap 'tis rusty but 'twill serve. 'Tis good enough for low Spanish dogs who invade my house.'

Blasco laughed. 'I see the Spanish dogs have robbed you of a leg, Captain. They let you go, I doubt not, knowing you for a worthless braggart. Mayhap they were saving your life that I might not miss a pleasure to which I had been looking forward these many years.'

'Come down,' said the Captain. 'Let us have deeds, not words!'

'You tore defenceless women from their homes.'

'Spanish women!' spat the Captain.

'You shall die for that.'

'You shall die for daring to step inside my house. Piller, why do you stand there? A sword, I said!'

'You must not,' said Pilar. 'You must not. You cannot.'

'Get it, girl,' he roared.

Blasco had started to come down the stairs. Pilar faced him, barring the way.

She said: 'Go away, Mr Blasco. You must not hurt him. You see he is sick and wounded. Once he would have killed you. But you must not hurt him, because he can no longer fight.'

'Stand aside, my child,' replied Blasco. 'You do not understand.'

There were tears on Pilar's cheeks. She cried: 'I understand

438

all. You love Bianca, and Roberto is your son. You have found them. Is that not enough? Must you kill my father too?'

Blasco wanted to push her aside; but she was appealing, standing firmly on the stairs, her arm thrust forward, the palms of her hands resting against his chest, her eyes dark with pleading, her light hair falling back from her lovely face. Blasco felt a great tenderness towards her; her beauty and courage acted like a douche of cold water on his burning hatred of this man.

He repeated. 'You cannot understand, child. This I have promised myself these many years.'

Bianca was beside him now. She caught his arm. 'Blasco, no, no, no! No bloodshed! It is done. What good can you do by killing him? He ruined those years of our lives. But it is done, and all over. And only harm can come to us all if you do aught against him now.'

The Captain said: 'Stand aside, woman. Do you think I need women to plead for me? Let him come down here. I'll tear out his heart with my hands. I have two of those left, aye, and I'll find much satisfaction in using them.'

He started towards the stairs, but it was not easy for him to mount them. Blasco stood very still, with Bianca clinging to his arm. Pilar had rushed to the Captain and put her arms about his neck. 'I will not let you go. You cannot . . . you must not. He is strong, and you are but an unseaworthy bucket. Captain, you must not. I'll not let you. I will cling to you thus, and if he kills you he will have to kill me first.'

'Piller girl,' said the Captain. 'Piller . . .'

Blasco had turned away.

He said: 'Come away, Bianca. You and the boy. Never set foot in this house again.'

439

He had started up the stairs, Bianca running beside him.

'Isabella,' he shouted, 'Isabella! Come . . . we will go from here. We will leave the English pirate with his one leg and his wheezy body. He is not worth despatching. Come! Come now. Let us go. Let us go!'

Pilar kept her arms about the Captain's neck as she waited, listening to the sounds above them.

'They are going,' she said. 'They are all going away now.'

The Captain growled but she saw how brilliant his eyes were, and they which had been burning with hatred a moment ago were soft with tears as they looked at her.

'Let 'em go!' he said. 'Let 'em think they can go. They'll not get far. We'll not let the dirty Dons strut on Devon soil, girl.' Then he put his arm about her and held her fast against him. 'He'd have got me then,' he said. 'He'd have got me. It's the second time in the space of a few months that I've stood close to a Don and seen death in his face, but each time there's been someone there to offer a young life for mine. It's something to remember, Piller girl. It's something to warm the heart of a man, no matter what's to come.'

❧ ❧ ❧

Isabella hurried out of the house. She ran all the way to Hardyhall. So many times she had dreamed it would happen, but never like this. Blasco had come, as she had thought he would come, but it was Bianca whom he had taken; and Bianca had walked out with him just as many years ago she had walked away from the gipsy tribe and into Isabella's life.

It was all so clear to her now. It was Bianca he had loved. When he had stood before her she knew Blasco, not as the hero of her dreams, but for the man he was; and her knowledge of the Captain had helped her to understand. It was the Biancas who were necessary to such men.

She came to the gate of Hardyhall and started to run across the lawns. Bianca must have been expecting her. She came out to meet her. They stood still, within a few paces of each other.

Bianca was young again; the shine in her eyes made them bigger than ever and there was a faint flush in her dark cheeks, so that she looked very like the gipsy who had first come to the house in Spain.

'Isabella,' she said. 'I am sorry.'

'Sorry that he has come back?'

'Sorry that you had to know.'

'All these years,' said Isabella, 'you kept that from me. I told you what I felt, what I hoped, but you kept that from me. I told of my foolish thoughts when you had his *son*!'

'We had been hurt so much. We could not hurt each other.'

'So now you are leaving me. We have been together a long time, Bianca. I cannot imagine my life without you.'

'I shall never be far away if you want me. If we go from here, you shall come with us.'

Isabella had turned away. 'I have come to confess my sins. I have come to take the Sacrament.'

'There is a new priest at the house, and you know who he is.'

Isabella walked slowly towards the chapel, and Bianca walked beside her.

'Go to the chapel,' she said. 'Wait there and I will tell him to come to you.'

Isabella obeyed. She entered the chapel, the door of which was open. Denuded of its vestments it seemed bare and cold. She shivered slightly and tried to pray. She was on her knees when Domingo entered. She heard his footfall and rose. They stood for a second in silence studying each other. Each saw the changes in the other, and yet it was the same Isabella, the same Domingo who stood there.

Domingo was the first to move. 'Isabella . . . after all these years! It seems incredible.'

'Domingo!' Her eyes searched his face, saw how the flesh had fallen away from his bones, realised that he had lived a life robbed of comfort.

'So often I have thought of meeting you,' he said. 'I believed that I should one day.'

'I believed it too, Domingo. I used to sit at my window looking over the sea. I used to dream that you came for me – you, Blasco or my father.'

'Your father lost his life in the search.'

She lowered her head for a moment.

Domingo went on: 'We went down to the coast when we discovered you had gone. He would not wait. He was anxious to put to sea at once. The English boarded the ship on which he was travelling. He picked a quarrel with one of them.'

'Yes,' she said. 'I see. And you became a priest.'

He nodded. 'It seemed as though God had ordained that this should be so.'

'You are a Jesuit, Domingo. You are a brave man to come to a heretic country.'

He wanted to tell her the truth about himself, but he lacked courage to do that. He could not bear to see the admiration in her eyes. He began to tell her about her mother and how she had rebuilt a new home on the ruins of the old; he told of Gabriel and Sabina and the child which had recently been born.

'It is all far away,' said Isabella. 'My mother has built a new life; I have a life here. I have a husband, Domingo. Did you know he married me? It was on account of our child – a girl.'

Domingo nodded slowly. He said: 'I had thought to take you home with me. I had thought that you would wish to go into a convent there and forget all this.'

'I have my daughter,' she said. 'I love her dearly.'

'And this man? . . . Isabella, you must hate him.'

'I have tried not to. He leaves me much to myself, particularly now that he has been badly wounded at sea. He adores our child. I could not bear to lose her, Domingo; nor could he. She binds us together in some way. We have no love for each other, but we each have a great love for our daughter. If you return, tell my mother that I have a daughter whom I dearly love; and because of this I know what terrible anxiety she must have suffered on my account. But it is all over now. She has Gabriel and Sabina and their children. I have Pilar. And you, Domingo – you will stay here for a while. You have taken Mr Heath's place.'

'Yes,' he said. 'I have taken his place.'

'Domingo, there is peril here. Mr Heath once was in danger of being caught. He managed to escape to the hole and was not discovered.'

'I know,' said Domingo.

'You know all that, and yet you come!'

Domingo bowed his head again, for he could not meet her eyes. He wanted to shout: I am a spy. I am not the holy man you take me for. I am a spy for the enemy of our Church and our country. And I became a spy because I was afraid not to do so. I disgrace the cloth I wear. And what I find harder to bear than aught else is the respect and homage paid to me by those about me.

Isabella said: 'There is much that goes on here. Sir Walter and Lady Hardy have to use the greatest discretion. They did not trust Mr Heath with all their secrets. But you have come here – you, Domingo, and Blasco – and because you are our very dear friend, the Hardys need have no fear of trusting you with all their secrets. Events are moving fast, Domingo. We hear great news from those who come from Spain. Soon this country will be free from the heretics who now rule it. The Holy Faith will be set up. We know it, Domingo, because we shelter those who come from Spain. Each day they bring fresh news; each day we hear that the great moment is coming nearer and nearer. And we shall feel happy now that you are here, Domingo – happy and safe because we know that we can trust you.'

'Do not, Isabella, say these things, I beg of you. I wish to be a priest . . . only a priest.'

'Oh, Domingo, brave Domingo, I am so happy that you have come.'

She covered her face with her hands and began to weep. He let her weep and, when at last she looked at him, she saw that his lips were moving as in prayer.

She did not know that what he said was: 'God forgive me. God forgive me.'

🌿 🌿 🌿

On the lawn the Captain sat, planning revenge.

Spaniards in Devon! That man had betrayed himself by coming to his house and openly defying him. He had taken Bianca and Roberto away. They were living at Hardyhall and he was going to marry Bianca. What was he doing at the Hall? Why had he come? What strange happenings were taking place not far from this very spot? wondered the Captain.

444

The sea belonged to the English, so reasoned the Captain. All those rich countries in the New World – they were England's heritage. But the Dons had got there first; they had the ships and the means to equip them. But that was all changed now. On the throne of England was a woman worth two of the pious monk of Spain. There were things she knew which that man had yet to learn. The Dons, with their instruments of torture, with their *autos da fé*, were not the men to hold what they had conquered. The Indians made good friends but bad enemies; and they were more ready to be friends with those who came to trade and live in peace among them, worshipping their own God, and not greatly caring what the dark men worshipped. The Dons came with fire and sword and the thumbscrews; they came with the red and white sarcenet and the Inquisitors. They did not want friends, they only wanted Catholics. They were making great mistakes which the English would never make.

'By God!' murmured the Captain. 'We'll wipe them off the seas. Give us time, and Spain will ere long be enfeebled; and the English shall have what is theirs by right of their courage and their seamanship. They shall inherit the New World and make it their own for ever.'

But what were Dons doing in Devon? He was a man who faced facts. They were formidable enemies and they knew that they faced an enemy as formidable as themselves. England's great sun had not yet risen; soon it would ride the sky, but as yet that sky was stained scarlet and blue and gold with its coming; England's glory had yet to be born.

And they knew it, the crafty Dons. That was why in the harbours they were building a great fleet of ships to sail against England; they had money at their disposal, and it was said by many neutral observers that their fleet was such as no other could stand against.

And now the Dons were here. The Dons were in Devon. Their spies were everywhere. They had even entered the Captain's house.

By God, they should be taken. They should die the traitor's death and he'd be there to see it. Then he'd go close to the scaffold and he'd laugh in the face of the Spaniard who had dared defy him and take Bianca away.

Bianca! The woman who had meant the most to him. He had often thought of what he would do if ever he came face to face with Roberto's father. Well now he had, but Fate was unkind. She had waited until he was old and maimed and no longer sea-worthy. She denied him one great pleasure for which he had longed. So the Spaniard had won, and he'd not be here to brood on it but for his girl Piller.

He could not think about his girl without deep emotion; and, when a man was getting old and he'd lost a leg and there was a crippling pain in his side from an old wound, he was softer than he had been. The tears came to his eyes as they never had before, not tears of rage but tears of emotion.

They saved my life – those two, he told himself. One day I'll see their children here . . . in this house, and they'll climb all over this old hulk and they'll call me Captain.

By God, that's worth living for, though a man has but one leg and a pain in his side and the tears come too easily to his eyes.

Petroc will be home mayhap next year and Piller will do as I want. And by that time that nest of spies in Hardyhall would be smoked out.

Perhaps he'd have Bianca back with him. She'd be glad to

come, for Roberto's sake. He'd promised Roberto a portion of his estate. Isabella was still here. She did not leave him. She was his wife and Piller's mother; and he would like to see them try to take Piller from him, he would!

Then they'd be as they were before, and he'd take Bianca and Isabella to see what loyal Englishmen did to Spanish traitors.

They would see then that he was still the Captain who had raided their coast, who had made them *his* women, and who took what he wanted when he wanted it.

For the time though, let them think they were safe.

The Captain had his secret thoughts. They amused him. It was not easy for him to travel, but he could go down into Plymouth where he knew men who could be trusted.

One of these had set out for London the day after Blasco Carramadino had invaded his house; and it would not be long, thought the Captain, before those activities which were going on in Hardyhall were looked into by men who understood such things.

🌿 🌿 🌿

The summer was passing. To Bianca and Blasco it was the most wonderful summer of their lives. They seemed to forget all else in the rediscovery of each other. They had married.

The Hardys had been surprised at such unconventional behaviour but in the strange circumstances they had done all they could to help, and the ceremony had been performed in the chapel by Domingo. They were prepared to believe that the coming of the brothers was a miracle; they interpreted it as a sign that God was pleased with them. Bianca was now living under their roof. Roberto could follow the religion of his father and mother. Had they but been able to have married Pilar to Howard and brought her and Isabella to the Hall, it would have seemed that their work was indeed blessed.

'We must have patience,' said Sir Walter.

And Lady Hardy with him was ready to give her blessing to the marriage of Bianca and Blasco, which they would in any other circumstances have thought of doubtful wisdom.

So Blasco and Bianca gave no thought during those summer months to anything but the rediscovery of each other, and for Blasco there was the additional joy of knowing his son.

To him and Bianca everything outside their little circle seemed vague and of small significance. But there was work to be done; Blasco did not forget that he was on a mission for the King of Spain. His task was to wander down to the town, to linger on the Hoe, to loiter in the cobbled streets, to lean on the wall and gaze at the ships in the harbour and gather any information useful to Spain.

Men would talk to him. 'You're a foreigner?' they would ask.

'Yes,' he would tell them.

'A Frenchman – we do know. And looking at our fine ships, eh! Know much about 'em?'

'Not much. But what a goodly sight!'

'You see what be lying there afore your eyes. She's one of the Queen's thirty-six-gun galleons. She's in the Dreadnought class. Why, we had the *Antelope* and *Swiftsure* down this way not long ago. I reckon there ain't no galleons the world over to beat them there.'

'Whither will they sail when they leave the harbour?'

'The Queen keeps 'em hugging the coast since we hear so much about these here Spaniards.'

Such information as this he gleaned; it was for this purpose he had been sent to England. He could see why it had been considered wise for him to accompany his brother. Domingo, with his thin ascetic face, could never have sat in taverns drinking with these men, could never have inspired them with such confidence that they dropped the secrets into his ears. Domingo looked what he was – a priest; and priests were suspect.

He would go back to Hardyhall and write his piece, and Domingo would put it into a code he had learned for the purpose; then Charlie Monk would ride with it to a house on the moors where it would be taken eastwards – perhaps to some messenger who on a dark night was about to leave England for Spain.

This was the King's work which he had been sent to do, and he did it because he considered it was his duty, but his thoughts were with Bianca and his son; and he grew to love the soft countryside with its temperate sun and its hedgerows decked with wild flowers, also to enjoy the continual bustle of the town which lay close by, and the activity of the port.

He felt that everything he had lived through was worthwhile now he had come to this. This was reality; all else seemed like a dream to be forgotten in daylight. Paris and the Rue Béthisy had grown dim; even the Carramadino estates seemed like something which belonged to another existence. One day he would return to them; but that was for the future; now he was following Bianca's way and living in the moment.

He was glad he had not killed the Captain. It would have been easy to have done so. Violence did not fit this peaceful scene. And the man whom he had hated all these years was the husband of Isabella and the father of the charming Pilar. If he could have asked for one wish to be granted, he would have

449

asked that Pilar be Roberto's twin, and both of them his children. He already loved the girl.

Roberto loved her. It was his one regret that he no longer lived under the same roof. Roberto and Pilar – they were of a kind and more suited to each other than the grave Howard who, though a pleasant boy, was dull compared with people like his own Roberto and the enchanting Pilar.

Often Blasco talked to Roberto of Pilar, and always he would see the look of great affection which would come into Roberto's eyes when her name was mentioned.

'I always thought she was my sister.'

'My son,' said Blasco, 'there could be a closer relationship between you two, if you so wished it. You love her; I am sure she loves you. Why should you not marry? I should be enchanted to welcome her as my daughter.'

'Marry Pilar? But she is to marry Howard, and I am to marry Bess.'

'A marriage is not a marriage until the ceremony has been performed. You planned your marriages before you knew that you were not brother and sister.'

' 'Tis true,' said Roberto.

Then he did not speak for a long time. Blasco watched him, and there was a smile about his lips.

❧ ❧ ❧

Pilar sat with the Captain on the lawn. There were many ships to watch in the bay now.

'By God,' cried the Captain, 'there lies the *Triumph*. She sails under Martin Frobisher himself. There's no English ship bigger than the *Triumph*. By God, what a sight! There are four cannons aboard her, three demi-cannons, and I'll swear there are sixteen or seventeen culverins. She'd blow any pox-ridden Spaniards out of the sea.'

'There are more ships in the harbour than there used to be,' said Pilar.

'By God, and need to be! They say the Spaniards are building them twice the size of ours.'

'If they have better ships, Captain . . .'

'Nay, nay! Better ships? They could build them four times the size of ours, girl, and they'd not have better ships. It's the men who sail in a ship who make her the ship she is. They've got fine ships, I grant you that, but by God, they've only Spaniards to sail 'em, and one Englishman is worth twenty-one of them.'

'And when they come here they'll bring their Inquisitors with them. That's what I heard, Captain. They'll sail, not only with soldiers and sailors, but with the instruments of the torture chamber.'

'We'll give 'em torture, girl. Not that they will ever land on these shores. We'll blow 'em out of the sea first. We'll sink 'em, whatever their size. They'll never land on English soil.'

' 'Tis a pity there should have to be this war between Spain and England.'

'A pity! It's as natural as the air we breathe. It's dog and cat, cat and mouse. Nature made us enemies. Nothing good could come out of the union of Spain and England.'

'I came out of a union between Spain and England,' she said.

That made him laugh. He could trust Piller to make him laugh. He continued to point out the ships in the bay.

And when she had left him, he thought of what she had said, and he laughed afresh. Then he remembered the Spaniards at Hardyhall and his anger was so great that he felt dizzy with it.

Why had nothing been done? He had told the right people in Plymouth that he suspected traitors were being harboured at the Hall; he knew them for Spaniards and he suspected them of coming to Devon to work against the Queen.

He was waiting to see them smoked out of their holes, but there had not even been a search at Hardyhall.

There was great activity throughout the town. In June, Sir Francis Drake dropped anchor in the Sound, and the crowds filled the streets to greet him. He brought with him a great ship full of gold and precious stones, silks, velvets, spice and ambergris. Her name was *San Felipe*, and even that seemed symbolic, for Felipe was the name of the King who was England's greatest enemy, and his people looked upon him as a saint, it was said. Drake was a legend. He had recently sailed the *Eliẓabeth Bonaventure* into Cadiz harbour where he had inflicted great damage on many of the ships he found there. He had stormed Cape St Vincent, and it was said that the very mention of his name – they called him *El Draque*, the dragon – made Spaniards turn pale.

But still there were tales of that great fleet, *Grande Armada Felicisima*, as the Spaniards called it; and when it was learned that Philip intended to start the invasion that September there was tension throughout the town. It was said that the Queen had refused money to repair the ships, that she would put another above Sir Francis Drake because Sir Francis, although the greatest sailor in the world, was not noble enough by birth to lead the English fleet to victory. There were murmurings among those sailors, who declared they would serve Sir Francis or no other; it was said, too, that there was disease in the English ships.

Through the summer, all waited for the sight of the first

Spanish galleon on the horizon; now the oaks were turning bronze and spiders' webs were glistening on the bushes, but the Spaniards did not yet sail up the Channel, and those who were living at the Hall – to the Captain's disgust and bewilderment – continued to live there in peace.

❦ ❦ ❦

The gales tore at the trees; the rain beat down on the grey sea; day followed day when the sun did not show its face.

As they lay in their bed one night, Bianca said to Blasco: 'We shall not stay here for ever, Blasco?'

'No,' he answered, 'I doubt not we shall go away one day.'

'Where shall we go? To Spain? To your home? What will your mother say when she finds a gipsy to be the wife of her son? She will never accept me, nor Roberto. A grandson born out of wedlock – the son of a gipsy.'

'That is all in the future and far away.'

'But I am afraid now. I see them coming here to take you away. We could not bear another parting.'

He took her into his arms and kissed her. It was as though they were back in those early days. They could almost feel the hot sun on the chapel wall, smell the orange blossom and feel the pomegranate bushes in which they were lying.

But later Bianca said fiercely: 'We must not be parted. We must never be parted again.'

❦ ❦ ❦

The Captain had gone on a journey. It was a long and arduous one for a man in his physical condition, and Pilar was anxious. She was afraid not only for the Captain but for others who were dear to her.

All her efforts to reconcile those two opposing parties were in vain. They would never be friends, she was sure; there would be strife between them until one of them was defeated; their differences were as great as those between England and Spain, and indeed they *were* the differences of England and Spain.

She knew on what mission the Captain had gone to London.

He was convinced that the authorities in Plymouth were not sensible of the havoc which a nest of Spaniards could wreak in a country soon to be at war. He had warned officials in Plymouth who should have taken measures and had apparently failed to do so. He cursed them for blind fools. He knew that many of the men in the English ships were sick; he knew that insufficient money had been provided for feeding them; he knew that, but for men like Drake and Frobisher who paid the sailors out of their own pockets, those sailors who were more than ready to fight for the Queen would have starved to death. There were many foolish mistakes being made during this most dangerous time, but the most foolish, in the Captain's opinion, was to allow those Spaniards to go on living in this very spot which was the centre of England's warlike activity in the West.

So he was determined to go to London to lay this matter before someone who *would* take notice.

Pilar wondered what the people in London would do when they had listened to his tales. What would happen to all her friends at Hardyhall? She loved them; she wanted to protect them no less than she wanted to protect the Captain.

It was growing dark as she stood in the garden looking over the sea. There were lights in the harbour, for men were working by flares and cressets down there. Sir John Hawkins was in charge of operations, and he had declared that the situation was urgent. As soon as the winter was over, the Spaniards would attack, and Her Majesty's ships were far from ready.

Down there they were carrying on with the work of scraping and tallowing all through the days, all through the nights.

Roberto came quietly upon her.

'Roberto . . . you here!'

'Yes, I heard the Captain was away. Where has he gone?'

'To London, Roberto.'

'To London? I thought he was too ill to make such a journey.'

'He goes because he thinks it necessary.' She was subdued, and that was strange for Pilar. But almost immediately she had turned to him crying passionately: 'I do not like it, Roberto. I do not like it since you went away.'

'No, Pilar.'

'You have a new father and you love him,' she said. 'The Captain was never a father to you, Roberto. But it is sad that you should have to go away from me to be with your father.'

'That was the only sad part about it for me.'

'We are not far from each other, Roberto, but sometimes it seems that it is a very long way. You are with them, and I am with my father. They are enemies, Roberto. It is like this war which everyone is talking about, and we are not on the same side.'

'It makes no difference, Pilar. We are just the same.'

'Yes, we are the same. You are Roberto – whether you take your lessons from Mr Heath or Mr West. I do not love you less because you are taught to believe one thing, and I another.'

'Pilar,' he said, 'I love you. I used to say that I never wanted to leave you. That's how I feel now. If we could go away from here . . . somewhere right away where there are no wars . . . where everybody thinks just what they want to think, and nobody minds, nobody tries to make them think something else . . . if we could all go away to such a place . . . my father, my mother, your mother, Howard, Bess . . . and you, of course you . . . it would not do if you were not there . . . that would be perfect.'

'I know,' she said, her eyes gleaming, 'Florida! Or Virginia. Those forests we heard of, do you remember? . . . all the fruits and the flowers – eglantine and tansy, honeysuckle and sassafras, and grapes and strawberries all growing wild. If we could all go away together – all of us – and not care what others thought, and build houses . . .'

'We'd have to cut down your forests to do that,' he said.

'You're laughing at me,' she said. 'You're laughing as you always laughed.'

'That's what I missed, Pilar – not having you to laugh at . . . to laugh with.'

He caught her by the arms and looked into her face. 'Nobody's eyes shine as yours do,' he said. 'Nobody else laughs as you do. No one else says those wild, fantastic things that make me laugh.'

'You laugh with scorn.'

'No, with happiness. I laugh because I say: "That's Pilar's talk. That's Pilar talking, and she's near me and that's where I want her to be." Pilar, now that we're not brother and sister, now that there is all this trouble around us, we could make sure of being together always if we married.'

'Married, Roberto! But I am going to marry Howard, you are going to marry Bess.'

456

'That was what we used to say. We divided ourselves as though for a game. We're older now. We know that living is not just a game. We were always together in the past. Do you want us always to be together in the future?'

She nodded slowly. 'Yes, Roberto, I do want that.'

He put his arms about her and kissed her. She withdrew herself and said: 'What of Howard? What of Bess? If they were not brother and sister they could marry each other . . .' She stopped short. She realised that she was thinking along the old childish lines, arranging their lives as she had arranged their games. Then she thought of the meeting she had seen between Bianca and Blasco, the way in which they clung together and held each other at arm's length, looking into one another's faces. She felt young then — young and bewildered.

She cried : 'I do not know, Roberto, I do not know. I want to be with you. I want to be with Howard. I love you both. It's so bewildering. And while we're talking here the Captain has gone to London. I love the Captain. I want to be loyal to the Captain, but how can I when I know what he has gone to do?'

'What do you mean, Pilar? What has he gone to do?'

She did not speak, and he went on: 'He has gone to inform against my uncle! He knows that he is a priest. But why does he go to London?'

Pilar shook her head. 'I do not know what I should do. That is what troubles me so. I feel as if we're caught up in things we don't understand. Is that growing up, Roberto? It was so easy before. Now I've got to be on one side, and sometimes I want to be on both sides. Roberto, I don't know what to do. Is everything going to be like this? I want to marry you, but I'm promised to Howard; and how can I hurt Howard? I'm the Captain's daughter, and I want to be loyal to him; but how can

457

I let him have men sent down here to take your uncle and your father and put them in prison?'

They clung together in the darkness.

🌹 🌹 🌹

Blasco was like a man awakened from a drugged sleep. He had realised that he had spent so long in brooding on the past that he had never greatly cared about the future; then, when he had found Bianca, the present had been enough. Everything seemed different now. He had found Bianca; he had found Roberto; and he wanted a future with those two.

He had often thought of taking them to Spain. But his proud and noble mother would never be reconciled to a daughter-in-law who would be known throughout the neighbourhood as a gipsy, and Bianca was not the woman to take insults calmly.

But at this moment he need not concern himself with future strife between those two; the immediate problem was to preserve himself and his family from disaster. These months of pleasure must not be an isolated period in his life; he was determined on that. He and Domingo were in acute danger and if they were taken and executed, what would become of his family? It now seemed not only a strange but a sinister thing that he and Domingo, having been arrested, should have been allowed to go free and carry on with the work they had begun – Domingo a Spanish priest, himself a Spanish spy.

It was even more strange that they had come as if by accident to this very spot where Isabella and Bianca were living, and which happened to be one of the most deeply involved in England's preparations for war.

Such things surely did not happen by chance. There was some deep meaning which could only spell danger – the most acute danger — and if Blasco was to save his family and himself he must discover that danger and act with great promptitude.

Domingo was writing many dispatches, which Charlie Monk took to a house on the moors; there Charlie handed these papers to a man who carried them to some destination which was unknown, Blasco believed, to Domingo as well as himself. Those dispatches were, Blasco had no reason to disbelieve, the information about English ships which he acquired in the harbours and about the town; this information, written in code by Domingo, was smuggled somehow to Spain, where Blasco could well understand it would prove of the utmost value.

Was it possible that the English were so foolish as to allow a man whom they had captured — a Jesuit whose one aim would be to spread the Catholic Faith far and wide — to be free to work against them at such a time? Was it possible that they would let him out of his prison to wander whither he would?

Another thought occurred to him. Information from both sides came into Hardyhall. The priests they received into the house brought information with them, information which was calculated to bring hope to all those in England who were working for the triumph of Spain over England and the establishment of the Catholic Church in the land.

Suppose those men who had allowed Domingo and himself to go free had not been so foolish as he thought them. Suppose they had known a great deal about Domingo's past! Was it possible that they could have known he was to have married Isabella, that she had been abducted by Ennis March and was living near Plymouth? And had they thought that it would be a masterstroke to send Domingo and his brother to Hardyhall where they might meet Isabella? Could they have known that

Isabella and some of the Spanish women from the Captain's house visited Hardyhall for the Confessional and to receive the Sacrament, and that any friends of these would inspire the greatest confidence, so that none of that information which was coming into the house concerning Spain would be withheld from them?

But of what use would that be? Suppose those dispatches containing the information collected mainly by himself and put into code by Domingo and taken to the house on the moors by Charlie did not go to Spain but to London. Of what use? They would merely prove that he and his brother were spies for the King of Spain. Surely they might guess that already. They had captured them; they could have put them to death as priest and spy in the name of justice.

No, it was the information about Spain which would interest London. Blasco tried to remember all he had heard: where the Spanish ships were assembled. How men were working day and night in Cantabrico and along the river of Sevilla. In what harbour Spain's biggest ship, the *Reganza*, was lying. How they were constructing *filipotes* and small craft suitable for carrying horses and artillery. They had heard, before it was generally known, of the death of Santa Cruz and the King's decision to put the Duke of Medina Sidonia in charge of the Armada. Useful information, vital information for those whose task was to prepare to meet the Spanish Fleet.

If someone in this house was working for England it must needs be someone who was in the confidence of those who had Spain's good at heart. That meant that there was an English spy in this house.

There was only one person who, in Blasco's opinion, this could be: Charlie Monk.

The more he thought of that, the more certain he was. He thought of how Charlie had met them in Paris, how he had brought them to England and led them to the house where they had been captured. Charlie was a man whose good humour and jocular personality inspired confidence. He would be a useful spy. How was it that he had been on the spot, so ready to leave the service of his good master and mistress to come with them to Devon?

This was a nightmare. They were fond of the man. He was so useful, so ready to serve them in a hundred ways, so good to talk to.

But the more he thought of Charlie the more suspicious Blasco became. Charlie had not the serious air of a Catholic. He heard Mass, he made confession; but he took his religion without seriousness. Yes, that was it. It was that lack of seriousness which seemed to confirm Blasco's suspicions. He thought of Charlie, genuflecting; Charlie on his knees. Never once had he seen Charlie without that secret jocularity which surely no true Catholic would bring into his religious devotions.

There was something else: that look of honesty, which they all trusted, succeeded because of its sincerity. Charlie had no guilt on his conscience. How could any of them have thought that he could be a traitor to his own country? This would explain why they were left in peace. The Captain had been to Plymouth to demand why Spaniards were allowed to live at Hardyhall, but nothing had been done. The Spaniards were left in peace because they were doing such good work for England. It might be that they were safe for a while; but war was coming nearer and when it appeared on the horizon all those, such as himself and Domingo, would be seized – he had

461

no doubt of that. And when that time came, there would be an end to his happiness with Bianca. They would take him and Domingo, and they would die the traitor's death.

He could not blame them. They would be just. The traitor's death was the reward of spies.

Oh, to be free of it all — to live one's own life instead of acting as agents and puppets of those in high places! Oh, to be free from the strife which hung like a black cloud over Europe! It would hang there until all the world was Catholic or all Protestant — or until they learned to live in peace with one another.

And I, he thought, could be completely happy living side by side with men who thought differently about their method of worship. I could be happy living near men who did not even worship the same god. He thought of Virginia then, and Florida, with himself, Bianca, Roberto, Pilar, Howard, Bess, Isabella, Domingo . . . a happy family of them, all living together in harmony; taking part in pleasant discussions now and then, putting forth their own points of view, harmoniously and peacefully.

He began to watch Charlie. Was he not always at hand when men came for a night's lodging at Hardyhall before passing on? Did he not serve them assiduously? Was he not of the party which brought them? Was it not Charlie who rode out for the first few miles with them to show them the way?

He listened to Charlie's talk to such men. Always it ran on the same lines: 'We're waiting for the great day, gentlemen. That's what we're waiting for. It warms the heart to hear how good King Philip is building his great Armada. And do you think it will be over soon? I reckon the Armada will be setting out if this fine weather lasts. I like to think of those ships lying there in Cadiz. I suppose it is still in Cadiz, gentlemen . . .'

Oh yes, he strongly suspected Charlie.

'Did you ever learn to read and write, Charlie?' he asked him once.

'Read and write!' Charlie shook his head. 'Now reading and writing, that's the privilege of gentlemen – not for the likes of Charlie.'

Yet he had followed Charlie on the lonely road to the moors, and he could have sworn – but he must necessarily keep his distance – that he saw him take the dispatch Domingo had written and peruse it.

He had to make sure of Charlie and he had to do so without Charlie's knowing.

🌿 🌿 🌿

There was little time, he was aware of that. The nights he spent with Bianca had seemed doubly precious. He believed they were numbered.

He would lie awake beside her and tell himself that he would not be cheated again. He would take Bianca and Roberto to safety, and he would live his life in peace.

He had a plan – a desperate one. But he was desperate. He believed that at any moment the pursuivants might make their appearance at Hardyhall and the search begin. Charlie would know of the hole under the chapel, and there would be no safety for them. That would be the end.

First then, he must make sure of his suspicions, and he could do that through Charlie.

In his quest for information he had visited some of the lowest taverns on the waterfront, and in one of these he met

463

Little Will, a man of great size who spoke hardly at all but who was reputed to be one of the most successful gentlemen of the road in the West Country.

Blasco drank with him and, when he considered the man to be mellow with drink, asked Little Will to walk with him up to the Hoe, where they might talk without being overheard.

❧ ❧ ❧

As Charlie rode out towards the house on the moors with the dispatch Domingo had given him, he heard a horseman behind him. He pulled up, turned and saw Blasco coming towards him.

'I thought to catch up with you before,' said Blasco.

'You seem in a hurry, Señor Blasco,' said Charlie with his ready smile.

'One feels the need to hurry when there is good news to tell.'

'Good news, eh? Charlie's ears are wide open for that!'

'I have heard that, besides the four Neapolitan galleasses and the four Lisbon galleys which are all but ready to start out, there are forty armed merchantmen and that Recalde, de Valdez, de Oquendo and de Bartendona are in command. They are assembling in Corunna. With them they are bringing Don Martin Alarcon of the Holy Office. His ships are being loaded with those articles which it will be necessary to use in order to persuade all those who will not willingly conform to Holy Church. There are shiploads of whips and branding irons that the obstinate shall be branded as slaves. As soon as the weather is clement, the Armada will sail.'

'Here's news that delights Charlie's ears,' said Charlie. But watching him closely Blasco believed he flinched at the mention of those branding irons.

'I could not resist riding after you,' said Blasco. 'I knew it would delight you to hear this news.'

'And you think that, with the wind right and the weather kind, they'll soon set sail for England?'

'There can be no doubt of it.'

'Just tell me about these men who are commanding the ships,' said Charlie. 'Tell me slowly. Those names of your countrymen are not very easy for a man like Charlie to get his tongue around.'

So Blasco repeated the names slowly, even spelling them out. 'But of course you don't write, do you, Charlie. I'd forgotten.' He told him how de Oquendo had made his name at Terceira, and how it was said that there was not a better sailor in Spain than Recalde.

'I will ride with you to the inn, Charlie. Then I'll have the pleasure of your company on the return journey.'

Charlie was grave. 'No, sir. Better not. You see, this is dangerous work we're doing. If anyone saw you with me – well, you know how it is. People get nervous. So, very much regretting the lack of your company on the return journey, Señor Blasco, I will say good-bye to you now.'

They parted, and Blasco turned and rode back to Hardyhall.

※ ※ ※

In the tavern late that night, Blasco met Little Will. They strolled out on to the Hoe together.

'I waited half an hour or more on the Tavistock side of the inn,' said Little Will. 'I got your man.'

The deal was completed, and Blasco walked away from the Hoe with Domingo's dispatch in his pocket.

His little ruse had succeeded. Charlie had handed the paper

to the messenger at the inn, the messenger had ridden away with it, and before he had gone many miles had been held up by Little Will and robbed of his purse and the dispatch.

Good work for us both, thought Blasco, as he unrolled the dispatch.

He knew as he looked at it that his surmise had been right for written at the bottom of the dispatch was a footnote, and it was not in Domingo's handwriting. It was in code, but it had been freshly added, and Blasco was sure that it contained that news which he had given Charlie on the road and which Charlie had thought should be sent to his employers immediately.

It was now clear to Blasco that Charlie was sending everything Domingo wrote, and which Domingo thought was going to Spain, to his English masters, and with it all the information he could gather. Hardyhall was therefore under close supervision. Evidence which could condemn them all to the traitor's death was passing into the hands of the English, and with it all that Charlie could glean concerning Spain.

There was no time to lose now. Blasco asked his brother to come to his room, and when he did so said: 'I have made a most alarming discovery. We must keep our voices very low. Charlie has deceived us. He is working for the English.'

There was no sound in the room for a few seconds. Blasco searched his brother's face, which he thought looked like a death-mask; now it seemed as though his brother was struggling for breath.

'Domingo, are you all right? This has been a great shock. Come, sit down. I should have prepared you.'

Domingo allowed himself to be helped on to a stool. His body seemed limp and lifeless.

Blasco went on: 'We are in acute danger. I see it all clearly. I cannot understand why I did not see it before. It is impossible that they could have been the fools we took them for. This is a plot . . . a plot against us. We are their victims. They are using us, Domingo. That is why they sent us here. Do not imagine that they are in the least foolish. They are diabolically clever. From the moment we left France – nay, before that – they have watched us. They have led us where they want us to go. They captured us and let us go, and they sent us here because they had discovered so much about us that they knew Isabella was here and that you were to have married Isabella all those years ago. How they could know so much, I cannot imagine. Except that they have spies everywhere . . . people you would least expect – like Charlie Monk.'

'Charlie is . . . is with them?' said Domingo.

'I've proved it. Charlie is collecting information about our country. That is his task. He has our confidence and because we have brought him here he has the confidence of everyone he meets at Hardyhall. All those dispatches you have written, which you believed you were sending to Spain, have gone straight to London to Charlie's employers, just as in the Babington plot every document written by Babington and answered by Queen Mary went straight into Walsingham's hands. Worse still, he is passing on all the news we get from Spain.'

Domingo said slowly: 'What will become of us, Blasco? What will become of us?'

'It is clear to me what will become of us. We shall be left here to work for them until we are no longer of use or they feel that it may be dangerous not to have us under lock and key. Then, my brother, we shall be tried for the spies we are; we shall receive the sentence of traitors. You know what that is. They hang traitors by the neck, cut them down alive and then . . .'

'Enough!' said Domingo. 'I know it. How well I know it!' He turned his tortured face to his brother. 'Blasco, I can keep this hideous thing to myself no longer. Charlie Monk may be working for them, but they are his own people. He is serving his country. To look at Charlie is to see a man who has no stain of guilt upon his conscience. But, Blasco, look at me. Look at me!'

'Domingo, what means this?'

'How many times, when we have lain in this room, have words come to my lips! So often I have nearly spoken. I must tell you now. I am afraid to tell you, Blasco. I am afraid of your scorn; I am afraid to share this with you, and I am afraid to keep it to myself. I feel like a man walled up in fear. I can never break away from it . . . never . . . never! I would I were dead, but how could I die with the weight of this sin upon me! I am a coward, Blasco. I made a mistake; I thought fear diminished with the years. Instead it has grown. It has become a monster. Blasco, you look at me strangely and no wonder! I must take off this *soutane*. I should never wear it. It shames me and I bring nothing but dishonour to it.'

'You should tell me, 'Mingo. You should tell me what is on your mind.'

Domingo said slowly: 'You are right. There is a spy in our midst. There is one here in this house who has taken advantage of the confidence he has inspired; he has learned all he could concerning affairs in Spain, and he has sent that information to Sir Francis Walsingham in London. You do not need to look far for that man, Blasco. He is in this room. I – God help me – am the spy.'

'You . . . Domingo . . .! You, to give our country's secrets to the enemy! You . . . a priest . . . a Jesuit! You have done this, even as Gifford did with Babington?'

Domingo nodded slowly. 'You must hate me. You must despise me. I have betrayed all these good people in this house. I have betrayed my cloth and my country.'

'Be calm, Domingo. Be calm. Why have you done this thing?'

'Because they came to me in prison. They took me out to St Giles's Field. They showed me how Ballard, Babington and the rest died . . . and they said to me: "Work for us and earn your freedom. Refuse, and die as these men died." Blasco, I have prayed. I have asked for courage . . . I have asked for guidance. But this was a decision I had to make myself and I feel that all my life had been leading to this one hideous climax. I made excuses. I have always made excuses. I asked myself to consider all the souls I could save, and while I told myself I could do God's work better alive than dead, I saw nothing . . . nothing, Blasco, but those men cut down . . . the ropes still about their necks, and the butcher bending over them with the knife. I heard their screams of agony and I could not endure that, Blasco. So I looked the other way and said, as I have said so many times: "This is God's will!" Help me, Blasco. For the love of the Holy Mother of God, help me! Tell me what I ought to do.'

Domingo could not bear to look into his brother's face. He covered his own with his hands, and great sobs shook his body although no sound came.

Blasco came and stood beside his brother.

'You do not touch me,' said Domingo. 'You find me loathsome. You are calling me Traitor in your mind. And you see me as one who has betrayed his country and denied his God.'

When Blasco spoke, his voice was full of pity. 'No, Domingo. I did not speak, because my thoughts were busy. I have become a traitor too. I think of the ships sailing here; I think of the officials of the Inquisition landing in this place; I think of those ships in which they will bring the *chevelet*, the bilboes, the whips and the branding irons. Then I too turn traitor. I am here to serve the King, but I no longer wish to serve him. I would not serve the Queen of England. I would serve freedom. I would embrace freedom, if I knew where to find her. Domingo, you have faced a terrible ordeal and you have betrayed Spain. Many have done it before.'

'I am a priest,' said Domingo. 'I love my Faith. I have betrayed my Faith because I could not die for it. I could have died if death were swift. It is the long, agonising torture which I can not suffer for its sake.'

'Domingo, you have always suffered from your conscience more than most men. You have asked too much of yourself. You are a man like the rest of us. You have been weak, some would say; but how many, do you think, in your place would betray similar weakness? Every day in our country the *chevelet* is breaking men's bodies till they deny their Faith. God will understand that you wished to serve Him; He will understand all that you have suffered, because you could do no other. We must get away from this place as soon as we can. We are in acute danger.'

'We are safe,' said Domingo bitterly, 'as long as I continue to betray my country.'

'We are safe only as long as they need our services. War between our country and this one is imminent. The Armada is ready to sail, and our King is eager for it to do so. As soon as that happens, I doubt not that we shall be taken. When the Armada is successful you will be cruelly tortured because you have worked against Spain. They discover these things. There will be those to remember. There are the incriminating dispatches you have written. It may be that these will fall into the hands of our own countrymen.'

'If they fail . . .' began Domingo.

'They cannot fail. We know, do we not, that they have the best ships that have ever been built; they have the mightiest armament that was ever put to sea; and they come in their Faith which is a different Faith from that of this land.'

'You mean God and His holy saints will sail with them.'

'I know not what I mean. I am a traitor too, Domingo. I no longer wish to serve my country. I felt thus when I was in Paris in '72. When I saw that bloody massacre. Now I feel the same.'

'You have become a heretic, Blasco?'

'I am no heretic. I am still a Catholic perhaps, for I observe the rites of the Church in which I was brought up, but I want to worship God in peace, and I want my neighbour to be able to do the same, even though he should worship different gods from mine. The religion practised in England, in Spain, in France during these times – what is it? It is but a cloak to cover a lust for power, a cloak to hide the truth. And, pity of pities, it is a cloak dyed scarlet with the blood of men who have dared hold an opinion which differs from those of their masters. But we are wasting time, Domingo. We have to get away from here.'

'Where should we go?'

'There is no place that is safe for us in this country or in our own.'

'I know it. There is nothing for me but death. Had I the courage I would take my own life.'

'Domingo, take off those things. Take off your *soutane*. Forget that you are a priest. You are a weak and sinful man. So are we all. You have one weakness, I have another. And there is no man living who has not committed his sins. You have been afraid of life. Now, Domingo, you must live. You must put these things behind you. We cannot return to Spain. We cannot stay here. There is no place for us in the old world. But there is a new world, Domingo.'

'What do you mean, Blasco?'

'Did I not always provide the solution? Even as I stand here my mind teems with plans. I too am afraid, Domingo. I am afraid that I shall lose the new life I have discovered. I want to live with Bianca and my son – my new-found son. I do not want to die. I have become so much in love with life that I fear death. I think something of this has always been in my mind. I have become more and more aware that we should have to get away. Domingo, one night in the future – the very near future – we will sail away from these shores. There is a whole new world waiting for us. Bianca, Roberto, you, Domingo, and myself . . . we will sail away and we will make a new life for ourselves. You will leave your fears and your conscience behind you.'

'I cannot throw away my sins as easily as that, Blasco.'

'Then you will take them with you; but there in the open country we will build a new life . . . a new world . . . where there would be peace and harmony, and each man's mind will be like his own plot of land which he will plant and weed as he thinks

472

fit.'

'These are dreams, Blasco.'

'The discovery of a new world was a dream before it happened.'

'How could we safely and secretly sail away?' said Domingo, his voice trembling with eagerness.

'In my wandering through the town I have talked with many people. I frequent the taverns. I have my friends down there in the town. I have often asked questions about these ships which leave the ports. It was part of my work, was it not? I think I always had this idea somewhere at the back of my mind. I want to cut myself off from argument, Domingo. I want to be free, and, I want to love my neighbour whether he be Catholic, Protestant or worships a totem pole which represents his god. You do not understand that. How could you, the priest?'

'I will try to understand. Blasco, look at me, brother. Do you despise me?'

'You are my brother,' said Blasco. 'How could I despise you? I know you for the good man you are. You had one weakness, Domingo. You were afraid of the dark. And you nourished that weakness. Like the roses in the garden it was cherished and shielded from the cold blasts which might have killed it. You allowed that tiny seed to grow into a great plant to entwine itself about you as the bindweed will about a tree. In the New World you will find a new life.'

🐦 🐦 🐦

Pilar watched the ships in the Sound. The sea enthralled her. Soon she would be sailing on it in the ship which would take them all to the New World.

It was like one of those childhood dreams about to come true. It was a great secret and no one but those who were going knew of it. There was acute danger near them and it was necessary for Domingo and Blasco to leave, and so they were going to form a little colony, just as they would have done in one of her childhood fantasies.

Blasco was busy. He was buying stores; he was discreetly making enquiries, and now in the harbour lay the ship.

The Captain was still in London. How was she going to bear parting from the Captain?

She made her own dream as she had done in the old days. When she saw the ship sailing the seas, the Captain was there, roaring, cursing, throwing his crutch at any who did not obey him promptly; when they landed in the New World, he was there also. She could not picture the future without him.

At dusk, they went down to look at the ship – she, Roberto, Bess and Howard; she felt excitement grip her and she was a child again, planning their lives for them. There was Bess, always close to Roberto; and there was Howard whose eyes were on herself.

How can I marry Roberto? she asked herself. He is for Bess. It would hurt Howard if I married Roberto, and how could I hurt Howard?

She loved them both, if love meant wanting to have people about you, wanting to scold them and bully them and hate them and be affectionate towards them, just as the emotion moved you.

She wanted them all to be close to her – all the people without whom she would be sad. But the Captain was also one of these.

She told herself: 'He shall come. When I go down to the ship on the day she's ready to sail, the Captain will be with me. He

shall stow away in the hold, and I'll see that he's not discovered.'

She imagined Petroc Pellering coming home to find them gone, and she laughed aloud to picture his discomfiture; then she was regretful because she would not be there to see it.

'We shall sail,' Roberto told her, 'before the Captain returns.'

❧ ❧ ❧

It was early April. They would leave in a day or two. Just a few more nights in this house, thought Pilar, and I may never see it again.

As she entered the house Carmentita came to her to tell her that the Captain had come home. Pilar ran to greet him. He looked older and tired and as she embraced him she thought: How can I ever leave him! And the tears gushed into her eyes.

She herself served him as he sat at table with good roast sirloin such as he loved, with pies and clotted cream. 'We can beat the Londoners at eating, girl,' he said. 'Give me the good pastry and cream of Devon.'

'Was your mission satisfactory, Captain?'

'That depends, girl. Have we smoked 'em out of their holes yet?'

'Things are still as they were when you went away.'

'Fools! Madmen! They let these dogs live among us!'

'Did they not listen to you?'

'Aye, they listened to me. They took me before this one and that. What I had to tell was of great interest. They would mark it well. They remembered I was the Queen's good servant. But they've left the rats in their holes.'

'Captain,' she said, 'would you like to sail the seas again?'

His eyes were glazed. 'Why, girl,' he said, 'if I could get my leg back, if I could rid myself of this accursed pain in my side, I'd be out and away, and this time you'd come with me. I'd be on my deck again. Aye, that I would.'

'Have you ever thought you'd go to sea in someone else's ship? As . . . as a passenger, say.'

That made him laugh. 'Nay,' he cried. 'I'd be master or nothing. I know what you think, girl!'

She flushed, and he went on: 'He'll be home soon. By God, he'll be home! He'll hear the rumours. They spread round the world. And Petroc would curse himself to his dying day if he was not here to drive the dogs away from our shores.'

The Captain sat laughing. He was old, and his life of adventure was over. But his eyes told her that he could still find life good while it held Petroc Pellering and his girl Piller.

The day came. The last day at home! thought Pilar. Tonight we shall sail away and I shall never see these cliffs again.

In the morning the Captain will stump through the house. He'll say: 'Where's my girl Piller?' And there'll be no answer. Then he will grow angry and they will show him the letter I have left for him, and there'll be nothing more in life for him. After that it'll be worse than the day he lost his leg and knew he would never sail the seas again.

The day was full of torments for her.

She knew she could not leave him. Roberto, Howard . . . they must go alone. Roberto must go because his father dared not stay, and how could Bianca stay if Blasco went away! They were a family now; they must be together. And Howard must go. The Hardys were in danger, and Howard was a man now;

he would be blamed for harbouring enemies of his country, even as his father would.

There was no safety in England for Howard.

She was so bewildered; she had always yearned to sail the seas; but if she went with them she would never as long as she lived forget what she had done to the Captain.

The time was passing. The tide would be right just after dusk. That was why they had chosen this day.

Soon the sun would be sinking below the hills. Soon it would be time to leave the house. Her baggage was aboard, yet she had not written her letter to the Captain. She had begun it, but her fingers refused to write, her brain refused to supply the words. Now she knew that she could never leave him, that she was more closely bound to him than to any of those who would sail on the ship.

She went to her mother's room and, as Isabella came quickly to her side, Pilar felt as though she were a little girl once more. She threw herself into her mother's arms.

'I know,' said Isabella. 'I know, *favorita*. You cannot go. You cannot leave him.'

'It is so,' said Pilar. 'I must be with him.'

'He is old, Pilar. You are young. Howard and Roberto must go.'

'I cannot leave him,' she repeated.

Isabella was silent. And if she stays, she was thinking, how can I go? How could I leave my daughter? She cares so much for him; she was born in hate and yet she has found so much to love in him that she will let us all go for his sake; and I, much as I long to go, cannot do so if she stays.

She is one result of the continual strife between our two countries, and yet we love her more than anything we possess in life. How strange that out of such hatred could grow this lovely girl!

Pilar was looking steadily at her mother, and was overwhelmed by her love for her.

Isabella said quickly: 'You must stay, my child. You would never be happy away from him. You love neither Roberto nor Howard – at least you do not love them enough. If you loved, you would give up everything for them. That is the way of love. But you will stay, and because I love you even as you love him, I will stay with you.'

❧ ❧ ❧

The ship sailed out of the harbour. On deck stood the little group, side by side, their eyes fixed on the land. They were adrift from the old life, and they were each aware that they knew not what the new one contained.

Bess was perhaps happier than any of them. She was with Roberto, and Pilar had stayed behind.

Blasco had Bianca beside him. But there was a shadow over their happiness. Bianca had been so long with Isabella. 'I felt that our lives were so close,' she had said. 'We were like two trees that grew side by side and what happened to one must affect the other.'

'We shall come back some time,' said Blasco to her.

That was what he had said to Roberto and to Howard. 'We shall come back.'

Both of them had declared their intention of staying behind when Pilar had made known her decision. Blasco had talked to them.

'It is Pilar's decision, not yours. She loves you as brothers – both of you. This is her answer to you. One day you can sail to England again. You can see Pilar grown-up; and then you can woo her if she is ready for wooing. Now she is too young, and she clings to her father.'

Blasco realised then that neither of them was the man for Pilar. Roberto's natural indolence did not accord with her fire. Howard's sense of the fitness of things, his calm acceptance of what he had been taught was right, his inability to reason for himself – that was not for Pilar either. Only a spirit as wild as her own could soar with her.

$$\textit{\S} \quad \textit{\S} \quad \textit{\S}$$

Domingo was riding to London. Beside him was Charlie Monk.

One hour before the ship was due to sail they had set out.

'I pray you tell my brother that I have had a sudden call to London,' he had said to one of the servants, who were unaware of that night's intended flight. 'Charlie and I must leave immediately.'

He had insisted that they set out at once. He was afraid to meet Blasco. He was afraid that he would break down under his brother's persuasion.

His spirits were uplifted as he rode towards London. The end could not be very far away now. He would steel himself to face it. Blasco would understand. He could not have sailed with them, for that would have meant that he would take his grim companion Fear with him. 'We are chained together, Blasco,' he had written, 'Fear and I.' He knew that there was only one way of severing those chains.

He must let Fear come close to him; he must look straight into Fear's eyes, he must feel the hideous breath on his cheeks; he must suffer all the torments against which his feeble body cried out.

Charlie was bewildered. He could not understand this sudden move. Yet what could he do about it but obey?

Charlie would understand soon.

When they reached London they put up at their old lodgings in Lad's Lane. And, leaving Charlie there, Domingo went out into the streets. First he went to St Giles's Field and stood there remembering. Then quickly he made his way to Seething Lane.

🌹 🌹 🌹

The harbour was alive with craft on that Whit-Sunday. From all the ships streamed the flag of St George. The wind was brisk, the sun brilliant.

The air was filled with the sound of bells; in the cobbled streets, on the Barbican, on the Hoe, the people were assembling. Many were making their way to the Church of St Andrew where Sir Francis Drake and Lord Howard of Effingham were attending the service together, to show all that there was no enmity between them and little jealousies had been forgotten in consideration of the great task which lay before them.

Pilar was there. The tension, the excitement of that morning was hers. She knew that she was living in one of the most significant periods of her country's history; and she had ceased to long for those who had sailed away.

On the water, swaying in the boisterous wind, were the proud ships of England – *Achates, Swiftsure, Nonpareil, Mary Rose, Elizabeth Bonaventure, Victory,* and the rest.

They were the invincible ones, she felt sure; and she thrilled to watch them riding at anchor.

She knew in that moment that this was where she belonged and that, although she would miss those friends whom she dearly loved, this was her home and she would not be anywhere else but here at this moment of her life.

They will come home one day, she told herself – for it was her nature to believe that what she wished would come to pass – or I will sail across the ocean to visit them. For when we have beaten the Spanish – and how can anyone doubt that we shall beat them? – the seas will be safe for travellers and there will no longer be wars on the land.

The Spaniards were the embodiment of evil, they who thought to come with their whips and their racks and their thumbscrews. She was the Captain's daughter and she believed this to be so.

That was why her spirits were lifted on this morning; her eyes sparkled and she wished she were a man that she might sail out in *Achates* or *Nonpareil* or any one of them to meet the enemy.

She turned and hurried to the Church of St Andrew. The Captain was already there.

'By God,' he cried. 'What a sight, eh? Who would not be an Englishman on this day! A pox on that fate which ties me to the land. I'd give all the rest of my life to sail out to meet them this day.'

There were the men of Devon, great names that would echo round the world. Martin Frobisher. John Hawkins. Lord Howard of Effingham – though he was not so popular here in Plymouth where every man believed that Sir Francis should have been Lord Admiral of the Fleet – and Sir Francis Drake himself, his sweeping moustaches curling nonchalantly, his beard aggressive above the lace of his ruff, his full-lidded eyes smiling at the people as he listened to their acclaim.

Then into the church for the solemn service; and those who

could find no place in the church, its being so full on such a morning, must stand in the square and pray for victory.

And when they came out of the church and gazed out to sea, many saw a new ship heading for Plymouth. They stood watching it, wondering whether it was the first of the Spaniards.

But no Spaniard this! She was flying the flag of St George, and she was alone and heading straight for the Sound.

The Captain and Pilar watched. And the Captain's eyes filled with pride and joy.

'By God!' he cried. 'What did I tell you, girl? Did I not say he'd hear the news and be home? Did I not, eh! Trust Petroc. England in danger, and he not there to save her! It could not be. I knew it. By God, I'm almost sorry for the Dons this day. What chance have they of victory, Piller girl? There's Drake to face 'em. And now Petroc!'

The Captain embraced Pilar; he was shaking the hands of all who came near him.

'By God, look at that! See that ship! That's my boy Petroc come home to fight for England.'

Pilar stood, her eyes shaded, watching the incoming ship.

❧ ❧ ❧

They had placed him on a hurdle. They were taking him to Tyburn Tree. In the streets the people jeered at him as he passed. A Jesuit! A Spanish spy! There was one word in England which was synonymous with Hate, and that was Spain. They threw stones at him; they picked up the muck in the gutters and threw it at him – they hated the Spanish spy.

He murmured to himself: 'Blessed are ye when men shall revile you . . . for My sake . . .'

It would be soon now. He would not have it otherwise. He

482

was at last face to face with the fear which had haunted his life. The worst was yet to come, but it could not last for ever. Now he prayed for courage to face his fear.

He had done that which he felt he must do. He could not have sailed away with Blasco, for to do so would have been to take his fear with him; he would have vainly tried to run away from fear as he had when he first rode north with Father Sanchez from Cadiz. There had been no escape, for the fear was part of himself. He had been born with it and it was said: 'If thy right eye offend thee pluck it out.' His fear was an offence to the man he longed to be, and this was the only way in which he could cast it from him.

They were shouting. He could hear their voices. They would crowd about the scaffold to witness his excruciating and most humiliating death.

But the end would have to come, and there was no turning back now.

He had faced the dark-eyed man in his house in Seething Lane.

He had said: 'I give myself up to you. I can no longer serve you as you ask. I come to say now what I should have said to you before. It is: "Take my body. Do what you will with it. I will no longer perjure my soul!"'

Sir Francis had lifted those rather sad eyes of his and said: 'You are a brave man, Señor Carramadino.'

'I had never thought to hear anyone say those words,' said Domingo.

'But it is so. You came among us – a hostile people – to try to foist your faith upon us. I would not condemn a man to die because of his faith. It is not so long ago that people of your faith were burning people of mine in Smithfield. It is something we shall never forget. I see that nothing but evil can come of such conduct, and I would not have people treated in such a way in the name of my Faith, in the name of my Queen. But you came to spy, and we must be harsh with spies. You know that, Señor Carramadino?'

'I know it,' said Domingo. 'That is why I have come back.'

So he had gone to his prison; he had heard the sentence; and now death was close, but before this day was over he would be at peace.

The pain will be prolonged and agonising, he pondered; yet it is the only way to peace. When it is over, my guilt will drop from me and I shall be cleansed.

They had taken him from the hurdle, and the rope was about his neck.

'Death to the Spaniard,' cried the people. 'Death to all Spaniards! Death to all spies!'

'God give me strength,' he prayed. His body swayed on the rope. He saw the butcher sharpening his knife. He heard the shouts of the mob.

He was praying silently.

'They are coming with their Inquisition!' someone close to him cried. 'Let them see that we can give as good as they would give us.'

A hostile crowd, he thought; and again he saw the butcher's knife gleaming as it caught the sun.

But Sir Francis had given special orders. He was a brave man, this priest. He had come back to face death when he might have escaped. It was due to some strange twist of the mind, something which was a part of his Faith.

'He will suffer many deaths in his mind on the hurdle,' Sir Francis had said. 'That will suffice.'

484

'*In manus tuas Domine commendo* . . .' prayed Domingo.

And he was dead when they cut him down.

🌷 🌷 🌷

All along the coast the people kept watch.

The battle had begun. Pilar and the Captain were on the Hoe. They were tensely waiting, and yet neither had any doubt of the outcome. The greatest Armada in the world had come against them. 'But what are great ships,' cried the Captain. 'It is the men who sail them who count. We've got Drake. We've got Petroc, girl. By God, 'twill not be long ere we set fire to these beacons. 'Twill not be long ere you will see them springing up all along the coast.'

And they waited while the battle raged far out of sight of the Hoe; they waited while Philip's great Armada was made great no longer, while the fireships were sent among the big unwieldy galleons of Spain, while the dream of Philip was dispersed, and the might of his great empire broken for ever.

🌷 🌷 🌷

Now the church bells were ringing and the bonfires were lighted. Men and women danced and embraced each other on the Hoe.

Soon ships were limping into the harbour. The victors had come home.

And there was one among them who now came striding up from the shore.

'Come, Piller girl,' said the Captain. 'We'll go and meet him. We'll go and tell him we're right glad to see him home. We'll set the cooks preparing such a banquet as never was. By

God, we'll let him see we're right glad and merry to have him safe with us.'

And Pilar looked at Petroc with the grime of battle upon him; and she thought of his riding the seas, facing death, snatching victory out of defeat; and she knew that he was her kind.

She marked the weary lines about his eyes, and she saw how those bright blue eyes gleamed at the sight of her.

'We're proud of you,' said the Captain. 'I'm proud and so is my girl Piller.'

Petroc caught her by the arms and, lifting her up, laughed aloud.

It was the laugh of the victor who has never had a doubt of the victory.